Hero Falling

By
Mark Barber

ZMOK
BOOKS

Hero Falling by Mark Barber
Cover from Mantic Ganes
Images by Tommaso Dall'Osto
This edition published in 2024

Zmok Books is an imprint of

Winged Hussar Publishing, LLC
1525 Hulse Rd, Unit 1
Point Pleasant, NJ 08742

Bibliographical References and Index
1. Fantasy. 2. Media Tie-In. 3. Adventure

Twitter: WingHusPubLLC
Facebook: Winged Hussar Publishing LLC

Timeline

-1100: First contact with the Celestians
  Rise of the Celestians

-170: The God War

0: Creation of the Abyss

2676: Birth of modern Basilea, and what is known as the Common
Era.

3001: Free Dwarfs declare their independence

3558: Golloch comes to power

3850: The expansion of the Abyss
  Tales of Pannithor: Edge of the Abyss

3854: The flooding of the Abyss, the splintering of the Brotherhood,
and Lord Darvled completing part of the wall on the Ardovikian
Plains.
  Drowned Secrets
  Nature's Knight
  Claws on the Plains
  Pious

3865: Free Dwarfs begin the campaign to free Halpi – the opening of
Halpi's Rift.

3865: The Battle of Andro;
  Steps to Deliverance
Several weeks after *Steps to Deliverance*
  Hero Falling
  Faith Aligned

3866: Halflings leave the League of Rhordia
  Broken Alliance

Thanks to Leo Barber for Z'akke, and Mantic Games for Thesilar and Ragran. I hope I've written them as the heroes they deserve to be.

The world of Pannithor is a place of magic and adventure, but it is also beset by danger in this, the Age of Conflict. Legions of evil cast their shadow across the lands while the forces of good strive to hold back the darkness. Between both, the armies of nature fight to maintain the balance of the world, led by a demi-god from another time.

Humanity is split into numerous provinces and kingdoms, each with their own allegiances and vendettas. Amongst the most powerful of all is the Hegemony of Basilea, with its devout army that marches to war with hymns in their hearts and the blessings of the Shining Ones, ready to smite those they deem as followers of the Wicked Ones.

Meanwhile, the Wicked Ones themselves toil endlessly in the depths of the Abyss to bring the lands of men to their knees. Demons, monsters, and other unspeakable creatures spill forth from its fiery pits to wreak havoc throughout Pannithor.

To the north of the Abyss, the Northern Alliance holds back the forces of evil in the icy depths of the Winterlands. Led by the mysterious Talannar, this alliance of races guards a great power to stop it from being grasped by the followers of the Wicked Ones. For if it ever did, Pannithor would fall under into darkness.

In the south, the secretive Ophidians remain neutral in the battles against the Abyss but work toward their own shadowy agenda. Their agents are always on-hand to make sure they whisper into the right ear or slit the right throat.

Amongst all this chaos, the other noble races – dwarfs, elves, salamanders and other ancient peoples – fight their own pitched battles against goblins, orcs and chittering hordes of rat-men, while the terrifying Nightstalkers flit in and out of existence, preying on the nightmares of any foolish enough to face them.

The world shakes as the armies of Pannithor march to war...

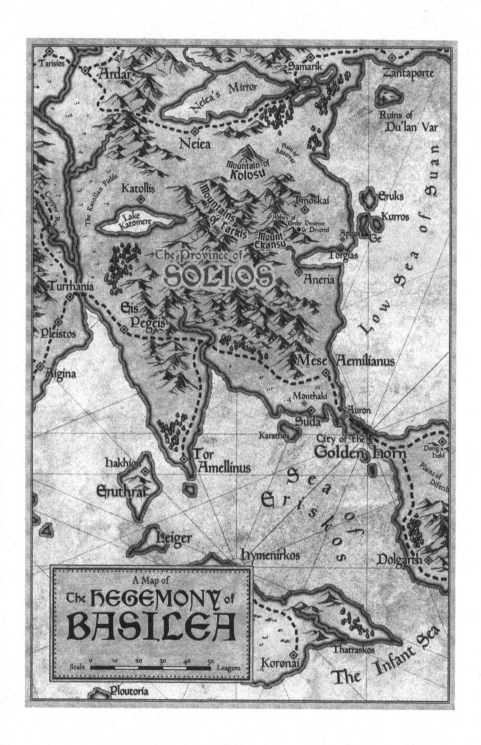

A Map of
The HEGEMONY of
BASILEA

Scale 0   10   20   30   40   5° Leagues

Chapter One

It was the smell that woke Khirius up before the noise. He opened his eyes and sat up in his lavish, four-poster bed, warily observing the hint of daylight that crept through the nearly imperceptible cracks between the wooden planks that boarded up the room's windows. His eyes came to rest on the letter on his desk and his unfinished reply, the source of his restlessness the day before. The acrid, smoky scent grew stronger. Burning. Then he heard the violent banging at the doors to his mansion. Leaping off his bed, Khirius quickly clothed himself and pulled a thick, dark cloak on over his silk shirt. The hammering at the doors grew louder. He heard a window smash somewhere on the ground floor and angry cries from the grounds outside his home's doors.

The banging on the doors to the mansion was now accompanied by the steady hacking and chopping of axes against wood. Khirius let out a snarl of frustration. Four years. Only four years in this house and he had already been discovered, despite his discretion. Once again, it was time to move, to uproot, to begin afresh. After two hundred years of it, he often wondered what the end state he was working toward actually was. Light footsteps drummed quickly up the main stairwell at the far end of the southern wing of the house and then padded on the thick carpet leading up to his door. An open palm slapped frantically against the door to his bedchamber.

"Master!" Hanna shrieked from the other side of his door. "Master! Wake up! Quickly!"

Khirius paced over to the door and unlatched the simple, brass lock before flinging it open. Hanna looked up at him, her face pale and her brown eyes wide in terror. Khirius' unnaturally attuned senses detected her quickly thumping heart and the rising pressure in her arteries. He saw a blue vein rise to prominence along the side of her slender neck, and he quickly turned away from her.

"Master!" the redheaded woman gasped. "There are people here, from Redworth Down! They're trying to burn the house! They must know who you are!"

"Calm yourself," Khirius commanded, placing his cold, gray hands on the young woman's shoulders, "I have seen this before. Even if we defeat them, they know who I am now. We must leave. We must leave and start again elsewhere. Find Tonnen and get to the cellars. Load all of the gold up into the wagons. I shall slow them down."

Hanna looked over her shoulder at the end of the corridor, where the grand, polished stone stairwell led down to the lavishly decorated main hallway and the source of the banging.

"But, Master," she protested, "there are many of them! Dozens! And you cannot fight them! It is daylight outside!"

Khirius smiled briefly, looking down in affectation at his loyal house servant. He had seduced many a young woman to his side over the decades, but Hanna was with him of her own volition. Of course, she was first drawn to his side out of her own desire to inherit a taste of his dark powers for herself, foolishly, but now he saw a genuine love and loyalty in her eyes.

"Hanna, go!" He smiled. "This is nothing I have not dealt with before! We are not alone here, at least not for long. The sun can slow me down, but it cannot stop what I can do from afar. Go now, quickly!"

Khirius' slower, heavier footsteps echoed along the corridor as he walked toward the entrance hall, watching as Hanna darted to the main stairs and down to the ground floor. Thin beams of sunlight penetrated the boarded windows, highlighting specks of dust that danced and twirled in the warm air. Khirius reached the balcony overlooking the main hallway and looked down below. Valuable vases from as far as Ophidia and Elvenholme lay atop small tables carved from precious woods from Galahir; long portraits of ancestors stared down gloomily from their ornate, brass picture frame prisons. All were fake, of course; even the fabricated relatives were purely for a show at normality. Whilst it certainly paid to maintain the illusion of riches and extravagance, Khirius had been forced to re-home himself enough times to know what happened when money was wasted on things that could not be moved in a hurry.

He glanced down calmly as thin strands of white-gray smoke wafted between the thick, oaken double doors of his mansion as another window was smashed in the south wing. They were trying to burn him out. How typically shortsighted. Khirius turned to regard the main doors and the gray stone walls flanking them. He could sense the hatred and anger from the men outside; simple folk with no education or fortune, easily terrified into attacking anything they did not understand. There was something else with them – a bright, almost painful sensation that spelled out the presence of divinity magic. A priest or cleric, perhaps, rallying the mob. If only they knew how selective Khirius was over whom he killed to exist, they would perhaps not be so quick to hunt him down. But many of those who he had killed were only yards away, buried beneath the dry earth of the picturesque gardens and hedge mazes flanking his courtyard, concealed only inches below the surface for a day such as this. Khirius closed his eyes and concentrated.

Unseen, inquisitive tendrils of arcane energy extended from his fingertips as he drew on his mastery of necromancy. Invisible coils of magic seeped through the stonework of the building's outer walls, past the flesh and blood of the angry mob outside, and into the dry earth beneath the green grass flanking the gravel courtyard. Khirius felt the limbs and trunks of the dead bodies beneath the gardens, as real and physical as if it were his own fingers delving through the crumbling soil. They were the corpses of the men he had fed upon and killed; dangerous or corrupt men who served him in their demise by sating his dark thirst. The dead bodies had been buried there with great deliberation, both to keep them hidden from inquiring eyes but also to lie in wait for when they could serve him a second time. Now was that time.

Drawing on a reserve of arcane power from his very core, Khirius gritted his teeth and winced as he emitted a pulse of dark power. The necromantic energy followed the probing coils through the walls and into the ground outside, connecting him to the carcasses of his victims. Like setting a candle alight, he drew on powers to rekindle the most minuscule essence of each of the dead bodies. A fraction of their soul, still bound to their decaying physical form, just enough to revive and revitalize the rotting muscle and sinew of each corpse. Fingers twitched, arms moved, and heads twisted in unnatural torture as the bodies exhibited signs of something akin to life once again.

A first zombie corpse broke through the thin layer of earth separating it from the fresh air above. A second, then a third followed. Even without the benefits of his unnaturally enhanced hearing, Khirius could hear the panicked cries of terror from outside the doors as the gang of village folk turned to witness the nightmare scene of the dead rising from the grounds behind them. The exertion of animating more than two or three corpses at one time was a great effort, even for a being of Khirius' power; he steadied himself against the smooth wall to his left with one cold, dead hand as he continued the gargantuan effort required to pervert the course of nature, raising more bodies to face his attackers.

Content that his would-be killers were distracted for a while at least, Khirius quickly made his way down the main staircase to the ground floor of his sprawling abode's entrance hall. He turned to pace across the smooth, polished floors to head to the northern wing, toward the stairwell leading down to the house's expansive basement. The dull, dry, rasping moans of the walking dead and the clash of combat sounded from outside as his freshly animated minions limped and stumbled toward the men and women besieging his home.

Adamant not to break into a run – despite being out of sight of any who might dare to judge him, running in what might be perceived to be a panic was unbecoming of a man of his status – Khirius walked quickly toward the basement entrance. He paused briefly at the next junction in the lengthy corridor, closing his eyes again and reaching out with his dark magic to raise another trio of zombified corpses to attack the villagers at the mansion's doors.

Up ahead of him, a window smashed. With a heavy thunk, a solid object impacted into the wooden boards his servants had nailed across the window opening. After a second slam, the wooden boards splintered and sunlight poured into the corridor. With a hiss of pain, Khirius leapt back from the bludgeoned opening. He glanced behind, briefly wondering if it would be better to attempt to re-trace his steps. No, the main doors would be open soon enough, and the basement was his only hope of escape in daylight.

A broad figure suddenly wriggled through the opening and jumped down into the corridor. The new arrival – a black-bearded man with leather armor and a heavy hammer, looked up in surprise at Khirius. Khirius narrowed his eyes in anger at the intruder, noting that aside from the armor, the man also carried a brace of throwing knives around his chest. This was no ordinary village peasant. This was a hunter. A moment later, a second man stepped through the window – taller, leaner, more agile, and armed with a short, broad-bladed sword.

With superhuman speed, Khirius leapt forward to attack. The dark-bearded man lunged out to meet him, swinging his hammer for Khirius' head. Khirius ducked beneath the attack and slammed a fist into the man's tubby belly, bending him over double with the force of the blow. His eyes wide with rage, Khirius stepped in to tear at the man's throat but let out a cry of pain as the second hunter's blade sliced across his back, opening a welt along his ribs. Khirius stepped back to avoid a follow up attack and yelled in agony again as he inadvertently jumped into the direct sunlight shining through the broken window, a sickening stench emanating from his burnt flesh as putrid smoke wafted up from his burning arm.

The big hunter swung his hammer down for another attack, but Khirius was again faster. He reached up and grabbed the weapon with one hand, stopping the attack dead. He lashed out his other fist, striking the bearded hunter with enough force to snap back his head with a crunching of bone before snatching the hammer from his hand and sweeping it down to crush the top of the man's skull. His comrade let out a yell of anger and lunged forward to attack again. Khirius batted aside the man's flashing blade and then stepped in to a deadly embrace, holding the writhing man still and overpowering him. Khirius leaned in to sink his teeth into the hunter's neck, tearing open a wound to the spurting jugular and drinking deeply. He instantly felt the lacerations in his arm and back healing as the revitalizing blood of his victim surged through dry veins across his body.

The hammer fell from Khirius' fingers to the floor with an echoing thump, followed a moment later by the corpse of the second dead hunter. He heard the thumping and banging on the main doors behind him resume, and he stopped again for a moment to raise another two bodies from beneath his macabre gardens, sending them limping into the fight outside before he resumed his fast walk toward the basement.

***

The resounding clashes of the small skirmishes between men and zombies receded as Khirius made his way cautiously down the stone steps into the dimly lit basement beneath his home. Lit torches bracketed the walls of the stairwell – not for his benefit, as he saw all in the darkness, but for his servants. It was immediately apparent upon reaching the top of the stairs that his home being besieged by ignorant village folk was not his only problem; a thin but persistent trail of blood led down the cold, gray slabs of stone.

Khirius knew what the problem was long before he reached the foot of the stairwell; his unnaturally attuned sense of smell picked up the stench of damp fur and feral body odors. This was an issue he had faced before, several times in the last month, and one that grew increasingly irksome the more his rules were ignored. Khirius could smell fear emanating from ahead of him as he rounded the last corner and could hear the guttural, heavy breathing of his vulgar houseguest.

The low ceiling of the basement curved down in sections to join up with the broad, supportive pillars of gray stone. Different sections of the cellars housed food and wine, hiding the chests full of gold and jewels behind them. Khirius' carriage and horses waited at the far end of the cellar, ready to take the short tunnel leading to the secluded exit from a hillside some quarter of a league from his home. He saw the hulking form of Garan stood by the carriage, one thick, furred fist wrapped around the neck of a much smaller being.

Stood in front of the two was Tonnen, Khirius' head servant. The aging man held his hands to either side, palms out, in a clear effort to appear non-threatening to the colossal wolf-man stood by the carriage. The trail of blood led to the werewolf and a corpse slumped at his feet, the body already half-devoured. Khirius walked out to assess the confrontation unfolding before him. He recognized the terrified, helpless captive held in Garan's claws. It was Hanna, his servant.

"Master!" Tonnen gasped as Khirius approached. "This beast, it has gone wild! It is dragging corpses in here to feed, again! It has Hanna!"

"Yes, Tonnen, I can see that," Khirius said coolly, stopping a few paces from the towering werewolf.

"She challenged me!" the huge, gray-furred beast uttered in his guttural tone through clenched teeth dripping with saliva. "She dared... challenge me!"

Her frail neck constrained by the deadly claw, Hanna could only look up at her master with terrified, pleading eyes.

"I would imagine that she challenged you on my behalf, Garan," Khirius replied, his tone more severe and threatening, "because you insist on breaking the rules I have laid out for you to follow if you wish to accept my hospitality. My protection."

"I do not need... to follow your rules!" the lupine creature snarled.

"Oh, but you do!" Khirius seethed. "You see, you have one of my servants by the neck. *My* servants. *Mine.* I respect loyalty, Garan. Would I die for my servant? No, of course not. Would I kill you to protect her? Yes... yes, I think I would. Let her go, now, or I will kill you. You live under my roof and accept my protection, so you will do as I say. More importantly, you have two months experience of the curse of lycanthropy. I have been a vampire for two hundred years. I could end you in a second."

The werewolf's yellow eyes narrowed and focused on Khirius' impassive stare.

"Try to stare me down all that you want!" Khirius spat. "You know full well that I can tear you apart in an instant!"

The werewolf looked down and released the terrified servant. The choked woman staggered over to Khirius, coughing desperately as her shaking hands clung to the folds of his cloak. She blurted out repeated thanks until he held up a hand to silence her.

"Hanna, go back upstairs and find as many of the servants as you can. Get them down here to safety. Tonnen, load the carriage."

The young servant girl staggered back up the stairs toward the ground floor as Tonnen warily edged past the werewolf to resume loading the chests into the back of the ornate carriage.

"What is happening?" Garan growled.

"What is happening?" Khirius snapped. "You dare ask that, of all questions? My home is besieged by a mob! Because of you! I warned you, Garan! I told you not to bring the dead back here! They have followed you and now blame me for your murderous indiscretions! I told you that this would happen!"

"Then let us go up and tear them all apart!" Garan roared.

"Until what?" Khirius retorted. "Until we have an entire army hunting us down? We are revealed, you idiot! We are known! We must flee and start again! Because of you!"

"Then we kill them all... before we flee!" the werewolf grunted. "We will kill them all for... daring to enter your house!"

Khirius opened his mouth to object to the ludicrous plan, but Garan had evidently already made his final decision. The hunched werewolf bounded past Khirius, leaning forward to prop up his heavily muscled torso with his long, powerful arms.

"Wait, you fool!" Khirius snapped.

With a roar that echoed through the cavernous cellars, Garan pelted up the staircase toward the ground floor with a speed and agility that seemed out of place from such a hulking monstrosity. Khirius let out a yell of frustration. Yes, the battle was already lost by sheer virtue of their discovery, but he did not want Garan killed. Khirius never had the choice in his curse; unlike so many of his servants over the years, Khirius never wanted or asked to be a vampire. Likewise, Garan never asked for the curse of lycanthropy. And such a curse made his vampirism seem like a gift in comparison. Khirius felt for Garan. He did not deserve to die. Swearing under his breath, Khirius dashed up the stairs after the werewolf.

The clashes of blades were louder; clear enough now that they could only be coming from within the house. Khirius arrived at the top of the stairwell and rushed back into the corridor leading to the main entrance hall. He swore in frustration as he saw Garan had already bounded halfway down toward a crowd of peasants in the main entrance hall. Some half dozen were already rushing up the main staircase to venture deeper into his home; perhaps twice that number were smashing decorations and setting fire to curtains and paintings. A few dead villagers and defeated zombies lay prone by the entrance; evidence of the ferocity of the final moments of battle between the attackers and Khirius' unholy resurrections.

Khirius darted off in pursuit of the werewolf, deftly avoiding the rays of sun pouring in through the smashed windows of the corridor and hoping that Hanna had succeeded in rallying together his loyal servants before the furious mob of villagers found any of them. Up ahead, the werewolf let out a furious cry that echoed along the corridors before leaping into the crowd of invading peasants, ripping open the guts of a tall farmer and lopping off the head of a terrified laborer. Khirius stood back and watched, holding his ground to summon forth his dark powers once more to bring a perverse form of life back to the dead that lay in wait beneath his gardens. Three more zombies clawed their way out of the earth and stumbled toward the mansion entrance.

Within seconds, Khirius' mental link to the zombies was severed as they were cut down. His eyes opened wide in surprise. Then he sensed the presence of divinity magic outside; the cleric he had detected earlier. No matter. Khirius merely needed to extract Garan from the fight and make his escape. Everything else could wait. He shifted his gaze back to the main entrance and saw the maddened, frenzied werewolf clawing apart another farm hand in a fountain of blood, spraying sheets of crimson across the white walls and blazing curtains.

Some of the invading peasants had already turned to flee in terror. From up on the balcony of the floor above, three more hunters appeared and brought crossbows to bear, quickly taking aim and then shooting their deadly weapons with a clicking of mechanisms and twanging of strings. Three bolts slammed into Garan's back, causing him to rear up and bellow out in pain, his immense, blood-soaked claws flung out to either side.

"Garan!" Khirius yelled. "Get back! Get away from them!"

The holy presence outside moved closer to the door. Khirius looked across. A slow, heavy thumping of metal on stone sounded from the steps on the other side of the broad doorway. An armored figure appeared at the doorway, silhouetted against the painful daylight. The man wore plate armor, dark in hue, with a surcoat of dark blue worn atop. His features were hidden beneath an all-enclosed great helm, and his shield bore the symbol of a tower. His broad, twin-edged sword was ornately engraved with a single word along its fuller. *Unworthy*.

"Garan!" Khirius repeated, recognizing the immense danger presented by the warrior leading the incursion. "Get away from him! Get away from that man!"   With another snarl from his blood-encrusted jaws, Garan surged forward to attack. Khirius sprinted down the corridor to the main entrance, snatching up a simple hand scythe from one of the fallen farmers and sweeping it around to slice open the throat of a bulbous, bearded villager who bravely stood his ground against the vampire. A brown-haired woman in the simple dress of green let out a cry of anguish and shot forward, lashing out at Khirius with a club fashioned out of a fence pillar. Khirius brought up a forearm to break the wood in half and then grabbed the pale woman by the throat. He snarled down at her impudence with rage-filled eyes and then threw her aside, flinging her into the base of the main stairs. In life and undeath, he had only ever killed one woman, and she thoroughly deserved it. He would never kill a woman again as long as he could help it.

An agonizing flash of pain shot through Khirius' shoulder as a crossbow bolt slammed into the side of his chest, spinning him around and forcing him to drop down to one knee. His suppressed hiss of pain immediately grew into a bellow of agony as the hunters on the floor above tore down the curtains, allowing direct sunlight to flood the entrance hall. A beam of white light sliced across Khirius' face, twisting and burning the dead flesh of his cheek and ear before he could leap back into the shadows. Up ahead, Garan ripped apart another villager as he fought against the armored knight, trading attacks between razor-sharp claws and the knight's heavy sword.

Khirius looked around frantically for a pathway through the pillars of sunlight so that he could dart forward to the werewolf's aid. Another crossbow bolt slammed into Garan, catching him in the thigh and causing him to drop to one knee. The knight quickly and skillfully lunged forward and, with a heavy slice of his sword, hacked off the werewolf's head. Garan's body remained upright for a moment, fountaining blood from the stump of his neck before crashing down at the knight's feet. Steam rising from his burning face, his head pounding with pain from sunlight all around, Khirius felt genuine fear as he looked up and saw the hunters above readying their crossbows whilst the Brotherhood knight paced confidently toward him, flanked by jeering, cursing villagers.

One hand pressed against his wounded face and blinded eye, Khirius turned and fled. He sprinted back down the corridor, his light feet accelerated to an unnatural swiftness by his dark powers. The corridor behind him echoed with screams and taunts as the hunters and villagers chased him like wolves leaping in pursuit of a wounded deer. Up ahead, Khirius saw Tonnen appear at the top of the stairwell to the cellars. The old man's eyes opened wide in alarm as he saw his wounded master pursued by the hate-filled mob. With a shaking hand, Tonnen unsheathed a small dagger from his side.

"Go, Master!" he yelled. "I shall try to slow them down!"

Khirius wrapped an arm around the old man's waist and yanked him off his feet as he sprinted past, dragging his loyal servant to safety as he pelted down the stone steps to the waiting carriage below. He reached the basement and saw Hanna by the back of the carriage, accompanied by two other servants. She looked up at her wounded master with agonized eyes.

"Get in the carriage!" Khirius screamed, running to the front of the wooden vehicle to unceremoniously shove Tonnen up onto the driver's bench.

"South, Master?" the head servant panted. "To the sea?"

"No! East! Basilea!" Khirius replied hurriedly, remembering the letter on his desk.

He clambered quickly into the back of the carriage and collapsed to the floor as the wooden cart jolted forward, Tonnen driving him and his surviving three servants to safety down the tunnel toward the secluded cave entrance in the hillside. Behind him, his home burned furiously. Khirius closed his eyes and sank his face into his hands, hoping that a small chance prevailed and his remaining four servants had managed to escape the inferno and baying crowd. He also hoped, as he accepted a well-meaning but useless hand pressed softly against his wounded face by Hanna, that the letter on his desk would burn with the house before the knight had a chance to read it.

Chapter Two

Ever since his childhood, Z'akke had always been an early riser. There was just too much excitement in life, and sleeping was a sure way to miss out on the myriad fascinating adventures the world had to offer. He opened one eye and saw the first rays of the dawn sun painting a blurred, orange line across the jagged horizon of the Mountains of Tarkis, visible through the opening in his small tent. He opened his other eye and shivered. Autumn in eastern Basilea was a far cry from the warming lavas of his homeland in the Three Kings. Clambering up and off his bedroll, Z'akke shuffled out of his tent to meet the new day.

The skies above were clear and cloudless, with a panorama of stars still visible across the azure heavens above. A gentle wind rustled the long grass and thistles of the mountainside, and a trio of hares snuffling through the foliage a few yards away elicited a warm smile from Z'akke's scaly mouth. He watched them hop away for a few moments, fascinated by their agility, before glancing down to the dead cinders of the previous night's campfire, sat in the middle of the three tents.

Z'akke held out a hand, spreading his clawed fingers over the remains of the fire. He inhaled deeply and concentrated. A warm radiance emanated in his very core, nurtured into greater life by the ever-present, fiery glow that resounded within all salamanders. He focused on the burnt wood, fixating on the few patches of brown that still existed amidst the charred black, willing the very essence within the wood to jump and dance, rapidly but subtly, at a level that no eye could detect. The imperceptibly miniscule particles of wood vibrated and resonated at his arcane command. Flames licked up from the wood once more. Z'akke allowed himself a smile.

After momentarily debating over and then deciding against taking breakfast so soon, Z'akke wandered over toward the edge of the small campsite. The three tents were pitched to one side of a narrow gully, the flat patch of land digging nicely into the natural, gray rock walls of the mountainside to provide shelter from the elements. Z'akke walked out of the gully to the edge of the patch of grass, staring down into the valleys below and marveling at the beauty of the serene scene laid out before him. Lush, green forests spread out in the ravines, easing gently up the foothills at the base of the mountains, a few sparkling rivers snaked their way along the lowest points of land toward the Anerian Wash and the Low Sea of Suan, just beyond sight to the east. The Mountains of Tarkis themselves reached up majestically toward the heavens, their caps white with snow, all seeming to lean ever so slightly toward the north as if in reverence to Kolosu, the largest of the mountains and the most sacred site in all of Pannithor to many millions of people.

Glancing across, Z'akke saw one of his two traveling companions crouched at the edge of the small outcrop of rocks, most of her form hidden beneath the folds of a thick, black cloak. Only Aestelle's head was visible outside the cloak, her blue-silver eyes staring off eastward toward the edge of the mountain range. Whilst Z'akke was the same as any salamander in being attracted to bold colors and textured scales, even he could see why practically every man they encountered was immediately drawn to Aestelle. Humans seemed to value perfect symmetry and gentle lines, and that adequately described Aestelle. Her face, normally alive with confidence and charisma, was now sternly set beneath intricate plaits of vivid, blonde hair, a few strands of which were interwoven with colored beads and small, precious stones.

"Have you slept at all?" Z'akke asked gently.

"Enough," Aestelle replied without looking up at him.

A hand, gloved in black leather, emerged from beneath her cloak, and she took a swig from a bottle of green glass. The harsh scent of the alcohol was enough for Z'akke to practically taste it. He momentarily contemplated confronting her on drinking so early in the morning but found his resolve instantly weaken at the thought of a potential argument.

"Thesilar did not come, then?" Z'akke asked.

"No," Aestelle replied quietly, "and yet, I do not find myself surprised."

The blonde woman rose to her feet, standing nearly as tall as Z'akke; taller than any other human woman he had encountered. But that was her lineage; she was only half human. The other half was something incredibly unique.

"Would you rather I make breakfast for us, or wake him?" Z'akke offered with a toothy smile, gesturing at the third tent.

"How about you go and wake him up and get him to make breakfast," Aestelle said, raising her bottle of wine to her lips again.

***

The wind picked up a little in intensity as the three companions continued north. Autumn in the Mountains of Tarkis was nothing to a man of Ragran's upbringing in the Howling Peaks; the only reason the winds elicited the barest of flinches from him was due to his choice of facing the elements with a bare chest, as real men of the north should. His last visit home had revealed that there were precious few of those in the latest generation to reach manhood. The mountain path wound gradually around the slope of Mount Fardis; gently enough that horses would and should have been an option. The problem with taking horses on an expedition was that there was a very real chance that once the three of them went underground, they could be stuck below for days or even emerge miles from where they entered. Horses were expensive, and leaving them tied to a rock to starve and then need replacing was no way to make money.

Ragran glanced ahead at his two traveling companions. Z'akke continued at a decent pace, his long snout turning from side to side as his twinkling eyes blinked, seeming to enjoy every moment of life as he took in the sights around him. Thick plates of boney, flame-colored armor covered his cream-gray, scaly skin, over which he wore a few pouches and pockets strapped around his waist and torso. The salamander's status as a mage-priest was defined by his long, ornate-headed staff, although for as long as Ragran had known Z'akke, the enthusiastic salamander had always insisted on fighting with a sword. Ragran laughed at the thought. In a world where magic was seen as the rarest of blessings by those who witnessed it, Z'akke the sorcerer wanted to be seen as a sword-wielding warrior.

Further ahead, Aestelle continued to lead the way, her dark cloak and long, blonde plaits billowing out to one side in the wind. She had sent out messages to three of her most trusted companions to meet for an expedition into the Mountains of Tarkis, promising a substantial haul of riches. Three companions. At least Ragran and Z'akke had bothered to respond. Ragran thought over the phrasing of the letter and the promise of riches. Every time Z'akke made money – and he managed to get his greedy claws on money with suspicious regularity – that money seemed to disappear sooner than he acquired it. As for Aestelle, now that she was a household name across all of Basilea following her escapades in the Battle of Andro, one would have thought riches would have followed the fame. Yet Ragran saw no evidence of treasures arriving with her new status; perhaps the money disappeared as swiftly as her fame would, given the fickle nature of the Basilean people.

And Ragran's money? Ragran prided himself on being a simple man. He fought hard for his pay, but he drank harder and had a taste for beautiful women. Neither hobby was cheap. But now, with his forty-second winter approaching and a body that did not seen to shrug off alcohol as easily as it once did, he found himself slowing down. The once ludicrous thought of retirement all of a sudden did not seem so ridiculous. He winced as he stretched out his right arm, rotating it in its socket. An old injury, the source of which was long forgotten, caused his shoulder to stiffen from time to time. This was not aided by the bandages around his upper arm that wound around a series of stitches from a vicious slash from a Peak Bear he had encountered two days before.

The pathway continued on through two peaks of jagged, moss-covered rock. Off to the east, Ragran saw the glinting waters of the Low Sea of Suan, their summer beauty now being replaced with the colder, grayer, and more foreboding waters of the fall. The path rounded a corner and suddenly increased its gradient markedly, forcing the three to lean forward as they continued up the slope. Continuing on for several hundred yards, the autumn chill wind increased in force as the trio hiked onward, the only sound accompanying the whistling gusts being the almost comedic bleating and shrieking of unseen mountain goats.

Up ahead, Aestelle stopped at the top of the path. Z'akke and Ragran caught up with her; the path terminated in a sheer cliff face, plunging down hundreds of feet to dark, deadly rocks below. A sturdy looking bridge made of rope and wooden planks, recently constructed, judging by the condition of the wood, tracked across the gaping chasm to the next slope.

"It is just up here," Aestelle said, "a little further ahead."

"How did you find this path?" Ragran asked, leaning over to further inspect the integrity of the bridge.

"The path has been in use for centuries," the tall woman replied, "less so in recent years since the coastal road has been improved. It's just the bridge that has been repaired recently. Come on."

The three companions made their way slowly across the rope bridge and up toward the next peak, Aestelle leading the way across confidently whilst Z'akke tentatively followed, his clawed fists gripping tightly to the bridge's rope rails as his eyes stared rigidly ahead. Ragran barked out a short laugh. He could not remember meeting anybody with more phobias than the gentle-hearted salamander.

Ragran was last off the steep bridge, following Aestelle as she led the other two off eastward and back down the steep incline of the new peak. A gust of wind shot along the valley leading in between the mountaintops, chilling Ragran again. Up ahead, Aestelle's cloak whipped out to one side to momentarily reveal her flawless, slim figure, further exaggerated by her skin-tight, black leather armor. Ragran grumbled in annoyance as he stared at her. One of the few conquests who escaped him. It would not have been so galling if not for the fact that in the four years he had known Aestelle, she had made little attempt to hide the fact that there were a fair number of men she had bedded. But despite his best efforts, Ragran had not made that list.

"Snack?" Z'akke offered, suddenly appearing at Ragran's side and offering him a chunk of crusty bread.

"I thought your lot just ate locusts?" Ragran grunted.

Z'akke blinked in confusion.

"Why would we do that?"

The burly salamander shrugged and bit off another mouthful of his bread, tilting his head from side to side with each loud crunch of his jaws as a blizzard of crumbs fell from his mouth. Up ahead, Aestelle turned off the narrow path and entered a broad-mouthed cave.

"This is it," she called back to the Ragran and Z'akke.

Ragran walked into the cave mouth, his eyes failing to pick much out in the darkness up ahead. He took his pack from his back and removed his cloak of coarse, brown fur. Z'akke followed him in, holding out one hand toward the tip of his ornate staff, the top of which erupted into flames to illuminate the cavern.

Ragran jumped and grabbed for his axe as soon as he saw the thin figure leaning against the cave wall, revealed by Z'akke's flaming staff.

"You lot took your time." Thesilar smirked as she stepped forward to meet the other three.

Ragran lowered his axe. Thesilar had not changed in any way since they had last crossed paths a little over a year ago. Her pale skin contrasted her dark hair that was tied back in a functional ponytail, with no additional effort at styling. She wore practical clothing of ruddy browns and greens that did little to compliment her figure, her drab appearance ornamented only by the addition of a small, green gem hanging from her neck. Despite this, she was, as were practically all of her elven kindred, possessing a grace in movement and gesture that no other race could match. Thesilar would be considered beautiful by any and all she met, if it were not for her present company. Stood next to Aestelle, she instantly faded into mediocrity.

"I said we would meet at Torgias." Aestelle glowered at the elf ranger.

"I arrived from the north, Petal," Thesilar beamed. "It would not make sense to track south all the way to your meeting place, only to track north again, would it? Now we are all here, you just do what you normally do and look pretty. Be a good girl and leave the thinking to me, alright?"

Aestelle's flawless features twisted into a mask of fury. She opened her mouth to respond, but Thesilar was quicker. She turned to regard Ragran and Z'akke.

"Mighty Ragran, we meet again." She smiled, slapping the back of one of her hands against his heavily muscled abdomen. "You're growing old, Northman. You're letting yourself go."

Ragran shook his head and smirked.

"Starting early on this one? You must be bored."

"I am sure it will all be nothing but excitement from this point onward. Hello, Z'akke."

"Hello, Thesilar," the salamander smiled, "it is good to see you again."

"Now that you have satisfied your insatiable ego with a customary grand appearance, shall we get down to business?" Aestelle growled, folding her arms.

Ragran followed Aestelle a little further into the cave, away from the driving wind in the valley outside. The fire from Z'akke's staff flickered across the rough, rock walls, light dancing along from the swaying flames with each enthusiastic step taken by the salamander sorcerer. The four adventurers crouched down at the far end of the cave, next to the entrance to a narrow tunnel leading deeper into the mountainside.

"So this is it?" Ragran asked, nodding to the tunnel. "This is what you brought us here for?"

"Yes," Aestelle replied, "this tunnel leads down to a network of catacombs that I believe dates back to the War with Winter, possibly even before that. Somebody important was buried down there. This is not like the barrows in the foothills. This is more than just another minor noble and his guard, animated by necromancy. There are very old and very valuable things down there."

"And these treasures," Z'akke frowned, "they are... defended?"

"Yes."

"So, undead, then?"

"That's correct," Aestelle answered coolly.

"Then it is just like the barrows used to be, back in the day." Ragran smiled, remembering the glory days of adventure and plunder in the foothills surrounding Tarkis, before all of the old tombs were bled dry. "Caverns full of walking dead and gold!"

A brief silence greeted his animated outburst before Z'akke spoke again.

"The gold part sounds wonderful," the salamander said quietly, "it's the tunnels crammed with zombies that I am less happy about."

"Don't be such a coward!" Ragran grumbled. "This is an opportunity to fight! And for somebody like you, it's a good fight with no chance of any of your moral uncertainty! Our blades against the evils of necromancy! What is there not to like?"

Z'akke looked across at Ragran. The sorcerer's fang-toothed mouth opened and closed a few times, but he said nothing.

"You are carrying a wound." Thesilar nodded to Ragran's bandaged shoulder. "That could slow us down. I have a potion…"

"Save it for when we need it," Ragran cut the elf off.

"You should not be starting this carrying an injury already," Thesilar warned. "We should be going in fresh and…"

"It's nothing," Ragran interrupted her again. "I shall be the judge of what constitutes a real injury."

Thesilar narrowed her eyes but remained silent. Aestelle rocked on her heels, clenching and unclenching her gloved fists impatiently. Z'akke idly picked at a tooth.

"I'll lead," Ragran announced to break the silence, adrenaline coursing through him at the thought of disappearing into the dark bowels of the mountains for fighting and fame. "Aestelle, you follow me up, and as soon as we have space, you get by my side. We'll form the fighting line. Z'akke, be ready to burn anything that opposes us. Keep your distance and leave the sword-play to me and Aestelle. Thesilar, you take the back and shoot anything you can from range. Keep an ear out for anything doubling around to attack from behind."

"Understood," Aestelle nodded.

"Yes," Z'akke swallowed uneasily, "yes, I'll keep my distance."

Ragran looked up at the elf ranger. The dark-haired woman folded her arms and stared through narrowed eyes at Aestelle.

"Somebody important buried down there, you say?" she sneered suspiciously at the blonde woman. "How do you figure on that?"

"By the sheer number of rooms leading up to the burial chamber," Aestelle answered.

"How many?" Thesilar demanded. "Exactly how many? And how do you know so much about what we are about to face?"

Ragran gritted his teeth as his fists clenched on the haft of his battle-axe.

"Come on, come on!" he growled. "We haven't traveled for miles just to reach this point and then let the blood go cold! Let's go!"

"He's right," Aestelle nodded at Ragran.

The blonde woman unfastened her cloak and removed it to reveal her form-fitting ensemble of black, leather armor. Tall boots were pulled up over tight leather leggings, with matching gloves reaching past her elbows in a series of crisscrossed straps, leaving her shoulders and a thin band of her midriff bare. Ragran caught himself staring as the tanned warrior folded her cloak into her pack and then drew a jewel-handled, two-handed sword from her back.

"Despite your attempts to woo us all with the latest in your long line of expensive yet impractical garments, you have still failed to answer my question," Thesilar said. "How do you know what's down there?"

Slinging her sword up to rest over her toned shoulders and tossing her head to flick a few strands of hair out of her face, Aestelle fixed her silver-blue eyes on the elf.

"Because I have been here before," she said. "The entrance I first used is collapsed now, which is a shame, as it cut straight through to very near the main burial chamber itself. Now that option is gone, this is the best I can find, and who knows where it will lead. Now, if you are quite done, shall we go?"

Aestelle barged past the elf ranger and into the narrow tunnel ahead. Ragran and Z'akke followed.

***

Thesilar was the last to drop down through the opening in the rocks to the dark tunnel below, her feet landing on the ancient flag-stones without a sound. The passageway was low enough to force each of the four adventurers to crawl, and narrow enough to keep them in single file. Only Z'akke's flaming staff illuminated the pitch black of their cold, claustrophobic surroundings. The floor beneath and the walls to either side were rough and functional, but clearly carved out without a thought for refinement. Thesilar had seen enough burial chambers to recognize an air tunnel, now long closed off but once built to keep a flow of breathable air from the outside world leading down to the workers who would have spent months constructing whatever lay ahead of them. Evidence of construction, yes, but so far nothing more.

Wafting back from up ahead, Thesilar could smell the unmis-takable stench of alcohol. One of her companions had been drinking already. That did not bode well. She heard one of her party drop down another level into a chamber a few feet below. A second, lighter drop sounded before Z'akke and his flaming staff followed. Thesilar reached the end of the old air tunnel and looked down below. Her three com-panions were in a much taller and broader passageway, the dusty floor beneath their feet decorated with age-old, faded patterns, all but com-pletely covered in dust and cobwebs. The distinctive doubled-curls in the tiles seemed characteristic of older Primovantorian designs, cer-tainly pre-War with Winter. That was Thesilar's first clue that they had, in fact, struck upon something worthwhile. She jumped down into the chamber below.

"Look at this," Ragran said from the cavern wall, one of his fin-gers dipped into an ancient torch attached to the cobweb strewn rock. "There's oil in here."

Z'akke walked over and held his burning staff to the torch, setting it ablaze. He then walked across to the next torch and repeated the exercise. Thesilar frowned. Setting up an ancient catacomb with a simple spell to set torches ablaze was a relatively easy feat of pyromancy, often used to dazzle visitors or scare away unwanted intruders. But this was different. This was normal oil, recently replenished. Thesilar looked down the corridor, to where it hit a junction and branched off to the left and right.

"Tread carefully," she said quietly, notching an arrow to her bow.

Ragran continued slowly ahead, his heavy axe held up and ready to strike. His dark eyes flitted from side to side beneath a mop of dirty, blond hair, most of which was tied up in a topknot. His thick lips were hidden amidst his scraggy beard, and his torso was clothed only in a demonic, horned skull that was strapped to one shoulder in the style of a pauldron. Aestelle followed half a pace behind him, her thin, bejeweled greatsword held ready in her gloved hands. Z'akke trudged carefully after their two leaders, igniting each wall-mounted torch as they advanced.

They reached the junction. Ragran stopped. Thesilar looked carefully to each side and saw a body fallen to their right, the ancient tiles beneath the corpse-stained rusty brown with blood. The corpse's clothes were vibrant enough in shades of green; the very presence of bright colors being evidence enough of how recent the death was. Thesilar took a careful pace forward, her narrowed eyes surveying the floor, ceiling, and walls up ahead. Aestelle walked forward to the junction.

"Wait!" Thesilar gasped.

She lunged forward and grabbed Aestelle by the back of her leather vest, yanking her back from the junction. Two faint whistles sounded in quick succession, and a blur of white ahead was the only visible evidence of the darts that shot out of tubes hidden in the walls. Thesilar shoved a hand against one of Aestelle's bare shoulders to spin her forcefully around to face her.

"What was that?" Thesilar spat. "Are you too drunk to see obvious traps, now? You're supposed to be a professional! An old hand at this! Wise up and act like it!"

Aestelle's silvery blue eyes narrowed in anger, but she said nothing. The tall woman turned and looked down at the broken darts and then across at the dead adventurer with a nearly identical dart protruding from his gray neck. Her anger faded away as her bleary eyes focused on the darts and the body that lay crumpled only a pace away.

Ragran carefully dropped to one knee and picked up one of the darts, sniffing it tentatively.

"No poison," he remarked, "at least nothing I can tell. Looks like this poor fool just ran out of luck and got it right in the jugular."

"It's not the dart I'm interested in," Thesilar said, carefully stepping across the trapped floor tiles to inspect the walls, "it's the mechanism. Judging by the design on these tiles, there's no way that a mechanically triggered trap would still work after centuries. No... this thing was magically triggered. Z'akke? What do you think?"

The burly salamander mirrored Thesilar's careful footsteps to safely traverse the junction and inspect the opposite wall. A barely perceptible gust of cold air wafted down the corridor from the darkness off to the left, causing Thesilar to spin on the spot and stare into the black void ahead.

"Aeromancy," Z'akke suddenly declared, "I can sense it now. These traps were charged with aeromancy. It makes perfect sense. If I was going to magically trap a location and aeromancy was my discipline, then compressing air to propel darts like this would be easy enough, I think."

Thesilar felt a chill again drifting down the corridor from her left. She looked into the darkness ahead for a second time but still saw nothing.

"Leave him be, Z'akke," Ragran warned the salamander as he crouched inquisitively over the dead body at the junction. "We don't know how many more traps like that are around here."

"Come on," Thesilar said, her eyes still fixed on the dark tunnel ahead, "this way."

Ragran moved carefully forward again, Aestelle following closely whilst Z'akke remained a few paces behind, lighting the torches as they went. The four continued slowly, silently for several minutes until up ahead, the corridor abruptly ended. The way was barred with two smooth stones, resting neatly against each other to completely seal off the corridor. Off to one side, an ancient, wooden door rested against a pair of rusted, failed hinges set into the rock face. Ragran moved up to the rock door, slowly running a hand across the dusty, ancient runes carved into the smooth face.

"Z'akke?" the muscular barbarian asked.

The salamander moved forward. Magically warded doors were a typical defense in the ancient tunnels and tombs found in the region, which was why a practitioner of the arcane with the ability to break such ward was vital to any group of adventurers, barrowers, and treasure hunters. Z'akke stopped by the sealed door. His azure blue eyes closed in concentration. One hand slowly raised. Nothing happened.

"I... I can't."

"What do you mean?" Thesilar hissed.

"I can't!" Z'akke repeated. "This is no normal ward! I can't break it!"

"You've never had a problem with these wards before!" Ragran exclaimed. "Can't you use one of those crystals you carry around?"

"Wards are normally just wards," the despairing salamander tried to explain desperately, "petty magic! From a common discipline known by all magic wielders! This is no common ward, and using an energy crystal won't make any difference! It's... aeromancy! Again, it's aeromancy!"

Thesilar exhaled in frustration. She stepped forward and looked at the runes etched in the smooth, gray rock. For all of her years of academia, the runes may as well have been from a language from another world. She prided herself in her several areas of deep expertise, but aeromancy was not one of them.

"Ooh!" Z'akke said as he stepped back and accidentally nudged the wooden door to one side, creaking it open by a foot or so. "What's this?"

"Z'akke, don't go wandering off," Ragran warned tersely.

"Ooh!" the excitable salamander repeated, poking his head curiously around the door. "Look at that!"

Ignoring the warning, the salamander mage-priest shuffled off into the darkness behind the ancient, wooden door.

"Z'akke!" Thesilar snapped. "Come back!"

She barged past Aestelle to follow Ragran in the salamander's wake. His blazing staff lighting up the cramped, little room on the far side of the door, Z'akke dashed over to a cobweb-covered, dusty wooden chest propped up against the far wall in the otherwise empty chamber. His eyes wide with excitement, the salamander leaned over to grab the lid of the chest.

"Wait!"

No sooner had the curious salamander flipped open the chest, then the air was filled with a flurry of frantic whistles. Z'akke stood upright, a dart protruding from the thick, reddish plates of his armored chest. He looked down and plucked the dart out with a curious wince, expending as much effort as if he were tweaking the petals off a flower.

"You nasty little sausage!" he growled at the offending weapon.

Ragran let out a choked, wheezing breath and then collapsed to the ground, laying deathly still save for a few jerking motions of his chest. Thesilar's eyes widened in surprise as she saw five darts protruding from bloody punctures across his chest and abdomen.

"Aestelle!" Thesilar yelled. "Get in here!"

Aestelle hurtled past Thesilar and dropped to one knee by the felled barbarian, quickly looking over his wounds. Sheer terror painted across his eyes, dark blood poured from the dart wounds in Ragran's gut as his chest crackled with each attempted breath.

"Can't... breathe!" he wheezed.

Aestelle swore viciously, grabbing at one of the darts lodged in the giant man's bare chest and yanking it out. She grabbed a second and pulled, but to no avail.

"This bastard's stuck in there!" she gasped. "Right in between the ribs!"

"I'm sorry!" Z'akke gasped, his face agonized with guilt. "I'm so sorry!"

"Never mind that now!" Aestelle growled. "Pull that dart out!"

The muscular salamander leaned over and grabbed the second dart in Ragran's chest, wrapping a powerful, clawed hand around it before pulling it clear. Aestelle placed one hand over the first wound and stared down in concentration. She removed her hand after only a brief moment and the wound was healed. Immediately, Ragran's breathing changed from barely audible chokes to pained gasps.

"His other lung is punctured," Aestelle said, "and I've got no more healing magic in me, not right now."

She reached into the top of one of her thigh boots and produced a bandage which she then proceeded to wrap tightly around the wounded man's chest before looking up at Thesilar.

"Give me one of your gloves! Quickly!"

Thesilar handed over a glove, which Aestelle forced beneath the bandage to cover the remaining chest wound. She then turned her attention on the cluster of darts emerging from Ragran's gut.

"Hold still," she warned, "this will sting."

"I'm sorry!" Z'akke stammered again. "I didn't mean to..."

Hisses of pain escaped from between Ragran's clamped shut jaws as Aestelle padded the wounds with a second bandage and then secured the pads in place.

"We need to get him out of here," she said, "he can't carry on. I don't know how serious these wounds are. We may even need to get him back to Torgias."

"Wait a moment!" Thesilar said. "Let's not rush into things! You've healed one of his lungs already, you can just rest up until you've recovered enough to use that healing magic again and then fix him up! I've got a potion or two with me."

Aestelle glowered up at Thesilar.

"Don't talk shit, you blithering idiot! He's got a punctured lung and three darts in his gut! He needs help!"

Thesilar dropped to one knee next to Ragran, flashing him an encouraging smile.

"What do you think, big man?" She grinned, producing a small bottle from a pouch on her belt. "Quick swig of some healing so we can keep going? Can you grit this one through so we can carry on?"

The barbarian stared up at her, wide-eyed.

"Get... me... out of... here!" he gasped.

Aestelle stood up.

"Z'akke, pick him up and follow me!" she ordered.

Begrudgingly, Thesilar followed her three companions back toward the blocked air tunnel leading to the surface.

Chapter Three

The foothills to the southeast of the Mountains of Tarkis swept down toward the Anerian Wash, providing a perfect mid-ground between the bitter chill of Tarkis in autumn and the still mild weather of the flatlands around the coast. A stiff breeze swept through the trees at the edge of the campsite as long, flickering shadows were cast from the campfire beneath a clear, starry night sky. Ragran turned awkwardly on his matt, hauling his rough blanket up over his shoulders again as pain gripped at his wounded abdomen. He reached for a water skin on the side of his discarded pack but then thought better of it as the challenge of standing to urinate against a tree pushed to the fore of his mind. Swearing under his breath, he sank back down into his fireside bedding.

His companions' empty bedrolls lay ready around the fire. With no sign of rain on the horizon and only a mild chill to contend with, there was no need to pitch tents, at least. Ragran tentatively moved a hand to his bandaged gut and winced again, the physical pain matched evenly by the mental turmoil over the shame of being dragged out of an exploration after being dropped by nothing more than a handful of darts. He swore again, remembering times when he would have shrugged off such superficial injuries. He closed his eyes as he recalled the last tavern he had spent the night in before finding Aestelle and Z'akke the previous day, and how he had smiled at an attractive serving girl only to be met with a look of revulsion. Growing older was worse than everybody had warned him it would be.

"Let me see those bandages," Aestelle said as she appeared from the far side of the small clearing, walking over to drop to her knees by his side.

"They're fine," Ragran grumbled.

"Shut up and show me the bandages," Aestelle snapped irritably.

Ragran pulled his blanket down past his waist. He was relieved that now at least he could do so – Aestelle had used her powers of divinity magic to heal his other punctured lung as soon as she had recovered enough energy to do so. This, assisted with a healing potion from Thesilar, had taken away the worst of the pain. But healing potions were of variable quality at the best of times. And healing potions, like divinity magic, were fantastic for the moment but did not solve problems in the long term. Severe wounds were only half-closed to the point that adrenaline would mask the remaining effects, but when that adrenaline wore off... middle-aged men past their prime would find themselves moaning and swearing in pain beneath an itchy blanket next to a campfire.

"It's fine, for now," Aestelle said, tugging on the edge of the bandages to check their security. "You should get some sleep."

"I told you," Ragran said, deliberately neglecting to mention the pain he still felt in his chest with every breath he took, "I'll be fine in the morning. Just keep that idiot gecko away from me."

"It was an accident," Aestelle narrowed her silver-blue eyes, "he didn't mean for anybody to get hurt."

"Oh, enough of defending him!" Ragran grimaced. "Every time we do this, we get the same nonsense from Z'akke! You remember Halpi, two years ago? He actually abandoned a fight and left us surrounded and outnumbered, because he saw a treasure chest! He's a greedy, selfish bastard, and if it wasn't for the fact that he could fry me with his unholy, Abyssal fire powers, I'd have strangled him by now!"

"Grow up!" Aestelle shook her head. "You know the risks in this business! You know that every time we go underground, there are no guarantees! You can't go blaming him because you are hurt!"

"I can, and I will!" Ragran grunted, his chest burning with pain. "We told him not to wander off! He set off that trap, not me! And I don't see him here apologizing, either! He's probably off somewhere drawing more of those stupid dragon pictures!"

"The pictures he draws are for his children, you heartless prick!" Aestelle spat. "Just because you and I, and Thesilar for that matter, have all got nothing waiting for us back home does not mean it is the same for him! He has children, a mate, parents he is still very close to. Every day he is here is torture for him! Torture that you and I can never understand! If you want to spend your life cutting things down with an axe and bedding every simple bar-wench with low enough standards to accept your ugly face panting on top of them, that's your choice! But don't go judging him for spending his time thinking of his family!"

Ragran opened his mouth to issue an angry response, something he had only half-thought through about Aestelle no doubt sharing those same regrets, but his response was cut off when four dead mountain hares were suddenly and unceremoniously dumped on the ground next to him.

"Don't get up, I'll get dinner for everybody," Thesilar sneered, appearing stealthily from the shadows at the edge of the clearing. "What's all the arguing about, then? You two bickering about who can wear less armor in battle to show off their enormous chests?"

"And the jealousy begins again," Aestelle sighed.

"Jealous," the elf smirked, "of you? My former apprentice? Not likely, Petal. I may have spent most of my life in human company to the point my own people think me crass and coarse, but the day I stoop to the shallow vanity of your kind, and you in particular, will be the day Z'akke thinks of his comrades before the contents of his purse."

Ragran let out a brief burst of laughter before the pain in his chest transformed it into an aching salvo of coughing. Aestelle raised herself to her feet, folding her arms and fixing the slim elf with a glare.

"People can change," she said quietly.

"Of course they can!" Thesilar beamed. "But not you! You are not capable of any positive change! You're honestly going to tell me that you're all grown up now? Tell me, simple 'yes' or 'no' answer: when you asked me for a glove to stay Ragran's wounds, given that you were wearing gloves of your own, did you make that decision because you did not want to spoil your own attire? Yes or no?"

Aestelle kept her eyes fixed angrily on the elf but said nothing.

"Thought so." Thesilar grinned. "Now be a good girl and go find Z'akke, I'm preparing our dinner."

***

The howling of wolves cut through the night air. The eerie pitch of the wails was identical to the wild beasts from the far north, reminding Ragran of his homelands in the Howling Peaks. The wolves were subjects of fear for any traveler in the peaks, but certainly not Ragran. He had killed enough of them. The only thing in this region that came close to inspiring fear was the notorious gur panther.

"Who is washing the tins?" Thesilar said suddenly from where she crouched on the other side of the campfire. "I caught dinner and I cooked it. Time for one of you to do something."

"I'll do it," Z'akke offered quietly.

"No, not you," Thesilar said, "you always offer and then do a half-arsed job of it."

Z'akke let out a quiet hiss.

"I heard that," Thesilar warned, "and I understood it. Remember, Z'akke, I have more than a passing familiarity with your language."

"Then I assume you are hinting for me to do it, given that Ragran is incapacitated," Aestelle said quietly, her eyes staring sternly through her locks of bright, blonde hair, interwoven with gems and pearls. "But I did it last night and I'm not doing it again."

"I said that I will do it," the burly salamander repeated, rising up to his impressive height and grabbing each of the adventurers' mess tins in turn.

After handling her tin over, Aestelle reached into her pack and produced a glass bottle.

"Leave off that," Thesilar commanded. "I've had quite enough of looking out for you today because you're half-drunk and off form. That goes for all of you. Today was an utter, utter embarrassment. Not one of you was performing like a professional."

"What did I do wrong?" Ragran snarled, forcing himself to sit up on his bedroll and pointing a finger at Z'akke. "It's not my fault if that idiot sets off a trap and I'm stood in the wrong place!"

"You blundered in there carrying an injury!" Thesilar leaned forward to stare him down through the flickering flames. "I tried to tell you before we went in, but you hit me with your now rather-tired non-sense about how manly you are! Man from north too strong! Mountain man no need to heal!"

Z'akke unsuccessfully attempted to suppress a chuckle at Thesilar's admittedly rather accurate impersonation of Ragran's distinctive accent.

"But the problem is," the elf continued, "that man from north is also getting old! And he doesn't carry injuries as well as he once did! You were all an embarrassment in there. An old man hobbling around with an arm hanging off, a drunken harlot too concerned with whether her armor was tight enough to show off her arse, and a selfish gecko who would let his entire group down if he could get a single coin out of it!"

"I'm sorry," Z'akke said sincerely, his eyes sorrowfully staring at his feet, "sometimes I just…"

"No, stop right there!" Aestelle seethed. "This little summary of the day's activities is missing one vital part – *you*, Thesilar! *You* were the one who tried to push on when Ragran had two punctured lungs! *You* were the one who has tried to take charge of this expedition at every turn!"

"As well I should," Thesilar replied, her tone patronizing, "because you are unable to…"

"This is my expedition," Aestelle interjected, her voice low and dangerous, "I invited you all along. I am in charge here. I am not your apprentice anymore, Thesilar. You have already ridiculed Ragran's culture a few times today, so allow me to lean on a part of it I admire greatly. Ragran, correct me if I'm wrong, but in the Winterlands, if a leader is challenged, it is to be done openly and contested physically, is that so?"

Ragran nodded.

"An expedition would be led by the hunt leader," he explained, "like a pack of wolves. If somebody wishes to challenge the hunt leader's authority, it is done as nature intended. With fists."

Aestelle leaned forward and stared at Thesilar.

"Sounds good to me," the blonde woman narrowed her eyes. "I'm the hunt leader here. You talk a good fight, Thesilar. You want to challenge me? You want to go fist to fist?"

Thesilar looked across at the leather-clad human warrior but said nothing. Aestelle stood up and stared through the flames of the campfire at the elf. Ragran grinned. Thesilar was perhaps the greatest archer he had ever seen. She was a peerless tracker and scout. Her knowledge of the undead rivaled that of great scholars. But in a fistfight, she was, perhaps, a touch above mediocre. Aestelle was the only one of the four around the fire who had spent years of her life at war, on campaigns. A soldier. It was the only experience of hers that Ragran truly envied. Aestelle would tear Thesilar apart, and all four adventurers gathered around the campfire knew that.

"You are uncharacteristically quiet, Thes," Aestelle whispered dangerously.

Thesilar leaned back and folded her arms defensively. Aestelle sank back down to her knees again and grabbed her bottle of wine.

"We're heading back to Torgias in the morning," Aestelle declared.

"I disagree," Ragran said. "I will be fine to fight after a good night's sleep."

"Oh?" Aestelle countered. "And that warded door we cannot break through? The one we need an aeromancer for? What is your plan there, Ragran the Mighty?"

Ragran winced at the ludicrous self-enforced moniker he had insisted upon in his youth.

"Well, you're all answers, it seems," Thesilar piped up again, "Z'akke knows no aeromancy. Magic users are rare enough; those who specialize in the art of aeromancy are rarer still. We are not just going to stumble across an aeromancer in the backwaters of rural Basilea. So what's your plan?"

Aestelle took a swig from her bottle.

"I know a man..." she began.

"Oh! Here we go!" Thesilar beamed. "Aestelle 'knows a man'!"

"Not like that," Aestelle said, "he's married with children. Even I have some moral boundaries..."

"Somehow I doubt that..."

"Thesilar!" Aestelle yelled. "If you don't shut that damn mouth of yours, I swear to the Ones above I'm going to break it for you! Shut up and listen! I know a man in the capital! An aeromancer, a good one! Tomorrow we will go back to Torgias. Z'akke can get a message to him and we will wait for him to come here. He will knock that door open."

The salamander mage-priest swallowed uncomfortably.

"It's not that easy," he said quietly. "Contacting another mage across the astral plain is a difficult undertaking. Messages of only a few words can be sent."

"It worked last time I was up here," Aestelle said. "That's how we got him to Tarkis in the first place."

"But who contacted him? Only the most skilled mages in all of Pannithor can contact complete strangers! Communications on the arcane plains are a... web. A spider's web where strands are connected only between those who know each other. Do I know this man?"

"I don't think so," Aestelle said. "His name is Valletto."

"Ooh," Z'akke's eyes opened wide with excitement, "like in your song!"

"It is not my song."

"Well, not 'your song', but... the song you are in..."

"Shut up about that damned song, Z'akke!" Aestelle spat. "Now look! You remember Borjia? The hydromancer who was with us at Difetth? He lives in Dennec. He is an old student of Valletto's."

"Dennec?" Z'akke nodded. "That is... a stone throw from here! I could contact him in the morning! Over such a short distance, contacting him would not be so difficult!"

"Then do it," Aestelle said, "after you have had some sleep. I shall take first watch."

Ragran watched as Aestelle picked up her sword and bow, and walked off purposefully toward the darkness at the edge of the clearing. Z'akke muttered something akin to wishing the others a good night under his breath and then crawled beneath his own blanket before curling up into a ball. Wordlessly, Thesilar removed her boots and produced a small, leather wallet from her pack, from which she found a small brush to clean her teeth. Ragran lay back and stared up at the stars. Not far away, the wolves continued to howl. He closed his eyes and thought of the rugged, unforgiving mountains of his homeland. Then he remembered Aestelle's threat to Thesilar and the thought of challenging a hunt leader. Memories from years past drifted through his mind...

His guard held up to protect his head and face, Ragran turned a broad shoulder on to face his attacker. A volley of three punches slammed painfully against his upper arm, even forcing him back a step, but for Ragran, it was nothing he had not weathered before. Moving his feet through the ankle-deep snow, Ragran turned in to face his attacker again, twisting at the hip to propel a clenched fist forward into his target's gut.

Gunnar let out a gasp and doubled over as the fist plummeted into his belly. Ragran followed up with another punch to the side of Gunnar's head, knocking him over into the snow with a cry of pain.

"Up!" Ragran bellowed, slamming a foot into Gunnar's stomach as he curled up into a protective ball in the snow. "Get up and fight me!"

Gunnar held his arms over his head and tucked his knees up into his gut as Ragran continued to kick him, only vaguely aware of the shouts of alarm from the village as figures ran over. A hand grabbed Ragran roughly by the shoulder and flung him away from Gunnar.

"Get off him!" screamed Frida, Gunnar's mother. "Get off him, you little thug!"

The short, graying woman pushed Ragran back as Gunnar's little sister rushed over to help the injured boy to his feet. Gunnar looked up at Ragran with tears in his eyes.

"What's all the commotion?" a familiar voice barked as a tall, muscular figure bounded over from the tavern.

"Your son, Taavi!" Frida pointed a finger in accusation at Ragran's father. "Your boy! Again!"

"My boy has done what?" Taavi sniggered as he paced across to tower over the two boys. "All I see are some high spirits! Some rough play!"

"Rough play? Look at the bruises! What sort of play is this? Ragran is twice his size! If your son..."

"They're both my sons, woman!" Taavi yelled deeply. "All I see is two boys of eight years each at play! Stop your whining! These are boys preparing to be men, and that is something you know nothing about! Now get back inside and mend some clothes, or whatever it is that you do know!"

Frida looked up at Taavi, fear and revulsion in her eyes. She pulled her two children into her and held them in an embrace.

"Yes, Taavi," she said quietly, "they are both your sons. But that bastard there is not by me and will never be a part of my family. He will never be welcome in my house."

Frida ushered her son and daughter back toward the village. Gunnar ran the back of one sleeve across his running nose as he passed, exchanging a brief smile with Ragran. Ragran watched his half-brother go as a fresh fall of snow began to drift down from the gray skies above.

"What was that about?" his father demanded, once they were alone.

"He challenged me," Ragran said. "It was my expedition. I was the hunt leader. He challenged me, and so I put him down in the dirt."

"Good." Taavi nodded, his thick lips twisted into a grin behind the course bristles of his long, black beard. "Good. You don't let anybody put you down, son. You stand strong. You're a Taavison. You always stand strong."

Ragran nodded, watching his half-brother as he was ushered inside his home by his mother. He felt a pang of regret but was not sure why.

"What were you playing?" his father asked.

"We were hunting a vampire!" Ragran answered excitedly.

"Vampires?" Taavi spat. *"I see no vampires here! So you were playing make believe?"*

"Well, yes, we were imagining that we were..."

"Imagining?" Taavi scoffed. *"Grow up, boy! You sound like a damn Basilean! It's good to see you fight. That makes me proud. Don't let me down by playing make believe like some soft southerner!"*

"Yes, Father."

Taavi looked down at Ragran. The clear disappointment in his eyes softened just a little as he dropped to one knee to regard his son eye-to-eye. The burly warrior clasped both of his enormous hands on Ragran's shoulders.

"You want an expedition, son? That's fine. It's nearly suppertime. You go run to the top of Black Peak and back again before this snow thickens up. That's an expedition."

Ragran's eyes widened. He turned in place to look up at the foreboding mountain peak that towered over their village. He looked back at his father.

"The top of the peak is nearly a league away!" he stammered. *"And it's getting dark!"*

"Don't be wet!" Taavi spat, standing up again. *"It's just a little run! It'll toughen you up!"*

"But Ashenn said there's goblins up there, and..."

Ragran's protests were cut off as Taavi leaned back and erupted with a loud, deep laugh.

"You think there are goblins up there?" he choked. *"Less than a league from our own village?"*

His face reddening, Ragran said nothing.

"You've never even met a goblin!" Taavi continued. *"You're already bigger than one! If you meet a goblin up there, then you smash its skull in with a rock!"*

"But what if there's more than one..."

"Then you fight harder!" Taavi snapped, his mirth giving way to anger. *"You tear them all apart! Are you my son? Yes or no?"*

"...yes..."

Taavi looked down impassively. Ragran looked down at his own feet.

"What's your hunt leader name?" his father demanded. *"In your silly games, what do you call yourself?"*

Ragran mumbled to himself in embarrassment.

"What did you say, boy?" Taavi boomed. *"Don't talk to your feet! Look up and speak like a man! What do you call yourself?"*

Ragran paused, preparing himself for the verbal onslaught from his father.

"Ragran the Mighty," he said quietly.

To his complete and utter surprise, his father did not laugh. For a few moments, he did not even respond.

"Ragran the Mighty," he finally repeated, "Ragran the Mighty is nothing. A child's dream. A stupid game. Nothing. But he can be something. Ragran the Mighty is waiting for you at the top of that peak. Right now. You ignore the snow, you push on through the dark, you ignore the fear of goblins, and you get to the top of that peak. Then you will be Ragran the Mighty. And I'll respect you for it. You brave everything that is worrying you, right now, and go up to that peak to claim your title. When you get down, son, you find me in the tavern. And you and I will celebrate Ragran the Mighty with my friends, and a pint of that grown-up drink I haven't let you have yet. Understood?"

Ragran felt a warmth in his chest, a determination to succeed, to impress his father. To win respect. He looked up at the peak again, the darkening skies above and the horizon disappearing as the snow grew thicker. His resolve began to crack. He looked up in despair at his father, desperate for some reassurance.

"But... what if I don't come back?"

"Then you were never any son of mine in the first place," Taavi grinned, "but I don't think that will happen. I'll be in the tavern, with two pints, waiting for your return. Waiting to tell the other warriors that you are now Ragran the Mighty. For real. Now go."

Ragran allowed himself a brief smile as he looked up at the stars, wondering if his father ever looked down at the man he had become. In the past few days, it seemed that everything he saw reminded him of Taavi. It had been a year to the day since the news caught up with him. Ragran was not given to faith and religion, but he still found himself muttering a brief prayer of thanks to his father for molding him into the man he had become before he drifted off into a restless sleep.

***

Letting out a pained breath, Valletto squeezed his eyes tightly shut and tried to will himself into calmness. He failed. The walls felt as though they were closing in. His temples pounded with a dull, relentless, tortured pain. He swore out loud. His eyes opened and focused on the bright sunlight pouring through the windows and illuminating the terracotta walled room, highlighting the lines running between the cold, simple tiles at his feet.

Jullia let out another high-pitched, ear-piercing scream of anguish. Valletto clenched his fists until they shook, the shrill yell seemingly piercing his very soul. He heard a commotion upstairs, on the floor above him. He swore again. The volume of the child's screams by his feet increased in response.

"Shut up!" Valletto whispered to himself, unable to hold in the frustration but adamant that his aggression would not be heard by his family. "Just... shut up!"

The footsteps hurried down the staircase and across the hall before his wife appeared at the kitchen doorway. Clera looked across at where he slumped over the kitchen counter, her arms folded across her sleek, white toga.

"What's wrong with her?" she demanded.

Valletto looked down at where his two-year old daughter sat by his feet, tears streaming down her face as she wailed inconsolably.

"She wants sweetbread!" Valletto exhaled wearily. "And I said 'no.'"

"Why can't she have sweetbread?" Clera asked irritably.

"She's had three pieces. She's had enough."

"You've given her three?!" Clera exclaimed.

"Yes! She was crying!"

"And how has that worked out now?!"

Valletto shot to his feet and slammed an open palm into the kitchen surface next to him. The force of the blow echoed around the terracotta kitchen, causing his daughter to somehow find it within herself to cry even louder. The world seemed to sway. Valletto felt a sickness in his stomach. One side of his ribcage ached. His head pounded. The yellow light of the morning sun was too bright, adding to the pains in his head.

"I'll take her," Clera said, rushing across the kitchen to scoop up the distressed toddler.

"I've got her," Valletto protested.

"Well, clearly you're struggling," his wife replied.

"You're looking after Lyius," Valletto grimaced. "I said I could take care of our daughter."

"I managed to take care of both of our children well enough on my own when you were off on the other side of the country for weeks on end!" Clera replied irritably.

"Whose fault was that?" Valletto exclaimed in genuine astonishment, bewildered at why his sudden and enforced front-line service in a military campaign would be used against him.

"I didn't say there was any fault!" Clera sighed. "I didn't accuse you of anything! You're just looking for offense in everything I say."

The moment Clera pulled Jullia against her, she stopped crying. Clera bounced up and down on the soles of her feet, shushing gently into the little girl's ear. The shushing now filled Valletto's world. It was somehow worse than the crying it replaced. His throat felt tight. He looked around for an escape but found none. Sparse lines of workers pulled grapes from the vines of his neighbor's fields, their simple existence devoid of the pressures of an irritable little girl only days after her second birthday.

"Can you stop the shushing?" Valletto exhaled, his shaking hands pressed against the kitchen counter.

"Do you want her quiet or not?"

Valletto found himself pacing almost uncontrollably across the room, as if somehow the distance of only a few paces would give him the peace and quiet he needed.

His wife scowled in disappointment and left the room, holding their daughter against her chest defensively. Valletto shook his head in anguish, taking several long moments to slow his breathing. The house fell silent. The birds chirped merrily in the morning sun in the picturesque but neglected garden behind their large house. He heard the gentle babbling of the little fountain in the garden. His head ached a little less.

As his breathing slowed, the realization of his ludicrous behavior sank in. He had fought to stop himself from shouting at a two-year old girl for asking for a treat. He had lost his temper with his wife for being protective over their daughter. He sank down to sit against the simple wooden cabinets of the family kitchen and closed his eyes. What an idiot he had been. He was numbly aware of light footsteps coming across from the kitchen doorway. A figure slumped down next to him and lay against him. He opened his eyes and saw his seven-year old son, Lyius, resting his head carefully against Valletto's shoulder before reaching across to take his hand.

"Are you alright?" the thin, frail boy asked.

"I'm alright," Valletto replied after a pause, "I'm just being an idiot. Again."

"You're not an idiot!" the brown-haired boy said defensively.

Valletto wrapped an arm around his son and pulled him in closer. He felt better instantly. It felt wrong, being a husband and father in his thirties, depending on a fragile seven-year old boy for support. Clera had voiced her concerns over that on more than one occasion. Lyius said he loved helping people and he loved to help his father more than anybody. It made him happy. It made Valletto feel like a parasite. He ruffled his son's hair affectionately and kissed the top of his head. He opened his mouth to speak. Then there was contact.

To describe a message across the arcane plains to a non-sorcerer would be like trying to describe color to a blind man. The closest thing, perhaps, would be to imagine an unseen hand, tugging gently at the cuff of a sleeve. A barely invasive attempt to grab attention. And then all that followed would be three, maybe four words. But those words came through, and they were whispered in Valletto's mind in a voice he knew well.

'Tarkis…undead…need…aeromancer…'

Valletto shot to his feet, his eyes wide with alarm.

"Father?"

He rushed off through the short, narrow hallway to the front door of his house and quickly pulled on his boots. Lyius dashed after him.

"Father?" he repeated.

"Tell your mother that something has come up," he said hurriedly as he grabbed his cloak. "Tell her I've gone in to the offices. To work. Tell her it is important."

Lyius looked up at Valletto, his eyes glazing over.

"But you said you weren't going to work today! You said…"

"Lyius!" Valletto urged. "This is important! Tell your…"

Valletto's instructions were cut off as his son squeezed his eyes shut tightly and began to cry. It was not particularly loud, yet somehow Valletto found it cut through the air to assault his ears, causing the pounding in his aching head to hit a new level. Squeezing his own eyes tightly shut as he took a moment to stop himself from shouting out in frustration, Valletto took in a deep breath and then quickly left the house.

Chapter Four

"How important?"

Saffus looked up from behind his untidy desk, his thick eyebrows furrowed suspiciously beneath his snow-white hair. Books lay piled up on one side of the birch desk; parchments lay scattered across the other. Sunlight poured into the oval shaped office, the low rays casting long shadows across the plethora of discarded letters, scrolls, books, and other assorted academia. Outside the office, the gentle chirping and singing of birds in the morning sun took the edge of the hustle and bustle of the center of the City of the Golden Horn, only a quarter of a league away from Saffus' office. Valletto swallowed uncomfortably from where he stood near the room's entrance.

"It's important," Valletto replied, "important enough to disturb you."

Grand Mage Saffus of Aigina, Advisor Primus of the Arcane to the Duma, gestured to the chair in front of his desk. Valletto walked across, spent a few moments wondering where to deposit the half-dozen parchments lying on the chair, decided to add to the dusty pile on the desk between them, and then sat down.

"Well? Go on."

"I've been contacted again by my man up near Torgias," Valletto began.

The old mage's eyes half closed and he let out a sigh of annoyance.

"Are we being invaded again, Val?"

"I don't know," Valletto answered truthfully.

Irritation, perhaps enforced for comic effect, was immediately replaced with a stern, severe look from the senior mage.

"What did he say?" Saffus asked.

"Tarkis. Undead. Need aeromancer."

Saffus leaned forward, planting his robed elbows on the desk in front of him and pressing his fingertips together in front of his wrinkled face.

"Alright. I'm less worried this time."

"Less worried?" Valletto exclaimed.

"Yes. It's only the undead. They're everywhere, like a disease. But a controllable one. We know there is this... Coven in operation across Basilea. But last time you came to me with a problem like this, it was the Abyss. Now those bastards, they have no business within our borders. Even a handful of those demonic shits are enough to concern me. Undead? Yes, yes, very dangerous... but also ubiquitous, if you look hard enough. You see?"

Valletto let out a breath between his clenched teeth.

"No!" he finally replied. "I don't see! This is Basilea, not Ophidia! Necromancy is outlawed! If there is a problem up in Tarkis that warrants Borjia sending a message to me across the arcane plains, then I think it warrants a response!"

"Oh, granted!" Saffus nodded. "Yes, a response. But last time you came in here with a warning from up north, it was regarding a potential Abyssal invasion, through portal stones! You see the difference? This could just be a country bumpkin with a spell book who has worked out how to raise a handful of zombies! This does not require me to go to the Duma and recommend that an army is sent north!"

Valletto shot to his feet, turning to pace across the office in frustration. He stepped over the first pile of books that he saw and then tripped up on a second, flailing across to throw a hand out to catch a bookshelf.

"Sir," he said, turning to straighten his shirt and compose himself, "if it was a country bumpkin with a spell book, Borjia would handle it. Also, he has specifically asked for an aeromancer? Why?"

"Why, indeed?" Saffus smiled. "Look, Val, I'm not ignoring the plight you have brought to me. Yes, this is odd and I will act. But your former student has asked for an aeromancer. So I shall send an aeromancer. And I'll let you know what he finds. All I'm saying is that on this occasion, we don't need to raise a cohort of legion soldiers."

Valletto sighed again, raising a hand to his pounding head. He looked across at Saffus, who had already resumed scribbling away on the parchment in front of him. He turned to leave. The stained, wooden door in front of him was shut, acting like a barrier between him and his problems at home. He thought of the ceaseless tears, the wailing and crying, the blame for every little problem. He thought of being woken every night and arguing every day. He remembered Clera's words. *"When you were off for weeks on end…"*

When he was off. Risking his life in battle to protect the country, as he was ordered to do. Not his choice. He resented the accusation, deeply.

"I'll go," Valletto declared, turning back to face the senior mage.

Saffus looked up.

"You've only just got back. And besides, you're in a teaching role. You're not eligible for deployment in your current job."

"I've been back for weeks now, I'm well-rested," Valletto lied, "I can go."

"Val," Saffus sighed, "aeromancers are as rare as any other mages, but not so rare that you are my only option. I can send some young, keen idiot to go off on an adventure. More importantly, last time I sent you off, I faced the wrath of your wife. She's absolutely terrifying. No, you go home. Gallivanting across the country isn't your job anymore."

Valletto took a step forward. All of a sudden, this seemed like the best idea in his world. In an instant, it had become absolutely crucial to him.

"If it needs an aeromancer, then this isn't a matter regarding petty, common magic. It needs a specialist. You don't want to send some freshly qualified youth, straight out of college! I'll go. I can be on the road north before midday."

Saffus leaned back in his chair, interlacing his fingers across his belly. His vivid eyes fixed on Valletto for a long, uncomfortable moment of silence.

"Anything you want to tell me?" he finally said.

"Nothing leaps to mind."

"People in your position rarely volunteer for time on the road, away from home, facing danger and discomfort. No, not rarely... *never.*"

Valletto folded his arms and exhaled. He thought through his words carefully. He considered blunt honesty; revealing that he was struggling at home, exhausted with domestic pressure, and wanted to teach his wife a lesson about how things were easier with him around. He considered playing the card of loyalty, integrity, and duty. He thought through half a dozen options in a few brief seconds before finally choosing his answer.

"I want to go."

Saffus eyed him, again with suspicion. Perhaps even a little disappointment, Valletto was not sure. He looked down and resumed his writing.

"Alright. You go. Report in via the normal methods. Off you go, then."

***

The road leading back down to Torgias was a dull, depressing affair now that the autumn rain had transformed the dirt into ankle-deep mud. The outskirts of the town appeared ahead; rickety miner's huts, seemingly constructed out of spare parts from the mine works that regularly punctuated the area, were dotted around haphazardly in the gullies and alcoves of the gray, rock walls. An offshore wind brought the unpleasant stench across from the smelting yards to the west. A little further ahead, the sturdy, wooden town wall and its four towers loomed up over the tumbledown mining huts outside the north gate.

An excited cry from one of the grimy children sat outside a hut greeted the four adventurers as they approached Torgias.

"The dragon-man! It's the dragon-man!"

A horde of half a dozen young children, screaming excitedly, ran out to meet them. A happy smile lit up Z'akke's face and he stomped comically out to meet the grubby children, his arms raised and claws extended as he let out a series of pathetic sounding growls and roars in imitation of a particularly unferocious dragon. The children gathered around him, some pretending to be scared and fleeing from him whilst others played as knights, whacking his thick, scaly armor with make-believe swords whilst he continued to stomp slowly after them and roar quietly.

"I hate children," Aestelle sighed, "but it is good that that loveable idiot can bring them some happiness."

"Well, 'tis early afternoon," Thesilar remarked, her hands placed on her slender hips, "so I assume the two of you will partake in that regular human ritual of drinking yourself into oblivion because you cannot be bothered to think of anything else to do. So with that in mind, I shall take my leave. Let me know when we have a plan."

Ragran watched Thesilar head over to the gateway at the town wall as Z'akke collapsed down to the ground, buried beneath a mass of writhing children who took it in to turns to take running jumps to elbow drop him as a second group of youths excitedly ran over to join the play with their beloved 'Dragon-man.' Ragran shook his head. Where he was from, a warrior did not degrade himself by rolling in the dirt with children.

"The Black Seam?" Ragran suggested to Aestelle.

"No," the tall woman replied, "I cannot stand that place. I'm going to the Trade Wind Inn."

"You waste your money there. It's overpriced for what it is."

Aestelle's response was cut off as an angry shout was issued from one of the miner's huts. A short, stout woman with curled white hair stamped over toward Z'akke and the playing children, rolling her sleeves up angrily.

"You lot!" she screamed. "Get off that thing! Get away from it!"

The children scattered, dashing off in every direction to disappear back into their huts, leaving one thin girl of perhaps six or seven years of age. The pale-faced girl looked up at the rotund woman as she approached.

"Lysa!" the woman yelled. "I said get away from that thing!"

The little girl looked up sorrowfully.

"But Mamma, he's the dragon-man," she protested quietly.

"He's my friend. He makes us laugh."

The woman grabbed her daughter roughly by the upper arm and dragged her back toward their hut, at a pace where the little girl struggled to keep up. Z'akke watched sorrowfully, his blue eyes doleful. Aestelle paced over and placed a hand on one of his scaly shoulders.

"You are not an 'it' to me, Z'akke," she said. "You're my friend, too."

The salamander looked over his shoulder at Aestelle and smiled.

"I have been called much worse," he said quietly.

The miner's wife and her daughter reached the entrance to their little hut. Ragran watched as the woman leaned over, holding up an admonishing finger at the little girl as she continued to scold her. The daughter said something, too far away for Ragran to hear, but he saw the woman raise her arm and then belt the girl across her face with the back of her hand.

Z'akke let out a loud gasp. The salamander stood tall, fists clenched and shoulders hunched. The scales along his spine lifted and flickered in agitation as steam began to waft up from his open mouth and nostrils. Z'akke bellowed a word in his own language with enough force than even Ragran jumped.

"Get your hands off her!" Z'akke roared, pacing purposefully over toward the mining hut.

"Wait! Z'akke! Stop!" Aestelle protested, rushing after him.

The miner's wife looked up furiously and somehow found enough bravery to take one step out toward the advancing, hulking salamander.

"Don't you dare tell me what to do with my own daughter!" she yelled.

Z'akke brought in a lungful of air, chest puffed up for a moment, and then flung his muscular arms to either side and leaned forward to let out a terrifying roar of anger. His mouth lit up yellow from the flames within his core as steam issued forth. The woman let out a cry of terror and grabbed her daughter before fleeing inside the hut and shutting the rickety door pathetically behind them.

"Get out here!" Z'akke bellowed, striding over to the hut. "You let that girl go! Now!"

Astounded by the display of unbridled rage in the normally placid salamander, Ragran followed Aestelle over in pursuit of the frenzied sorcerer. Aestelle placed a hand on Z'akke's shoulder and tried to stop him; the furious salamander grabbed her by neck, lifted her off her feet with one hand, and threw her aside like a discarded toy.

"Get out here!" he roared again, his tone guttural, and slammed a fist into the wooden support beam of the porch outside the hut.

The wooden pillar splinted and snapped with the force of the blow, and the entire porch collapsed in on itself. Z'akke raised a clenched fist as he reached the flimsy door to the hut. Ragran grabbed his wrist solidly. He was surprised by the sheer force Z'akke now displayed, but despite the pain from his wounds, he still found himself able to overpower the raging salamander.

"Enough!" he snarled. "Z'akke! Enough!"

Wrapping his arms around Z'akke's waist, he dragged the crazed salamander away from the hut, just as two halberd-armed men wearing the tabards of the Torgias Guard arrived by them.

"You there!" the taller of the two guards yelled. "Stop! Right now!"

"She was hurting a child!" Z'akke said desperately, the fire in his throat now dying away as his voice became more sorrowful than angry. "The little girl needed help!"

"We're taking you to the cells! You can explain this to the magistrate!" the guard said.

"Wait!"

Aestelle walked over, her leather-gloved hands held passively to either side.

"Wait!" she repeated. "Come on, Sancos, it's Z'akke! You know he would never hurt anybody!"

"I know what I saw, Aestelle!" the guard replied. "He just knocked half a house down! He's coming to the cells!"

"Don't take him in!" Aestelle urged.

"I can't ignore what I saw!"

Aestelle winced as if in pain and buried her face in her hands for a second before looking up again.

"I'm not asking you," she said sternly, "I'm ordering you. You're not taking him in."

"Ordering me?" the guard repeated incredulously. "On what authority?"

Aestelle paced over to her discarded pack and recovered a crumpled sheet of parchment from within it, which she then presented to the guards. The taller man read through it and then stared up at her, eyes agog.

"Is this real?!" he exclaimed.

"Yes," Aestelle sighed in frustration, "yes, it is real. As Viscountess of Monthaki, I am your legal superior. Do as I say and release him."

Ragran watched in astonishment as the guard handed the parchment back to Aestelle.

"I'll need to check this with the guard commander," he said. "This is not over yet."

"I'll be at the Trade Wind," Aestelle replied coolly.

The two guards walked cautiously away, exchanging muttered conversation with each other. Ragran eased the pressure off Z'akke. The salamander collapsed down to sit miserably amidst the rubble of the porch he had wrecked. Tears filled his eyes.

"She is just a child!" he said quietly. "A culture is defined by the way it cares for its own weak! The Deliverer herself said that! We must take care of our children and our elderly! We must! She can't hit her own child! Only a monster would do that!"

Aestelle dropped to one knee by the miserable salamander.

"It's her child, Z'akke," she said, "it is not up to us!"

"I have children!" the salamander sobbed. "I have three of my own! I miss my children! I miss my mate! I miss my parents! I don't want to be here! I want to go home!"

"Come on!" Ragran found himself growling in frustration. "Pull yourself together!"

"Shut up, you oaf!" Aestelle snapped.

Ragran watched uncomfortably as Aestelle sat down next to Z'akke, slipping an arm around his quivering shoulders. The salamander rested his head against Aestelle's, sniffing quietly as tears rolled down his dry, scaly face.

"I miss my children," he whispered. "I should be with them. I shouldn't be here."

Ragran let out a breath. He felt a pang; a tiny shred of sympathy when he thought of the support his own father had shown him in his youth. He had no children of his own that he was aware of, so could not say anything of comfort to the distressed salamander. But there was one other thing Z'akke talked about incessantly, aside from his family, and there Ragran could help. Clutching his chest, he limped over to his own pack and fished out a small, curved object from the bottom. Something interesting to him, but not nearly as interesting as discovering that Aestelle was suddenly a titled member of the upper classes – but that conversation would have to wait.

"Z'akke," Ragran said, "look at this. It's a tooth from a blue dragon."

Z'akke's eyes shot open.

"D... dragon?" he gasped.

"Only a young one and only a small tooth from the back of the mouth somewhere. But still rare. I won it in a game of dice against Semential Curnis. I was going to make a necklace out of it, or something. I never got around to it. Anyway. You have it. Here."

His jaw agape, Z'akke reached out with a shaking hand for the dragon tooth.

"R... really?"

Ragran nodded.

His face alight with joy, Z'akke examined the tooth in minute detail.

"Thank you!" he gasped. "Thank you, thank you, thank you!"

"Come on," Ragran grunted to Z'akke and Aestelle, pain flaring up in his wounded chest again, "let's go to that overpriced tavern and get something to drink."

***

"Master?"

Khirius slowly opened his eyes.

"Master?" Tonnen's hoarse voice repeated. "We are here."

Khirius sat up in the back of the wagon. Many days had been spent on the road now, moving steadily eastward to cross the border into Basilea and navigate onward toward the coast. The hours of sunlight were spent traveling in the back of the cramped wagon, squeezed uncomfortably between several chests of gold and riches, and two of his servants, whilst Tonnen drove the wagon with the third. Several chests of gold; all that was left of his family's fortune. Khirius smirked wryly. Perhaps he should count himself grateful even for that. Not just for his recent and fortuitous escape from a violent demise, but also for the help in the early days, when he finally escaped from the clutches of the vampire who made him into what he was. The smirk became a genuine smile of gratitude as he remembered the kindness of Lord Eldon, perhaps the only other vampire he had encountered who possessed the kindness to assist a fellow creature blighted by the curse of undeath.

Khirius and his servants stopped at coaching inns during the night, with Khirius' servants taking the opportunity to sleep in the rooms he paid for, whilst Khirius wiled away his waking hours unsuccessfully trying to find a good book or occasionally sustaining himself with the blood of some hapless character he found in the taverns or roadsides. Khirius made sure to spend some time evaluating potential victims, ensuring at best he was killing individuals who were particularly unpleasant; at worst, when desperation set in, he confined himself at least to those without dependents.

But now, after so many uncomfortable days of travel, they had reached their destination. Khirius stepped down from the back of the wagon and regarded his new surroundings, the thoughts of his lost, most likely dead, servants at his former home still nagging at his conscience. A waning moon gleamed down through the broken clouds of the crisp, night sky above, illuminating the surrounding foothills and small copses of autumnal trees. The horizon to the northwest was dominated by sweeping, majestic mountains that reached up through the layer of cloud, their jagged tops hidden in the clear skies somewhere up above. A wolf howled, probably a good quarter of a league away, but at a pitch that was exactly right for Khirius' attuned ears to make it seem as if it were only a few paces.

"The Mountains of Tarkis," Khirius nodded, taking in the resplendent view.

"Yes, Master," Tonnen nodded, "as you commanded."

Khirius again remembered the letter left on his desk, the day he had been forced from his home. It would be an overstatement to say that he had been summoned to Tarkis – it was more of a stern and pointed request – but he could be economical with the truth enough to make it appear that he had dropped everything out of respect to the Coven. That was far better than the actual truth; that he was a vampire on the run from hunters, left with only four servants and a wagon full of two centuries of accumulated riches.

"You have a proposal for a place to stay for the night?" Khirius looked across at his aged servant before nodding to the tired-looking women huddled together in the wagon. "They need rest."

"Yes, Master," Tonnen said, "I made some inquiries at a farm complex we passed perhaps three hours before sunset. There is a town not far ahead. A port called Torgias, just up on the coast."

"Torgias," Khirius repeated. "Well, it is as good a place as any. Hopefully it will have some better accommodation than the last few country inns we have frequented. But if we are stopping here for some time, you know the hazards we face. If we move fast enough, I can afford to leave a small and discreet trail behind us. If we are staying put, things get a little harder."

"Of course, Master," Tonnen cleared his throat. "We shall make the usual inquiries in town to ascertain what options we have open to us."

Khirius noted the small clouds of white that briefly appeared in front of the mouths of his servants as they breathed out into the cold, night air. He, of course, had none. There was no warmth within him, body or soul, assuming he still possessed the latter.

"Back on the road to Torgias, then," Khirius declared. "We shall find lodgings for the night and then set about finding some help."

***

Aestelle flung the doors to the Trade Wind Inn open before swagger-ing toward the bar, allowing the last rays of the evening, summer sun to pour into the tavern. Brimming with self-importance, she removed her greatsword and bow from her back as she paced across the wooden floor, all eyes upon her. All conversation died as she entered, and the eight or nine patrons barring her way stepped aside wordlessly to allow her through.

"Henry!" she called out. "Drinks for all my friends, here! Drinks for everybody! We have met with success again!"

A cheer erupted from the two dozen patrons. Aestelle held her hands up and twirled in place, arrogantly beaming from ear to ear as she accepted the praise and adulation of her sycophantic admirers. Ragran followed her in, leaving his pack and axe by the door as a barmaid whose name he did not remember walked over to him with a purposeful smile. Aestelle leaned back against the bar as the landlord set about bringing over bottles of wine. She propped one booted foot against the bar behind her, crooking one leg to allow a bare thigh to part the strips of her leather armored skirts. She was immediately surrounded by a crowd of admirers.

Guraf grumbled to himself as he paced over to a quiet table in the corner. Z'akke followed him, sitting down to fish a piece of parchment and a stick of charcoal from his pack before he continued on another of his drawings. A peal of laughter erupted from the crowd of men encircling Aestelle as she described the party's latest adventures in the barrows of the foothills of Tarkis. Ragran smiled down at the nameless, raven-haired barmaid. He would at least observe the formality of buying her a drink first...

Ragran opened the doors of the Trade Wind Inn, greeted by a warm blast of air from the hearth to combat the chilly, evening wind. Good quality furniture of oiled cypress furnished the neat alcoves surrounding the hearth and central bar. Perhaps twenty or so patrons were in the tavern; some were officers of merchant ships in the port; others were wealthy mine owners. A motley group of four armed men in the far corner exhibited every sign of amateur adventurers, from their cheap but pristine weapons and armor to the map of the local area they all argued over. Aestelle, Thesilar, and Z'akke followed Ragran in silently, a far cry from the theatrical entrances Aestelle used to make in that very tavern in years gone by.

"Ragran!" Henry, the landlord called over from behind the bar. "Been a long time! You still on ales?"

"Yeah, ale," Ragran smiled a greeting at the tall, pot-bellied tav-ern owner.

All eyes were on Aestelle and Z'akke as they followed Ragran in; some curiously eyeing the red-scaled salamander; most lecherously leering over the tall, blonde adventurer.

"You want the normal sending up to your room?" Henry greeted Aestelle as she leaned across the bar.

"No," Aestelle yawned, "I'll stay here for a while. Do you still do those platters? The bread with the olive oil? And cheese? But not one that stinks. Enough for the four of us."

"Which bread?"

"The nice bread."

"They're all nice, or I wouldn't sell it."

"You know!" Aestelle sighed impatiently. "The... *nice* one!"

"We've just had a crate of Melisian wine shipped in," piped up Fran, the landlady's burly wife, with an oddly unsettling grin. "Good stuff! Twenty years old! If you've got the coin for it!"

"Coins!" Aestelle snapped irritably. "If you pluralize the singular concrete noun 'coin,' you add a sodding 's' on the end! Coins, Fran! Coins!"

The wart-faced woman stared at Aestelle incredulously throughout her outburst, pausing for a few moments in silence with her fists planted on her broad hips before she responded.

"Do you want the wine or not, you skinny bitch?"

Aestelle glowered back at her.

"Yes, I'll take the damned wine!"

Aestelle stomped over to a quiet alcove and sat down moodily in the corner, staring out of the steamed-up window at the drizzly evening outside. Z'akke followed her.

"What's up with her, then?" Fran scowled.

"Don't know," Ragran shrugged, "don't really care, either."

"She's been like this ever since that battle up at Andro. Ever since she got famous," Henry remarked dryly as he began to fill a wooden tankard up with ale from a barrel behind him.

"She's probably upset that she has to share the lyrics of those atrocious bard's songs with other people," Thesilar said bitterly. "Now enough talk about Aestelle. Could I get some service, please?"

Ragran slid a pair of coins across the bar to pay for his tankard of ale and then made his way across to sit with Aestelle and Z'akke. Thesilar soon joined them as Fran brought across their bread, oil, and wine.

"I'm sorry," Z'akke said quietly, once the landlady had moved on to serve another alcove, "about all of that outside the town. I just... I sometimes forget how different the customs are here."

"It's alright," Ragran said, taking in a mouthful of the bitter ale and relishing the oaky aftertaste, "it's not for me to interfere. But I can see why you did. Even where I'm from, the bond between a parent and child should be... better than that."

"Oh?" Thesilar raised an eyebrow as she set about slicing up the warm loaf of bread. "Did I miss something?"

"No, no," Z'akke said awkwardly, "nothing."

The conversation was interrupted momentarily as the door to the inn opened, admitting a tall, pale-faced man of middling years with piercing eyes and an expensive-looking linen shirt visible beneath an equally grand cloak. He was followed by an older man and three women whose plain attire marked them out as his servants. Ragran watched them for a moment with disinterest. His thoughts were otherwise occupied and had been for the past couple of days. He entertained the notion of sharing his thoughts with his companions, as seemed to be the fashion in the soft societies of Basilea, but then decided against it. He then saw Thesilar open her mouth to begin talking, her eyes lit up with a mischievous playfulness that could only mean her words would be at Z'akke's expense. Ragran, even in his own mind uncharacteristically, decided to speak up so as to save the salamander from further persecution.

"It's a year since my father died," he said suddenly, "it has been on my mind."

"Oh, I'm sorry," Z'akke said sincerely, his scaly brows sinking in sympathy. "I am so very sorry. There is a prayer... a rite of honoring the dead I could say for him if it is not disrespectful. I am sorry for you."

Ragran mused over the offer. It was easy to forget that Z'akke was a mage-priest, as he rarely discussed the spiritual side of his vocation. In fact, Ragran thought, he could barely remember seeing Z'akke do anything priest-like at all.

"Yes," Aestelle looked over from the window, "I'm sorry, Ragran. Were you close?"

"Once," Ragran admitted, "when I was younger. I was one of four boys, but I always thought that I was the favorite."

"Was he a good man?" Thesilar asked.

"I thought so. Where I come from, he was respected. He could fight better than any other. And he could drink more than an ox. He was a good man, in my eyes. But to you lot? Probably not. To people like you, he was probably a complete bastard."

Z'akke raised his tankard and gave a respectful nod.

"To your father's memory," the salamander mage-priest said solemnly.

Ragran reached over the table and clinked his own tankard against the salamander's, finding some comfort in his words.

"To his memory," he said quietly.

All four adventurers drank in honor of Taavi and then fell silent. Predictably, it was Z'akke who was the first to break that silence.

"Now that I have heard back from Borjia and we know that this Valletto is on the way to us, what is the plan now?"

"We wait," Aestelle answered simply. "We pay for rooms here for a few days, and we wait. As soon as he arrives, we go back up into the mountains and we break that door open."

Ragran looked across the table at his companions. Z'akke gazed thoughtfully out of the window at the dark, rainy sky outside; Aestelle sampled her wine, appeared unimpressed, and then turned to adjust her hair in the reflection of the window. Thesilar stared across the tavern, watching the pale man who had entered the building a few moments before. The elf woman placed one clenched fist into an open hand and rested her chin on them, her narrowed eyes concentrated on the tall man's every move.

"Thesilar?" Ragran asked.

She glanced across.

"Yes, I heard," she said. "We wait here until this grand sorcerer arrives. Fine. If you'll excuse me, I'm going to get an early night."

***

On a visit to Ophidia in his childhood, back in the simple days of mortal life, Khirius' father had once taken him and his sister to see a wealthy man's collection of exotic animals. From all across Pannithor, the rich merchant had collected everything from a lion to a bear, even a gur panther and a ferocious tyrant lizard. But the jewel of his collection was an adolescent red wyvern. Khirius recalled his boyish fear as his father ushered him to the edge of the creature's enclosure – a very cramped affair, as if the wyvern had enough room to build up speed, things would quickly become problematic for the owner. Khirius looked down to see the majestic creature, beautiful in its sweeping lines and long, graceful limbs that bristled with muscular power and ended in razor sharp talons. The monster was inherently evil, that much even the young Khirius could tell, yet it possessed an otherworldly beauty and a rich intelligence that hinted toward something far deeper than simple malevolence behind its resentful eyes.

As Khirius sat on the simple chair by his dresser, holding position so that Hanna could finish her sketch, that was precisely how he felt. Of course he knew he was evil. He existed by draining the blood and the very life of others. But he liked to think that there was something deeper, something more spiritual behind the centuries' long anguish that tormented his soul in the sheer act of continuing to exist.

"Finished, Master," Hanna smiled briefly, placing down her charcoal stick.

Khirius held out a hand. His servant walked across the creaking floorboards of the inn room, a nervousness in her eyes as both of her small hands clutched tightly to the yellowed piece of paper before her.

"No need to be scared," Khirius said honestly, "I have told you before. I am not here for flattery. You serve me with your honesty."

Khirius took the piece of paper. The portrait, as always, was elegant in its simplicity yet displayed the talent of its artist via the bold contrast of the shading within the accurate outlines of shape. Being devoid of a reflection, it was the only way Khirius ever knew what he looked like. And, judging by the deathly pale skin and the deep shading beneath his eyes, he knew that he did not look well. He glanced up at Hanna.

"You need to... to..."

"Kill again," Khirius helped the young woman with her words.

Before she could reply, Khirius flinched for not the first time that evening as he sensed something akin to brightness close by. He turned his head to look at the door of his inn room, as if that would somehow assist him in seeking out the source of the unnatural sensation.

"Master?"

Khirius held up a hand to silence Hanna as he slowly stood.

The sensation was similar in many ways to what he had detected shortly before his home at Redworth Down was attacked. The divinity magic used by the Brotherhood knight had made him flinch in pain just by being a handful of yards away. This, however, was different. This was not painful. Almost... pleasant to be near.

"Divinity," Khirius muttered to himself, "there is somebody in this inn who is, perhaps, not what they claim to be."

"You can sense a priest?" Hanna asked.

"No. Something different. Something more powerful and yet... I don't know... an untapped resource. Unrefined. Unaware, almost."

The sensation drifted away again. Khirius turned to Hanna and offered her the portrait with a gentle smile. She accepted it with a courteous bow of the head.

"Can you sense every magic, Master?" she asked suddenly.

Khirius laughed.

"Oh no! Far from it! Divinity, in many ways, opposes what I am, so that is what I sense. I can sense beings similar to myself but in a different way. That is the way this curse has chosen to manifest itself in me."

"Chosen, Master?"

"It is one way of describing it. Over the last two hundred years, I have encountered several vampires. But never have I encountered two alike. Our powers and our vulnerabilities are all unique. What you see in me will not be the same as you see in the next vampire you cross paths with, should that ever occur."

Any further conversation was stifled as Khirius heard two sets of heavy feet thumping up the creaking staircase from the ground floor. He turned again to face the door as the two figures made their way along the corridor before stopping outside his room. By this point, even Hanna could hear the steps. She moved quickly over to the polished dresser by the window and recovered a slim knife from the top drawer.

"Master?"

Khirius heard Tonnen's voice from outside. The tall vampire nodded to Hanna, and the servant walked across to open the door. Tonnen stood outside with a broad-shouldered man of perhaps thirty years of age, his dark hair cut short and his thick features partially hidden beneath a gruff beard that fell down over his brown cloak. Khirius momentarily sensed the brightness of divinity again, but it was far enough away to eliminate any chance of it emanating from the newcomer accompanying Tonnen.

"Somebody to see you, Master," Tonnen announced, "this is…"

"My name is not important," the dark-haired man snapped confrontationally. "I am here to speak with your master. You may leave."

Khirius folded his arms slowly and narrowed his eyes. Tonnen looked at him expectantly. Khirius shook his head once, and Tonnen remained in place.

"Shut the door," the newcomer commanded Tonnen.

Again, he looked to Khirius for guidance. Khirius nodded.

"You have, no doubt, received the letter from my superiors within the Coven," the bearded man said, his tone a little more hushed. "You are expected, tomorrow night."

Khirius stood up and looked down at the young man. Sensing undeath in others was far from sure, as was even the dark stench of necromancy; but even with those two inconsistencies accepted, Khirius could sense nothing abnormal or special in the man stood before him.

"You seem confident that I am the person you think I am," Khirius issued a thin smile, "which seems rather risky considering…"

"I know exactly who you are," the dark-haired man interjected. "Our people have followed your movements since you crossed the border into Basilea. There are people within the Coven who are more than capable of sensing a being such as yourself."

"Can you?" Khirius challenged, finding it some effort to keep his voice impassive in the face of the rude newcomer.

"I cannot," the young man raised his bearded chin defiantly, "I..."

"...have talents in other areas, one presumes." Khirius took a step forward.

"My talents do not concern you," the man replied with some venom. "What does concern you is that you arrive at the village of Aphos, three leagues to the north of here, two hours after sunset to-morrow."

Khirius took a few slow paces up and down the center of his inn room, his feet causing the dry boards to creak, his hands clasped behind his back. He mulled over the man's words, actions, attire, and general demeanor. After a few moments, he turned to address the visi-tor again.

"You're nothing more than a servant," Khirius declared. "Ad-mittedly a trusted one, but you have no powers. Arcane, necromantic, even worldly authority. No, no... do not interrupt me again, for your life may depend upon it. You have burst into my chamber, treated my servants – your equals – with contempt, and then your manner with me, your superior, has been deeply inappropriate."

"You are not my superior," the man grimaced. "I am the head servant of Lord Annaxa himself. You should consider yourself privi-leged that he sent me personally to talk to you."

Hanna let out an audible breath. Tonnen frowned, shook his head, and then quietly locked the door behind Annaxa's servant.

"I died a little under two centuries ago," Khirius explained, "but in life I had a younger sister. I doted upon her, especially when we were children. She married a military man. He treated her well enough and they seemed to enjoy a good life together. I miss her dearly. But I digress. One thing she learned the hard way was that it does not do to wear one's husband's rank."

"I have no idea what you are..."

"A man, or equally a woman in this day and age for that matter, works hard to achieve ranks and status. Simply marrying them does not give you the instant right to the marks of respect they have earned. It is the height of bad manners for an individual to talk down to anoth-er based solely upon a link they have with a third party. Do you see? Even worse if that link is one of servitude rather than marriage. Alas, you have learned the hard way also. And a little too late, too."

Baring his fangs, Khirius leapt forward to seize the terror-strick-en servant.

Chapter Five

There was at least an empty market square near the center of Torgias. That allowed the settlement to officially call itself a town, but in Valletto's eyes, the settlement was little more than a large village. The perimeter walls encircled a motley collection of wooden and stone buildings, ranging from homes and taverns to cobblers, blacksmiths, and farriers. But, even with everything a coastal settlement in mine-country could need, it all seemed very backwater and miniscule when compared to Valletto's life in the City of the Golden Horn, or at least living on the semi-rural outskirts of it. Only an hour after sunrise, the streets were all but deserted, but the few early risers still managed to remind him of his outsider status by eyeing him suspiciously. This elicited a wry grin from Valletto; not only was he human, he was also a fellow Basilean. Where he was from, the streets bustled with dwarfs, elves, and ogres alongside humans from every kingdom in Mantica. Yet here, within the same borders, his attire marked him out as neither a miner nor a sailor; so to these simple, secluded people, he was somehow worthy of a second glance.

Following the directions from the guards at the town's south gate, Valletto threaded his way past shops as their wooden shutters were opened for the day's trading, sailors heading to the docks on the eastern side of the town, and affluent mining supervisors who left their townhouses to head off into the hills to the west, past the shanty town outside the settlement wall made up of the homes of their subordinates.

The Trade Wind Inn was easy enough to find, the neat collection of buildings occupying their own cobbled enclosure not far from the town hall. A carriage drawn by two horses plodded away from the inn's stables and past Valletto as he approached, a chill autumnal wind blowing through the streets from the snow-capped peaks on the northwestern horizon. Valletto saw four figures waiting by the wooden bench seats in the small garden to the side of the inn's main building. He immediately recognized one. Aestelle stood with her arms folded across her chest, leaning back on a wooden beam supporting the slated roof over the short row of bench seats and tables. Although it had only been a few weeks since they had last crossed paths on the return journey to the capital after the Battle of Andro, it somehow seemed longer. Far longer.

The tall woman – standing the same height as Valletto, himself relatively tall for a man – was clad in her signature garb of tight black leathers, covering her entirely save for her head, the eye-catching but deeply impractical low neckline of her light armor, and her bare shoulders. Her bright, sandy-blonde hair was worn up, complementing her tanned skin, and punctuated along one side of her head by neat rows of sparkling precious stones. The handle of a greatsword emerged from over one shoulder; a bow and quiver of arrows over the other to bracket her flawlessly beautiful face. That beauty momentarily reminded Valletto of his wife – even Aestelle's unearthly perfection was not enough to force his eyes to wander – but the reminder of the terms under which he left his home and his family left his stomach knotted and nauseous.

Sat on one of the benches was a truly gargantuan man – some six and a half feet of solid muscle – a weathered, middle-aged face hidden behind a scraggy beard of graying dirty blond and long hair tied up in a top-knot at the crown; a style openly mocked in the capital and the punch line of many jokes, marking the man out as a foreigner. The giant's dark, heavy brow, tree-trunk like bare arms, and long double-headed axe immediately dissuaded Valletto from any temptation to crack jokes about the top-knot. The horned skull of some horrific beast was worn on one shoulder in the manner of a pauldron.

Opposite the yellow-haired man-mountain was a complete enigma. Valletto had encountered a handful of salamanders in his travels – even a few of their mage-priests – but nothing quite like the creature sat at the end of the bench. Valletto could sense the arcane energies flowing around the salamander – even before he saw the wizard's staff – strong enough that they could even be narrowed down to flowing from the pyromancy discipline; a sphere of magic that dominated the ranks of salamander mages. Yet the creature before him did not wear the robes of a mage-priest. He glanced across at Valletto as he approached, his large, blue eyes blinking, his jaw set in a curious way that hid his sharp teeth and set his mouth so that it gave the impression of a friendly smile. That inane smile, coupled with the large, almost naïve eyes, made the powerful salamander appear more like an oversized infant's toy dragon rather than a fire-wielding sorcerer from a race that Valletto knew to be bold and dangerous.

The final figure, perched at the end of one of the tables, was remarkable in her normality. The tall, slim figure wore ruddy greens and browns; tough, practical clothes that looked ideally suited for the inclement weather that Tarkis in autumn was known to bring. A green gem hung from a cord around her neck – Valletto sensed the mild flow of magical energy from it and identified it as a bond-stone. She also carried a bow and quiver over one shoulder, and would have been inconspicuous beyond this if it were not for the delicately pointed tips of her ears that protruded through her roughly scrapped back, dark auburn hair. From Valletto's experience, elves commanded attention even in the capital, let alone out here in the backwater streets of a Basilean mining town. The drab attire of the elf archer highlighted her pale complexion, and an air of almost mischievous humor lit her eyes as she watched Valletto approach.

"Val," Aestelle issued a slight smile, offering a leather-gloved hand, "it is good to see you."

Valletto took the hand and shook it. Aestelle's grip was firm but not strong. In his experience, most fighting women he had met had handshakes that could crush bones. Valletto had no doubt that Aestelle could do so if she chose, but the decision not to spoke more about her self-confidence and lack of any need to prove a point. Still, her warm greeting seemed odd enough. Yes, Valletto knew Aestelle from the Battle of Andro. Yes, they had spoken several times on the ride back to the capital after their victory. But beyond that, they were all but complete strangers. Certainly not friends.

"How is your wife?" Aestelle inquired. "Clera, isn't it?"

Valletto respected her for at least committing that detail to memory, but the mention of his wife's name amplified the churning in his gut. He remembered the bitter disappointment in her eyes as she watched him leave the house for the last time, their children crying as they clung to her. She knew he had volunteered to go. He had not told her, but she knew.

"She is well," Valletto said, "well enough, at least. And you?"

"Oh, I'm just dandy," Aestelle smirked, her eyes half-closed. "Back here again, as if I never left. Come on, I shall introduce you to the others."

Valletto followed Aestelle over to the benches as a cart packed with casks of ale clopped across the cobbles to head around to the back of the inn. The salamander stood up and nodded his head in greeting. The barbarian and the elf remained seated, watching the newcomer in silence.

"Valletto, this is Ragran. You've no doubt heard of him."

Valletto's eyes widened in surprise. Ragran the Mighty was a name known well enough in song and tale. Stories of his daring had graced the halls of nobility and the campfires of the peasantry for nearly twenty years. Contrary to expectation, Ragran was every inch in reality the gargantuan warrior that was described by the bards.

"An honor," Valletto chose the word carefully based on what little he knew of the cultures of the north.

Ragran returned the nod with a vague hint of a smile.

"Thesilar," Aestelle gestured to the elf, "the self-confessed mastermind behind the plan to take down Thrundak Skullsplitter."

Again, Valletto found himself shocked to be in the presence of a famed adventurer whose stories had entertained him even as a young man. Thesilar was one of the four who had fought their way into Thrundak's fortress and eliminated him after his reign of terror across the Ardovikian Plain and into the outskirts of the Forest of Galahir itself.

"And if that leaves you wondering whether the salamander here is the famed Hrrath Flamespitter himself, you will be disappointed." The elf smirked with a malicious glint in her eyes. "This is just Z'akke. You won't have heard of him."

The friendly looking salamander had already taken a few paces across to meet Valletto, offering a hand in honor of the human custom of greeting. His warm smile instantly faded at Thesilar's words. Valletto looked across at the smirking elf and instantly formed a judgment. It was far from positive and left him sympathetic to the evidently bullied salamander. He looked back at the glum-looking mage and saw something of his son, Lyius, in that forlorn expression. He leapt out and shook the salamander's hand warmly.

"You are Z'akke?!" Valletto exclaimed. "By the Ones above! What an honor!"

Z'akke looked down at the human mage in confusion.

"You… you've heard of me?"

"Of course!" Valletto lied, picking out the most generic adventuring archetype he could think of before continuing. "Who was the human warrior who used to accompany you? The fellow from the humble background."

"Saltius?!" Z'akke exclaimed in surprise. "You've heard of him?"

"Only in passing, but your adventure off to… the south is one of my favorite stories of all."

"That little crypt outside Ul'Arah?" the salamander grinned in blissful ignorance. "My gosh! How did anybody think that was worthy of a story?"

Thesilar smiled wryly at Valletto, evidently seeing right through his series of white lies. Valletto folded his arms and met her glare.

"It may only have been a little crypt," Valletto said, "but two unknown heroes facing it was always more impressive to me than four famed adventurers wandering through a forest and killing an orc."

Z'akke's jaw hung open and silently, his eyes wide, he looked from person to person in quick succession, joy painted across his scaly features. Ragran watched the exchange without emotion. Aestelle exchanged a brief conspiratory smirk with Valletto. Thesilar eyed him angrily.

"Well then," Aestelle said, "now that the introductions are done, we should be going. The crypt is not far from here."

"Crypt?" Valletto asked. "What crypt? I don't even know why I am here. And are we really leaving now? I've been on the road since well before dawn. Can't this wait until tomorrow?"

"We've been waiting for days already," Ragran grumbled, standing up and lifting a large pack onto his back. "Enough with the waiting. We're going."

"Come on," Aestelle said, "I shall explain all on the way."

***

Aestelle dropped down from the air tunnel and into the passageway below, landing lightly in a squat with her sword held ready. Her eyes flitted from side to side, examining the stony corridor. It was as they had left it, save one worryingly noteworthy change. The torches hung from the walls were illuminated. Standing up, Aestelle took a careful pace forward as Ragran dropped down behind her, his heavy frame causing the thud of his feet to echo along the corridor. Wordlessly, the two stood shoulder to shoulder and advanced cautiously along the corridor as Z'akke, Valletto, and Thesilar dropped down to follow them.

Cold air wafted past Aestelle's bare shoulders, chilling her skin as she stepped carefully forward. Learning her lesson from their last aborted attempt at invading the tunnels, Aestelle had drank significantly less than normal the previous night but now found her throat dry and her temples throbbing with a dull ache. The group advanced carefully to the first junction where last time they had encountered the first trap. Aestelle looked down at the tiled floor.

"Wait," she breathed.

"What?" Ragran demanded.

"The body that was here last time. The dead man. He is gone."

A hushed commotion sounded behind Aestelle as Thesilar pushed her way past the two mages.

"What's the problem?" she demanded. "Are you blundering into traps again?"

Aestelle gestured at the floor with the tip of her greatsword.

"The body is gone."

"So?"

"So!" Aestelle growled. "The torches are lit and a dead body has disappeared! We are not venturing into tunnels left undisturbed for centuries! There is activity down here!"

"The question remains," the elf raised one eyebrow, "so?"

"So we need to think this through!" Aestelle hissed, fighting the urge to punch the self-righteous, conceited elf in the nose. "We..."

"We what?" Thesilar interrupted. "Leave? Because somebody lit a torch? We carry on, precautious pretty. *You* should be exercising supreme caution at all times down here regardless! Not upping your game just because something has changed! Now stop complaining and get that mage of yours to the door."

In direct contrast to the agreed plan, Thesilar pushed her way past Aestelle to step over the trap they had discovered on their last journey to the tunnels, to then take lead and make her way forward. Aestelle stared at the elf's back, momentarily imagining whipping her pistol up from her belt and shooting Thesilar in the spine.

After only a few more paces, Thesilar stopped dead in her tracks. Wordlessly, the short precession behind her halted. She dropped to one knee and looked down at a marking on one of the stone slabs beneath her feet. Aestelle walked over to examine the find. Three marks were drawn in what looked like charcoal on the ground; two crossed lines and a triangle on top of them.

"What is it?" she asked the elf.

Thesilar turned to look over her shoulder.

"What is it?!" she spat. "Have I taught you nothing? It is a necromantic rune. A placeholder, until the real thing can be transcribed here. This place has been measured and assessed for necromancy to be used so that a bunch of corpses can be dumped here, and the next idiots like us who wander through will activate the dormant magic and raise them. I have taught you this before, Aestelle."

"*You* are the one who knows about undead!" Aestelle snapped. "I am the one who knows the demonology! This looks new! This is all the more evidence that things are developing here!"

"But it has not been implemented yet," Thesilar frowned, "so I suggest you dig deep, find some courage, and we move on. Alright?"

After only a few more moments, they reached the door that had barred their progress on the previous expedition. The two huge, smooth stones stood exactly where they had left them, fitted perfectly to the rough walls of the rocky passageway. Dust-filled runes were etched to either side of the wavy split between the rocks, now overgrown with moss and fungi. Valletto stepped up to examine the runes.

"Well?" Ragran demanded. "Can you open it?"

"I'm still working that out," Valletto replied, his voice distracted as he ran a hand across the runes. "These are old. That obviously won't come as a surprise to you, but... this is an old form of aeromancy. More of an art rather than the science we see it as today. It's like... studying an old text written in original Primovantorian.

"I don't care about that!" Ragran growled. "Can you open it?"

Valletto stepped back from the rocky door, cleared his throat, and turned to look up at the gargantuan barbarian.

"Before we go on, let's get one thing clear," the aeromancer stated coolly. "I'm well aware that you can break me over your knee or cut me in half with that axe. You're a big man with a big reputation. But you need me. I don't need you. I'm here to help you, and I can walk away at any time I like. So from this point forth, you don't speak to me like I'm your whipping boy. You show me the same base level of respect that I am showing you."

Valletto turned back to the stones. Z'akke let out a half-choked snigger.

"Shut up, Z'akke," Ragran grunted.

Valletto looked over the stone doors, starting at the ceiling of the passageway and scanning his eyes down to the dusty floor. He placed a hand against one of the runes, and Aestelle saw a smoky, blurred tendril of energy snake out of his palm. Nothing happened. Valletto swore under his breath. The aeromancer tilted his head to one side, his eyes narrowed. He reached up again and, to a non-mage at least, appeared to carry out the exact same procedure. Again, the blur of arcane energy surrounded Valletto's outstretched hand.

Dust coughed up from the edges of the stone slabs and small rocks fell from the ceiling above them. A blast of stale air blew between the two stone slabs, dislodging a handful of moss. With a dry creak and groan of stone against abrasive stone, the two slabs rolled apart to disappear into channels cut into the tunnel to either side. The tunnel continued ahead into the darkness, Aestelle's vision without the benefit of the blazing torches along the walls quickly being obscured by the blackness ahead.

Aestelle could smell them long before she could see or even hear them. The overpowering stench of decay and rotting flesh wafted down from the tunnel ahead. Thesilar was the first to react, snatching an arrow from the quiver on her back and notching it to be bow before loosing the deadly projectile into the darkness. Ragran let out a booming yell that echoed down the rocky tunnel, raising his huge axe above his head and pelting away into the darkness. Aestelle raised her sword and sprinted off to follow him, now aware of familiar choked and rasping moans ahead as another arrow whistled in between her and Ragran to thud into something in the darkness before them. Through a combination of her eyes quickly adjusting to the darkness and their sinister adversaries limping out of the shadows toward the light, Aestelle saw the hunkered, shambling forms of the undead up ahead.

Ragran met the first zombie like a hurricane tearing through a barn, his axe whirling down to slice through the pale creature from hip to hip, sending the upper half of the body toppling back to land behind its own feet. Aestelle caught up and lunged forward to lance the tip of her greatsword through a second zombie's chest with clinical precision; she twisted the blade in place to open a greater wound, yanked the weapon free, and then planted a booted foot on the creature's torso to kick it down to the ground.

More of the undead monsters staggered toward them; from what she could make out in the shadows, perhaps another five or six. Each fixed her with a deathly gaze from their vacant, milky white eyeballs that stared unblinking from within gaunt, putrid faces beneath dank, limp hair. Shaking hands reached out for her and Ragran at the ends of thin, rotten limbs covered in scraps of cloth whose color had long ago bled away. The closest zombie opened its mouth to display a jaw of broken, green-gray teeth and then half-lunged, half-fell toward Aestelle. She sliced both of its arms off at the elbows and reversed her strike to hack open the creature's chest, but still it moaned and rasped, flailing out at her as, by her feet, the first zombie she had attacked crawled on and reached out to grab at her ankles.

***

Valletto watched as Ragran and Aestelle tore into the advancing zombies, axe and sword felling the undead monstrosities that poured through the stone passageway from the darkness ahead. His feet somehow remained firmly rooted to the spot as he watched, numbly aware of the fear rising in his gut as he realized that he had placed himself in mortal danger for absolutely no good reason. Only a handful of strangers – themselves skilled and experienced with fighting in dark, damp tunnels, admittedly – stood between him and his beloved son and daughter growing up without a father. All of this because he could not check his temper. At that moment, Valletto would have given anything, absolutely anything below the heavens, to be tucked up in bed next to his son, reading him a story as he drifted off into a contented sleep.

"Behind us!" Thesilar yelled, loosing off another arrow that shot through the air with unerring accuracy to thread between Ragran and Aestelle and plant squarely in the forehead of a zombie. "There's more of them coming from behind us!"

Galvanized into action, Valletto turned and looked back down the corridor they had taken to reach the sealed door. He heard the chilling, deathly moaning of more zombies as shuffling, twisted bodies limped down toward them on rotten limbs, silhouetted by the flickering flames of the wall-mounted torches. Z'akke held out a clawed hand, and Valletto sensed the sudden surge of magical energies manipulated around the salamander mage-priest. The entire corridor ahead lit up as a pillar of flame erupted from the ground beneath the nearest zombie, shooting up to blossom out over the ceiling. A wave of intense heat smashed against Valletto's face from the arcane flames as the zombie attempted to stumble on through them. The undead creature took a single pace and then collapsed forward, its long dead skin and flesh burnt to blackened cinders and ash by the ferocity of the magical flames.

Valletto held out a hand toward the advancing trio of remaining zombies. He concentrated, assessing the composition of the air around him, taking in every detail of its temperature, moisture content, and mineral composition in the briefest of moments as his own arcane training surged to the fore. Satisfied that he knew exactly what tools he had at his disposal in the surrounding air, Valletto let out a rush of invisible, magical power to manipulate the air around the zombies. His powers excited the molecules into a frenzy as he heated up the air violently, causing a massive and sudden difference in pressure in the stony corridor.

Focusing and intensifying the pressure differential, Valletto used his powers to create the force of a hurricane in the tiniest of spaces and, in less than a second, forced it through an area no larger than a fist. The air howled and rushed, smashing into one of the zombies with unnatural force. Even from this distance, Valletto heard the creature's ribs buckle and one arm snap as its head twisted around. The hideous being was lifted from its feet and, bones snapping in mid-air, was flung back down the corridor to smash against a wall and fall with a thud to the ground.

An arrow thumped into the torso of one of the two remaining zombies but did not slow it. Z'akke again let fly with another spectacular display of pyromancy as flames leapt from his staff to surge down the corridor, setting fire to another of the undead abominations. However, this time the blazing, moaning creature continued to limp and stumble on toward them regardless of the inferno that melted away its long dead flesh.

***

Letting out a grunt, Ragran brought his axe up over one shoulder and then swung down, cleaving the blade into the zombie that faced him. The blade tore straight through the abomination's arm, severing it halfway between the wrist and elbow before cutting cleanly through the creature's body to spill out its odorous entrails. Somehow the zombie continued to move on another step, still flailing at him with its one remaining fist before its half-severed spine gave way and it folded over in two.

Clear of any adversaries, Ragran looked across at Aestelle as he heard a whoosh of magical flames erupt from somewhere behind him. The blonde warrior lay on the floor, two zombies on top of her, both creatures tearing at her with their rotting fingers and frantically leaning in to bite her. Her teeth bared as she shouted out a string of obscenities, Aestelle flung an elbow into the face of the first creature to create an opening before reaching down to the small of her back to recover one of her throwing knives. Aestelle plunged the small blade up through the creature's chin, through its mouth, and into what remained of its brain.

Ragran took the opportunity to lumber over and swing his axe into the second zombie, batting the flat of the twin-headed weapon into the undead creature and propelling it through the air to crash against the crumbling wall behind. As he paced over to finish off his foe, he felt icy cold fingers clamp around his forearm, and the zombie Aestelle had stabbed suddenly fell down onto him, sinking its broken teeth into his shoulder and drawing blood. Ragran let out a yell, more from surprise than pain, and watched as Aestelle grabbed the creature by the hair, flung it off Ragran, and then decapitated it neatly with her greatsword. Seeing the last of their adversaries twitching against the wall where he had flung it, Ragran stepped over and kicked the zombie down before stamping a booted heel into its skull.

The corridor fell silent. Ragran looked behind him and saw Thesilar, Z'akke, and the human mage whose name he had already forgotten checking over the defeated second wave of zombies at the far end of the passageway. Ragran hesitantly brought his eyes across to look at the wound on his shoulder. Blood ran down his bicep and across his elbow to drip onto the dusty floor.

"Aestelle?" he called shakily.

The tall woman looked across from where she knelt to recover her throwing knife.

"Aestelle?!" he repeated, panic now surging up from his gut as the realization of his predicament sunk in.

"What?" Aestelle snapped as she walked over.

"I... I think I'm infected," he stammered, keeping his voice down so as not to alert the others at the far end of the passageway. "One of them got me."

Aestelle's silver-blue eyes narrowed, and her lips broke out into a smile.

"Do you have any idea how necromancy works?" She folded her arms across her chest.

"This isn't funny!" Ragran hissed. "I've been bitten! Can't you do something? You know divinity magic! You know all that holy healing stuff from when you were a nun! Do something, would you?"

Aestelle fought to keep her expression even and bit back a sarcastic comment. She found herself surprised that Ragran did not know better after so much experience fighting against the undead, but then again, the warriors of the north were famed for their superstition.

"Look, zombies don't pass on infections by biting! Zombies are simply dead bodies that are raised and animated by necromancy! They do not infect people!"

"I know how necromancers raise and control zombies," Ragran retorted, "most of them, anyways! But I've heard about some zombies that can pass on an infection with a bite! The wounded person drops dead and then becomes a zombie themself! What if these zombies can do that? What if I'm infected?"

Aestelle swore and placed a gloved hand over Ragran's wound. She closed her eyes and Ragran felt a wave of cooling, soothing energy wash over his shoulder. The pain faded away. The wound stopped bleeding. When Aestelle removed her hand, there was only bruising where the ragged wound had been seconds before, as if it had had weeks to heal.

"There, if it makes you feel better." Aestelle shook her head. "That is not easy for me, you know? I can't just go pacing around, healing wounds and diseases like some sort of prophet! But yes, that is divinity magic – holy magic – so if there were any sort of ridiculous, undead plague coursing through your veins, that would have healed it. But there wasn't, so you've wasted my valuable energy with your hysteria."

Ragran watched as their three companions made their way over from the far end of the shadowy passageway.

"Thank you," he muttered quietly to Aestelle, with real sincerity.

"Come on," Aestelle said as the others arrived, "whatever is animating these bastards knows we are here now and is watching us. Let's keep moving until we find a defendable position we can lay up for the night."

***

Valletto removed his hand from the ancient, oak door and turned to face the others. Flames crackled from the fire in the middle of the low-ceilinged chamber, illuminating all but the corners of the room and sending shadows from the five adventurers dancing across the crumbling stone walls.

"That ward will hold the door until morning," Valletto announced, "unless something comes looking for us that knows how to break a ward, of course."

"Same on this one," Z'akke called from the far side of the chamber, where he had just cast the same, simple spell to magically lock the room's second door.

In the center of the ancient, dusty chamber, Ragran had gathered some broken wood from an old, empty chest that Z'akke had discovered, which the salamander then set ablaze to warm the room. Aestelle and Thesilar set about preparing bedrolls whilst Ragran readied their food; some lean looking, dried meats and mushrooms from the depths of his pack. Valletto watched them wordlessly at work, fighting to keep thoughts of his family locked at bay. He paced around the dim room, trying in vain to muster up some interest in the ancient patterns painted onto the stone tiles on one of the walls.

"They are Primovantorian," Aestelle said, appearing by his side. "Whether that means that these burial chambers were once within their borders or that the individual buried here is of Primovantorian origin is yet to be revealed."

Valletto nodded. The flames in the middle of the room cast half of Aestelle's face in darkness, accentuating the perfect symmetry of her flawless features. She glanced across at him.

"Do you... hear from any of the others?" she asked, her voice strangely hushed a little. "Any of those we fought with at Andro?"

Valletto knew exactly where she was going with the line of questioning even before he formulated an answer. But to cut straight to what he believed she wanted to talk about, or more precisely who, would feel perhaps... awkward.

"Tancred was given command of a cohort not long after he met with the Hegemon. They were all sent out westward after that. Some uprising on the border near the Western March. Orion has written to me twice since. He sends a letter to me and a separate one to my son. I think he is a lot... softer than he would like people to think."

Aestelle issued a slight smile and nodded. The smile itself failed to match the sorrow in her eyes. That sadness echoed the feeling gnawing away at Valletto, the bitter regret clawing at his soul that was suddenly intensified when he mentioned his son. Walking away from home was a stupid idea. He tried for a brief moment to divert his thoughts elsewhere but then decided that the pain and turmoil was deserved. Self-inflicted. He owed it to his son, and to the rest of his family, to think of them and feel that pain.

"He's not soft," Ragran grumbled from where he sat by the fire.

"Pardon?" Aestelle looked across.

"Orion. He's not soft. I crossed paths with him once."

Aestelle darted over and dropped down to kneel by the fire.

"You know Orion? You never told me."

The barbarian looked up, his heavy brow furrowed.

"You said you hated the songs about Andro. I respect you enough not to bring up anything in them. Or anyone. But I wouldn't say I know him. Years ago I was traveling near Turrhania. I stopped for the night where a group of paladins had set up camp. I had a falling out with your Orion. He won that one. Big fellow, very big for a Basilean. He can take a punch, to his credit. I've been hit a lot harder, but the thing I remember is his speed. No man that big should be so light on his feet. So fast. Yes, that bastard won that one. But he was a rude, disrespectful prick. And coming from me, that's saying something."

"He is different now," Aestelle said quickly, "he isn't like that anymore."

With a theatrical flurry, Thesilar dashed across and took her place, cross-legged, in front of the fire.

"And there it is!" the elf beamed, pointing at Aestelle. "There is the big reveal!"

Aestelle looked across at the elf wearily.

"I know better than to rise to your poisonous little challenges, but go on. What is the big reveal?"

"Why you have been moping around like a sullen adolescent ever since we got here," Thesilar replied gleefully. "Why all of your flair and arrogance is gone, replaced by petulant sulking. For the first time in your life, a man has rejected you. Those stupid songs make the two of you sound like a match made on the peak of Kolosu itself. You are here, pining away, clinging to every word said about this fellow. It is clear how much he means to you. It did not end well, then? Aww. What a shame, what a shame!"

"I was not rejected!" Aestelle spat viciously. "I have never been rejected! I never will be! Take a good look at me!"

"Perhaps this paladin really is as noble as the songs say," Thesilar shrugged, "and perhaps he could see past the pretty face and big breasts to the rotten, ugly core underneath."

"It is jealousy that drives you on to be so unpleasant, isn't it?" Valletto snapped. "I don't know you at all, but it certainly comes across that way. Jealousy or insecurity. Maybe both."

The elf looked up at Valletto in silence. Her narrowed eyes fixed on his. The lull in the conversation seemed to drag for hours before she finally spoke.

"The great academic speaks," she sneered, "but perhaps it is best that you stick to matters arcane rather than the inner workings of the mind. You judge me on human societal norms. I am not human. I would never, in a thousand years, feel envy toward... *her.* Your societal failings are what drive you to defend her now. The noble hero leaping to the defense of the damsel, based solely on the need to impress the pretty girl with the big breasts."

"Could be that," Valletto shrugged, "or it could be that I've just taken an instant disliking to you because you are a complete bitch."

Z'akke's fanged mouth dropped open and he emitted a series of choked clicks which Valletto realized after a few moments was laughter.

"He's right!" the salamander grinned.

"I'm not defending Aestelle," Valletto continued, "I barely know her. No, not defending her. I'm attacking you. Because you are a bully."

Thesilar burst out laughing.

"A bully?!" she exclaimed. "Absolutely! Let us all tread in trepidation, lest we invoke the wrath of the willowy she-elf!"

"You don't need brawn to bully people," Valletto folded his arms, "you can do it well enough with words."

"Only in Basilea!" Thesilar continued to laugh. "Across all of Pannithor, all other peoples are somewhat hardier! Do you think there are orcs queuing for an audience with their warlords to issue complaints about harsh words wounding their feelings? No! Only within your borders are people so soft! And perhaps the salamanders, too. But I do not count them as they are not really people. More... animals."

"Thes is right," Ragran grunted as he removed a spit of charred meat from the fire. "Only in Basilea have I encountered your ways. Where I am from, 'bully' is not an insult. A bully is strong. A bully knows that sometimes ruling through fear is what gets things done. A bully rises to the top and knows that strength in unity is more important than something so pissy and unimportant as feelings."

Aestelle stood and glowered down at Ragran.

"A bully is strong?" She shook her head in disgust, her voice shaky. "Yes, Ragran the Mighty, you are strong! Stronger than me. If we went head to head in anger, I know I would lose against you. But physical strength is not what made Valletto, me, and the others stand fast at Andro. Brawn is not what made us turn back an Abyssal invasion. It was courage. That's the Basilean way. That's the way of Z'akke's people, too. And of the five of us in this room, I know whom I would rely on to stand firm in the face of the Abyss itself. You, Ragran, and you, Thesilar, you would have been the first to turn and run at Andro. Because you have no heart. No soul. There is nothing to you, nothing beneath the surface. You would both run, and that is no reflection on elves or men of the north. I would never be so crass and judgmental as to besmirch an entire people. You would run because of your personal failings, not those of your people."

Ragran inhaled deeply and nodded. He looked up at Aestelle.

"You take offense too easily," he said impassively, "where there is none intended. I state plain fact, not insult. For that, I will not apologize. But your people are, in general, weak and needy. But there are exceptions. Your man Orion did not knock me on my arse with Basilean courage. He did it because he is a bully. And for that, I have some grudging respect for him."

Thesilar burst out laughing again. Aestelle looked across at her with rage in her silver-blue eyes. Thesilar was nimbly on her feet, ready to defend herself before Aestelle was even halfway to her. Aestelle flung out a punch that Thesilar quickly deflected to one side. Aestelle's knee came crashing up into Thesilar's gut, bending her over double as she let out a choked gasp of pain. A fist slammed down into the side of the elf's face, the thud from the blow echoing around the chamber as Thesilar was knocked to the ground.

Valletto remained fixed in place, watching in alarm as Z'akke moved in to break up the fight whilst Ragran remained by the fire, watching calmly. Thesilar batted away an intervening arm from the salamander mage and then brought her elbow arching across into the human woman's cheek. Aestelle's head snapped back, but she was moved only half a pace. She retaliated with a rapid volley of punches, smashing hammer fist blows into Thesilar's face and abdomen, forcing her back until a powerful swing connected with the elf's nose and audibly broke the bone. Blood streaming from both nostrils, Thesilar collapsed to the ground.

Issuing a torrent of violent curses and challenges, Aestelle stepped in and slammed a booted foot into the elf's ribs repetitively.

"Get up!" she yelled. "Get up and fight me!"

Z'akke managed to wrap his trunk-like arms around Aestelle's, holding the frenzied warrior woman in place as Thesilar crawled away, blood dripping from her mouth and nose, and leaving a crimson trail across the ancient tiles. Even Ragran jumped to his feet.

"Enough!" the barbarian yelled. "You want to fight a little, that's fine! You're going to kill her, you fool!"

Valletto watched helplessly, frozen in place still by the sudden display of violence. Thesilar crawled away, clutching her ribs with one arm, her eyes fixed on Aestelle in alarm.

"Come on!" Z'akke urged the kicking, swearing woman. "Come on, now! It is finished! Stop now!"

Valletto dashed over to the door he had sealed, breaking the magical ward to give the salamander somewhere to drag Aestelle off to calm her down. He saw Ragran crouch over Thesilar to examine her wounds as Aestelle finally gave in to Z'akke's overpowering grip and allowed herself to be dragged off into the adjoining chamber. Quickly picking the duo of strangers he felt more loyalty toward, Valletto followed Aestelle and Z'akke, sealing the door behind him.

Chapter Six

Aphos was a village not unlike many others for leagues around. A central cluster of buildings consisted of two or three permanent shops and a blacksmith to augment the trade provided by visiting merchants. A ubiquitous tavern – evidence if any was ever required to non-humans that the society of men would not function without the consumption of alcohol – was tucked away to the east of the village, near one end of the palisade wall of wooden stakes that formed a neat but barely defendable perimeter.

Khirius' suspicion was aroused when the night watchman did not challenge them. He, a stranger mounted on horseback, with a servant walking at his side – both of them clearly armed – entered the village well after sundown. If that was not worthy of challenge for any night watchman, what was?

"What now, Master?" Tonnen asked quietly, one hand resting on the pommel of the shortsword at his side.

In his day, Tonnen had been a skilled enough fighter. It was a requirement for a man who, like his father and grandfather before him, was committed to a life of servitude to a vampire. But Tonnen was no longer in his day. The requirement for Khirius to respond to his question was negated by the arrival of two men with torches from the direction of the tavern. Despite his powers and decades of survival in his undead form, the flickering of flames always left Khirius on edge. Nervous.

"Lord Khirius," one of the two men greeted formally as Khirius dismounted and handed the reins of the horse to Tonnen.

He looked across at the duo. With only broken clouds above and a waxing moon illuminating the star speckled sky, Khirius would have been able to see that both men were young, even without his gifts augmenting his sight.

"There is no need to fear your identity being compromised," the second of the two said, a thin man with fair hair and a clean-shaven face. "Your kind are quite safe in this village."

Khirius could not help but sigh in despair as he glanced across at Tonnen. Clearly the two youths had mistook his brief silence for apprehension at the situation he found himself in. In addition, the amateur theatrics surrounding the notion of the 'village of the damned hiding in plain sight' were clearly tedious enough to Tonnen, let alone Khirius. From where he stood, Khirius could sense villagers asleep in their beds in the small cottages and huts on either side of the muddy lane leading to the tavern. Normal folk who had most likely been threatened into keeping their business to themselves and not inquiring about what went on long after dark in their village. Simple people who were easy enough to intimidate into looking the other way.

"Wait here with the horse, Tonnen," Khirius instructed as he walked toward the tavern.

"Lord Annaxa has instructed us to escort you both inside," the first man said coolly.

Khirius and Tonnen were ushered inside the tavern. The interior was just like any other in a small village; a low ceiling punctuated with thick, wooden beams to support the floor above, a short bar with tapped barrels of ales lining the wall behind, and a crackling fire providing warmth and light to the main room. Khirius and Tonnen were escorted into a long room behind the main bar. Moonlight poured in through the bay windows at the back of the room, silhouetting two figures that sat in darkness at the end of a long, polished table. The torches held by the two men who had escorted Khirius and Tonnen in provided the only other light in the room.

The taller of the two figures at the head of the table sat on a less ornate chair and, partially illuminated by the moonlight behind, was revealed as a man of perhaps thirty years of age, his beard neatly trimmed and his long hair pulled back severely into a short ponytail. Even from where he stood, Khirius could sense the deathly aroma of necromancy around the man. The second figure, who could only be Lord Annaxa based on the seat being set at the head of the table, immediately grabbed Khirius' attention for two reasons.

Firstly, even though blanketed in darkness to the mortal eye, Khirius could make out enough of the figure's form to deduce that Lord Annaxa was, in fact, a woman. Second, and of far greater concern to him, was the aura that seeped across the room, overriding the darkness emanating from the necromancer sat to one side. The woman was a vampire. That changed everything. All of the false mystery, the pathetic theatrics, the threats issued by underlings – they were all real.

"Lord Khirius," the necromancer at the far end of the table greeted, "my name is Cane Levia. I am here to speak on behalf of Lord Annaxa. My lord apologizes for being unable to converse in your tongue, but as I am sure you have already ascertained, Lord Annaxa is not a native of these lands."

Khirius suppressed a smile and seated himself at the end of the table nearest the door, directly opposite Annaxa. He doubted very much that Annaxa could not understand them. It was all part of the ruse, all there to confuse the scent of anybody who might pose a threat to her.

"I received your letter," Khirius said.

Cane opened his mouth to reply but was stopped when Annaxa held up a hand. The vampire leaned over and whispered in his ear for a good few moments. Even with his own vampiric hearing and highly attuned senses, Khirius could not make out a single word of the conversation. Cane looked down the table again, pulling at the bottom of his neat tunic to straighten it.

"Lord Annaxa is very keen to discuss the letter with you but commands me to first address a trivial but more immediate matter. That of the servant you killed yesterday."

The statement elicited a raised eyebrow from Khirius.

"Loyalty is paramount," Cane continued, "you do not need me to point out the folly of villagers' yarns and tall tales describing how cheap life is to a vampire. No life is ever cheap. All life serves purpose, particularly when a bond of loyalty between servant and master has been established. That life was not yours to take. And now you owe my lord a debt."

Sadly, Khirius could not fault that logic. He found himself off guard, perhaps as he had not expected to find himself facing another vampire. Encountering another of his type was something that happened only every few decades. Cane nodded toward Tonnen.

"Your servant there will suffice to even the debt owed. My lord commands you to kill him."

Khirius sprang bolt upright in his chair. He looked across at Tonnen. The old man looked down with a kindly smile but betrayed no sign of fear. His eyes, if anything, showed an acceptance of the situation. As if this was, somehow, fair. He remembered Tonnen's father and grandfather, both with their years of loyal servitude. He even remembered Tonnen as a baby, meeting him two nights after his birth, congratulating the happy parents. Khirius looked back at the necromancer at the far end of the table.

"No," he said simply.

"No?"

"Don't make me repeat myself."

"My lord has made it quite clear…"

"Shut up, boy!" Khirius snarled, his lips curling back to display his sharp teeth as all pretenses at civility melted away. "I shall speak now! You have made demands of me with no authority. I come here to speak with you, nonetheless. You send a rude, obnoxious buffoon to deal with me, and he insults me time and time again. I still come to converse with you with cordial intentions. You now have the sheer arrogance to demand a man, whose family has three generations of loyal service to me, killed? Let me forego the pleasantries and articulate words one might not normally expect from a man of my social standing. If you threaten me or my house again, I will rip your spine out of your throat. I know what you are and what you are capable of. But I know that you also can sense what I am. We both face each other knowing who is the more powerful. Consider that the end of the matter."

Annaxa immediately held up a hand to stop Cane from responding. She turned her head slowly to face her lieutenant and issued a simple nod.

"Lord Annaxa is satisfied with your explanation. For now," Cane said.

Khirius suppressed a smile. Not only was Cane's response a rather forced threat that came across to him as a desperate attempt to conceal the fact that they had backed down in the face of his aggression, but also Annaxa's instant intervention was proof that she was not left at the mercy of some language barrier; she understood every word that was being exchanged.

"To the matters of real importance, then," Cane continued. "The Coven has information regarding a burial site of critical importance. Not far from here. This is the reason why you were summoned to Tarkis."

Khirius interlaced his fingers and rested them on the table in front of him. He sensed somebody on the floor above suddenly wake from a restless slumber whilst outside a patrolling guard was momentarily frightened by an owl rustling in the trees just outside the village. He filtered out all of these things and resumed his attention on the two figures sat opposite him. Keeping his eyes fixed on Cane, he avoided the temptation to regard Annaxa in an attempt to learn more about the mysterious vampire.

He knew well that she could clearly see his every move in the moonlight flowing in from the windows behind her, including the direction of his gaze. Tonight, would not be the night to learn about her. He would have to content himself with what he sensed, and from that he took away nothing more than the sensation of real power; something he had not sensed like this for nearly two hundred years.

"You have heard of the expedition that passed through here in summer," Cane continued, "the Basilean military expedition to hunt down Captain Dionne of Anaris?"

Khirius shook his head.

"The minutia of minor details in eastern Basilea did not reach me."

"Those minor details led to a major battle that thwarted an Abyssal invasion of the most powerful nation in Pannithor," Cane frowned, "but regardless, that matters not. What does matter is that during the pursuit, scouts from the Basilean expedition attempted to cut through an area of the Mountains of Tarkis – Mount Ekansu, to be precise – on the far east of the range. Part of the tunnels they used collapsed and they discovered a burial site. An ancient and important one. A one in a million chance, if one believes in chance dictating the turn of events."

Khirius caught himself leaning forward eagerly as his interest was piqued and slowly leant back again to resume his earlier, more casual pose.

"Undead guards were aroused from their rest by the intruders," Cane said. "Many were slain but some remained active after the Basileans had moved on to the north to carry on their pursuit. There was enough of a presence to be detected by our Coven. We carried out our own investigations of the site and blocked up the previous rock fall to protect it."

Cane paused, perhaps expecting a torrent of questions from Khirius. Whilst he certainly had many, he knew better than to show his enthusiasm to these strangers.

"I have one question," Khirius said. "Why have you brought me all this way to discuss this? I am not a member of your Coven. I am not even Basilean. What does any of this have to do with me?"

"That part of it is really very simple. My Lord Annaxa is a member of the Coven's council. The council has heard of you – a two hundred year old vampire existing on the edge of our area of influence will hardly escape our notice. This burial chamber that has recently been discovered... this is of immense importance. The individual buried in Ekansu is a necromancer, and one with both great power and historical significance. This is a real opportunity for the Coven to forge a link that will be of benefit to us all. The council has decided to expand our influence. That is where the invitation to you comes in."

Khirius nodded slowly. The proposal came as little surprise to him; there were only a handful of outcomes he had considered viable on the long journey across to Tarkis. Certainly there was some attraction in the thought of assistance or shelter being on hand from a powerful organization. At least, he assumed it had some power.

"In short," Khirius summarized, "your Coven is an underground company of necromancers, vampires, and anybody who toys with the undead. You have seen an opportunity to expand and solidify your power. Now that opportunity is there, you want me within your ranks to bolster that power."

"Yes."

"And who exactly is up that mountain, half-dead and halfway to being brought to undeath?" Khirius insisted.

"Join us, and I will tell you," Cane shrugged.

"And If I don't?" Khirius narrowed his eyes.

"Then feel free to walk out of here," Cane said dismissively, "we are not your enemy. We have not brought you here to issue demands upon pain of death. Or undeath. But let us be perfectly clear; the letter was sent to you when you enjoyed a peaceful existence living in luxury. We made this offer of friendship to you when you had so many other options. Now that the proverbial mob has burned down your house and you have no home, the Coven still extends this exact same offer of friendship and hospitality. Even though we know full well you have no other viable options open to you. The terms remain the same. As a gesture of good will. We are not here to capitalize on your misfortune. Simply agree to join us, swear as a gentleman that you will tell no others of our existence, and work with us toward a common advancement. Nobody loses."

Khirius rhythmically tapped the fingertips of one hand against the knuckles of the clenched fist of his other hand. This organization knew too much. But Cane was entirely correct. This was his best option. He could ask for time to think upon it, he could leave the uncomfortable silence for longer still to put up the pretense of mental turmoil and debate, but the simple fact was that it was an easy decision.

"I think I will join you," he said after a pause, "but I would like to know your Lord Annaxa's true identity first."

"Don't push your luck," a feminine voice whispered from the head of the table.

"Well," Khirius smiled, "I suppose now at least we can dispense with the theatrics surrounding the supposed language barrier. Alright. On my word as a gentleman, I am in. I will join you."

"Good," Cane issued a thin smile, "then you shall be working alongside me in the service of Lord Annaxa, ensuring all goes smoothly in the tomb. As agreed, you are owed the name of the necromancer who is being raised there. The body in the tomb is Arteri SeaBreeze."

Khirius found himself on his feet before he even realized how surprised he was at the mention of the name.

"Arteri the Plague?!" Khirius exclaimed, pointing a finger in the vague direction of the mountains. "He is up there?! Now?!"

Cane nodded calmly.

Khirius remembered momentarily what it felt like to be breathless in mortal life. Arteri the Plague. Elven aeromancer turned necromancer and chief lieutenant to none other than Mhorgoth the Faceless himself.

***

Gritting her teeth, Thesilar snatched another arrow from the quiver on her back, notched it to her bow, and brought the string back until the familiar ache of tension shot across her forearm and shoulder. She lined the tip of the arrow up on her target, paused for a moment to make sure of her shot, and then let fly. The arrow shot away, straight and true, directly toward the zombie lumbering down the passageway. Darting in between Ragran and Aestelle as they charged past the blazing torches on the narrow walls to either side, the arrow struck the lead zombie square in the forehead. A perfect shot – surpassing all of the protection provided by the creature's rusted coat of mail and battered, bronze breastplate.

The armored zombie stopped in place, two of its undead comrades shuffling past it as the thing appeared almost to have a moment of recognition, of consciousness. Its rusted short sword and round shield dropped to the floor with a clatter, and the creature pitched forward on its face. Thesilar had, by this point, already notched up another arrow and taken aim. A roaring rush of wind plummeted down the corridor, the ferocity of the magical blast of air extinguishing the torches on the walls until it slammed into the leading two armored zombies in the column, slowing their pace as they struggled to push against Valletto's magic. Almost simultaneously, a column of fire sprouted up at the rear of the undead group, incinerating another armor-clad zombie in a ball of flames.

Ragran smashed into the group of undead monsters, planting a skull-encased shoulder into the first creature and toppling it before slamming his axe into another. Aestelle hit a moment later, ducking deftly beneath a sword strike before bringing her own blade arching up to carve off half of a zombie's face with the tip of the weapon. Thesilar's second arrow thudded into the zombie's chest, cutting through the rusted armor but failing to drop the creature.

"Force them back!" Ragran yelled over the roaring winds created by Valletto. "Don't let them get a foothold!"

Aestelle hacked down again into the zombie opposing her, cleaving off an arm before a creature in the second rank lurched forward to strike. A rusted sword bit into her shoulder and she let out a cry of pain as blood spattered against the wall next to her. Her sword fell from her fingers, but before it had even hit the ground, she had snatched up the pistol from her belt and shot the zombie in the face, sending it staggering back into the blazing rank behind in a cloud of black powder. Thesilar loosed another arrow into the same rank for good measure as Aestelle quickly dropped down to retrieve her sword.

A blast of wind of renewed ferocity impacted the closest of the zombies, smashing the monstrosity into the wall to one side with enough force that all four of its limbs detached. Ragran was forced back a step as two of the long dead corpse-soldiers combined their assaults in an attempt to overpower him whilst Aestelle blocked the attack from a third creature, dropping her sword for a second time and clutching at her wounded arm in pain.

"Z'akke!" Thesilar yelled. "Burn that front rank! Burn them!"

A torrent of flame roared along the corridor past Thesilar, the blazing heat feeling as though it would blister her cheek as it passed. It raged up to hit the ceiling above, tongues of flame licking along the top of the corridor and whooshing over the heads of Ragran and Aestelle, before then likewise streaming straight past the half-dozen remaining zombies facing them. Valletto stepped forward and held out a hand. Within an instant, reacting to his unseen commands, the flames turned around and fell down on the zombies, engulfing the first two in flames. The creatures continued to stumble forward, still stubbornly hacking and lashing out with their ancient blades as Ragran and Aestelle backed away from the inferno.

The two burning zombies fell down, but the next pair was quick to step through the flames to attack their foes, the first of them striking out with a vicious lunge that succeeded in passing Ragran's guard and piercing his thigh. The gargantuan mountain man lashed out with his axe, cutting down his assailant. Thesilar aimed her bow again, but the ferocity of the blaze ahead obscured her vision with writhing figures in the flames, heat haze, and smoke that blurred her eyes with tears. Coughing, she returned her bow and arrow to her back and drew her sword. Through her blurred vision, she saw Aestelle smash a zombie in the face with the pommel of her sword before following up the attack with a neat strike that decapitated the monster. Another was instantly in its place, viciously attacking her with a flurry of blows that forced her to step back, desperately bringing up her sword to defend herself.

Valletto advanced toward the fire, holding both of his hands out. With a sudden whoosh, the flames ahead erupted into a fireball, and an invisible fist of energy emanated out, knocking Thesilar onto her back. The skin on her face felt unbearably hot, her eyes streamed from the smoke and her lungs struggled with the thin air as coughs wracked her body. She dragged herself up to one knee and looked ahead. A colossal pyre continued to burn, blocking the way. Ragran staggered back away from it, dragging Aestelle with him as he retreated. Valletto, seemingly untouched by the heat or smoke, calmly stood his ground as he stared into the flames, clearly ready for any zombie that may somehow have survived the onslaught. Thesilar continued to look around her.

"Z'akke? Z'akke!"

The salamander mage was nowhere to be seen. Staggering to her feet and rubbing at her streaming eyes, Thesilar looked around desperately. A refreshing gust of air suddenly wafted past her face to cool her skin, clear her eyes, and make breathing bearable again. Taking a moment to compose herself, she looked across at Valletto to nod in gratitude for his intervention. That was when she saw the open door behind him, leading off the narrow corridor that had served as their battleground.

Barging past the aeromancer, Thesilar stomped through the door and into the room. The chamber was relatively small, with a low ceiling similar to the passageway outside. An ancient table lay collapsed in the center of the room whilst an age old weapon rack hung from one of the other walls, housing an array of rusted blades; on the far side was an old chest of draws, similarly ruined and crumbled from the ravages of time. Knelt by the ruined furniture, his clawed fingers frantically scrabbling through the wreckage, was her salamander companion.

"Z'akke!" Thesilar yelled. "What in the Abyss do you think you are doing?!"

"Just a moment!" the mage-priest chittered. "I'm just finishing sorting this out into piles for us all!"

Swearing angrily, Thesilar paced over to the salamander sorcerer and stood in front of him.

"Again!" she growled. "You're doing this again! We were fighting for our lives!"

"I know what this looks like," Z'akke said, quickly pocketing something fist sized and standing up, "but the fight was won. I saw that Valletto was using his own powers to manipulate the flames I had already created. Genius, really! You had it all covered, you didn't need me anymore! Then I saw this door and the cabinet, and I realized that it was perhaps an old storeroom. So I thought I could best make myself useful by..."

"Getting in first and helping yourself to the spoils!" Ragran boomed, appearing at the doorway like a demon of the Abyss, silhouetted by the glowing flames in the passageway outside.

"No!" Z'akke pleaded. "No! I..."

"We've done this before, Z'akke!" Ragran thundered, pointing a thick finger in accusation at the salamander. "I warned you! We share the spoils equally when we get home! You don't rush in and help yourself whilst your comrades are still fighting! You don't get to choose what you want because you ran from a fight and left us!"

Her eyes narrowed in pain, one hand pressed against her bleeding shoulder, Aestelle followed Ragran into the room. She looked across at Z'akke and then closed her eyes, shaking her head in disappointment.

"Z'akke," she exhaled quietly.

"I found an energy crystal for Valletto! A good one! And I found this potion." Z'akke held out a small bottle to Thesilar. "I think it is for healing. Magic potions keep, almost indefinitely! I think it will still work! I kept it for you!"

"And what did you put in your pouch?" Thesilar pointed in accusation. "I saw you hide something for yourself!"

His eyes open wide in fear, his mouth agape, the salamander looked around the room in desperation at the angry and disappointed faces of his companions.

"What is in that pouch?" Ragran roared.

Z'akke's broad shoulders slumped. He looked at the ground in defeat and reached inside his pouch. Thesilar let out a gasp when he produced a large gem of glittering green.

"That gets split," Ragran insisted immediately, "five ways!"

"No," Z'akke shook his head, "I found it. It's mine. I found this potion for Thesilar."

"A potion?!" Thesilar exclaimed. "That may or may not work! If you sell that gem and give me a one fifth share, I could buy ten potions! No, Z'akke! You don't get to run from a fight and leave us just so that you can take what you want! You complete bastard! I cannot believe you are doing this again!"

Ragran spat out a word that Thesilar would never herself repeat and made directly for the salamander. Aestelle rushed to stand in front of him.

"Wait! Wait!" the blonde woman insisted.

"You're going to defend him, still?!" Ragran spat in disgust.

As if hearing Aestelle's voice somehow reminded her of their fight the previous evening, the pain in Thesilar's broken nose suddenly flared up. She heard her breathing coming out in disgusting wheezes and whistles, and she remembered her sorry reflection, with her two black eyes, crooked nose, and blood encrusted upper lip. She looked at Aestelle and felt nothing but hatred.

"Z'akke," Aestelle said gently, "you have to split our findings. We agreed on it. You have to sell that gem. If it means that much to you, you can take my share. You take two fifths, but you give the others what they are owed."

Seeing the blood still dripping down Aestelle's arm and deducing that she must be too weary to use her divinity magic to heal herself, Thesilar quickly snatched the potion from Z'akke. Given that Aestelle had angrily refused to mend Thesilar's broken nose even the following morning, she felt no guilt in depriving the arrogant woman from the potion that might heal her shoulder. Thesilar popped open the bottle and took a swig before pouring the rest of the contents over her mangled face.

The liquid tasted rank, like wine that had turned to vinegar, only mustier and more with an aroma of oil. Still, she felt the familiar surge of arcane energy flowing gently through her. Her eyes cleared a little. Her nose hurt less. She felt a bone click. Reaching up, she found only tender flesh and bruising where moments before there had been broken bone and scabs.

"There, you see!" Z'akke forced a nervous smile. "That's worth more than money!"

Thesilar sighed, flicking a hand out dismissively in disgust at Z'akke as she turned back to face Aestelle. Somehow, with her facial wounds now all but healed, she felt less embarrassed. More like facing her rival again.

"Easy for you to offer to give up your share of that gem." She folded her arms. "How much were you paid for turning up at Andro?"

"That gem is hardly worth a fortune," Aestelle scowled, "but I know that it is the principle that matters. But if you must know, all of my money is gone. I've already spent it all. Every last coin."

The room fell silent. All eyes now fixed on Aestelle.

"I bought a title and some land," she continued, "I have a large house. It is crumbling to ruin. I could afford to repair the bedroom. I am the Viscountess of Monthaki. I have a mansion that is falling to pieces. Within it, I have one room that is decorated to royal standards. The rest is falling to shit. So no, I do need money."

Thesilar felt like laughing. The thought that Aestelle's arrogance had taken a once in a lifetime opportunity and wasted a senator's ransom of gold on a title for nothing more than vanity gave Thesilar a warm glow inside. But she found herself too weary to argue again.

"I'm not giving up my share," she said to Z'akke, "I'm not giving you a single coin that I am owed. You are a selfish bastard, and once we are done here, I never want to see you again. Come to think of it, I never want to see any of you again. Come on. Let us get this damn job finished and go our separate ways."

Pushing her way past Aestelle and Ragran, Thesilar returned to the blazing passageway outside the ancient storeroom.

Chapter Seven

The crackling of the fire was accompanied by a slow, steady dripping of water from the cracked ceiling above. Z'akke sniffed miserably to himself. Another night underground, another night of sleeping in a locked room crafted centuries ago, defended from undead monstrosities by people who hated him. He wanted to go home perhaps now more than ever before. Z'akke tucked his knees in toward his chest and wrapped his arms around them, the cold stone of the ancient wall behind him pressing against his back.

Ragran sat stoically by the fire in the center of the room, staring silently at another small hunk of charred meat as it slowly roasted above the flames. Thesilar crouched in the opposite corner of the room from Z'akke, scratching away with a stick of charcoal against a sheet of parchment as she mapped out their progress in the catacombs. Aestelle lay on her bedroll, pretending to be asleep; probably to avoid any further arguments, Z'akke thought. He had seen her asleep enough times whilst he was guarding camps to know that when she was truly collapsed in slumber, she spread out to cover an astounding amount of room for somebody so slim.

Z'akke looked down again at the little book of his sketches sat on his lap. Perhaps twenty pages of dragons, ranging from majestic monsters looming over mountains and seas, to more thoughtful drawings of how Z'akke imagined these incredible creatures might spend their time in more mundane settings. He had, of course, only ever seen a red dragon soaring above the fires of the Three Kings back home, and was left to wonder over what other species would look like. He told himself that the sketches were for his children – Z'annde, X'orther and V'yaal – but he wondered if that were true. Realizing that tears were welling in his eyes again at the thought of how much he missed his children, he quickly turned away from Ragran and Thesilar, in case they saw him and began to ridicule him again. Sometimes it was easier to shrug off the insults than others, and now was not one of those times. It would all be so much easier if he could tell them why it was so important for him to raise the money. Selfishness and greed had nothing to do with it.

He stopped to think on how his life had led him to Basilea. His calling reminded him of his duties as a mage-priest, and in turn, his prayers and his faith. The role of a mage-priest was so different to the equivalent in human societies; it did not stop merely at faith but also extended to providing wisdom and advice to society's greatest leaders. The problem there was that Z'akke had never been particularly wise.

He was a mage-priest in title, but when he stopped to think on what duties had been asked of him, he was little more than an acolyte in human terms. An acolyte with over ten years of experience. Still, being away from the Three Kings and away from the priesthood had made him lazy, in his own mind at least. Prayer had ceased to form a part of daily life, and that was something he needed to remedy.

"How do you do it?"

Z'akke looked up and saw Valletto walk across to sink down and sit next to him against the crumbling wall.

"Do what?" Z'akke asked defensively.

"I've studied with human sorcerers from a dozen nations. I've studied with elves. Even a dwarf mage, once. But never a salamander. How do you manipulate the elements the way you do? Do you use magic the same way I do?"

Z'akke let out a sigh of relief. He considered himself self-aware enough to realize that Valletto knew he was miserable and was simply trying to distract him from his woes, and for that he was truly thankful.

"It is very similar, I think," he began hesitantly. "I have had a few conversations with graduates of your colleges, and it certainly seems that Basilean sorcerers see magic as more of a science these days than an art, but I think a salamander mage-priest sees it a little differently. I don't know how much you know about our faith and spiritual beliefs, but when Kthorlaq led our people to the Three Kings and gave her life for us, the fires of the Three Kings became far more than just lava. I... I'm not really answering your question."

"No, go on." Valletto smiled encouragingly.

Z'akke eyed him suspiciously. He was not used to kindness from humans. Aestelle was normally kind to him – normally – but she was an exception. Most humans were scared of the sharp teeth and the scales. Those who knew Z'akke seemed to treat him dismissively, as an idiot and the butt of jokes. But Valletto seemed genuine enough.

"The fires of the Three Kings hold great significance," Z'akke carried on carefully. "Winter cursed our people with a cold that... eats away at us. This much is fairly common knowledge. The journeys back home to the fires of the Three Kings are both spiritual but also necessary for physical survival. But the fires there... they are made up in part of the essence of every one of our kind who has survived to take on the final pilgrimage. That last journey where instead of laying in the fires to rejuvenate, they lay down to die. To allow their physical form to be absorbed by the flames. That must sound awfully grim to an outsider, but to us, it is beautiful. Your relatives are never truly lost; you need only visit the fires to feel their presence. And it is those flames that give us our powers. The essence of our forefathers. It is that power that the mage-priest manipulates. It is done using the same techniques your science teaches. But it... perhaps *means* more to us when we do it."

"So," Valletto narrowed his eyes in concentration, "you still feel for the elements? You still send out a check, that... pulse to see what surrounds you before then manipulating it?"

"Oh, absolutely!" Z'akke nodded enthusiastically. "And for an aeromancer, you would understand pyromancy more than any other discipline, I think. Air is a huge part of what we need to make our magic work. Without air, the fire starves. I could never bend the air to my will like you do, but I need to do it enough to fan the flames. But air and heat is the easy part of pyromancy. It is making up a source, the wood of the fire, if you like, that is the hardest part. To make that up from nearly thin air, that is the real magic."

Valletto looked ahead, nodding slowly as his eyes drifted a little out of focus. The chamber fell silent as the two mages stared across to the far wall. Z'akke noticed Valletto's eager smile fade away, replaced by a frown slowly filled with anxiety and turmoil. The pained look in the human mage's eyes made Z'akke briefly wonder what he was thinking about, until that very look reminded him of his own anguish over missing his mate and children.

"I always wanted to be a mage," Valletto suddenly said, his voice hushed so only Z'akke could hear. "I've sometimes wondered if... well... not everybody can wield the powers of the arcane. With all of the study and training in the world, it comes to nothing unless you are lucky enough to have that gift in the first place. I wonder if I wanted it so badly that I somehow made my own luck. Changed my stars to give me what I always prayed for as a child. There isn't really any history of magic in my family, in our line. My grandmother's uncle. That's about it."

"It was in my family from the start," Z'akke replied, "from my mother. My birth mother that is, not my clutch mother. But she isn't a pyromancer. She is a healer. I always took it for granted, magic. When I was young, it never excited me so much. All I ever wanted to be when I grew up was a father. Other hatchlings thought me strange, I remember, but I was so close to my father. I still am."

"Z'akke!" Ch'annde looked down at him, a kindly smile spreading across the eternally friendly features of his teacher. "I know it is an exciting day, but don't forget your pouch!"

Z'akke wandered off to the back of the classroom within the small, wooden school building. He threaded his way through the bench seats, momentarily distracted by the bright, colorful images painted on the walls by him and the other hatchlings, before he retrieved his pouch and his few belong-

ings within. Outside the school hut, he could hear the commotion as the other young salamanders from his class saw out this momentous day in their lives, both exciting and terrifying.

Z'akke would always love and cherish X'marta, his clutch mother. X'marta had raised him from birth for these past five years, helping him through the trials and ordeals of youth, showering him with love and support despite his differences and unique outlook on life. X'marta would always be there, and he would always love her, but today was the day that he met his birth parents. There was no grand ceremony, no ritual, just a quiet introduction to the couple who waited patiently in the small crowd outside the school hut.

Yet when Z'akke stopped to think about it, he cried. He wanted X'marta. He only needed one mother, and she was all he had ever known. Z'akke sank down into the corner of the hut, hugging his knees and sobbing. Ch'annde, ushering out the last of the hatchings to the last of the waiting parents, did not hear his cries. So he cried louder.

"Z'akke!" Ch'annde rushed over. "Come on, now! It will be fine! This should be exciting! There are two people out there who love you very much and have been waiting for years to have you back! Are you not excited to find out who your birth parents are? To see if it is somebody you recognize?"

Of course the thought was curious to Z'akke. With a couple of thousand salamanders of his clan in the sprawling temple-city at the edge of the jungle, there was a fair chance that he had never even laid eyes on his birth parents. But they knew him. They had been watching him from afar, he had been told. But they were not X'marta. Nobody ever could be.

"I don't want to go," Z'akke sobbed. "I want things to stay like this!"

Ch'annde crouched down and gently ran a clawed hand across his snout, smiling sadly.

"Everybody else has gone," she said. "Your birth mother is right outside that door. She hasn't held you since the day you were born. She hasn't held you for five years. Come on, Z'akke. This is a wonderful day for you both."

Z'akke reached up and allowed his little hand to be enclosed in the careful grip of his teacher. He tottered after her, following her to the rickety door that led out into the playing yard outside his school hut, overlooking the temple-city and the beautiful beach that ran around it, all nestled beneath the watchful gaze of the ever-guarding peaks of the Three Kings above.

Ch'annde opened the door. Z'akke saw her and recognized her at once. He saw past the sunlight above, the tall mountains reaching up from the center of the island toward the blue skies of the heavens, the neat buildings of light wood at the bottom of the gentle, sandy slope; all of the things he had known all of his short life. He did not know her name but remembered her from the infirmary when he had once fallen and cut open his head. She was a healer, a wonderfully kind salamander with beautiful colors to her scales and warm eyes *that instantly made him smile. He walked over quickly, nearly running, and beamed up at her.*

"Mother?" *he asked hopefully.*

The healer smiled and nodded, tears streaming down her face as she reached out to embrace him. Z'akke reached up to hold her, confused as to why she was crying so much; equally confused as to why he was not surprised to find her waiting for him, as if he somehow expected it. She said nothing. She just cried and held him tightly. He was happy and comfortable being held by her. It was safe.

Then Z'akke heard the footsteps behind him. The slow, heavy thuds of feet impacting against the sand of the school's play yard. He turned slowly in his mother's embrace and saw a newcomer. A huge salamander walked slowly across to them from the settlement at the bottom of the peak. He was tall and broad, and he wore a coat of dark blue that Z'akke had seen worn by the salamanders that came in to the temple-city on the fighting ships. He had a sword at his waist. The salamander's eyes were black, narrow, and complimented a broken horn on his snout in adding to his grim frown. He walked over with a slight limp that added to the air of peril that surrounded him.

In an instant, this near stranger who was Z'akke's birth mother became his only protection from this terrifying newcomer. Z'akke let out a whimper and shot around to hide behind his mother's legs, wrapping his little arms around them. The healer let out a gasp.

"You arrived!" *she said excitedly.* "I didn't think you would! I didn't think you could get here in time!"

The sailor's frown gave way to an almost timid smile. It did nothing to alleviate Z'akke's fear. His mother looked down at him.

"Don't be scared," *she said gently,* "this... this is your father."

Z'akke hid, burying his face in the back of her legs. He could hear the sailor walk across with that ever so slight limp before dropping down to one knee right in front of him. Z'akke looked up. The sailor was next to him, his face down at the same level as Z'akke, the timid smile gone.

"Are you scared of me?" *he asked quietly.*

Z'akke nodded.

"That's alright," *his father said gently,* "because I'm scared of you, too."

Z'akke blinked and looked across incredulously at the broad, armed salamander with the limp and the broken horn.

"You... you're scared of me?"

"I'm scared of what you are," *the sailor smiled gently.*

He carefully reached out to take one of Z'akke's hands.

"I've seen a lot of the world," *the sailor said,* "I've seen giant sea monsters, terrible storms, and huge battles. But none of that scares me nearly as much as the thought of ever letting you down. You are my son, and you are* *everything to me."*

The fear melted away in an instant. Smiling, Z'akke reached up and held his father's huge hand in both of his.

Z'akke smiled at the memory of his first meeting with his birth parents, as clear to him now over three decades later as it was on that sunlit afternoon. It was quickly replaced with the bittersweet thought of home; the comfort in knowing his parents lived a mere stone throw from his mate and children and were there to support his family in his absence, marred by the gnawing guilt of that very absence itself.

"Yes." Z'akke nodded, realizing that he had fallen silent for a long time, as he had mulled over that special memory. "Yes. To be a father. More special even than magic."

Valletto continued to stare ahead in silence. Z'akke looked across and saw a thousand thoughts run through the human sorcerer's head in the briefest of instants. None seemed good.

"I'm in a bit of a mess," Valletto said, "and it's not about money. This whole thing the others were talking about, with splitting the spoils we find five ways. I'm not really interested. I just need to get home in one piece. You take my share of the spoils, Z'akke. I don't need it. You... get some sleep."

Z'akke opened his mouth, every strand of decency within him urging him to turn down Valletto's kind offer. But he remained quiet. The human mage walked over to his bedroll and recovered a small wooden box from his pack.

"Sleep well!" Z'akke called out after him, eliciting a despairing shake of the head from Ragran.

After a few moments of quiet reflection, Z'akke made his way across to his own bedroll to ready himself for the perils of the next day in the ancient catacombs.

***

With a roar, Ragran flung himself into the trio of skeletons. His axe swung around in a wide arc, cleaving through the first of the magically animated warriors and sending it cluttering to the floor in a pile of bones. The remaining pair reacted quickly, the first lashing out with a bronze short sword and forcing Ragran to bring his weapon up to defend himself, whilst the second leaned in to slash a vicious cut across the barbarian's exposed ribs.

Forced almost back-to-back with him by the first wave of skeletons, Thesilar brought up her own sword to defend herself from the closest of the undead soldiers.

"This is not a fair fight!" Thesilar gasped as she dropped a shoulder to avoid another attack from her long dead assailant. "I rather feel our opponents have a lot less to lose than we do!"

"Not now!" Ragran grumbled, slamming a fist into the bony face of one of the skeletons to force it back to create an opening. "Less jokes, Thes! More dropping these bastards!"

A second skeleton warrior caught up with the first facing Thesilar, forcing her to shift her guard and alternate between fending off savage blows from both opponents, left without a chance to attempt an attack of her own. Then, seemingly from nowhere, a heavy blade descended onto one of the skeletal warriors and cleaved it apart, giving Thesilar the opening she needed to hack down into her second opponent and lop off its head.

Z'akke, her unlikely savior, brought his heavy blade up again and charged over to attack the trio of skeletons swarming around Ragran, an odd grin plastered across his scaly face as he emitted a chittering laugh.

"Use the magic, not the sword!" Thesilar snapped angrily at him as she sheathed her own blade and recovered her bow.

At a range of only a few feet, an archer of Thesilar's skill could not miss. She quickly notched an arrow to her bow and let fly, sending the deadly projectile flying into the back of a skeleton's skull with enough force to shatter the bone. Ragran and Z'akke were able to dispatch the final two undead warriors with ease, allowing silence to descend within the dusty chamber. Slowly lowering her bow, Thesilar looked around the dimly lit room.

Valletto was near the half-crumbled doorway they had entered via, one hand pressed against the wall by his side as he took in a series of deep breaths. Aestelle stood next to him, her greatsword held ready in both hands as her eyes flitted from corner to corner of the room, warily watching each pile of bones from their defeated adversaries. On the other side of perhaps a dozen felled skeletons, Thesilar waited hesitantly by Ragran and Z'akke.

The room itself split apart at the far end, a portion of wall having collapsed into two separate segments that led on to a further two doors. Valletto and Aestelle made their way over. Thesilar looked back to the far end of the room, dropping to one knee and running a hand across the ancient tiles at her feet. Sweeping away some of the dust, she saw squares of dark red, carefully laid, the precision of their lines and level indicative of skilled artisans' work. She glanced at the fallen ceiling ahead and then back at the half collapsed doorway they had entered by.

"What is it?" Ragran asked, his hands twisting in place on the haft of his axe as he looked around the room helplessly, "What's the problem?"

Aestelle carefully made her way across to the northern wall and slowly ran a gloved hand against the neat brickwork. She was looking for traps, just as Thesilar had once taught her to. She was wrong; that was not the threat. Thesilar had taught her much, but not everything.

"Aestelle, you said that when you first found this place you think you were in the inner guard chamber for somebody important?"

"It had all the hallmarks of it," Aestelle replied, "relatively grand architecture, long..."

"Yes, yes," Thesilar snapped irritably as she examined the floor leading up to the fallen rocks, "but how did you get there? We've been down here for a couple of days now and haven't found the inner guard chamber."

"That's because half of the corridors we try to take are caved in," Ragran grumbled.

"That's precisely my point," Thesilar said as she slowly stood up.

Aestelle's eyes narrowed as she nodded.

"We ended up finding our way straight to the inner guard chamber," she said quietly, "because of a rock fall. The tunnel we were in collapsed."

Z'akke suddenly pivoted his head and stared at the southern wall.

"What was that?" the salamander mage asked.

"I didn't hear anything," Ragran said.

Thesilar heard a dull thump from not far away.

"There!"

"I heard it that time," she exhaled.

The room fell silent once more.

Then the wall behind Valletto opened up. Ancient slabs of stone were smashed to powder as a gigantic fist plummeted through the masonry, filling the room with clouds of dust. Thesilar briefly saw Valletto thrown back before she was forced to turn away and close her eyes to protect them from the plumes of grit blossoming across from the collapsed wall. She heard a dry rasp, almost like a pained cough, which then amplified quickly into a terrifying roar.

Turning back around, Thesilar looked to the far wall and saw the giant, crouched figure of a hulking monstrosity silhouetted in the torchlight and half-hidden in the slowly dissipating plumes of smoke. Standing easily at twice the size of a man, as broad as it was tall and with a hunched back rippling with torn, decaying muscles, the hulking creature stepped forward into the room. A zombified troll. Shuffling and limping past it came another four zombies, heads lolling from side-to-side atop rotten necks as their flesh-peeled fingers clutched ancient swords and axes. The vacant-eyed, pig-snouted troll stared across at the five adventurers.

"Z'akke," Thesilar yelled, "set fire to the big bastard!"

Thesilar immediately notched an arrow to her bow and shot the projectile, sending it straight into the neck of the towering troll. The creature did not even notice the impact. A gunshot erupted from her left, the staccato bang echoing around the room as smoke and a brief burst of flame shot from the flint-lock pistol held in Aestelle's outstretched arm. A hunk of flesh was torn open in the troll's chest, and the gargantuan creature staggered back a little from the impact; but within seconds, the hole in the dead flesh began to visibly fill in and become smaller as the notorious regenerative powers that the troll possessed in life proved to be just as effective in undeath.

Flames spewed forth from the salamander mage-priest, roaring along the center of the room to envelop the zombie troll. The monster let out a yell, demonstrating to Thesilar that it could somehow still feel pain, whilst the flames scorched its broken, decaying flesh. Two of the zombies staggered toward Valletto who, one hand pressed against a wound on the side of his head, held out his other and sent one of the monsters flying back in a tornado of wind. Z'akke drew his sword and rushed across to assist his fellow mage against the other.

Ragran bounded across the room, his axe held across his bare, barrel chest. One zombie shuffled out to face him, and Ragran cut it down with a heavy strike, without so much as slowing his pace. With a roar, the barbarian leapt in to attack the zombie troll, swinging out with his axe to embed the blade in the creature's knee. The troll retaliated by bringing a clenched fist sweeping down at Ragran. The huge mountain man jumped aside to avoid the first blow and brought up his axe to block the second. With a near unbelievable show of strength, Ragran met the attack with even force, the troll's fist impacting against his axe with a blow that sounded like a clap of thunder. Gritting his teeth, Ragran swept his axe back and then in to strike again, tearing a huge gash across the troll's abdomen and spilling out a stream of cold, rotten entrails.

With a rasping roar, the troll lashed out with a vicious backhand blow, catching Ragran's axe and snapping it in half. A follow up strike caught the barbarian in the side of the head and tossed him across the room with the ease of a petulant child throwing a doll in a tantrum. Another wave of fire swept across from the far corner of the room, setting alight to the troll's back. Thesilar loosed a pair of arrows in quick succession, the first catching the troll in the gut whilst the second flew true and pierced one of its eyes. From Thesilar's left, Aestelle also loosed off an arrow that hit the troll in the flank with an audible thump. Clawing at the arrow in its eye, the zombie troll staggered forward drunkenly, lashing out blindly with its other hand. Thesilar reached for another arrow from her quiver but stopped when she saw Ragran was still lying motionless where he had landed, face down against a wall.

"Aestelle," Thesilar yelled across the room, "see to Ragran!"

As Thesilar loosed off another arrow to ineffectually dig into one of the troll's arms, Aestelle sprinted across the room toward Ragran. Another blast of deafening wind smashed through the room from Valletto's outstretched hands, smacking into the troll with a clap and forcing the gargantuan monster to lean forward and struggle against the wind in an attempt to lunge at Aestelle. Thesilar's eyes opened in surprise as the troll seemed to suddenly fight past the effects of the wind, just as Aestelle was dashing in front of it. With another echoing roar, the troll charged at Aestelle. Perhaps alerted by a warning cry from Z'akke, the blonde woman looked across and saw the troll heading her way. She dived aside at the last moment, and the troll ploughed shoulder first into the wall behind her.

The world collapsed into a confusion of darkness and weightlessness. Thesilar grasped frantically to either side in panic, plunging down into darkness as she heard stones clattering against each other all around her. The two seconds of free falling seemed like an age in the darkness, but her feet hit solid rock beneath her and her legs gave way. Letting out a cry of pain and alarm, Thesilar crumpled down to the ground. The rocks continued to fall all around her. Clouds of smoke and dust, invisible in the darkness even to elven eyes, enveloped her and forced her to cough uncontrollably. She staggered up to one knee, hiding her mouth and nose in the crook of her elbow as she fought to control her breathing.

The cacophony of noise around her stopped. The chamber, or wherever she was, was plunged into silence. Her eyes streaming with tears from the grit and dust, her lungs burning from the coughing, Thesilar reached into her belt and struggled for her flint and steel fire starter. Recovering a bandage, she struck the two together to set it alight.

Now partially illuminated, Thesilar saw through her tearstreamed eyes that the room was tiny, with a rock fall of smooth, light gray stones covering half of its area. The rock fall formed a slope, a ramp of sorts, leading back up to the room above where she had been only moments before. She heard muffled shouting. It sounded like Valletto. Groggily, Thesilar looked around her. She let out a gasp when she saw Ragran's prone body in the corner of the tiny chamber. Rushing to his side, she set the burning bandage down and rolled him over. Ragran was bleeding from the side of his head and one shoulder, but his eyes blinked and he looked up at her.

"What the... what happened?"

"Ragran?" Valletto yelled from somewhere. "Aestelle? Thesilar?"

"Down here!" Thesilar called back. "I'm down here! I'm with Ragran!"

There was a momentary pause.

"I'm with Z'akke!" Valletto shouted down from somewhere above, his voice only just traveling through the rock fall. "We can see daylight up above us! The whole place has collapsed!"

"Yes, I know that!" Thesilar snapped.

For a moment, her attention was caught by something in the corner of the room. Something pale blue. The tiles on the floor were different. Her eyes opened wide. They were elven.

"Is Aestelle with you?" Z'akke shouted down.

"No!" Thesilar called back, her throat hoarse from the dust and the shouting. "I thought she was with you!"

"No!"

Thesilar paused. She remembered Aestelle sprinting across the front of the troll toward Ragran. Glancing down at the wounded barbarian and looking around her to ascertain her bearings, she mentally calculated approximately where Aestelle must have been when the floor collapsed. That placed her...

With a panicked cry, Thesilar ran over to the rock fall and began tearing at the stones with her bloodied fingers, desperately trying to rip them out of her way.

"Help me!" she screamed. "Ragran! Help me!"

The barbarian staggered over, dropping to one knee by her side and grabbing at fistfuls of rock with his huge hands.

"What's going on?" Valletto called down. "What's happening?"

Thesilar heard another muffled call.

"Wait!" she held up a hand to Ragran. "Stop! Stop a moment!"

There was silence for a second. Water dripped somewhere and another minor slide of stones and rocks echoed from somewhere above.

"What's going on down there?" Z'akke called from somewhere above. "Where's Aestelle?"

"Shut up, Z'akke!" Thesilar snapped.

She heard the muffled voice again from below the rock fall.

"Stop... stop digging."

"Aestelle?" Thesilar shouted.

"…Yes…"

"Are you hurt?"

"…Yes…"

There was another moment of silence.

"I'm in a tunnel," Aestelle called up. "I've got about half a foot of room above me. If you keep digging, it will collapse."

"What's going on?" Valletto called.

"Aestelle is below us!" Ragran shouted back up. "She's trapped under a rock fall!"

"Then dig her out!" Valletto yelled back down.

"Everybody shut up!" Thesilar shouted. "Just… shut up for a second! Aestelle! Can you move?"

Water dripped. The tiny room fell so silent that Thesilar thought she heard the smallest rush of a breeze. Either that, or something moving not far away.

"I can move a little," Aestelle said. "Just… got to get past the troll."

"It's down there with you?" Ragran yelled.

"Yes. But its head has come off, so I'm not too worried. The tunnel carries on ahead. It looks like its natural… a stream, maybe. That's all there is. I can just about fit through."

Thesilar wrapped the blazing bandage around one of her arrows to form an improvised torch. She looked across at Ragran.

"Aestelle, we need to dig you out," the barbarian called down.

"No!" Aestelle shouted up. "You move another stone and this whole thing will cave in! Do not dig!"

"What's going on?" Z'akke called down again.

Thesilar looked up.

"We're on three levels!" she shouted back up. "Ragran and I are just below the room we were fighting in! I think we can get back up! Aestelle is well below us and we can't get to her!"

"Then we have some real problems!" Valletto called down. "We can see clear skies! The whole thing is caved in! We can't get back to you!"

Ragran looked across at Thesilar again.

"We can't carry on," he said quietly, "not like this."

Thesilar looked up again.

"Get back to Torgias!" she called up. "Get up to that clear sky, work out where you are, and get back to Torgias! We'll meet you there!"

There was nothing for a few moments until the question Thesilar was struggling with herself, the question she was dreading, was shouted down from above.

"What about Aestelle?"

Thesilar looked across at Ragran. The barbarian's face dropped.

"Look," Thesilar said quietly, "if we get back to where we were, we might be able to carry on forward and find a way down a level. If we do that, we can hopefully drop down further and find this tunnel Aestelle is stuck in."

Ragran met her desperate eyes with an impassive expression. His bushy, blond eyebrows lowered.

"We can't just leave her!" Thesilar exclaimed.

Ragran looked away.

"I don't know what to do, Thes."

Thesilar looked across at the rock fall again. There was no plan, no way ahead. The facts were simple. Aestelle was buried alive.

"Thes," Aestelle called up, "I'm going now. I've got to move. I've got to try to get through here."

Thesilar nodded. Tears still streamed down her face. The dust clouds were long gone.

"Thes," Aestelle shouted up again, "I'm... sorry. About the other night. I'm sorry."

Thesilar felt a sudden sickness flare up in her throat. Ragran placed an arm around her shoulders. She did not push him away.

"Just... get to Torgias!" Thesilar called down. "Follow that tunnel, get clear and get to Torgias!"

"Right," Aestelle replied, "I'll see you there. I'm going now. Thes?"

"Yes?" Thesilar called down weakly.

Her hands shaking, Thesilar brushed away a tear as she waited for the response from Aestelle.

"Take care of Z'akke for me."

***

It was close to midnight by the time the two weary adventurers managed to stagger back out into the fresh air of the mountainside. The skies were clear, illuminated by a partial moon and a speckled heaven-scape of twinkling stars, but a stiff wind whistled through the craggy rocks like a herald of the harsh winter only weeks away. Ragran stopped by the entrance to the catacombs, taking a few moments to tighten the ragged and rusty-brown stained assortment of bandages covering his body and limbs. He found himself glad of Thesilar's company. Even with an entire childhood and adolescence spent in the mountains, he knew well that he was not immune to the unique dangers posed by that familiar environment. And having an elf with eyesight so good that she was practically able to see in the dark significantly reduced those threats.

Wordlessly, Thesilar led Ragran along the narrow, winding track leading down the dark mountainside toward Torgias. The wind picked up, funneled mercilessly through the narrow ravines between the peaks. Knowing well when it was time to swallow pride and admit that showing off bulging biceps and pectoral muscles was secondary to life itself, Ragran produced his fur cloak from his pack and wrapped it around himself. Much of their supplies had been lost with their smaller packs during the cave in, but their traveling packs did at least remain untouched at the entrance to the catacombs. Ragran was relieved to see that Z'akke and Valletto's packs were gone; a positive sign that they had made it that far and were most likely well ahead on the same mountain track. Thesilar had spent some time staring at the solitary pack left behind at the entrance.

It was perhaps two hours before Thesilar stopped abruptly on the mountain track. She folded her arms and turned her back to the wind, staring up at the mountain they had spent the last couple of days exploring.

"I don't know where it all went wrong," she said quietly.

Ragran tentatively scratched at the scab forming on the wound at his temple.

"The place caved in," he shrugged, "you couldn't have seen that coming."

"That's not what I meant," Thesilar carried on staring up.

The winds continued to howl, their icy fingers snatching at the ends of Ragran's gray cloak. He waited for her to speak again.

"This expedition," she said, "the whole thing was a disaster from start to finish. We were a disaster. Do you remember Arianya? And Tharn? We're no strangers to working with difficult people. Foul tempers. But this? We were at each other's throats!"

Ragran sighed and shook his head.

"You've known me for long enough to know that I am not afraid to speak my mind," the barbarian said, "and the truth of the matter is that of all of us, you were the one who was driving that. You were the one constantly looking to upset others. For your own amusement. You've changed, Thesilar. You used to make us all laugh. Now you just look to drive the knife in to everybody you know."

The slim elf span around.

"We've all changed!" she exclaimed, her eyes pained. "The world has changed, Ragran! Since they flooded the Abyss and the borders changed, nothing has been the same! Look at you! You used to have more fire than a volcano!"

"I grew up, Thes. I got older."

"I know! And it's killing me to watch! I'm no elf, Ragran, not anymore! I had to run from my people nearly half my life ago! I've spent more time in the company of humans than anybody else for over a decade now! And all I do is watch the people who mean something to me grow wrinkled and gray. I stand back and watch my friends wither, knowing that the next wave of friends will come along, and the next and the next. I shall be the constant, forever young in your eyes. Forever alone, because of what I did to my own kin. Even though it was morally right."

Ragran remained silent still, content to let his old friend talk. He still did not know what drove her to a life of adventuring. Nobody knew. The few words she uttered to him there and then, on the side of the mountain, were the most details she had ever shared.

"But what really hurts," she continued, her eyes glistening, "what really kills me is that Aestelle is still alive. Right up there! Right where we are running from! Not for long, but she is alive right now. In the dark, alone, scared, and dying. If she had taken a sword to the head and died up there, yes, I'd be upset! But this? This is sickening! This?! I do not know how to... I... she used to look up to me. She used to hang on my every word. She was so eager to learn! And then she changed too. Like the rest of you. If anybody should have stayed the same, it should have been her, because... well, you know what she is."

Thesilar fell silent. Ragran watched her, willing enough to let her release her anxieties and frustrations. It meant little to him. Losing somebody was something he had rarely stopped to think about. Up until recently, at least. Losing his father changed everything. Ragran looked across at Thesilar. Her shoulders were shaking. She took a handkerchief from her belt and wiped her nose.

"She's still alive up there," Thesilar repeated.

"Do you want to go back and look for her?" Ragran offered.

"Do you think we stand a chance?"

"None," Ragran replied honestly, "absolutely none. But perhaps you will face her loss better in the days to come knowing that you tried."

Thesilar looked back up at the lonely, windswept peak. After a few moments, she turned without a word and resumed her trek back down the slope toward Torgias.

***

A sliver of light appeared in a crack in the rocks above. That narrow glimmer of daylight changed Aestelle's world. For what could have been hours, days, or even longer, she had tried to edge her way through the rocks, feeling desperately in the cold darkness around her. The Shining Ones seemed to favor her with that first fall, where the rocks crushed the troll but only succeeded in trapping one of her arms, with injuries that a wave of divinity magic was more than capable of healing. But the real providence lay in the still blazing torch that had fallen down with her. But once that had burned out, her determined efforts to escape her rocky tomb had slowly descended into a miserable panic.

It was a truly terrible way to die. She could breathe, the injuries from the past two days were not at all severe; she was in good health. That made the prospect of starving to death in complete darkness all the more terrifying. A thousand thoughts ran through her head in the hours spent tentatively feeling the rocks around her in an attempt to find a way through.

Since she left the Sisterhood, she had taken part in many expeditions in long forgotten places. She had encountered countless examples of dead bodies; frozen in place or bones bleached by the sun. Skeletons devoid of any life or clue to their former identify. Was that her fate? To die alone down here, only to be discovered five, six hundred years later by some expedition, without a clue as to who she was? That was the only time she laughed. Out of nowhere, a thought forced itself to the front of her mind. *You can't die like this. What if somebody were to discover your bones and not know how amazingly beautiful you were?* She had laughed at herself for her ludicrous, incurable, but certainly valid vanity.

That laughter would, at times during the night, nearly become tears. There came a point where she turned to faith. Yes, she had left the Sisterhood, but that was due to her problems with the Shining Ones' representatives on Pannithor – mortal people. She had never lost her faith in her deities. That was when she remembered that her Eloicon – her holy book and one of her last memories of her life in the Sisterhood – was gone. Given as a gift to a friend.

Aestelle remembered her last meeting with Orion. He still had her Eloicon chained to his waist, to replace the one he had lost in battle. That last meeting was a disaster. Of course she knew he was in love with her – she was fairly sure that most men she encountered were – but he did not *say* it. His words proved it, but there was no declaration. No grabbing her to kiss her, no clear statement of undying love. And if he was not willing to do that? She would be damned if it would come from her. So despite his desperate pleas for her to stay, she did what had to be done. She had no choice. She turned her back and rode away.

But what if she had stayed? What if she had taken the initiative, agreed to one of his suggestions, even kissed him? Would they be together now? At this very moment, would she be watching the sunrise on some exquisite veranda, overlooking the sparkling coast of the Infant Sea, hand in hand with the man she also loved? Would swallowing her pride on that last meeting have changed the course of her life for the better, putting her in a perfect place instead of dying slowly, miserably and alone, forgotten in a tunnel within a mountain?

It was at that moment, with those agonizing thoughts racing through her mind, that the first ray of sunlight broke through the crack in the rock above. Aestelle watched as the blackness ahead slowly morphed into a thousand shades of blue and gray; just enough light creeping through for her to see her own hands ahead of her. Then light seeped through a second crack. And a third. She looked up at the white cracks of light above but saw there was no way of climbing up; and even if there were, there was certainly no way of breaking through rock. As the light continued to intensify, she saw that she was in a low cavern, not far from where she had dropped out of the first tunnel she had navigated. Only a few feet ahead of her was another hole in the rock face, all this time hiding in the darkness was another route to explore that might take her to the surface.

Carefully willing her aching limbs back into motion, Aestelle crawled to the hole in the rock. It was another natural tunnel, even narrower than the last but with a flicker of light at the far end. Hunkering down to drag her weary arms and legs forward, she slowly crawled through the tunnel, gritting her teeth as jagged rocks scratched at her back and tugged at her clothing.

Then she sensed it. A familiar warmth. A glow, a comforting brightness to accompany the light at the end of the rocky tunnel. Was it her prayers being answered? Were the Shining Ones guiding her to safety? Or, more likely, was her exhausted mind playing tricks on her? She carried on with slow, careful determination, her knees and elbows painfully driving her through the cold tunnel. Her head began to pound again as it often did when she went a long time without drinking.

The tunnel turned a corner and stopped abruptly. Below her, at the end of a short drop, was the surface of a cavern. Lit by gaps in the rocks far above, pillars of dawn sunshine illuminated a pool of water below her, perfectly still and undisturbed. On the far side of the water was a rocky outcrop; an island of sorts in the water-filled cavern. Aestelle stared at the smooth rocks. Again, her mind played cruel tricks on her. She blinked and re-focused. The shapes were still there in the shadows. There were dead bodies on the rocks. She sensed the presence of divinity again. She heard a low grumble; a growl that could not come from anything human.

Gently lowering herself down from the mouth of the tunnel, Aestelle dropped into the pool below. The near freezing water immediately soaked her, seeping up and over her belt to run inside her boots and leggings, causing her to stifle a gasp. Reaching to her shoulder, she unsheathed her greatsword and waded cautiously forward. The pool grew shallower as she approached the smooth rocks, now only up to her thighs in the water. There was blood in the water ahead. As her eyes adjusted to the darkness, she saw the bones of at least a dozen bodies scattered around the rocks. She waded closer, her fingers tightening around the handle of her sword. It was closer to two-dozen skeletons. She heard the inhuman growl again.

Icy water dripping from her, she edged closer to the rocks. There, in the very center of the mounds of bones, were three bodies of very recently deceased warriors. The skeletons around them still clutched weapons and were positioned such that they had clearly attacked from all sides, advancing out of the water. Aestelle's eyes widened in shock as she drew close enough to identify the bodies of the dead. Two wore robes of white and blue. One was clad in ornate, steel armor wrapped in a surcoat of white. All three were women. She recognized the colors, the cut of their attire and their weapons. They were warriors of the Sisterhood. Just beyond where they had fallen was the crumpled body of an enormous, powerful gur panther. Its chest weakly rose and fell as it let out low moans of pain; the source of the inhuman groans.

Aestelle dashed over to the rocks. She sensed it again as she approached the bodies, that familiar glow of divinity magic. The body in the armor moved. She was still alive. Aestelle dropped to one knee and carefully turned her over to face her. The woman's face was pale, with dark hair plastered across her cheek. Her green eyes were half-closed. Blood seeped from terrible wounds across her body. The green eyes flickered and slowly drifted across to focus on Aestelle. The warrior's eyes widened in surprise as she weakly drew in a breath.

"...Aestelle? It... cannot be..."

Aestelle's jaw dropped open as she recognized the voice. "Joselin?!"

Chapter Eight

Prioress Marilla closed the door gently behind her before walking into the center of the room, showing the due respect to her hierarchical superior with a sincere bow. The very action sent a flare of pain up either side of her spine, although she certainly needed no reminder of her advancing years. The office was austere, as one would expect; the white pillars holding up the walls lacked any detail or design, and the room's only furnishings were made of the simplest wood, again without any features beyond what was required to function.

Abbess Vita looked up from behind her desk as Marilla stood up straight again. The younger, higher-ranking nun lowered her quill and pushed the scroll on the desk in front of her to one side. Even with the low sun directly behind her, almost haloing her head in a warm yellow, Marilla could see the lines on Vita's face. She wore simple robes of blue and white, with her graying hair tied up severely in a plain bun. She remembered Abbess Vita as a mere novice some three decades ago, a determined, devout, but introverted girl. Now she stared up from behind her desk with unmatched confidence practically emanating from her dark eyes as she regarded the older nun.

"Prioress Marilla," she greeted coolly, "how pleasant to see you again."

The tone of her voice did nothing to convey that pleasance.

"Reverend Mother," Marilla bowed her head again, "thank you for agreeing to see me at such short notice."

"I gather it is of some importance," Vita said, declining to offer Marilla a seat or even inquire as to her health in the year since they had last crossed paths, "so please go on."

Marilla forced a smile, wincing as the fierce rays of sun blurred the mountainous horizon through the window behind the abbess.

"I have with me a young girl," Marilla said. "I believe her place is here. With you. I believe she is something special."

"Oh?" Vita leaned back in her chair.

"Yes. She..."

"I have no capacity to take on new aspirants," Vita declared. "Even if I did, any girl wishing to join this abbey would need to go through the same process as the near endless queue of youths wishing to accept the hospitality of this Order."

"I... I appreciate that, Reverend Mother," Marilla nodded, again forcing a smile at the younger woman, "but, as I say, she is special. I believe."

Vita pushed her chair back and stood. Her broad shoulders and muscular frame showed, even when partially masked by her simple robes.

"She is recently orphaned," Marilla smiled sadly. "The plague took her father a year ago. She lost her mother only this month."

"There are countless orphaned girls in this province." Vita tilted her head slightly to one side. "The plague has been cruel. It is your job, Prioress Marilla, to provide care and hospitality to the sick, poor, and needy. That is what your priory is charged with. My abbey has a military function. My sisters are soldiers. Our duty is to fight."

Marilla stopped. Was this the right thing to do? Was committing an orphaned girl to a harsh life of danger really what the Shining Ones above would want? She took a breath.

"Reverend Mother. You should see the girl yourself. She is just outside. I knew her mother, briefly. She was a mill worker in Martia. I knew her long enough to know she had an honest, devout heart. I believe what she told me about the girl's father. And that being the case, this girl belongs with the Order. She will be capable of great things."

The graying abbess' eyes narrowed momentarily. She silently gestured to the door. Marilla walked over and opened it again, admitting the youth she had traveled to the abbey with. The girl was five years old but was tall enough to pass as a few years older. The simple clothes of a mill worker's daughter and the grime on her face did little to lessen the impact of her features. Bright blonde hair crowned a face that was perfect in all proportions, with dazzling eyes of silver-blue. Vita looked down at the girl. Her eyes narrowed again, but this time, with clear interest rather than suspicion. Marilla smiled. She could sense it, too.

"Why are you here?" she demanded.

The girl looked up, her unnaturally colored eyes a combination of nervousness and defiance.

"'Cause my mamma is dead, an' I've no place to go."

"*Because* my mother died, *and* I have no place to go!" Vita corrected sternly. "Annunciate your words properly, girl! Stand up straight!"

The girl did as she was instructed. She looked across to Marilla, who smiled down encouragingly.

"Prioress Marilla tells me that your father was special."

The girl shrugged.

"Dunno. I don't remember 'im much."

"I do not *recall*! I do not remember much about *him*! Pronounce your 'T's!"

"I don't know. I don't remember him much."

"What do you remember? What did your mother tell you?" Vita demanded.

The girl looked up at Marilla again. Again, she smiled and nodded. The girl looked back at the towering abbess.

"Mamma told me he came from the heavens. He was an Elohi. He changed 'cause he loved her."

Vita's eyes widened. Her nostrils flared as she stared down at the girl and then across at Marilla.

"Lies!" she finally declared.

"If the girl was lying, we would both sense it!" Marilla retorted, her temper finally giving way.

"Not her! The mother! She lied to the girl!"

"She did no such thing!" Marilla folded her arms. "I was with her when she told me! My command of the powers of divinity is more than enough to detect an untruth!"

The girl took a step forward and pointed a finger up at the abbess.

"Don't you talk 'bout my mamma like that! My mamma was no liar!"

Marilla rushed over and placed an arm around her shoulders.

"Alright, dear, alright. Nothing was meant by it."

Vita paced up and down in front of her desk, her eyes flitting from side to side as conversations played through her head. She stopped after several moments to regard the aging nun and the little girl again.

"I do not doubt the sincerity of the girl or her mother. But I do doubt the validity of the information which her mother believed to be true!"

Marilla stepped across in front of the muscular abbess.

"Vita! Look at her!" she growled. "Use your eyes, woman! Use your senses! Tell me in all honesty that you cannot feel the powers of the divine literally flowing from her! She is the child of an Elohi! She is half-divine! Half-immortal! She is descended from the angels of Mount Kolosu, and it is our responsibility to take care of her! To raise her! Now, you have far better facilities and resources here to do it! But if you do not take her in, then I will! Even without your approval as my superior, I will do it if you do not!"

Marilla stared up at the younger woman. Vita's mouth opened to issue the inevitable reprimand to the insubordinate prioress. She stopped. Perhaps she recalled the years of loyal service Marilla had provided to the Order. Perhaps she remembered the help Marilla had given to the young Novice Vita so many years ago. She stepped past Marilla and looked down at the girl.

"I like your attitude," she smiled faintly, aggressively, "I like your spirit. You shall need it with what awaits you. But let me be clear. I am your abbess now. This entire abbey is under my charge. You do as I say, and you do as my subordinates say. But I am willing to take you on as an aspirant. That means that you shall live here whilst I consider whether you shall be permitted to attempt to join the Order of the Penitent and the Devoted. If I deem you worthy, you will be permitted to take the First Step. Do you understand?"

The girl again looked across to Marilla for approval. She nodded.

"Yeah. I mean, yes, milady."

"*Reverend Mother*," Vita corrected. "Now tell me, aspirant. What is your name?"

"Aestelle."

***

Aestelle leaned in closer, staring in disbelief at the face of the dying warrior before her. It had been some eleven years since they last crossed paths, since Joselin had played that instrumental part in Aestelle leaving the Sisterhood. The years had changed Aestelle's memories of Joselin from a stern, but fresh-faced senior sister in her mid-twenties to, judging by the badges of rank etched on her heavy belt buckle and right pauldron, a veteran Sister Superior. Aestelle looked down at her wounds. She let out a breath and swallowed. Despite the severity of the injuries, she held up her hands and concentrated to bring forth the healing surge of divinity to her fingertips.

Joselin reached up and weakly batted her hand to one side.

"No..."

"No?!" Aestelle gasped. "What do you mean? You're dying!"

"No... do not try to heal me... I am gone, Aestelle... you will... only prolong my suffering. Please... no..."

Aestelle lowered her hands and took in a deep breath. She knew Joselin was right. Looking down at her wounds and the amount of blood she had lost, she was beyond help from even the most skilled of healers. Despite the clear evidence before her, Aestelle wracked her mind for a solution to the problem, but her thoughts were cut off when the mortally wounded woman spoke again.

"How can it be you?" Joselin whispered weakly. "How are you... of all people, here... at my end? What are the Shining Ones trying to tell me?"

"Well, you must have really screwed up somewhere if the last thing you'll see is a bitch like me!" Aestelle offered an apologetic smile.

Joselin's pained brow lowered; a look somewhere between anger and disappointment that Aestelle had seen a thousand times in their youth.

"You… haven't changed… Aestelle…"

That familiar look of disappointment brought back a flood of memories from her childhood. None of them pleasant. Joselin looked up at her.

"I have something to ask of you…"

Aestelle's face dropped. She looked down at those horrific wounds again and thought on Joselin's words. She wanted the suffering to end.

"No," Aestelle shook her head, "no, Joselin. Please don't ask me to do that."

The dying Sister Superior smiled weakly.

"I am not asking you to end… my suffering, Aestelle! Although eleven years ago, at the foot of these… very mountains, I think you hated me enough… to do it then!"

Aestelle screwed her eyes up tight for a second, sickness rising in her throat.

"We both hated each other, Joselin."

"I… never hated you. But listen… I have a lot to say, still, and not long left. It heartens me to see you still… have the faith to heal. Please… heal Seeba…"

Aestelle looked up at the fallen bodies of the two battle sisters who had accompanied Joselin. One stared up to the heavens above, her eyes wide-open, skin deathly pale and throat slit. The other lay face down, half on the smooth rocks and half-floating in the cold water, surrounded by masses of fallen undead.

"I'm sorry," Aestelle said, "your sisters. They are both dead. I'm sorry."

"I know…" Joselin whispered. "Shining Ones rest their souls… I know… Seeba is my panther. Heal her and… take her home to the abbey."

Aestelle looked up at the wounded, growling gur panther. She felt a shiver of fear when a long-forgotten memory flooded to the fore of her mind, images of a young sister mauled to death by a gur panther during training. She looked down at Joselin again.

"You want me to take… *that* back to the Abbey of the Penitent and the Devoted?!"

"*Her*," Joselin corrected sternly. "Seeba is just as much… a part of our Order as any sister."

"I'm not really a cat person…"

"Aestelle! I am dying! Do this for me!"

Aestelle leaned away instinctively, surprised at the force in the dying woman's voice.

"Alright," she replied, "alright. I shall take the panther back to the abbey."

"Listen… there is more… this place, what is going on here… why I was sent here… there is more that you need to know…"

Aestelle looked away. She found her mind drifting, half through the sheer shock of encountering Joselin again after so many years, but also due to the task that lay ahead of her. Returning to the abbey. Returning to what had been her home for over fifteen years of her life. She closed her eyes and shook her head. Home. That place could never be associated with the word 'home'…

***

Their footsteps echoing along the dim corridor, the two novices walked briskly from the Sister Superior's office toward the dormitory. Both were dressed in the same simple robes of white, brought in at the waist with a belt of woven hemp strands. Flickering candles illuminated the small, neat alcoves cut into the white walls of the cloisters, some with simple statues of worship; others with dried flowers or framed pages from holy books. Aestelle suppressed a smirk as Joselin struggled to keep pace with her. Even though Joselin was twelve years of age – two years older than Aestelle – she was shorter and could not keep up with her deliberately long stride.

"Things will change for you now," Joselin declared, her eyes fixed at the end of the long corridor, her aloof manner increasingly annoying to Aestelle. "You may have been moved up a year early, but there will be no special measures for you. You will be expected to meet the same standard as the rest of us."

"Yes, yes," Aestelle rolled her eyes, "I have been here for five years now. I rather fancy that I understand how this place works."

"*Senior Novice*," Joselin said. "You have been placed in my dormitory. I am the senior novice. In the absence of any of the sisters, I am in command of the twenty novices there. Understood?"

"You are twelve," Aestelle suppressed a yawn, "so drop the pretense. I am not impressed."

The older novice looked away and took in a breath. The door of the dormitory was only a few paces away now.

"We have all heard of you, Aestelle," Joselin said. "Everybody in the abbey knows that you think you are something special. Perhaps you are – and if you are, it was handed to you rather you earning it through any hard work. More likely, you are not. So to manage your expectations, let me be perfectly clear. I expect you to do exactly as I tell you to."

Joselin opened the door and pushed past Aestelle to walk in first. The long dormitory was similar in appearance to the corridor leading to it; plain white walls, smooth in texture but with a few rough lines where repairs had been implemented over cracks in the plaster. Two rows of ten beds lined the longer walls, with a simple wooden chest at the foot of each bed. Aside from a handful of religious symbols nailed to the walls, there was nothing else adorning the room. As soon as Joselin entered the dormitory, the eighteen girls in the room dashed over to stand up at the foot of their beds. All were eleven or twelve years of age and dressed in the white robes of order novices.

"Novices," Joselin announced, "this is Novice Aestelle. She is now one of us. Novice Aestelle, that is your bed. Clean your area and then go and get new linen. You will lead us in evening prayer tonight. Morning prayer is at four bells. Weapons training is immediately afterward. Go."

Aestelle walked over to her bed and placed down her bag. The other novices resumed their previous activities; mainly cleaning or studying. Only one other girl offered her a smile. The remainder ignored her. Aestelle unpacked her bag onto her rough, straw mattress. Robes, fighting attire, Eloicon, prayer book...

"What is this?"

Aestelle turned around.

Joselin reached into Aestelle's open pack and took out a small, white band. Aestelle let out a breath. Joselin held it up, high above her head.

"Give that back," Aestelle warned.

"What is this?" Joselin repeated.

Aestelle looked up at the simple, woven bracelet with the tiny sunflower stitched into it. Her mother's. The last physical link she had to her family before the Order.

"It belonged to my mother. Give it back. Now."

Joselin turned to face the girl who had smiled to Aestelle; a short youth with auburn hair.

"Novice Antonia," Joselin stared down at the girl, "inform Novice Aestelle of the Order's rules regarding personal possessions."

The brown-haired girl swallowed nervously.

"*The Order provides all that is needed,*" the girl recited mechanically. "*The Shining Ones provide. Those blessed with the good fortune to be nurtured within the Order's ranks need no personal possessions. To do so would be to spurn the charity and good grace of the Order's love.*"

Joselin looked back at Aestelle. She raised one eyebrow, smiled, and tore the cloth bracelet into pieces. She opened her hand and let them twirl slowly down to the stone floor.

"Clean that up," she ordered Aestelle, "and as you are new here, I shall extend the courtesy of keeping this transgression within these walls."

Aestelle watched the little, white pieces flutter to the floor. She remembered her mother's gentle face. She remembered evenings with her family, just enough that she could even just about picture her father's smile. She looked up at Joselin.

With a snarl of rage, Aestelle leapt forward. She brought a clenched fist back and then propelled it forward with all of her anger, smashing it into the senior novice's face. The blow echoed across the chamber, and Joselin was flung back. She fell to the floor, blood streaming from a split lip and tears already forming in her eyes. With shock plastered across her bloodied face, Joselin opened her mouth but only managed to burst into tears. Aestelle flung herself down on top of her and brought her fist hammering down into Joselin's face again, and again, and again...

***

Aestelle hesitantly edged across toward the wounded gur panther. The creature was truly colossal, perhaps as large as a bear, the gently shade of brown covering her flanks and fading into the white fur on her belly giving an elegant appearance, a gentle beauty that Aestelle knew from memory could not be further from the truth. The wounded panther watched Aestelle approach, her yellow eyes tracking the former battle sister as she edged closer.

"I know you can understand me," Aestelle said, her voice low, her gloved hands held out to either side. "I am here to help you..."

The wounded creature forced herself up onto one bloodied paw and bared her dagger-like, razor sharp teeth with a low, threatening growl. From her distant past, Aestelle remembered her lessons on how to deal with these lethal creatures. Gur panthers were native to the Tarkis region of Basilea and, due to their rare ability to combine near unstoppable fighting strength with an intelligence that lay almost halfway between beast and human, those that could be tamed were used by the fighting arm of the Sisterhood. Many were used as cavalry mounts, some pulled chariots into battle, whilst the most fearsome of all, the ones that could only be half-tamed, were unleashed in groups to fight with their own deadly claws, too feral and ferocious to allow a sister to ride them. Aestelle noted with rising terror that this particular beast wore the shoulder plates of just such a creature – a fighting panther, too ferocious to be tamed for the cavalry.

Blood still flowing from the cuts on her head and belly, the panther struggled to stand to face Aestelle, who turned to look at Joselin. The pale, fading sister shook her head weakly.

"Do not... show fear..."

Aestelle remembered that much. She recalled seeing the cavalry sisters, the panther riders, breaking in the new cubs. It took a certain kind of woman to want to take those risks. Aestelle, consequently, had never volunteered for the cavalry. Nonetheless, she pushed her fear away and stood up straight.

"Do not look at me like that!" she leaned in, staring eye to eye at the gur panther. "I said that I was coming here to help you! Now get back down before I kick you in the damn teeth!"

Aestelle never decided on whether she believed gur panthers were intelligent enough to actually learn the meaning of words. But she had certainly seen enough evidence to know for a fact that they fully understood the meaning behind a human's tone of voice. The panther struggled up, sucked in a lungful of air, and let out a deafening, terrifying bellow that reverberated all around the small cavern. The petrifying creature then let out a groan and collapsed back down to the ground, her chest heaving unevenly.

"I told you, you bloody idiot!" Aestelle snapped, fighting to control her rising fear as she approached to within swiping range of the lethal claws. "Now stop that pathetic mewping before I slap you on the nose!"

The gur panther looked up at Aestelle, her eyes pained. They moved across to regard Joselin, and Aestelle saw an utter sadness, a more complete image of despair than she had ever seen in any human. The panther let out a quiet, agonized cry and then closed her eyes. Aestelle seized the opportunity to drop to one knee by the huge beast, gently running her hands across the wounds and allowing the divine powers of healing to close up as many of the injuries as she could before exhaustion clawed at her core and she was forced to stop. Almost immediately, the panther's breathing seemed to even out.

Still trailing blood, the deadly creature crawled over to flop down next to Joselin, resting a huge paw over the dying sister's belly. Joselin smiled weakly and reached up with a shaking hand to stroke the panther's head affectionately. Her hands shaking with fear, Aestelle stared incredulously at the unbelievable display of gentleness and affection the deadly creature treated Joselin with. It was the closest she had ever been to a gur panther. She thanked the Ones above that she had never volunteered for the cavalry.

***

The bells rang out above the precession of sisters, the melodious tolls reverberating down the bell tower and into the chapel itself. Sun poured through the tall, stained-glass windows over the altar to paint the Chapel of the Sacred Devotees' floor in shades of red, blue, and gold. The fifteen novices filed in silently to form a line in front of the altar and then drop to their knees as one. Aestelle bowed her head. This was it. Finally, after ten years of toil, pain, and anguish, in a few moments she would no longer be a novice. The Ceremony of the Second Step.

At fifteen years of age, Aestelle was technically too young to become a sister. But she had heard all of the rumors and seen all of the anxiety and concern on the faces of those in positions of command. The abbey was filled with talk of nothing else. Unexpectedly high casualties on campaign against the orcs in the northwest. Critical shortages of fighting men and women across all of Basilea's fighting arms. It came as no surprise to her when she was informed that she had been granted special dispensation from the head of the entire Order to qualify and go to war, even though she was a year underage. Aestelle, like all the other novices, was not concerned by the worries of command. Casualties and logistical woes meant nothing to her. Only the chance to finally go to war.

The chapel filled with the familiar scent of incense as the service's opening hymn was struck up. The congregation – some two hundred made up of sisters and young novices alike – filled the building with song to accompany the somber blasts from the chapel organ as Abbess Vita led the main precession up the central aisle toward the altar. Aestelle knew the hymn well, but the graduating novices were to remain silent, on their knees, until the moment they would be invited to stand and have their title conferred onto them. Just as importantly, the novices would find out what role they had been selected for.

For the overwhelming majority, it would be in the battle line. Infantry, going to war with flail or sword. Some – those of a strange disposition, Aestelle felt – would be chosen to begin their specialist training in the cavalry, riding the terrifying gur panthers into battle. That left only two other specialist roles within the Order's battle ranks. The elite role of demon hunter was ruled out immediately. There was no such thing as a novice initiated straight into such a dangerous role; only veterans of many campaigns were approached and asked to consider the task of demon hunter. But with the mounting casualties the Order had suffered in recent months, there was one opening. One extremely rare opportunity for the very best novice to be permitted to join the elite ranks of the Sisterhood scouts. Skilled, disciplined, feared masters of stealth and bow. Aestelle smiled at the thought as the opening hymn drew to a close and Abbess Vita began the service. That one hallowed, esteemed place in the scouts belonged to Aestelle. She was sure of it.

The service droned on. The second hymn began. Aestelle, lost in the fantasies of the adventures ahead, had not heard a single word of the welcome, readings, or the sermon. Knelt next to her was Joselin, her rival of half a decade now. Whatever test or trial was put in front of the novices, it would always be Aestelle or Joselin who would come out top. Knowledge of scripture, mastery of divinity magic, tactical aptitude in maneuvering soldiers in battle – Joselin won at all. But when it came to the things that really mattered – skill with a flail, blade, bow, or unarmed combat – it was always Aestelle whom was the last woman standing.

Aestelle risked a glance across at Joselin. The seventeen-year-old woman remained motionless, head bowed in prayer, eyes gently shut. Aestelle remembered her last words before they walked in for the service.

"Forget being a scout, Aestelle. The scouts want discipline, commitment, and obedience. You are incapable of any of these."

She smirked to herself. Joselin actually believed that one opening in the scouts was hers.

The second hymn ended with a high note from the wailing organ. The Abbess walked down from the edge of the altar toward the line of kneeling novices. This was it. This was the end of turgid, backbreaking chores and study. This was the beginning of real life. The Second Step was moments away.

"Novice Antonia, arise," Vita called, her powerful voice echoing throughout the chapel.

The young woman stood. Vita held up her right hand to bless her as a young novice sprinkled holy water across Antonia. She then handed over Antonia's Eloicon; her own personal copy of the holy book that would guide her for the rest of her life. The full, weighty tome of unparalleled spiritual significance that replaced the simplified, almost childish version of the sacred texts that was given to the young initiates on entry into the Order.

"I bless and anoint you, Sister Antonia of the Order of the Penitent and the Devoted, battle line."

Aestelle nodded to herself. She was, like the others, surprised that Antonia had managed to survive the grueling years of training, but she was happy for her nonetheless. Perhaps they had lowered the standards in anticipation of all the casualties...

"...I bless and anoint you, Sister Sarai of the Order of the Penitent and the Devoted, lancers."

Sarai had been selected for the cavalry? Aestelle exhaled sharply. The thought of the frail woman attempting to master a gur panther was tear inducing. Abbess Vita continued to move down the line, anointing novices to sisters in turn, all to the line of battle with only three sisters selected for the cavalry. Vita stopped by Joselin. Only Joselin and Aestelle remained.

"Novice Joselin, arise."

Doubts flooded into Aestelle's mind. What if Joselin was right? What if the scouts were after dedication to duty over actual ability? Aestelle knew she had a reputation for being reckless and disobedient. She had been punished many times, more than any other sister she was aware of by some margin. At that moment, she regretted it more than any before. Surely Joselin would not be made a scout? *She* would be the logical choice for cavalry. She was bossy enough to master a gur panther. She liked to look down on everybody else and could do that even better from up in a saddle. She was perfect for the cavalry. Surely?

"I bless and anoint you, Sister Joselin of the Order of the Penitent and the Devoted, battle line."

Aestelle suppressed a gasp of astonishment. They had made Joselin a soldier of the line of battle? Just like the others who barely passed the training? She would be furious! But... that left only her. Only Aestelle. And only one space for the scouts. She knew it! She knew that raw ability was what mattered! She knew they saw something special in her!

"Novice Aestelle, arise."

Aestelle stood up. She smiled down at the aging abbess, a warm glow of confidence in her heart. The incense wafted into her nostrils. Holy water flicked across her robes. Abbess Vita looked up at her coolly.

"I bless and anoint you, Sister Aestelle of the Order of the Penitent and the Devoted. Battle line."

With shaking hands, Aestelle silently accepted her Eloicon from the grim-faced abbess.

***

"...this place," Joselin gasped, the voice growing weaker with each passing minute, "I... I was sent here to investigate... we... interrogated a messenger... there is... an organization. The Coven..."

Aestelle leaned in closer, trying to make out every word Joselin spoke. The gur panther lay down next to her, the forlorn paw still draped over her dying master, the eyes sad.

"The Coven may operate over all of Basilea... there have been... suspicions for years now... we believe it is orchestrated not far from here. But this place... Mount Ekansu... something was awoken here..."

"I know," Aestelle exhaled, "it was me. I awoke it. I do not know what it is, but I did it. It is why I am here. To fix my mistake."

Joselin reached up with one hand and took Aestelle's. Even with such little strength left, her grip was tight. Joselin leaned her head forward.

"You came back to do the right thing," her eyes drifted open and closed as she spoke. "You... always did. Aestelle... stop the Coven. Find out what is happening here... and stop it..."

Aestelle nodded.

"I can do that."

Joselin lay back again, a look of relief passing over her.

"Then they have not won," she whispered. "That is why the Shining Ones put us together... a last time... you can stop the Coven, like you did with the demons at Andro..."

Aestelle slumped forward, shaking her head. She remembered the lines of red-skinned Abyssals at the foot of the hill, the hundreds of Basilean soldiers passing in the night as she held her torch and banner up high, screaming with all her might to attract their attention...

"I did not do much at Andro, Joselin," Aestelle confessed, "not like the songs would have you believe. I... wanted to be a hero when I left the Order. But I fell. I am falling still. I failed to become that hero I wanted to be."

"Did you... stand next to that paladin atop the hill?" Joselin asked. "Did the two of you face the demon, Dionne... did you stop the invasion of our lands?"

"Yes," Aestelle answered after a pause, "yes. That part is true."

"Then you are all you set out to be." Joselin offered another weak smile as her eyes grew duller, less focused. "You are... you are a hero. You did not fail. My time... is nearly up... take Seeba home for me. Follow the passageway behind me... an hour... our packs are at the entrance..."

Aestelle looked down at the gray, deathly complexion of the woman she had known and resented so much as a child.

Aestelle knelt upright, shaking her head.

"I cannot, Joselin! I can't go back there! I walked away! I was disgraced! I turned my back on you all! I cannot do as you ask!"

"You were not disgraced. You were... forgiven... I was there, that day... the abbess forgave you... you are still one of us..."

"I am no holy woman!" Aestelle gasped, tears in her eyes.

"We were never holy women... we were soldiers..."

***

Rank after rank of orcs and goblins stretched across the green fields in front of the Basilean force. Formed up into untidy squares of dozens, even perhaps a hundred here and there, some one thousand greenskins dominated the far side of the valley floor. The fields, until yesterday ploughed and prepared by dedicated farm hands, were now deserted save the two opposing armies. The Basilean line held place as the allied force of orcs and goblins moved down the valley and into position; hulking, axe-wielding orcs in the center with gore riders and bow-armed goblins forming the flanks. Enormous, lumbering trolls towered above even the mightiest of orcs at irregular intervals within the army whilst three catapults were wheeled into position behind the ranks of infantry and cavalry.

Facing them, determined to defend the northern border of the Hegemony, stood the Basilean force. Neat, well-drilled squares of legion men-at-arms formed the backbone of the thousand-strong human army; some units armed with broad-bladed koliskos spears, others with daga swords and shields, and others still with heavy crossbows. Ready to face the threats on the flanks were the legendary knights of the paladin orders; their shining armor and blue surcoats making them seem every part the noble warriors of song and legend that sprang up across Basilea after their exploits. But not all of the Basilean army was made up of professional soldiers; on the left flank, a furious, doom-spouting zealot stood before three ranks of a hundred penitents – fanatical and devoted peasants who had followed the army north with nothing more than hammers, pitchforks, and zeal to face the evil ahead.

A roar suddenly erupted from the center of the orc force. It rippled outward, growing in intensity as the green-skinned savages bellowed and screamed, banging their axes into their shields. The guttural yell was accompanied by the high-pitched shrieks of goblins to form an unholy cacophony that echoed across the valley. The roar was opposed by the legion soldiers; men-at-arms took up a rhythmic banging of weapons into shields – two bangs followed by a shout – that rapidly grew to even rival the cries of the greenskins. From the far left of the flank, the sound of the paladins singing rousing hymns from their saddles was just about audible over the top of the shield-banging men-at-arms and the zealous leader of the penitents delivering his near foaming mouth sermon of hatred for the enemy.

From her position on the front rank of the forty Sisterhood war-riors near that left flank, Aestelle turned to look over her shoulder at the top of the valley behind them. The command tents were set up, messengers at the ready and order flags in position. She saw the ab-bess' tent, pure white and defended by a unit of panther lancers, near the dictator's command post in the center. The order flags were clear for all Basilean forces. Hold position. Aestelle turned and looked for-ward again. Her first ever battle, thrown her way when she was only fifteen, was against orcs. Now, at eighteen years of age, she was one of the most experienced and blooded sisters in the entire army.

"Will we have to charge them, or will they attack us?" Aestelle heard a frightened whisper from one of the new sisters on the rear rank.

"Shut up!" Senior Sister Decima, the unit commander, bellowed from the middle of the front rank.

Aestelle looked forward at the endless line of orcs across the valley and drew her greatsword from her back. The wind whipped at her long, blonde hair tied in a ponytail with a simple band of light blue. She wore the same garb as her sisters; a tunic and leggings of white, augmented with a surcoat of light blue that fell down into a long loin-cloth. Her only armor was a tight bodice of tanned leather and tall, bat-tered boots of the same color that extended half way up her thighs. She looked down the front rank of sisters. Decima glanced across and gave a slow, grim nod, a brief mark of respect from the dark-skinned, shav-en headed Senior Sister. Aestelle returned the nod and looked ahead again.

A single enormous orc, seemingly half the size of a troll, strode out in front of the sprawling army. The creature held up a double-head-ed axe and let out a long, guttural roar. With that, the army of orcs and goblins charged forward. Aestelle turned to look over her shoul-der again. A precession of flags appeared above command tents along the ridge to the south, conveying orders down to the Basilean troops waiting in the valley. On the flanks, bugles blasted and lines of paladin knights rode out to position themselves ready to charge the exposed sides of the enemy force. Drums sounded their staccato beats, and le-gion men-at-arms marched neatly out to face the foe. A red and blue pennant was raised above the abbess' command tent.

"Sisters," Senior Sister Decima yelled, "advance!"

The fighting nuns paced forward across the green fields. To ei-ther side, the drums and bugles continued. The maddened voice of the penitent leader rose into a frenzied series of incomprehensible screams. The orcs drew closer, quickly covering the distance as they sprinted into attack. Aestelle slung her heavy, crude greatsword up over her shoulders as she walked. She was on the front rank; nobody stood between her and a thousand greenskins. With her allies outside her line of sight and only thin, flimsy robes and a cheap, issued leather breastplate to defend her, she felt more vulnerable than ever before.

Behind her, one of the new sisters began singing a hymn. Nobody else joined her. The bugle blasts on the flanks sounded the charge, and with a great roar, the paladin knights thundered across the fields with their lances lowered. A series of loud thunks echoed from the slope to the south, and steel-tipped bolts, larger than a man, whooshed through the air and over the heads of the advancing Basilean soldiers from their own heavy arbalests. The huge projectiles tore through the front ranks of greenskins but were immediately answered by the enemy's catapults, flinging enormous boulders up across the cloudy sky above. Huge rocks fell down into the midst of the advancing men-at-arms, crushing soldiers as they slammed into the dry earth with plumes of dust and dirt.

The greenskins were close enough now to make out individuals within their front ranks, towering orcs made up of muscle and crude armor, fanged jaws, pig-snouted faces, crude axes, and frenzied eyes. The familiar sound of bowstrings twanged from somewhere behind the orcs' first rank, and the sky filled with dark blurs as scores of arrows arched up to the apex of their deadly journeys before falling down to plummet toward their targets. A sister on the front rank to Aestelle's right let out a gasp. They had been targeted. With a gentle whistle that sounded in stark contrast to the death they would bring in moments, the arrows shot down into the Basilean front ranks. Men-at-arms raised their shields. Aestelle stared straight ahead and carried on walking. There was nothing else she could do.

Arrows tore into the forty lightly-armored sisters. Aestelle heard a scream from next to her and saw a comrade drop to her knees out of the corner of her eye. More cries of pain and some of panic reverberated from the rear ranks.

"Advance!" Decima screamed again. "Keep going! Forward!"

Aestelle looked dead ahead. The front rank would not stop. It was down to the rear ranks to pause and help the wounded. Aestelle's task was to keep going. No matter what the casualties, no matter what the threat. Keep moving forward. With a chorus of savage shrieks, the huge mob of penitents broke ranks and charged forward to meet the orcs.

A second salvo of arrows fell from the heavens, again tearing into the sisters. There were more cries and screams. Aestelle made the terrible mistake of turning in place and looking behind her. Perhaps a dozen of her sisters lay on the ground, their white and pale blue robes covered in blood. Some lay dead where they fell, others cried out for help, holding on to where arrows had pierced their bodies and limbs. The youngest of the unit, the new girls of sixteen who had arrived only three days before, either looked around in stunned helpless silence, openly wept, or dashed in a panic from casualty to casualty, desperately trying to lend aid.

Decima lay fallen on one knee, an arrow protruding from a bloody wound in her hip. The veteran warrior gritted her teeth as she yanked the missile out in a spurt of blood before placing a hand over the wound and healing it. No sooner had she stood up than another arrow struck her in the chest. She looked down at it for a brief moment, her face somewhere between surprise and confusion, and then toppled over to the ground. Aestelle saw Sister Claudia, a kindly but determined woman she knew from her childhood, staggering up to her knees next to Decima. Claudia weakly grasped at an arrow in her chest, her breathing wheezed and labored. The young sister looked up at Aestelle, her eyes pleading, and reached out toward her with one blood-soaked hand.

Aestelle turned away again to face the enemy. The front rank carried on. That was her task. Aestelle failed to take even a single step before she changed her mind. Dashing over to Claudia, she dropped to one knee by her wounded comrade.

"Stay still!" Aestelle urged, raising her voice over the screams of the wounded as the booming, thunderous yells of the orcs drew nearer still.

Aestelle pulled the arrow clear and then placed a hand over Claudia's holed lung, sending a burst of healing magic across the wound. The pale-faced sister immediately took in a long, deep breath.

"Th... thank you..."

Before Aestelle could reply, an order was yelled from the center of the decimated, stalled unit of warriors.

"Fall back!" Joselin yelled, moving to the front of the unit. "Sisters! Fall back to regroup! Carry the wounded! We must retreat and regroup!"

A hand slammed painfully onto Aestelle's wrist before a grip like iron clamped around her. Aestelle looked down and saw Senior Sister Decima staring up at her with pained eyes.

"Don't... retreat..." the veteran warrior hissed through bloodied teeth.

"Senior?" Aestelle gasped.

"Orders... are to advance..." the gravely wounded sister choked. "Aestelle... take command... lead the charge..."

Aestelle nodded and leapt to her feet.

"Reform the line!" she yelled over the din of battle. "Fighting line! Two ranks!"

"Aestelle! We are falling back!" Joselin shouted, pacing over to confront the taller sister. "We are being cut to shreds! Armored infantry need to take the front! We must regroup before we can be of any use!"

Aestelle rushed out to meet Joselin at the front of the lines of dead and wounded sisters as ranks of orcs and men-at-arms clashed into each other only a few dozen yards away.

"The order is to advance!" Aestelle shouted. "We have enough here in fighting shape to make a difference now!"

"I am in command!" Joselin screamed. "I am senior to you!"

Aestelle grabbed Joselin by the throat and dragged her in to shove her face into her old rival's.

"The senior sister has placed me in command, and you will do as I say!" she thundered. "You will follow me into the fires of the Abyss if I tell you to! Get in line and prepare to charge those bastards!"

Aestelle flung Joselin down to the ground and turned to face her unit.

"Get in line!" she repeated. "If you can walk, you are fighting! If you can't walk, then see to the wounded! Form up!"

Aestelle turned to look to the north. There was no longer two distinct forces closing in on each other, but a mass of fighting bodies to the left and to the right as the savage, ill-disciplined orcs surged against the tightly packed ranks of legion soldiers. With battle raging in every direction, there was no way of ascertaining who was winning or losing, or even if there was any plan left at all. All she could see was the fighting immediately around her, and the terrible, bloody casualties inflicted by each side. Up ahead, there was a gap in the fighting where a horde of perhaps forty orcs, each bearing an axe and spiked shield, thundered across the fields toward the sisters, their feet drumming on the ground like a herd of charging animals.

Aestelle held her broad-bladed, straight edged greatsword above her head and walked out toward them. Her walk picked up in pace. She broke into a run. Whether or not her sisters were following her she did not know, and she dared not look back to find out. The deafening sounds of battle faded away until she was aware only of her feet on the dry earth beneath her, her knees skimming through the long grass and the pounding of her heart in her chest. She let out a growl through her gritted teeth, growing in intensity until it became a roar.

Aestelle planted a hand on the top of a dry stone wall cutting across the edge of the field and vaulted over it, picking up her pace again to a sprint. The orcs charging down on her were only a single field away, the details of their crude, black armor and battered weapons now clearly visible. The first orcs reached the final barrier between them; a half-collapsed wooden pole fence of waist height. Aestelle reached the fence and with a final yell, jumped up to plant one foot atop it, and then hurled herself down into an attack.

Hacking down with all of her might, her first strike tore open the chest of the closest orc and sent him falling back into his unit, fountaining up dark blood from the gaping wound. Aestelle linked her attack into a second strike as soon as her feet touched the dry earth again, the edge of her blade catching a second greenskin and ripping open one of his arms. The orcs swarmed forward around her, two charging in to attack her directly.

Screaming curses at them, she deflected one heavy axe strike that left her blade ringing with the force of the blow before lashing out with a clenched fist to punch her assailant in the nose. The second orc bore down on her and batted aside her blade with his shield before slicing down at her with his axe. Aestelle nimbly stepped aside and brought her own blade up to bite deeply into the orc's gut, bending the creature over before she kicked him off her blade and delivered an arcing, overhead strike to slice down through the top of his head until her blade became lodged in the orc's neck.

Before she could dislodge and recover her sword, a fist slammed into her face and knocked her clean off her feet. Aestelle fell crumpled to the ground, her ears ringing and her vision blurred. The white sky above was instantly obscured as her attacker knelt above her, two enormous, powerful hands grasping her throat. Aestelle flung an elbow around into her orc assailant, thrashing and kneeing the creature until the iron grip slackened just enough for her to fling her head forward. She sunk her teeth into the orc's nose, bit off a chunk of flesh, and spat it out before headbutting the greenskin directly on the wound. The savage creature let out a yell and punched Aestelle again, smashing her senses into nothingness.

Aestelle lay back helplessly as the orc scrabbled around for his axe to finish her. The greenskin's entire head exploded into a mass of bloody flesh as the metal ball of a flail smashed through the side of it. Aestelle looked up and saw Joselin stood above her, drenched in orc blood. Joselin reached down and grabbed Aestelle by the scruff of the neck, hauling her roughly back to her feet.

"Get back into the fight!" she yelled before turning and charging headlong into the orcs, surrounded by the advancing sisters from their unit. Aestelle numbly recovered her sword and charged back into the fray.

***

Wind whistled through the cracks in the rocks above. Water dripped slowly and rhythmically into one of the many puddles surrounding the main pool. The lumbering gur panther breathed in and out, her paw still draped affectionately over her dying master. Aestelle sat to the other side of Joselin, her knees drawn in to her chest.

"Aestelle," Joselin breathed, "I'm scared."

"You have nothing to be scared of," Aestelle replied, as matter of factly as if they were discussing the day's weather. "You did everything right. You followed all the rules. If you do not receive favor from the Shining Ones, then nobody can. You have nothing to fear."

The subterranean chamber fell silent again. Aestelle stared up at the cracks of light above, the nausea in her throat perfectly accompanied by the hollow emptiness in her chest as she processed a hundred long suppressed memories.

"Can you... read the Litany to me?" Joselin asked. "Can you give me my Third Step?"

Aestelle shut her eyes and hung her head. The bitter irony that she would be delivering the Third Step – the soul's transition – to the same woman who was her accuser in both her Fourth and Fifth Steps – the path of damnation.

"I... do not have an Eloicon," Aestelle replied honestly, "I gave it away."

"Take mine. Keep it."

Aestelle looked down at the holy book hanging from Joselin's armored waist. It was the same book that Abbess Vita had presented to Joselin when they knelt next to each other in the chapel sixteen years ago. She unclipped it from her dying sister's waist. The book fell open on the first page. Aestelle saw an old, faded inscription written neatly inside.

> *'Dearest Joselin,*
> *You never fail to make us proud,*
> *With love,*
> *Ma and Pa'.*

"I am so sorry," Aestelle said, her hands shaking as she turned to find the Litany of the Soul's Transition. "I am so sorry that you face your final journey with me by your side instead of somebody you love."

Joselin looked up at Aestelle, smiled, and then closed her eyes. She reached up and took Aestelle's hand.

"I am not sorry, Sister," she murmured.

Aestelle swallowed and took a few breaths before looking down to begin reading the familiar lines.

"The light above guides us through darkness. The light above leads us home..."

Aestelle closed the book. She had heard the words so many times during five years of fighting within the ranks of the Sisterhood. She had lost count of how many memorial services she attended, head bowed in fields and hills across a dozen nations and kingdoms, how many bodies of young women she had seen carefully lowered into the ground, a hundred leagues from home and their loved ones.

"Your holy light strengthens our souls," she continued from memory, "the light of your love will overcome all darkness. From the first to the last days, our faith and your love will guide us and strengthen us. Shining Ones, accept your daughter Joselin into your hearts, prepare a place for her at the peak of The Mountain, let her soul transition to you to rest in a place of love and holiness. Bring her home to your love and your holy light."

At some point during the recital of the words, Joselin's grip on Aestelle's hand eased off and gently fell away.

Chapter Nine

The sandstone tiles stood out in stark contrast from the dull gray of the previous chambers, centuries of dust brushed away to reveal the intricate craftsmanship behind the delicate etchings. Khirius ran a hand along a wall tile, marveling at the display of ancient history at his very fingertips. Two hundred years of existence had given him ample time to learn the basics of several elvish dialects, but the text cut into the orange stone before him was utterly alien.

"Incredible, is it not?" Cane smiled, the first real show of emotion that Khirius had seen from the necromancer. "These tiles were smuggled halfway across Pannithor to get here, under the very noses of the Primovantorians who killed Arteri in the first place."

The two stood alone in the long, well-lit outer guard chamber. Khirius' fascination in the relics of the outer chamber faded away as he focused on his own hand in front of him. The skin was gray and taunt, receding back to turn his fingernails into hideous claws. It had been too long since he had fed. If he left it much longer, his form would twist so much that passing by in mortal society even under the cover of darkness would not be an option.

Cane paced around the ancient, subterranean chamber, past the skeletal elven guards stood rigidly at their places in wall alcoves – their bronze breastplates, glaives, and shields cleaned of cobwebs and dust but still pitted and stained with the effects of nearly an age of time passing by. In the center of the room stood a gold-trimmed sarcophagus, adorned with gems and similar etchings; a guard commander, no doubt, perhaps one of Arteri's greatest soldiers who was willing to go to his death to serve his master in another age. Cane stopped and looked up at one of the skeletal guards waiting in a wall alcove, flanked by two quietly blazing torches.

"Hmm... this one will have to go..." the necromancer mused aloud. "The incantations must not have been completed correctly. A little amateur, really. The passage of time has not been slowed nearly well enough on this one. Look at the rot on the bones! This one will snap as soon as it attempts to walk."

Khirius glanced across. The dark-haired necromancer winced in distaste as if he were sampling an unsatisfactory wine rather than looking at the remains of a person. A being once alive, with aspirations, fears, family. A life.

"What will you do with him?" Khirius asked.

Cane looked across and raised an eyebrow, his thin lips twisting into an amused grin.

"Why, throw it away and replace it with a better example. What would you have me do?"

Khirius paused. Part of him bowed down to the contempt displayed by the necromancer, bullied into a silent submission by Cane's callous display. Then he remembered his own power, his own status, and felt free to speak his own mind.

"I would have you bury him," Khirius folded his arms, "decently. He was loyal to this cause. Loyalty is a concept that should be rewarded in all cultures; even ones that revel in the dark arts. If we do not recognize loyalty, we are no better than orcs."

Cane barked out a quick laugh and then raised a fist to his lips to stop himself.

"Quite right, quite right!" he beamed. "If only time were infinite enough to allow us to do so! But, given the rather substantial number of corpses we utilize here and at many other sites across Basilea – and now across the borders, too – I'm afraid that sentimentality is a luxury we simply cannot afford. Raising Arteri from the grave is no simple task. It requires weeks of preparation. If anything is carried out incorrectly... we will raise nothing more than a mindless zombie. All of his skills, abilities, memories – all gone."

Khirius watched in annoyance as the patronizing mortal moved on to inspect the next dead guard. He looked to the far end of the chamber at the impressive steps leading up to the grand double doors, locked shut with an ancient ward.

"Considering how long it must have taken to build this entire mausoleum," Khirius said, looking up at the impressive roof above them, "why did Arteri's disciples not just raise him back then? Why go to all this trouble if the plan was always to bring him back anyway?"

Cane issued a thin smile.

"Why indeed." The necromancer shrugged. "The answer to that lies with the Coven's Council if, indeed, it has been uncovered at all. But if you want my theories, it is either because the art of necromancy was more primitive and embryonic back then, and such an undertaking was beyond their abilities, or..."

"Or?"

"Or for whatever reason, Mhorgoth did not allow it."

Khirius paused for a moment to consider the two theories. The latter seemed more likely to him.

"Is Arteri through there?" Khirius asked, nodding his head to the end of the chamber.

Cane looked back across at him.

"There are several outer chambers," the necromancer explained, "and they all eventually lead in to the central hub and then the main burial chamber. That is where Arteri lies. The rituals to raise him correctly are still on going. That is as much as you need to know."

"Then why bring me here at all?" Khirius frowned. "If all this secrecy is in force to prevent my knowing more, why have you brought me here?"

Cane walked back over, running a hand across the gems of the central sarcophagus.

"The master's orders," Cane shrugged, "we cannot expect you to willingly carry out tasks for us if we don't even show a little faith in you by including you in what is going on."

Khirius raised an eyebrow.

"Tasks?"

Cane issued a mischievous smile.

"I'll get onto that shortly. What do you know about barrowing?"

Khirius paused.

"It's just another word for tomb robbing, is it not? I recall some years ago that this region became something of a center of that business for all of Upper Mantica."

"Quite, quite. The vein of tombs in Tarkis has been bled, but not quite dry. It's a dangerous business, given that it was the norm for centuries to defend ancient tombs with traps and leave undead guardians in place. Fortunately, it is such a dangerous business that not many survive. Unfortunately for us here, those who do survive become very… problematic. Difficult to exterminate. I trust you know of the more famous names?"

Khirius shook his head.

"I've never really had any interest in following the exploits of self-styled adventurers. It always seemed rather petty to me."

"Petty it may be," Cane continued, "but the most successful become famed across all of Pannithor. There are perhaps a dozen who are truly notorious for their skill in the business. And here lies our problem. This very tomb we now stand in, this most important of discoveries for the past century, has already been raided four times. In the past month."

Khirius suppressed a smile. He was not sure why the Coven's woes amused him so much, but that little spark of mirth brightened his evening.

"How do so many people know about this place already?" he queried.

Cane folded his arms.

"A small army moved through here when this place was discovered. One would assume that word traveled fast after those scouts stumbled upon the tomb. That, and the fact that our initial attempts to lay claim to this tomb and shore up the initial rock slide were... less than subtle. The culprits have been dealt with. But yes, four incursions. The first was a simple enough affair to deal with. Barrowers with little experience. Their bodies are part of our outer guard now."

"And the others?" Khirius asked, sensing that the answer would not be so confident.

Cane paused.

"One came from an abbey of the Basilean Sisterhood. I'm not sure how they knew about this place. I fear we may have an informant in our ranks. That raid has been dealt with for now – that small expedition was eliminated. That just leaves the third and fourth incursions. The real problem. A group of five barrowers has been in here twice. On their second attempt, they reached the barrier of the inner guard! They were about five minutes' walk from where we stand now! It was only the providence of a cave in that stopped them. But not for long, I fear."

Khirius raised his brow in interest. Yes, it was a privilege of sorts to be allowed access to this ancient tomb and to see the marvel of such an endeavor with his own eyes. But his actual interest in raising Arteri was minimal. He paused on that thought. On reflection, his interest was not, in fact, minimal. He thought it was a terrible idea.

"This brings me back to what I said earlier about the dozen or so most successful and most dangerous adventurers in Pannithor. Two of them were in that expedition of five, from what our sources have told us. A northerner named Ragran, and an elf called Thesilar. Ragran is absolutely ferocious in combat. Thesilar is deadly with a bow and, unfortunately for us, something of an expert in necromancy and the undead. The third is a woman named Aestelle – a native of Tarkis and something of a local hero. Her skill with a blade and ability to use divinity magic makes me fairly certain she is formerly of the Sisterhood. The final two are of little consequence."

Khirius raised a fist to his pale lips.

"You still haven't described this task I am expected to achieve."

Cane smiled broadly.

"I was just getting to that part. You see, Ragran and Thesilar are far too dangerous to be allowed to roam at will around these tombs. Our job – you and I, that is – is to draw them out. They are staying in Torgias, so the plan is simple. You and I are going to lead a force down there to assault the town."

Khirius grimaced and lowered his brow.

"You want to risk our discovery and to massacre a town full of bystanders?"

"No, no. Of course not. We're not savages. No, the town garrison is small enough. We will lead a force down to scare the townsfolk away. When these famed adventurers come in to clear the town of our abominations, we will then strike and kill them all."

***

An owl hooted from one of the trees behind the Trade Wind Inn. Valletto stared up across the night sky in an attempt to see the bird in the darkness but failed to make anything out in the shadowy foliage. He raised his brows in interest, having only ever heard owls in the wild, rather than near the center of an admittedly rather quiet town. Then again, having spent the majority of his life in the sprawling City of the Golden Horn, any settlement seemed tiny, quiet, and practically rural by comparison.

He glanced down into his glass of rum again. The autumn night was unseasonably mild, with a warm breeze blowing from the south, as if summer had sprang back from the onslaught of the change of seasons to insist on one last wave of warmth before winter expelled her.

"I thought rum was a sailor's drink," Z'akke remarked, leaning across to peer into Valletto's glass.

The two sat outside the inn on a sturdy, wooden bench, listening to the owl hoots and gentle rush of wind. Conversation and mirth continued from inside the tavern, as normal. Z'akke glanced across at Valletto, his clawed hands toying idly with a blue energy crystal – one of the artifacts used by mages to increase the potency of their spells.

"It's not exclusively a sailor's drink," Valletto replied, "but it is certainly associated with sailors. I'm not sure why."

"My father is a naval man." Z'akke smiled proudly. "He taught me all about fighting ships. He has some great stories! I think I told you that already."

Valletto smiled. Their journey down from the mountains to Torgias had certainly given them a lot of time to talk, and he felt he knew Z'akke a lot better. The salamander certainly seemed kind and well-natured, but he did like to talk a great deal – almost always about himself and his own passions rather than showing much of an interest in others.

"My wife has a little brother in the navy," Valletto remarked as he swilled the contents of his glass absent-mindedly. "He's a nice enough fellow. A bit wet at times. No pun intended. He's been threatening to leave the navy for years now. I don't think he ever will."

"Why not?" Z'akke asked, poking his snout inquisitively into his own mug.

"He's a pirate hunter out of Thatraskos. My wife received a letter from him a few weeks ago. They just promoted him to captain and gave him a frigate. I have no idea what a frigate is, but it's certainly enticed him to stay in."

"A frigate is a medium sized but fast warship, typically characterized by having a single, continuous gun deck, at least in human navies," Z'akke explained with a proud smile. "My father taught me all of this! We are very close, my father and I."

Valletto smiled and shrugged. The salamander was correct. He had indeed already told Valletto that during their trek down from the mountains. Twice. Valletto's response was disturbed as he saw two figures emerge from the shadows at the far end of the inn's courtyard by the large, gated entrance through the perimeter wall of the site. A massive, lumbering man of six and half feet and a slim figure moving with an inhuman grace. Z'akke looked across and smiled, his eyes wide with excitement.

"They're back!" he beamed, leaping up from the bench and rushing across the dimly lit courtyard.

Valletto downed his drink and walked off after the salamander.

Ragran emerged into the lights cast by the torches hanging from the lip of the inn's roof; the long shadows cast across his heavy brow, flat nose, bone pauldron, and the bulging muscles of his chest gave him a near demonic appearance.

"I'm glad you have made it here safely!" Z'akke greeted, almost hopping from foot to foot with nervous energy.

Ragran offered him a small but genuine seeming smile. Thesilar stepped across after him.

"It is good to see you are both here," she greeted, her tone guarded, almost nervous, immediately prompting Valletto to wonder exactly what words had been exchanged between her and Ragran on the return journey.

Z'akke peered past both of the new arrivals.

"Is Aestelle just catching you up?" he asked.

Ragran and Thesilar glanced at each other. The look they exchanged told Valletto all he needed to know.

"We have not seen or heard from her since we were all separated at the cave in," Ragran said.

"Alright!" Z'akke smiled. "I am sure she will be along shortly! Probably with some story to tell of her adventure, no doubt! Come on and sit down, I shall fetch you some drinks!"

The salamander wandered off back inside the inn. Valletto turned back to the two veteran adventurers.

"Is he right?" Valletto asked. "Do you think she will be along shortly?"

Ragran shook his head.

"No. I don't think she will."

"You're certain?" Valletto asked.

"No. Can never be certain. But from experience, when you get separated in places like that, it rarely ends well."

Valletto looked from face to face at the forlorn barbarian and elf ranger.

"Then we should go and look for her," he declared sternly.

Thesilar stepped forward.

"We have talked about little else on the journey back here," she said gently. "We have discussed all of our options. You and Z'akke could not see down to our part of the cave in. There was no way through to her. None. If we had tried to dig down, the whole place would have collapsed. Yes, we could go back and look for her now that we are four again, once we have refreshed our supplies, but the rather callous fact of that matter is that by now one of two things has happened. Aestelle has found her own way out, or she has died of cold, thirst, suffocation, the undead, or a dozen other things up there."

Z'akke appeared at the inn entrance again, shuffling out to open the door with his back whilst he carried four mugs of drinks.

"Are you telling him that?" Valletto asked Thesilar, nodding at the salamander mage. "That we have all just abandoned a comrade and now you think she is probably dead?"

"No," Thesilar shook her head, "because at this stage, I am rather hoping that, against the odds, Z'akke is right."

"Look," Ragran grumbled, "I understand that you are a military man. Your view of danger is that it is shared amongst comrades. You stand in line to defend against a common foe, shoulder to shoulder with soldiers. People you trust. I respect that, but this business is not the same, Valletto. We are all here for the money and the fame. That is what adventuring is. No noble cause, no unbreakable bonds of comradeship. We all know that. We are all honest with each other about it. We are all honest with ourselves. But this is not the legion. If one of us falls, we don't risk four lives to see if we can help. We move on. We wish them all the best in our thoughts, and prayers if so inclined. But we move on."

Valletto grimaced and nodded slowly, an anger tearing at his gut.

"Understood," he hissed through gritted teeth, "and that makes you a pair of complete, utter, and irredeemable bastards. So I'll be leaving at first light to go back up there. I'm entirely confident that Z'akke will come with me when I ask him to help. Why don't both of you famed heroes just sod off, take your egos with you, and go find somewhere else to look for your gold and fame?"

Without giving either adventurer a chance to reply, Valletto stormed back over to where Z'akke was setting the four drinks at the table. Valletto grabbed his and downed it in one.

"Thank you for the drink, friend," he smiled grimly but sincerely to the salamander. "I'm going to get some sleep. At first light, I'm going back up there to see if I can help Aestelle. Are you coming?"

"Oh!" Z'akke blinked. "Yes! Good idea! Yes, let's go and see if we can help!"

"It's just the two of us," Valletto added as he walked away, "I'll see you at dawn."

***

The mild dawn followed on from the gentle night, with the sun peering over the horizon to illuminate a clear, hazy sky reminiscent of summer. His pack on the same table he had shared drinks with Z'akke the night before, Valletto checked over his various pouches and provisions. He tutted to himself as he did so, wondering how he had ended up in such a mess. Put simply, he was not an adventurer. The previous expedition to the mountain catacombs was unlike anything he had ever experienced; up until the Battle of Andro, he had never faced an enemy face to face, only supported soldiers from behind the line of battle. These past few days had seen him fight undead and venture through the dark bowels of a mountain littered with ancient traps and threats – something he never thought he would be involved with.

A crow cawed from a tree at the far side of the inn courtyard. Valletto looked across at the copse of trees and then up at the hazy sky. The weather in southeast Basilea was predictable – mild winters and hot summers punctuated with very occasional heavy downpours. But northeast Basilea followed almost extreme seasonal weather. Hot summers just as in the south, but winters were cold enough to bring snow. An outsider might think that was connected to the proximity of the Mountains of Tarkis; an educated outsider might even go as far as claiming that the autumnal cold winds were related to the funneling effects of the mountainous terrain.

However, to a skilled aeromancer such as Valletto, that interesting seasonal weather was physically tangible. On the ride north along the coastal road, he even felt it. There was something that happened in the atmosphere around him, something that caused the air to want to rush upward toward the heavens. The result of that was that surrounding atmosphere needed to fill the gap; and so the hot air of the south moved upward whilst the cold air of the north moved down, and the two met in the middle. Wherever that upward rush moved would dictate whether the Tarkis region experienced hot southerly air or cold northerly flows. It was the subject of a friend of Valletto's thesis at the College of Aeromancy. Nobody knew for certain what caused it. It fascinated Valletto but was no doubt as dull as dwarven discourse to anybody else.

Valletto was interrupted from his academic thoughts by the inn door opening behind him. He smiled a greeting to Z'akke; the smile instantly faded as he realized that Ragran and Thesilar followed the salamander. Valletto folded his arms. Thesilar took in a breath and then walked briskly over to Valletto.

"I owe you an apology," she greeted, "two, in fact. You are entirely correct. We should not have left Aestelle up there. We are all coming with you to try to find her. And... I have been less than kind to you. For that, I apologize."

"Give your first apology to Aestelle and your second to Z'akke," Valletto replied, turning his attention to Ragran as the huge mountain man made his way over.

"You're coming as well?" Valletto asked.

"Might as well," Ragran grunted. "I stand by my words last night, but I have nothing else to do."

"Thank you, Mighty Ragran." Thesilar shook her head. "That delicate display of northern sentimentality is precisely what we needed to set the emotional tone for this journey."

Ragran looked over the heads of both Thesilar and Valletto, his eyes focusing on the far side of the courtyard.

"I don't think we need any tone for any journey," he remarked. "It looks like we're not going anywhere."

Valletto span around. Her shoulders slumped, her feet dragging wearily across the gravel courtyard, Aestelle walked over from the direction of the stables. She wore a blue cloak, lined with white over her black leather attire, and carried a light pack over one shoulder.

"Oh!" Z'akke remarked with a broad, toothy grin. "I told you she would not be far behind us!"

Aestelle stopped by the four other adventurers. An uncomfortable silence descended.

"We were just coming to look for you!" Z'akke nodded enthusiastically. "Valletto said we should, just in case you were in trouble."

"Thank you, Z'akke," Aestelle smiled wearily, "but it is quite alright. I have had rather a long night to get here. But here I am."

She turned her gaze to Thesilar and narrowed her eyes.

"Are you off, then?"

"No. I was coming to look for you."

"Because you said you were leaving. You said you never want-ed to see any of us again. You were very clear on that point."

"Aestelle," Ragran rolled his eyes, "come on. We all say things in moments of anger. Don't drag this up again."

Aestelle looked at the graveled ground, paused, and then nod-ded.

"You are right. I'm sorry. All of you. I… something happened before I found my way out of the mountain. I have had a long journey back here. I have not slept and I have had a great deal on my mind. I am going to go to get some sleep. If any of you are still here this evening, I shall see you for drinks then."

An ear-piercing scream of unbridled terror emanated from the stables. Two young stable hands sprinted out of the doors, yelling in panic. Ragran and Thesilar had already drawn their weapons by the time Aestelle held up her gloved hands to stop them.

"One other thing," she yawned, "I forgot to mention. I have put a gur panther in the stables. I shall explain it all later."

Valletto's eyes opened wide in shock.

"A gur panther?!"

"Is that safe?" Z'akke ventured.

"No, not remotely," Aestelle replied wearily. "Val, may I have a word, please?"

Valletto followed the tall woman along the side of the inn's main building until they were out of earshot of the others. The blonde warrior turned to face him.

"Was it your idea to come to look for me?" she asked. "That is what Z'akke seemed to think."

"Yes," Valletto said, "I suppose it was my idea."

The young woman smiled wearily and shook her head.

"Alright. Look, Val. I know I have a reputation for leaving a somewhat lengthy trail of broken-hearted men across Pannithor. But… you are married and have children. That is crossing a line for me that I am completely and utterly unwilling to cross. You understand?"

Valletto narrowed his eyes.

"No. Not really. No. I have no idea what you are trying to say."

Aestelle exhaled in frustration.

"I'm not going to sleep with you, Val," she said bluntly. "This whole thing of trying to impress me by leading an expedition to come to my rescue. It is…"

"You egotistical bitch!" Valletto snapped. "Who the hell do you think you are? My wife is ten times the woman you are! No, she is *one hundred* times the woman you could ever even aspire to be! I wasn't coming out to find you to impress you! Are you really that stupid that you can't comprehend a basic act of kindness when you see one?"

"Right." Aestelle folded her arms and raised one eyebrow skeptically. "Because you would risk your life for any of us?"

"Z'akke, yes!" Valletto replied honestly. "Those other two? Probably not so much, no... but I'll tell you now that I deeply resent the accusation that any act of nobility going on here is influenced solely by everybody wanting to bed you! Do you even hear your own arrogance? I suggested it because it was the right thing to do! I may not be much to look at – I might not have your perfect face and body and charisma – but I have things that some people respect! Responsibility, loyalty, things meaningless to an immature girl who dresses like a..."

"Alright!" Aestelle took a step back. "Alright! You don't need to..."

"Shut up, Aestelle, I'm not finished!" Valletto snapped. "Because you need to be careful! Z'akke is a very loyal friend to you! He tells me how much he thinks of you because you are always kind to him. You always defend him. Now, those two famous bastards over there were very clear last night in telling me that they are in this for the fame and the money. Nothing else! They accuse Z'akke of the same, but that doesn't wash for me. There's something else going on with him. He is far too apologetic to be as selfish as he is being accused of. He needs the money for something. That much should be obvious to anybody with even half a brain!"

Aestelle opened her mouth to speak; clearly thought better of it, and then closed it again. Valletto mentally formulated his next sentence but then decided against it, taking a deep breath instead. He was no longer sure where he going with his stream of accusations or, more importantly, why. She was not his friend. She did not care what he had to say, and he had no reason to lecture her.

"I..." Valletto sighed, "it doesn't matter. I'm so utterly confused by this whole... adventuring way of life. I don't understand any of this. I don't understand you. I don't understand why Orion was so taken by you."

Aestelle's eyes widened.

"He spoke to you?" she demanded. "About me?"

"Yes," Valletto exhaled, "of course he did! You strung him along! What did you expect?"

Valletto took a few paces backward, giving Aestelle a chance to speak. She stared to one side, her jaw slightly agape, her eyes narrowed. Exasperated by the whole ridiculousness of his experiences since arriving in Torgias, Valletto snatched up his pack and walked out of the inn courtyard.

Chapter Ten

Even a restless, disturbed four or five hours of sleep left Aestelle feeling entirely more human. Rising from her bed at the inn, her mind was instantly troubled by the same thoughts that had prevented a proper sleep. Her encounter with Joselin had sparked a thousand memories, practically all of which were unpleasant – some she would go as far as to consider traumatic. All had been well and truly packed away, buried deeply from the moment she walked out of the abbey's gates for the final time, until her chance encounter in the mountain.

Well aware of her rapidly dwindling financial resources, Aestelle nonetheless elected to take advantage of it being market day by purchasing a new and suitably revealing red silk dress of elven styling before heading back to the Trade Wind Inn to use the bath house for a long overdue, thorough wash. After an hour spent on her hair, her thoughts still dominated by old memories, Aestelle pulled on the new, figure-hugging dress and headed down to the main bar for her evening meal.

"A platter of the nice bread," Aestelle greeted Fran as she arrived at the bar, "and a bottle of white. Something I haven't tried before."

"Oh yes, milady!" the rotund landlady threw on a sarcastic smile as she curtseyed.

Aestelle swore at the cackling woman, thoroughly regretting her choice to spend so much money on a seemingly useless title, before she walked across to an empty booth in the corner of the inn. Idiots like Fran finding out about her buying an elevated position in society was, unfortunately, an inevitability.

The skies had darkened outside, and the brief period of unseasonal warmth was already replaced by a stiff breeze, whistling past the walls outside the grimy windows of the inn. Aestelle seated herself, taking a few moments to subtly position her dress to ensure it exposed every inch of one thigh when she crossed her legs, well aware that as always she was attracting the gazes of every occupant of the inn. Satisfied that she was center of attention, she cast her gaze outside at a flickering torch on the inn's exterior wall as her mind fell back to that final exchange with Joselin.

"Can we talk?"

Aestelle looked up.

Thesilar stood at the edge of the seating booth.

"I thought you were leaving," Aestelle remarked dryly.

Thesilar glided gracefully across to sit on the bench seat opposite Aestelle.

"I wanted to apologize," the elf said. "I have been less than kind to you. To all of you. I... have said a lot of things I should not have."

Aestelle leaned back in her seat and folded her arms, eyeing the elf ranger suspiciously. She momentarily considered demanding an explanation for Thesilar's maliciousness but then realized that she herself was on less than firm ground. Aestelle, too, had played a large part in the group's lack of cohesion.

"Apologize to Z'akke, not me." Aestelle shrugged. "I have been... difficult. Z'akke has not done anything wrong. Except turn his back on us and leave us defenseless whenever he sees something valuable. Aside from that."

Thesilar smiled. It was a smile Aestelle had not seen in some time now. The malicious smile that was issued as a precursor to a spiteful comment was one she was well accustomed to. But not the genuine smile Thesilar briefly gave.

"What changed?" the elf asked, seemingly half to herself. "Why are things so different?"

Aestelle looked down at the dull wood of the table between them. She had much on her mind, but how much she was willing to share with Thesilar was another matter entirely.

"Why did you change?" Thesilar asked. "When you first appeared within the adventurers' circles, you were the life and the heart of any room you occupied. You captivated audiences. Even though you were raw and had so much to learn, you were still the center of attention."

"That's because I used to dress less conservatively." Aestelle smirked.

Thesilar glanced down across her attire.

"Only marginally, there really isn't much in it. But seriously, why so solemn now? What changed?"

Aestelle hugged one leg to her chest and rested her chin on her knee, turning to look out of the window again.

"I started to wonder what it was all about," she began hesitantly. "I... left the Sisterhood. I discovered freedom. Alcohol. Sex. All the things that were forbidden for so long. Then the novelty wore off and I realized how trivial so many of these things were. I looked up, and a decade had passed. I was on top of a hill with a dead Abyssal demon at my feet, back on the battlefield for the first time in years. Then bards began to sing songs about me. I... it was what I wanted. But then when it arrived, I... I hated it."

Thesilar nodded but remained silent.

"It took me quite a while to work out why I hated it," Aestelle continued, "you see, I left the Sisterhood under poor terms. I think I was eager to show them they were all wrong. To show them that I could do something good, something honest, something heroic even following my own ideals. I could still change the world for the better without wasting my life slaving under their rules. Their discipline. Then the day came when bards sang songs about me. But... those songs needed to be correct. Political. It simply would not do to describe me as I am. So the songs described me as I was. Or as I should have been. Pure, noble, chaste, a true Sister of the Order. It... I don't know... it hurt. It felt like they had won."

"It is just a song." Thesilar shrugged.

"No. No. It isn't. It was the apex of my journey. The pinnacle of my achievements. And I was described to Basilea as what they wanted me to be all along. The exact opposite of what I set out to prove I was. And now I am left wondering what comes next. Valletto said that you and Ragran told him this business was all about the money and the fame. Alas, I think that is all I have wanted, deep down. The fame part, at least. To be a hero. To be... loved. But the world wants me to be... I don't know, I'm just going around in circles now."

Thesilar leaned back. One of the inn workers knelt by the hearth and set about lighting it for the night. Fran finally appeared with Aestelle's bottle of wine and platter of bread and oil. She left again without a word.

"And this paladin?" Thesilar asked. "The one who is troubling you?"

Aestelle placed one fist within the other and leaned across the table.

"I am not talking about that with you. You are not the last person in Pannithor I would talk to about men in my life. But you are one of the last."

Thesilar shifted in her seat.

"Why?"

"Why would I?" Aestelle insisted. "Do you honestly think that purely because we are the only two women in this group that we have some sort of understanding? Some sort of kindred approach to romance? We may both be women, but that is meaningless. You are not even human. We have nothing in common, and that is even if I wanted to discuss my feelings with anybody else. Which I do not."

Her cheeks burning, Aestelle looked away again and grabbed her glass of wine.

"Half-human," Thesilar corrected calmly.

"Pardon?"

"Half-human. You are only half-human. I think that is my problem with you. It is your other half. You see, you being here with the rest of us is rather like turning up to a game of cards. Except your personal deck has nothing but emperors. Your heritage means you are cheating at life. Everything is easy for you. And it is very easy to resent you for it."

Aestelle slammed her wine glass down on the table.

"Easy for me?! Coming from a damn elf?! Your people are more intelligent than humans, faster... by the Ones above! You live for a thousand years! And you want to sit there and tell me *I* have it easy?"

Thesilar tilted her head and shrugged calmly.

"When providence fails and all around you falls, leave your glades and visit the human halls."

Aestelle sank her glass and poured another.

"What?"

"Ellentithe," Thesilar explained, "one of our poets. The rhyme is far more delicate in our language. What it means is that if life ever becomes painful, it pays to spend time with humans. The reason for that is that the most mediocre, middling, and unexceptional elf will instantly be seen as an intellectual giant and pinnacle of physical beauty when in the company of humans. Even for an elf, that can soothe the ego magnificently. All of that is fine, of course, right up to the point that a half-Elohi goddess with the golden face of an angel atop a body of physical perfection shows up. Everything you touch turns to gold, Aestelle. How many of your type are there in this world? Two? Three? And you have to be here to visit my human halls. I may have an edge in the game of cards, but you have cheated your way to victory before the first hand is even dealt."

Aestelle took in a breath and exhaled slowly. She passed the bottle of wine over to Thesilar. The elf took a swig from it.

"It does not work like that," Aestelle said quietly, "not really. I have not told many people about being half-Elohi, but I describe it as being faster and stronger. That is... an oversimplification. There are humans who are both faster and stronger than me. But it takes years of dedication to achieve what they achieve. For me, it is much easier. A little practice and things fall into place. I have no magical powers or strengths, not beyond what the Sisterhood taught to me. I can just achieve the pinnacle of human limits without trying nearly as hard as others. So yes, I suppose you are correct. I am cheating. But all of that head start does not stop Ragran from putting me on my arse every time we spar. And if it makes you feel any better, it has not made me happy. Not in the slightest."

Thesilar drew from the bottle of wine again. A waft of hot air blew across from the now blazing hearth on the far side of the room.

"I never said I wanted you to be unhappy," Thesilar said. "I have just found it more difficult to work with you since you have come into your own. Since you have mastered so many skills required of one in our profession. Since... you stopped needing me."

Aestelle raised her brow in contemplation and looked down at the bread and oil platter in front of her. It was her favorite food. She had not eaten properly in nearly two days, yet she could not stomach the thought of a single mouthful. She momentarily contemplated telling Thesilar about her encounter with Joselin in the mountains but decided against it. She looked back up at the elf ranger.

"Why do you do this? Is it really for fame and money?"

Thesilar rested her chin in the palm of one hand and looked across the table.

"You know I am not really keen on talking about things like that."

"One would imagine that you are equally less enthralled by admitting to feelings of jealousy and insecurity to a mere human," Aestelle countered, "yet here we are."

Thesilar leaned back again. Her brow fell and her features darkened. The table fell silent. A trio of weary looking merchants entered the inn through the main door and walked over to the bar. A table of sailors in the far corner shared a joke as a tray of drinks was brought over to them. For a moment, Aestelle felt uneasy, almost as if she was being watched. Being stared at by everyone whenever she entered a room was something Aestelle was accustomed to, something that, if she was honest to herself, still left her smugly satisfied in her narcissistic arrogance. But this was different. This did not feel natural. Thesilar looked up at Aestelle again.

"My father was a self-made man." Thesilar looked down at the bottle in her hand. "He made his fortune by capitalizing on trade routes across the western reaches of the Infant Sea. We moved to Therennia Adar when I was very young. I barely remember life before that move. Our family grew rich from trade to the north. Elven trade to and from the Successor Kingdoms was relatively limited. You know how your kind can view elves."

"More so, I know how your kind can view humans," Aestelle remarked, noticing a series of glances from one of the merchants at the bar and rewarding him with a brief smile before turning her attention back to Thesilar.

"Regardless," the elf continued, "my father made his money in precious stones. Shipping them south to Elvenholme and then transporting elven jewelry back up to the Successor Kingdoms. The demand for that never ended. That was where the real profit came from. My father personally oversaw much of the dealings with the human traders. When I was old enough, he took me on the business journeys with him. I think that was what sowed the seeds for me. The excitement of travel and of seeing other cultures. The Successor Kingdoms seemed so... blunt in comparison to home. There was something fascinating about the bare honesty of the human way of life. Aestelle, I am telling you something I have not spoken about for over a decade – are you even listening?"

Aestelle looked back across from exchanging subtle smiles with the handsome merchant at the bar.

"Yes, I am listening," she said, "I have the capability of listening to somebody without the need to stare at them."

"But eye contact in conversation is still considered polite."

"Sorry. Go on."

Thesilar took a breath. One hand toyed with the jade colored gem suspended from a thin cord around her neck.

"When I came of age, my father welcomed me into his business. I tried to apply myself for about three years, but it simply was not for me. I enjoyed the traveling, but the rather mundane complexities of mathematics and business management did not appeal to me. So with his reluctant blessing, I traveled east to Ileuthar. I became a ranger in the Twilight Glades. It was on a visit home that a conversation set in motion a series of events that would eventually lead to me being here..."

A gentle breeze pushed the dead leaves across the smooth path leading up to the house, every shade of brown swirling around in small vortices as the dry leaves scraped across the rough tiles. The tall house, resplendent in its isolation even in such a large city, was just as immaculate and well-kept as Thesilar remembered it as she approached the sweeping front porch. She was somewhat taken aback when the front door was opened for her to reveal an elderly human male in a crimson jacket, trimmed with gold. The man stood rigidly to one side to allow her through.

"Good afternoon, ma'am, and welcome home," the white-haired human announced formally.

Thesilar followed the stranger up the winding, spiral staircase, confused as to how a man she had never laid eyes on before was welcoming her 'home' to the very house she spent her adolescent years in. Her eyes danced from painting to painting hung from the smooth walls, momentarily lost in not only the depictions of the far flung corners of the world – deserts, mountains, forests, and oceans – but also the differing styles of artistry displayed by human, elf, halfling, and even one dwarven artist. Some of the paintings were new. All, she had no doubt, were expensive.

The stranger led her across the second floor landing, his footsteps muffled on an exquisite rug of Ophidian origin – also a new addition to the house. After a gentle knock at the study door, followed by a bark of acknowledgement from within, the door was again held open for her. Smiling, Thesilar glided across the well-lit but untidy room to embrace her father, Dalofir, momentarily. The tall, auburn-haired elf returned the gesture before stepping back a pace, his gray eyes regarding her contentedly. He wore the same holed tunic of gray wool that she had pictured him in every time she thought on her family during her absence.

"Thesilar! I was not expecting you until this evening! I am afraid your mother has not returned yet. How was your journey?"

"Oh, well," Thesilar beamed, "it is good to be home again."

She checked over her shoulder to ensure the door had been shut behind her and the strange servant had disappeared.

"It certainly seems as though a few things have changed in the last year."

Her father's pale face twisted in confusion for a moment.

"Oh! You mean Hector? The frequency of my dealings with men and dwarfs has increased of late. For dealing with them it pays to, how to put it, look the part. But enough of that, what of you? You are a trained ranger now? I hope you have not yet been forced to use that blade."

Thesilar looked down at the slim shortsword hanging from her waist.

"No," she admitted with some regret, "I am an archer, first and foremost. We wear the blades in Ileuthar as more of a status symbol. So yes, I have been involved in a minor skirmish or two already but certainly nothing of note."

Dalofir's face dropped.

"It pains me to hear this. Your mother will tell you the same. You have chosen a dangerous path, Thesilar. How long must you keep this up for?"

"Father!" Thesilar sighed. "I shall keep it up for as long as it pleases me! The life of a trader is not for me! We have been through this! I am home for seconds few and this begins already?"

"You are correct," Dalofir nodded in apology, "of course, you are correct. Let me go and fetch you some tea."

"Do you not have a man who can do that for you?" Thesilar smiled mischievously.

Her father returned the smile and departed the study. Thesilar looked around the room; the skylights on the low, angular ceiling above allowing sunlight to illuminate the sprawling table that dominated the study. The table was haphazardly covered in maps and charts, with routes between ports and cities highlighted in different colors, and calculations scribbled in at various waypoints.

Thesilar traced a finger across the route to the Port of Lantor and the road up to her father's mine in Nyssia. She recalled the spectacular views on that last journey they took together and the look of disappointment and hurt on his face when she told him that she had sent a letter for apply to consideration to be taken in and trained as a ranger.

Thesilar stopped. There was another leaf of paper beneath the maps. A coat of arms, the colorful nature of which was what had caught her eye, showed through the thin paper full of messy calculations above it. Thesilar pulled the paper out from beneath the charts and scribbles and held it up to the light. Her eyes widened. It was a neat representation of several lines of genealogy. A family tree. Her own name was on it. Thesilar placed the paper down on the table and planted her fists to either side of it, her eyes narrowed in concentration as she leaned over it. Messy, haphazard notes in her father's handwriting were scribbled all over the document – particularly focused around the coat of arms on the left side of the paper. A decidedly human looking coat of arms.

Thesilar and her older brother, Bannien, sat beneath their father, Dalofir Searite and their mother, Loswithen. Neatly drawn on the line above were her grandparents, Nyarin and Oliyana. It was their influence in the Twilight Glades, and most likely her grandfather's tragic sacrifice in battle against the forces of the Abyss, that resulted in her first application to become a ranger being a success. Thesilar followed the line back down and stopped. She blinked in surprise and looked again.

"Here we are," her father smiled warmly as he backed into the study, carrying a tray with a steaming pot and two stout, gold-trimmed dwarven mugs. "I have some sugar from the Three Kings. You must try it."

"Father," Thesilar said, staring down at the paper, "who is Halofir Moonsight?"

Dalofir's smile instantly faded. He walked slowly over to the table and placed the tray down carefully.

"What do you have there?" he asked, a darkness in his tone that she had never heard before.

Thesilar held up the paper. Her father's frown darkened further still.

"Don't you worry about that," he said coldly.

It did not feel like paternal care. It felt like a warning.

"Who is he?" Thesilar insisted. "Because it says here that he is your brother. My uncle. You have never mentioned to me that I have an uncle."

"He disappeared," Dalofir said, his tone still unnerving, "a long time ago. Before you were born. That is why I never mentioned him to you."

"How?" Thesilar demanded. "How did he just vanish? And what of this? It says here that he had a daughter. Your niece. My cousin. Where is she?"

Her father drew himself up to his full, impressive height and folded his long, slim arms. His gray eyes, normally the color of a cool, gentle ocean now seemed as hard as granite.

"Listen to me, Thesilar," he half-whispered, "and listen carefully..."

"...he told me to listen carefully," Thesilar said, her eyes half-glazed over in recollection as she stared out of the window, "he told me that the search for his missing brother had consumed him for ten years. He told me that..."

Aestelle jumped when Ragran lowered himself down unceremoniously on the seat beside her and slammed down a tankard of ale.

"I, too, have decided to stay," he declared with a nod. "I am not leaving here with a job only half done. I have visited the market today and I have bought a new handle for my axe, and... I... I am not a man of great skill with conversation, as you both well know. But I think I have interrupted something important."

"No, no," Thesilar smiled, quickly cutting off Aestelle's response, "we were just discussing archery. Aestelle was asking for some training tips from one of her betters. Me. Isn't that right?"

Aestelle looked across at the elf. Her glare was somewhere half-between pleading and threatening.

"Yes. Right. Go on, Thes, explain to me again about the breathing and the posture."

She sank back into her seat. Again, as before, she had the feeling that she was being watched. Closely.

***

Valletto allowed himself a smile as he gazed out of the window by the booth and into the darkness. The hearth roared away from next to the bar, providing the perfect amount of warmth for the half-filled room. The unique scent of the burning logs and the gentle crackle of the wood splitting in the heat added a homely feel to the inn's interior. The cold, night winds whistled outside, making the Trade Wind Inn seem all the more cozy for the contrast. Valletto was briefly reminded of a rather insignificant occurrence from his childhood when, on a dark night whilst returning from the theater with his father, he had looked up at a ridgeline to see a coach being driven along a dusty road by two horses.

He recalled asking his father if he could have a night journey in a coach. His father said that one day he could. Valletto lost count of how many times, as a legion battle-mage, he had been driven across the country in a coach at night, staring down at regular people – including fathers and sons looking up at him – wishing he could be going to a theater or out for drinks at a tavern instead of traveling in a coach. And now he was here, he did not wish to be. It was not that he wanted to be in a coach. He wanted to go home.

"Same again!" Ragran smiled wildly as he returned from the bar, sliding a rum across to Valletto, a bottle of wine and two glasses for Thesilar and Aestelle, a flavored water for Z'akke, and an ale for himself.

He returned to his seat at the edge of the round table packed into the booth where they had found Thesilar and Aestelle earlier in the evening.

"So tell me!" Ragran boomed. "About this gur panther! Where in the Abyss did you find that?"

"Yes," Z'akke smiled across to Aestelle, "the grrr panther!"

"Gur panther," Thesilar corrected.

"Grrr panther," Z'akke repeated, confused, "like I said."

Aestelle topped up Thesilar's glass with the new bottle of white wine and then her own. She flashed a half-smile uncomfortably.

"I do not wish to bring the mood down," she shrugged, "suffice to say, I ran into the aftermath of a confrontation. With a sad ending. That animal was the only survivor. She is a Sisterhood panther. I need to take her back there, to an abbey a few days travel from here. My former abbey, in fact."

Thesilar sucked through her teeth. A table of richly dressed mine owners near the hearth exploded into laughter. The next table along, made up of amateur looking adventurers, eyed Ragran with interest.

"Well, we can worry about that in the morning," Thesilar offered. "Right now, we have drinks and our health. Let us be thankful for that."

"Aye!" Ragran beamed, slamming his tankard on the table for effect before taking a long swig of the musty-smelling ale.

Thesilar looked across at Z'akke.

"It is a gur panther. Gur."

"That's what I said," the salamander frowned.

"Never mind," Thesilar exhaled, "I rather suppose some words from our various languages are difficult for you."

Z'akke narrowed his eyes and tilted his reptilian head to one side.

"Well... some," he agreed, "human words, at least. Human things all sound the same to many of us. Humans have a certain... I don't know... style to their words."

"What?" Valletto asked, leaning over his tumbler of rum. "Human words? I would understand if you found that with dwarfs or elves. But humans? We are the most widespread race in all of Pannithor! And the most eclectic! No two human kingdoms are alike!"

"They are to me," the salamander shrugged, "especially your place names. All these 'heims,' 'grads,' and 'stadts.' Back home, there is a fictitious human city that is the sort of butt of jokes about your people. Cravendor! That sounds like a human city, doesn't it? Cravendor! Your towns and cities all sounds so miserable… I think, perhaps, the humor is lost when I translate it."

Ragran's face dropped in confusion. Thesilar placed her glass down.

"It is similar in meaning to the dwarf slang, *'mullen'*," Thesilar explained, "that perhaps sums up the sentiment more succinctly. Mullen – as sullen as man."

"Those miserable, testy little bastards think *we* are sullen?" Ragran exclaimed angrily.

"Well, not all of them," Thesilar shrugged, "it is not oft used. And it is aimed more at the Successor Kingdoms rather than all of humankind."

"Cravendor. I do not think it sounds anything like a human city," Aestelle said.

"I… think there is a Cravendor in Menanica," Ragran offered.

"No, that is Cravenheim," Aestelle shook her head, "near Gloomsdor."

"There's a Cravendor in Primovantor, definitely," Valletto declared as he sank his rum.

"Cravendor," Z'akke sniggered, "grrr panther. Anyway! Your names are difficult, too! Aestelle was one of my first human friends, and I could not pronounce her name for a long time. I used to call her…"

Z'akke stopped dead. His face dropped.

"Never mind."

"No, no!" Thesilar insisted. "Go on! What did you call her?"

Z'akke's brow dropped. His eyes opened wide.

"The Drinky Lady."

Thesilar spat out a mouthful of wine in laughter at the same moment Ragran noisily erupted with mirth. Both stared across at Aestelle, pointing and laughing. Z'akke sank lower into his seat.

"Dee Drinkee Yaydee!" Thesilar repeated, imitating Z'akke's accent. "That is perfect!"

"Dee Drinkee Yaydee!" Ragran boomed. "Because you drink so much!"

Valletto leaned across the table, debating on whether to intervene. He had seen alcohol addiction destroy lives. It was no laughing matter to him.

"That is fantastic!" Thesilar beamed, pointing at Aestelle's frowning face. "Cheer up, Aestelle! You have two defining characteristics to your personality and he picked the better one to name you by! Imagine if he had called you a..."

"Yes, yes," Aestelle rolled her eyes, "I see where you are going with this. Again. But I do not think it is a crime to be inundated with male attention. And I do have standards."

"Unless you want something from them," Thesilar beamed, "like how you acquired that greatsword of yours, for example."

Clearly an outsider to the group, Valletto was left wondering why he did not find any of the banter between them humorous. Was he being too uptight? Had society in the Basilean capital moved past such cruel jokes? Having spent years on campaign in the company of soldiers, he was no stranger to harsh banter. But he certainly never enjoyed it. The others seemed to think it was funny. Being on the fifth round of drinks possibly helped with that. Ragran had been drinking at double the pace of the others. At least they had all moved away from the more serious conversations of earlier. He appreciated that much, at least, certainly after having to report back to Saffus earlier and inform the grand mage that there had been next to no progress.

"Oh, I should let you talk more often, Z'akke!" Thesilar sank back down into her seat in the booth.

"Yes, you should!" Z'akke urged. "I have many funny things to say, if you would give me the chance!"

Aestelle leaned across the table and smiled venomously.

"Oh? Go on then, Z'akke. Tell us something else. Tell us something funny about... I don't know... Thesilar."

Thesilar's smile faded. Ragran's grin spread as his eyes opened wide in anticipation.

"Alright," the salamander shrugged nervously, "do you remember Hrrath Flamespitter?"

Valletto glanced across. Even he had heard of Hrrath Flamespitter. The most famous salamander adventurer alive, he was notorious for his fighting skills as a gladiator in his earlier life and as an adventurer thereafter. He was one of the three adventurers who accompanied Thesilar years ago on her famed expedition to Galahir to defeat the orc warlord Thrundak.

"Yes..." Thesilar grimaced suspiciously. "I remember Hrrath. Go on."

"Well," Z'akke said, "he... had not spent much time in the company of humans. Or elves. You'll remember that he never learned how to speak your tongue."

"I know," Thesilar grumbled, "I had to translate for him. Your language is not easy to learn, Z'akke."

"You see," the salamander continued uneasily, "Hrrath loved Upper Mantica and everything about it! Including the people. He thought the elven folk were so different and graceful and beautiful! All that time you were struggling to learn our language, and he couldn't understand you and the others... well... he actually spoke common fluently. He was just pretending he couldn't understand so that he could spend more time with you."

Valletto leaned back instinctively as Ragran burst into laughter again. The mirth of the giant mountain man was infectious, and Valletto somehow found himself laughing, too. He realized, again, that the drinks probably helped. Ragran pointed a finger directly into Thesilar's stony face.

"The gecko thing was in love with you!" The inebriated barbarian boomed. "And all that time you were learning a nearly impossible language, for nothing!"

Aestelle leaned back and issued a dark smile, chuckling into her glass of wine.

"Well, *love* isn't the word I'd use," Z'akke muttered awkwardly.

"Regardless," Thesilar flashed a brief, acidic smile, "when it comes to romantic liaisons, you'll excuse me if I confine myself to my own people. It's not a slant or insult towards any species' physicality; it's purely intellectual, you understand."

"Right," Valletto sneered, "calling every other race stupid is far less offensive."

"Besides," Thesilar continued, "racking up a tally of different species is more... well, the territory of the Beauty of Basilea here, is it not?"

Thesilar narrowed her eyes as she turned to face Aestelle.

"Well, I haven't added an orc to my list yet," Aestelle shrugged with a smile, "but there's time. I'm still young."

Again, the bellowing laughter from Ragran all but physically knocked Valletto back in his chair.

"Another!" Ragran insisted. "Another drink! I shall buy!"

"You have bought the last three rounds," Thesilar said. "Six of your own, in fact. I shall get these."

"Cravendor," Z'akke muttered thoughtfully.

"Not for me, thank you," Aestelle said, finishing her drink and standing up. "I think I shall retire for the evening. If you will excuse me."

"Oh, come on!" Ragran boomed. "Live up to your nickname! Have another!"

"No, thank you," Aestelle said, "I have a little on my mind. I shall quit whilst the atmosphere is good and I have a fighting chance of walking in a straight line tomorrow morning. Excuse me."

"Good night!" Z'akke smiled.

Thesilar exchanged a small but sincere smile and a nod with Aestelle. Valletto let out a breath as Ragran's hand thumped into his shoulder.

"You still drinking?" he demanded.

Valletto smiled.

"Perhaps one more."

Aestelle turned to leave. Thesilar looked over at Z'akke and issued a series of strange hisses and breaths. Z'akke burst out laughing.

"True!" the salamander grinned. "That is very true!"

His face then instantly grew serious again.

"But your pronunciation is terrible..."

***

Aestelle walked away from her comrades, content to hear laughter erupting again as she approached the bar. She yawned, desperate to plunge headlong into a good night's sleep. The rooms at the Trade Wind Inn were certainly the best in Torgias, but she yearned for something more comfortable still. She exchanged smiles with a young merchant who had bought her drinks a few nights before and then looked up at Henry, the landlord, who leaned across the bar with two thick fists planted on the wooden surface.

"I think I shall take the master bedchamber tonight," Aestelle decided. "Could you be a dear and have one of your minions move my effects into it?"

Henry frowned.

"You still owe me for the last two nights' room and board, Aestelle," Henry grumbled, "and now you want me to put you up in the best room? And then there is the matter of that bloody panther you have shoved in the stables! I've had to have my lads build a temporary wall to separate it from the horses! And I don't think a thin plank wall will stop that animal if it gets aggressive! Who is going to pay for all of that?"

Aestelle suppressed a smirk. With divinity magic and time to heal wounds, Seeba was already close to a full recovery. Aestelle leaned across the bar to look him eye to eye, fixing him with a sultry stare.

"As you know, I always find some way to pay my debts," she said huskily, "one way or another."

Henry's eyes opened wide. He looked up at the nearest of his serving staff.

"Tomas? Tomas! Go and move the lady's things from room three to the master chamber!"

Chuckling to herself, Aestelle walked toward the narrow door leading to the inn's accommodation just as Fran, the landlord's wife, shot out from the storeroom behind the bar and set about belting Henry around his shoulders, shouting a series of threats and insults at him. Aestelle shut the door and headed up the stairs. All pretenses at elegance and seduction were instantly dropped now she was out of eyeshot of anybody else; her proper, upright pose and deliberate swing of her hips was replaced with a tired slump and heavy footfall as she dragged herself up the stairway.

The corridor above led past the normal, but certainly high, quality rooms and through a small, enclosed walkway to the adjoining building. She stopped to look through the glass windows of the walkway, down at the stable block below. She would have to take the panther to the abbey the next day. There really was no way around facing that challenge. All of the mirth and alcohol-fuelled humor of her evening with the others instantly faded away as she stood, lost in thought, again remembering Joselin's words in the mountains and the horrific memories from her childhood that they had sparked. Finally, yawning again and after a good several minutes' contemplation, she carried on forward to the master bedchamber.

The master bedchamber was more a suite of rooms, all in its own separate building. A small anteroom consisted of a polished table and four chairs with ornately carved backs; behind the anteroom was the bedroom itself, dominated by a grand, sweeping four poster bed and an impressive fireplace. Two doors led from the bedroom; one to a balcony overlooking the slope leading down to Torgias harbor and the bay, the other to a private bath chamber. Aestelle smiled as she entered the rooms. A few years ago, this place had been her home, back when she had climbed to the top of the ladder of the most successful adventurers in the Tarkis region.

They were good times in many ways. Celebrating her newfound freedom from the Sisterhood, she had enjoyed a life of adventure, uncovering riches in the mountains to then spending it all on fine living in these very rooms, living off equally fine wine and enjoying the male company that had been forbidden to her at the abbey. The thought of the abbey reminded her again of Joselin's death and the myriad emotions associated with it. She exhaled and shook her head as she kicked off her shoes and pulled her clothes off, throwing them into the corner of the main bedchamber, noting that the fire had already been lit for her.

Her bags, weapons, and armor lay against a chair in the corner of the bedroom. Aestelle retrieved a short, satin night dress from her bags and pulled it on over her head. Learning from past mistakes, she then took one of her throwing knives and placed it under her pillow before propping her greatsword up against the side of the four-poster bed. She grabbed her pistol from her pack but remembered that her powder had become soaked and useless in the mountains, leaving the weapon completely ineffective until she could acquire more.

Dismissing the notion of taking a bath at such a late hour, Aestelle clambered into the plush bed, letting out a long breath as the familiar comfort of the thick mattress and expensive sheets enveloped her. The fire crackled gently from the far side of the bedroom, painting the chamber in flickering shades of amber and red. The heat built rapidly in the room. The thick bedding soon became stifling. Aestelle closed her eyes. Sleep refused to bless her with its embrace. Her mind raced.

In her thoughts, she saw Joselin dying before her; she remembered the panther in the stables and the journey to the abbey that could not be avoided. She would have to tell some figure in authority of Joselin's death. They would, no doubt, blame her. Then she would need to argue her case. A verbal clash would ensue. Would it come to fists? She thought through a thousand different conversations that could take place at the abbey, ruminating on every possible outcome. They all ended badly. She opened her eyes. Perhaps an hour had passed, wasted in anxious mental turmoil.

The room felt like a furnace. Aestelle threw off the bedding, save a single thin sheet. Poking one leg out in an attempt to cool down, she closed her eyes again. The memories of the Sisterhood returned instantly. Her eyes ached with fatigue. Sleep drifted close, again and again, but constantly evaded her at the last moment as she tossed and turned in the bed, trying and failing to expel the memories from her mind.

Aestelle opened her eyes wide and sat bolt upright. The room was freezing cold. The reds and ambers were all gone, replaced with a hundred shades of pale blue and black shadows. The fire was extinguished and the doors to the balcony were wide open, white curtains fluttering in the whistling night wind. She shivered as beads of icy sweat rolled down her skin. Something felt wrong. Her pulse quickened. She heard her heart hammering in her chest and short, sharp breaths escaping her lips. The sensation was there again. Being watched. She looked around the empty room as the wind whistled through the open balcony.

A shadowy figure sat on the chair on the corner of the room, staring at her. Her eyes wide with shock, Aestelle moved quickly away from the figure to the other side of the bed. She reached for her greatsword. It was not there. Aestelle shivered, the freezing air of the room combining with a genuine feeling that had escaped her at this intensity for many years. Fear. The figure stared at her silently, dark eyes boring into hers. She could sense the sinister energy flowing from it; tangible, real, not just a mere suspicion. As an apprentice demon hunter in her final year in the Sisterhood, she had been trained to sense the dark energies of the denizens of the Abyss. Whilst that fleeting ability was now long gone, she recalled the sensation. This was not it. This was something else entirely.

The creature's dark eyes continued to stare at her. She found herself transfixed, mesmerized by the black orbs within the face of the tall figure hidden in the shadows. Moonlight poured in through the open balcony. Aestelle saw her jeweled greatsword in its scabbard, resting against the chair where the dark figure sat silently.

"I took your sword," a voice whispered. "You understand, of course."

The voice was perfectly normal, natural, lacking the disturbing and otherworldly edge normally behind the voice of anything from the Abyss. There was an accent; somewhere from the eastern end of the Successor Kingdoms. Aestelle swallowed as she thought through her options. If a creature exuding dark, powerful energies appeared in her bedchamber in the dead of night, there could be few motivations behind the visit.

"Are you here to try to kill me?" she finally spoke, succeeding in keeping her tone calm and confident despite her hammering heart.

"I don't know," the creature replied, his tone reasonable despite the implied threat. "I have not decided yet. A lot depends on you."

Aestelle remembered the knife beneath her pillow. On the far side of the bed. Too late, her eyes drifted over to it. In an instant, the dark figure moved in a blur to sit on the bed next to her, blocking her path to that one accessible weapon. The moonlight caught just a little of the creature. Tall, thin, deathly pale skin clothed in a cloak of black. The eyes bored into her again.

"I would rather keep things civil between us," he said quietly, "without weapons. Just you and I."

Another gust of wind blew in, chilling the sweat running down Aestelle's arms and back. She shivered and turned away.

"You have been watching me for some time now."

"Yes."

"Who are you and what do you want?"

The figure reached across, and a deathly cold hand pressed against her cheek. Her face was tilted back to face the intruder.

"You may look on me," the figure said, brushing the cold hand down her neck and along her shoulder. "If I wished to mesmerize you with my powers, I would have done it by now."

Anger rose, slowly beginning to override her fear. She glared into the intruder's eyes but exercised enough self-control to bite back a heated response. She took a breath, calmed her racing mind, and rapidly thought through her options. The threatening figure sat between her and her weapons; rushing for her greatsword or the door would result in her being intercepted before reaching either, judging by what she had witnessed of his speed. Then there was the unwelcome hand that lingered against her. That left her normal secondary plan of seducing anybody she could not defeat; long enough at least to distract him and then retrieve the knife beneath her pillow.

She stopped. She was not dealing with an oafish bandit warlord or enraptured, lovesick youth who she could easily bend to her will. This was far more dangerous. Someone powerful, wise, intelligent enough to instantly detect an obvious attempt to trick him. Somebody capable of moving with an inhuman speed, mesmerizing mortals with an otherworldly stare. The wind rushed in through the balcony again, pushing aside the curtains and allowing a beam of moonlight to momentarily illuminate the intruder. White, wrinkled skin clung tightly to a gaunt face. Pale, almost colorless eyes stared into hers. The eyes were reminiscent of the zombies she had faced only days before; dead, unfeeling, yet these held a fierce, deep intelligence behind them.

"You are a vampire," Aestelle breathed.

"Yes."

She had only ever seen two vampires before; one on the other side of a battlefield during her time in the armies of the Sisterhood; the other in a deep catacomb explored with Thesilar and some others perhaps four years ago. On both occasions, she had seen how astoundingly powerful and dangerous these creatures were.

"Listen very carefully," the undead creature spoke softly, "for lives depend upon it. There is a body, a secretive society of necromancers at work in your Hegemony. The Coven. There are things about it that you must know."

Chapter Eleven

Smiling down at his breakfast plate as Fran shoved it unceremoniously in front of him, Z'akke regarded the colorless combination of bread, cheese, and fried fish. A cockerel crowed from somewhere on the other side of the stables, loud enough to traverse across the courtyard and into the Trade Wind Inn as the dawn sun rose into a cold, blue sky. Having left the bar a little after midnight – encouraged by Ragran's increasingly boisterous behavior – Z'akke had managed some six hours sleep that, by his standards, was certainly enough. Better to skip a little sleep than miss out on the day. Or night.

Z'akke leaned over to begin his breakfast when out of the corner of his eye he observed Thesilar sat alone on a bench on the edge of the courtyard. Grabbing his plate and mug of water, he wandered out of the inn and walked across to her. Thesilar looked up at him and issued a faint smile as he approached. Contrary to her normal garb of drab, practical, and loose-fitting leggings and a tunic, she wore an elegant but simple dress of pale blue, matched with a thick, fur-lined cape worn off one shoulder.

"Good morning!" Z'akke greeted, placing his breakfast down on the table between them. "You look… graceful? I hope that is a compliment. It is so difficult to compliment people in this part of the world. So easy to accidentally cause offense. I hope that calling you graceful is…"

"Thank you," Thesilar held up a hand to save him, "graceful is fine, Z'akke. Sometimes it makes a nice change to shrug off the ranger attire and dress in something a little more… graceful. I don't think we have much on today, so it seemed a good day to do it. Although the winds are coming from the north, again, so it is certainly getting colder. Winter is not far away."

"Do you mind if I eat here with you?" Z'akke asked. "I saw that you are not eating, and my father used to tell me that I can make an awful lot of noise when I eat sometimes."

"It is quite alright."

Z'akke slowly and hesitantly bit into his fish. It was too dry and unseasoned, which seemed to be a norm for human preparation of seafood. But it was functional and it would be rude of him to complain, he thought.

"Have you seen any of the others?" Z'akke asked.

"No," Thesilar shook her head, "I called it a night not long after you did. Ragran and Valletto were still going strong. I don't think we shall see them any time soon."

"Hmm... I don't think drink really... affects Ragran too much the next day. Not that I've seen. Perhaps he will be along shortly."

Thesilar shrugged.

"What is your plan then?" she asked. "Aestelle is going to the abbey to take their panther home before it eats a horse here. Are you going back up into the mountains with her after that?"

"Yes," Z'akke nodded, "I think so. We should finish what we started."

He worded his response carefully. It would not do to tell her the whole truth. It would not be right to tell her that the catacombs they had explored showed great promise of rich treasures, giving him his best chance to carry out the task that had hung over his head for four years now. The task, of which he was sworn to secrecy, that prevented him from going home to his mate and offspring. He was interrupted from his thoughts when he saw Aestelle pacing purposefully over from the master bedchamber block on the other side of the inn's stables. Z'akke immediately noticed that she wore her leather armor and carried her greatsword, bow and quiver slung over one shoulder. He opened his mouth to ask why she was fully equipped for a fight at dawn in their inn but was cut off by Thesilar.

"You look like shit," she greeted. "What happened to you?"

"Haven't slept," Aestelle replied, "an hour at most, perhaps. I am not sleeping at all at the moment."

Z'akke regarded her curiously but could not detect any degradation in the normal pristine care she took over her plaited, bead-woven hair and dark eye make-up. Then again, his human and elf companions would no doubt fail to recognize much visible change in the health of a salamander.

"Why are you carrying your sword?" Thesilar asked.

"There is a fight coming," Aestelle answered, keeping her voice low, "here. Today, perhaps."

Thesilar glanced across at Z'akke and raised her brows before looking up at the tall woman again.

"You both need to get armed up," Aestelle said, "and we need to wake the others."

"How do you... know this?" Z'akke asked.

Aestelle leaned back to sit on the edge of the table between Z'akke and Thesilar, and she folded her gloved arms across her chest. She looked down at the ground by her feet.

"Somebody broke into my room last night," she said quietly. "He told me that an attack was coming."

Thesilar smirked and narrowed her eyes.

"Aestelle. Normally when you spend a night with a man in your room…"

"Not now, Thesilar," Aestelle exhaled with a glare of warning. "I am very serious about this. It was no ordinary man that visited me. It was a vampire."

Z'akke's eyes widened in surprise. Thesilar frowned and shook her head.

"Aestelle," she smiled softly, "despite the fantastical stories depicted in the theatres of the City of the Golden Horn, vampires are not romantic creatures that visit beautiful women in the middle of the night to woo them. Vampires are deadly, heartless bastards that kill without remorse. They do not engage in friendly conversation. They kill. And it is highly unlikely that there are any within a hundred leagues of here, unless we have woken one up in that mountain. I don't think you saw a vampire. I think you need some sleep."

Aestelle looked down at Thesilar.

"I know what I saw," she said evenly, "I saw how fast he moved. I saw… his eyes. They were dead. He was a corpse. A talking, intelligent corpse who could move faster than even you or I. I am not theorizing, Thesilar."

"Alright," Thesilar sighed, "so this man who appeared at the side of your bed at midnight… let us call him a vampire, if you like. What did he want with you? Something surprising?"

"He told me that there is a society of necromancers operating in Basilea. It is called the Coven. It knows about the catacombs. He knew about us, Thesilar. He knew about that cave in that forced us to leave."

Z'akke watched as Thesilar's smile quickly faded.

"Go on," the elf said seriously.

"He said that he has no interest in helping the Coven. He said the Coven wants us dead because of our interfering at the catacombs. He told me two things that we really need to know. First off, the Coven plans to attack Torgias to drive us out into the open. To kill us. The vampire has been ordered to be a part of that. That is why I am armed and that is why you should both be armed right now, too."

Thesilar stood and looked up at the mountains looming on the horizon to the northwest. She clamped her hands behind her back. A horse and wagon crossed the inn courtyard with the Trade Wind's morning supply of fresh food and provisions.

"What was the second thing he warned you of?" she asked quietly, once the wagon had passed.

Aestelle narrowed her blue eyes.

"The thing that I awoke up there. He said its name was Arteri."

Z'akke's eyes widened. He looked up at the two women stood by the bench.

"Arteri the Plague?" the salamander asked, his voice hushed.

"I don't know," Aestelle shrugged, "the name means nothing to me."

Thesilar turned back to face the others.

"Thesilar?" Z'akke asked. "Have you heard of…"

"I know who Arteri SeaBreeze was," the elf replied seriously, her face a little paler than normal.

She paused for a moment and then looked across at Aestelle again.

"You should go and get some sleep," Thesilar said.

"Sleep?" Aestelle grimaced. "Do not be ridiculous! Have you not listened to a word I have just said?"

"Oh, I have listened," Thesilar replied calmly, "and I am thinking through various courses of action as we speak. None of them require you for the next few hours, and all of them would benefit from you being well-rested and fighting fit. Go to sleep."

"And when the attack comes?" Aestelle growled, her voice low as two stable boys walked across from the inn's main building to the stables.

"It won't come today," Thesilar shrugged, "if it even comes at all. Let us assume for a moment that every word your vampire has told you is in fact true – an assumption that I have not accepted as fact, yet – but that indeed he will be a part of an attack on this town. The earliest it can take place is tonight."

"How do you know?" Aestelle insisted, her gloved hands planted on her slim hips.

"Because vampirism does not grant those cursed with it a uniform, standardized set of ailments and abilities. Every vampire is different. I'm sure you have heard of some being unable to walk in sunlight. If this man wished to talk to you, it would have been far easier to do so in daylight. Yet he chose – or was compelled to choose – to meet you after dark. I don't think the attack will come today because your vampire cannot move in daylight."

Aestelle folded her arms again.

"That is a fairly large assumption, Thesilar. And the stakes are rather high if you are incorrect."

"There are no stakes. If the attack comes, we respond."

Z'akke, following the conversation eagerly but reticent to offer his own opinions, finally found he felt compelled to speak out.

"We only respond if the town is attacked?" he asked. "But… that is too late! We need to tell the town guard now! To prepare defenses!"

"Exactly!" Aestelle agreed.

Thesilar shook her head and moved closer to the other two.

"And tell them what?" Thesilar scowled, her voice in a low whisper as she checked over both shoulders. "That Aestelle spent the night with a vampire who told her that the chief lieutenant of Mhorgoth the Faceless himself has risen from the grave on the top of that mountain, and that a swarm of undead will be here any moment? They would have her locked up as mad, or worse! No! A proactive approach to this is not an option! Not overtly, anyway!"

Aestelle took a step back.

"Mhorgoth?" she breathed. "Nobody mentioned that name! Where has this come from?"

Z'akke looked across at Thesilar. Mhorgoth, the most powerful necromancer to ever walk Pannithor, was a name feared and despised by every race and every nation. Z'akke knew little of Mhorgoth's past – few people did – but he knew that the most common theory was that Mhorgoth was raised and educated in the arcane arts by elves.

"Arteri was an elven aeromancer who turned to necromancy," Thesilar explained. "He was alive at the time of Mhorgoth. At least, back when Mhorgoth lived as you and I do now. But just because your visitor has mentioned his name does not mean that this is true. Any of it. But if it is, you need to be ready to fight as soon as night falls. Aestelle – go and get some sleep."

Z'akke looked up at her.

"I will guard you!" he offered with a nod. "I saw you have those expensive rooms again. You go to sleep. I will sit in the anteroom. If anything happens, I will wake you. If anybody tries to attack you whilst you sleep... I will burn them."

Aestelle looked at Z'akke, and then across at Thesilar. She finally held her hands up in surrender, nodded, and walked back over toward her rooms. Z'akke grabbed his plate of breakfast and stood to follow her. A cold hand grabbed his wrist firmly. He looked across at Thesilar. She clung to him, her face white.

"Z'akke," she said, her voice hushed, "be on your guard. Just before the cave in, I saw something new in those catacombs. Elven tiles, their designs looked about right for the age of Arteri and Mhorgoth. And then there were the obstacles that stood in our way – aeromancy and necromancy. That tomb up there has links to the right age, aeromancy, necromancy, and evidence of elven craftsmanship. Everything agrees with this having a possibility of being Arteri. Which means I think Aestelle's story could well be true."

Z'akke nodded.

"If it is a vampire and it comes back, I'll burn it."

"If it is a vampire, you get Aestelle and you get out of there!" Thesilar urged. "Ignore what you've read! Ignore these ridiculous stories from the past few years about romance and gentlemen undead tortured by their morals! It is all lies! These things are evil incarnate! And if one has taken a shine to Aestelle, it will try to seduce her and turn her against us, if that process has not started already! Z'akke, stay alert! If there is anything out of the ordinary, get Aestelle and get out of Torgias!"

"And you?" Z'akke asked, his heart thumping within his chest.

Thesilar took a step back. Her eyes darkened and a look of grim resolve fell across her graceful features.

"I'm going to get the others."

***

His cloak whipping out behind him in the slowly intensifying wind, Khirius looked down the slope at the coastal town sprawled out to the southeast. A trio of small fishing boats drifted into the protection of the small harbor as the final light of the day disappeared beneath the misty horizon, and hanging lanterns illuminated along the narrow streets as the progress of four lamplighters could be tracked even from the slope outside the town. A handful of lights illuminated in the scruffy collection of miner's huts outside the town walls. Khirius looked to the wealthy area of the town near the harbor, and where he had paid for room and board along with his servants at the Trade Wind Inn. With his unnaturally augmented sight, he could just about make out the separate block and the room he had visited Aestelle in the previous night. He shuddered as he recalled touching her. Her aura, exuding divinity, had drawn him to her, but it was her sheer, unrivalled beauty that made him feel... nearly alive.

"Lord Khirius," Cane called over from the other side of the hill, "it is time."

Khirius looked behind him. Lined up in neat rows, stood upright and ready, were the forty skeletal swordsmen that had been entrusted to his command by Lord Annaxa. That trust and authority came in the form of a written letter rather than a face-to-face interaction, but his orders were clear. Attack the town, drive the adventurers out into the open, and kill them. Khirius winced at the thought. Naturally, he had already made his mind up that he would assist Aestelle in any way he could. Likewise, he knew the salamanders to be a race of noble heart and fierce morals.

But the others? The elf, the lumbering barbarian, and the mage?

He would be content enough to kill them off to ensure Annaxa believed he was loyal to the Coven. But only if it came to it. The ideal solution would be for the attack to utterly fail – and for the five adventurers to continue to threaten the return of Arteri and all the darkness that would follow with him. But Cane's earlier words to Khirius were true. He was in a desperate situation. He had lost everything and now found himself fighting for his very existence, and the Coven was his only viable chance of achieving that: the right to carry on existing. That forced his back against a wall. If the Coven said he needed to cause terror and anarchy in a town and then kill some people he had nothing against, then… kill them he must.

Khirius glanced to his left and saw Cane vault up onto his horse. He sensed the emanation of arcane power from the dark-haired necromancer, and Cane's own unholy contingent of forty skeletal troops began their march down the hill toward the northern gate of Torgias. Behind them, lurking in the darkness was the real threat that would be unleashed once the skeletal soldiers had succeeded in drawing out their prey. But for Khirius, his task was equally clear. Take the southern gate and prevent the adventurers from escaping. Transmitting a command into what remained of the minds of the long dead soldiers, Khirius walked down the slope with his undead horde close behind.

***

Ragran leaned across the table in the booth, his dark eyes regarding the sketch map of the town drawn by Thesilar. Outside the Trade Wind, a stable boy walked around each of the buildings to light the hanging lanterns for the evening as a small crowd of raucous sailors piled into the inn. The breeze was already picking up beneath a heavy, leaden sky. Inside the inn, business carried on as normal with the same faces of regular, wealthy clientele wandering through the doors at the end of a hard day's work. Valletto leaned back in his seat and waited for the towering barbarian to voice his thoughts.

"I'd go for the Town Hall." Ragran shrugged. "If I was attacking this place and trying to cause as much trouble as possible, I would cut the head off the dragon."

Thesilar shook her head irritably.

"The dragon?" she repeated. "Ragran, less of the melodramatic! This is a small town of a few hundred people! We are not talking about a seat of government or a major military position! This place will take practically nothing to descend into chaos! Furthermore, we need to remember that none of us have any useable military training or experience! I served very briefly as a ranger in the Twilight Glades, but all I did there was follow orders. I never learned anything about setting up a viable defensive position! No, Ragran, we need to keep this simple because we don't know what we are doing!"

Valletto scratched his bearded jaw thoughtfully as he looked down at the map. He had been here before – recently, too – in the unenviable position of battle approaching, and the mental war raging in his thoughts between turning and running so that his children grew up with their father, or standing and fighting to protect those who needed it. The decision was a little easier to make second time around, but not much.

"What about the town guard?" Valletto asked. "There must be some ex-legion soldiers in their ranks?"

"I have already spoken to Vendis, the guard commander," Thesilar said, "at least, as much as I could. Without risking panic or committing to something we knew nothing about, I merely advised him that a contact of mine had warned me to be vigilant for violence tonight. I daren't risk any more than that. But Vendis is not a man of war. He and his guards keep the peace when the taverns throw out aggressive drunkards or chase down petty thieves stealing from markets."

"That may be," Valletto said, "but the town charter here will be, I'm sure, as clear as any other. The guards are responsible for public safety. If anything happens, they will have to stand and fight."

"Against what?" Thesilar snapped, attracting turned heads from surrounding tables before she lowered her voice to continue. "Have you ever seen a vampire? Do you have any comprehension about how dangerous these things are? If that thing swoops down into this town tonight, it will cut through the guards like a kraken through a fishing fleet!"

"She's right," Ragran nodded grimly, "there are not many creatures in this world that I am apprehensive of facing in single combat. A vampire, however, is one of them."

Valletto nodded. He looked around the room, content that the normal assortment of mine managers, trade ship captains, and wealthy merchants were no longer regarding the adventurers in the corner. Then he saw the four young adventurers they had seen several days before, still in their same booth. Still with pristine, unbloodied weapons and immaculate armor.

"What about them?" Valletto asked.

Ragran looked over his shoulder.

"What *about* them?"

"It's four more swords," Valletto said, "why not give them a warning that something might be happening tonight?"

Thesilar shook her head.

"If their mettle is up to the task, they will do the right thing. If not, they will run. Our words will not change that. Look, we have talked our way in circles for two hours now. We need to focus and get back to the plan. We need to keep it simple. And the simple fact is this – if an attack comes, we do not know what strength it will be or from where it will arrive. My guess is that stealth will be in order, and that vampire will look to pick us off one by one."

"No," Ragran shook his head, "they have a tomb full of undead guards. They will attack in force. They will come in rank and file."

"Ragran!" Thesilar shook her head in despair. "I have told you! This is Basilea! Undead armies do not simply stomp through Basilea!"

"They might if their leaders do not care about casualties," Ragran offered, "and no undead general cares about the welfare of his soldiers. I do not have your intellect, Thes. I do not have your knowledge of the undead. But I also do not have your morals. I am callous enough to think a little like they might. If I wanted to draw us out, I would attack in force. And if that happens, we need to get every last woman and child out of this town."

Thesilar leaned in and eyed her old comrade indignantly.

"We are not planning a mass evacuation of commoners, Ragran. We are planning a way to defend ourselves from something awful, something horrific that will strike from the shadows. We are looking to keep ourselves alive. No more."

Valletto opened his mouth to intervene. His response was cut off by a sound drifting across the cold, night breeze from the center of the town. A sound that had no place in the streets of Torgias after sunset on a weekday. The chiming of church bells. The whole inn fell silent instantly. Ragran stood and calmly picked up his axe.

"That's our song," the barbarian grunted, hefting the heavy weapon up over his huge shoulders. "Time to go and be heroes."

***

Khirius heard screams from the northern end of the town, drifting to him across the chill winds funneled down the mountains and across the foothills surrounding Torgias. His skeletal horde obeyed his command to follow the mining path through the darkness, leading to the shanty village that occupied the dirty ground just south of the town wall. The church bells rang, announcing to the town's inhabitants that there was a threat – be it fire, flood, or invasion, something was wrong. He doubted that many would expect to see lines of ancient, sword-wielding skeletons filing neatly down the miners' paths to their very homes. It saddened him. But he had a plan and, despite the requirement for some blood to be spilled in executing that plan, it was certainly the lesser of a number of evils.

The path wound gently down through the foothills to join the main coastal road leading up to the southern town gate. Khirius looked ahead, past his marching skeletons and to the road, where it ran through the frail, rickety wooden buildings of the miners and their families. There were at least a hundred figures packed together in the darkness ahead, dimly illuminated by a handful of torches. Men looked to the town, to the south, and toward the Low Sea of Suan to the east, frantically searching for the source of the unknown threat. Children were grouped together by adults, women carried crying babies. Khirius had not accounted for any of that. He was no stranger to killing, but he certainly had no desire to lay waste to a hundred innocents. His thoughts were interrupted as he felt a pulse of necromantic energy whoosh out from the north; a familiar spell. Cane was raising zombies from the town's graveyard.

Screams from up ahead brought Khirius' attention back to his immediate surroundings. His skeletons marched around a corner in the path and into clear view of the assembled mining families. The terrified shouts of panic quickly rippled back through the small crowd as the skeletons approached. Within mere moments, a hastily assembled group of burly miners gathered together in front of the women and children, mining picks held at the ready. There were about twenty men, ranging in age from those barely out of childhood to some verging on elderly, all dressed in grubby, drab clothes.

Their group grew slightly in size as a few of the women rushed forward to join them with improvised weapons of their own. Khirius smiled slightly in relief. His plan to sabotage the assault on the town would look all the more convincing if there were a few dead bodies left in the wake of the advance from his skeletal soldiers. Sad, but a necessary price to pay for the Coven's trust and his continued existence. Khirius concentrated and issued a mental command to the skeletons to form four ranks and then charge the miners.

***

Staring from side to side in confusion, Ragran paced slowly along the town square with his axe held ready across his gut. The church bells continued to call out as small groups ran seemingly in all directions. Townsfolk sprinted in threes and fours away from the northern gate, sailors made their way rapidly in small groups toward the harbor, whilst town guards rushed both toward the northern wall and, worryingly, some also dashed away from it. Ragran found himself turning toward Thesilar to question her on her thoughts but stopped himself. She had spent far too long in her self-appointed leadership role in the last few days. All evidence pointed toward a threat from the north. That was all Ragran needed to know.

"You there!" a voice called out. "Stand fast!"

Ragran turned.

He saw the familiar figure of Vendis, the guard commander, rushing toward him from the direction of the town hall with two of his guards in tow. Vendis was a shortish, middle-aged man with a waxed moustache and beard, whose belly was evidence that his best years were behind him. His rich, red cloak with gold trim marked him out against the more plainly attired guards accompanying him.

"You!" Vendis called to the trio of adventurers as he approached. "You can fight! I need you to help the guards!"

"I am already heading that way." Ragran nodded to the north. "What do we face?"

"A full on attack!" Vendis exclaimed. "I have not seen it for myself, but my men say we are being assaulted by walking dead! Corpse soldiers, here! At Torgias! There are attacks at both the north and the south gates! And the cemetery by the miners chapel!"

Ragran glanced down at Thesilar and flashed a smirk; content in his rare victory following on from their earlier debate over what form the attack would arrive in. Thesilar did not respond but instead turned to address the guard commander.

"Where do you want us?" she asked.

"I... I've heard back from the harbor already – all of the boats are already full and the ship captains have evacuated everybody they can! I need to locate the remaining townsfolk in one place to mount a defense! I think the south. That way we can maybe get the miners and their families from outside the wall inside to try to protect them. I... can you defend the northern gate so I can pull back some of my guards to the main defense at the south?"

Ragran grinned.

"Aye, commander, we can do that."

"Wait!" Valletto held up a hand. "You want us to defend the gate by ourselves so that your men can fall back? What exactly do you think we are capable of?"

Vendis blinked in confusion.

"You are adventurers? Your vocation is to fight monsters like these! You are the best I have!"

"We fight small numbers of them in enclosed spaces," Thesilar corrected. "You are asking us to take on the role of an entire army, and in open ground. That, we cannot do."

"If you don't, then who will?" Vendis snapped in frustration, his sweating face pale. "The closest major legion presence is at Tmoskai, and the Abbey of the Penitent and the Devoted is days away! We need to try to fight this off with what we have!"

Ragran growled and rolled his eyes, his annoyance at Thesilar and Valletto rapidly rising. The guard commander was entirely correct. A stand needed to be made, and Ragran was confident he could do just that. His response was cut off as three newcomers sprinted over to join them. Ragran was not surprised to see Z'akke and Aestelle; the enormous, hulking gur panther with them was less expected. The panther stopped by the gathering and immediately fixed her eyes on Ragran, narrowing them and issuing a threatening growl.

"Steady!" Aestelle shouted at the huge creature. "Wait! You wait for my order!"

Ragran met the deadly creature's glare head on. The panther took a pace forward with a pad of one huge, clawed paw, and the growl grew in intensity. Aestelle barked a command at the panther again but was completely ignored.

"There is an attack to the south!" Z'akke announced. "A guard told us that there are skeletons attacking the miners!"

Vendis swore and dabbed at his brow with a handkerchief.

"What is that thing doing here?" he gasped, backing away from the gur panther.

"She will help!" Aestelle nodded. "You just watch! These things can fight!"

"Alright!" he held his hands up, perhaps calming himself more than any of the others. "Alright! We need to defend the south! Can you go to the northern wall and stop anything coming through? I… I don't know what strength they have! But we have to try!"

"As I said," Ragran repeated, taking a wary step back from the panther, "we can do that!"

"And the chapel cemetery?" Thesilar asked.

"Z'akke and I can handle that!" Valletto offered. "If these bastards are raising the dead right here, we might be able to nullify their magic. Z'akke and I are best to clear the cemetery."

"Right," Z'akke nodded, "agreed!"

"Then go!" Vendis stammered.

Valletto and Z'akke sprinted off toward the west and the path leading up the slopes to the little chapel sitting just inside the town wall. Vendis turned back to face the others. His eyes fell on Aestelle.

"You! You're a Viscountess now! I heard about that! You have the right to assume command of the defenses here!"

"Take command?" Aestelle's eyes widened. "It is quite alright! I do not feel the need to carry out that particular privilege!"

"But you were a soldier," Vendis continued, "a fighting sister, of the order? Is that rumor true?"

"Yes," Aestelle replied uncomfortably, "but... I was no leader! I was a senior sister – a sergeant, in effect. Vendis, I cannot perform a miracle and save this town!"

Vendis dabbed at his neck and nodded.

"Right!" he gasped, looking around desperately as the lines of panicked townsfolk continued to come and go from every compass point. "Then... we need to head south! Ragran, Thesilar! Go and do all you can at the north gate! Aestelle, come with me! We will hold the main defense to the south!"

Ragran watched as Vendis, Aestelle, the two guards, and the panther pelted off toward the south gate. Save the incessant screams of terror from every direction, the town square fell relatively silent. The wind whipped through the narrow alleyways to the north. Ragran grinned at Thesilar.

"Ready?"

Thesilar took her bow from her back.

"Bloody stupid way to die. Defending a Basilean mining town in the middle of nowhere. This is a stupid way to die, Ragran, after all we have done."

Ragran laughed and shoved a comradely fist into the lithe elf's shoulder.

"There is only one way to die that isn't stupid. With enemies ahead of you and a blade in your hands. If it happens, this is as good a way as any! Come on, Thes. I am in the mood to spoil their plans!"

Chapter Twelve

Orange light leaked through the thin gaps in the wooden blinds, illuminating the cool bedroom as the dawn sun slowly rose. Valletto opened his eyes, his head aching dully from the fatigue of another restless night. The culprit – Jullia, his one-year-old daughter – lay sprawled out on the bed between him and his wife, somehow taking up more space than either adult. Careful not to disturb either, Valletto slowly sat up and cast his eyes around the cool dark of the bedroom, across the rough, white walls and smooth, polished stone floor. It was such a far cry from the nights spent traveling, at best in a country inn but more likely on a bedroll in a military encampment, constantly under threat from Abyssal invaders.

But that was all in the past now, memories that seemed years ago, even though he had been home for only a single week. He closed his eyes as his head pounded, raising a thumb and forefinger to his throbbing temples. The action, that barely perceptible movement of a single limb, caused the boards of the bed to creak. Valletto looked across in the darkness, the shadows of the room slowly illuminated by the dawn sunlight penetrating the gaps between the blinds over the windows.

The little bundle between him and his wife, Clera, stirred. Jullia let out a choked snuffle and then a moan of discomfort. Groaning wearily, Valletto reached across and picked Jullia up. She immediately flopped down against his chest, wrapped her short arms around his neck, and settled into a contented silence as her eyes opened to greet the day. Long moments passed. She did not drift off to sleep again, yet she remained perfectly happy in his arms, her eyes peering into the darkness around them. She looked up at him and smiled. Despite the ceaseless weariness caused by the sleep she robbed from him, Valletto looked down at his daughter and loved her completely, and unconditionally.

The two mages sprinted through the narrow lane, long shadows cast along the cobbles from the flickering flames of the lanterns suspended from the cracked, plaster walls of the buildings to either side of them. Screams continued to drift across the winds – mainly from the south – but the clash of blades could also be heard intermingled amongst the panicked cries. Valletto emerged from the end of the narrow lane and into a small square. He looked up the shallow slope leading to the western end of the town and saw the chapel at its peak, just inside the town's perimeter wall.

"There's something up there!" Z'akke confirmed as he bounded after Valletto. "Can you sense that?"

"Not yet," Valletto replied.

He saw Z'akke reach into one of the small pouches on his belt and produce an energy crystal. A handful of the crystals being at the ready to augment the power of his spells would have been comforting, but Valletto had none of his own.

A small figure appeared on the meandering path ahead. Valletto and Z'akke rushed over and up the winding dirt path, the suspended lanterns soon revealing the newcomer to be a boy of perhaps twelve or thirteen years of age, clothed in the plain white robes of a church acolyte.

"Run!" the boy gasped, tears streaming down his pale face, half turning to point behind him. "Run, quickly! The dead are rising from their graves!"

"Head to the south gate!" Valletto urged the boy, turning in place to face him as they passed. "Head south! You will be safe there!"

Doubting his own statement, Valletto continued up along the path with Z'akke close behind. He, too, felt it now – the dark, claustrophobic sensation of necromancy at work, the sickening, unnatural feeling that could practically be tasted on the tongue by an experienced mage. He shuddered as the aberrant sorcery threatened to surround him and envelop him.

"It's coming from the north!" Z'akke hissed as they continued up the path, smoke wafting up from his nostrils in excitement as they threaded their way through the overhanging trees to either side. "Whoever is raising them is near the north gate!"

Valletto heard the dry, rasping groans before he even saw the walking corpses. Likewise, the unique, nauseating stench of rot and decay invaded his nostrils moments before he reached the top of the path. The little mining chapel sat at the crest of the small hill; a tiny, rectangular building adjoined by a simple tower and spire surrounded by haphazard rows of graves within an old, broken wooden fence ringing the consecrated ground. Crooked and crumbled headstones of gray stone marked older graves; newer graves were marked by crossed wooden poles forming rough triangles.

Illuminated by the lanterns hanging from the chapel, eight or nine shadowy figures shambled through the long grass surrounding the unkempt resting places, some brandishing wooden poles torn up from the graves to wield as weapons. The closest of the creatures limped toward Valletto, fixing him with vacant stares from the blank, cream-colored eyeballs sat deep within gray-green faces of dead, rotting flesh.

Valletto held out a hand and summoned his powers to create a whirling vortex of unstoppable wind. The torrent of arcane energy shot from his outstretched palm like a hurricane, smashing into the closest of the lumbering zombies and sending the walking corpse flying back through the air to impact heavily against the stone corner of the chapel tower. The impact snapped the zombie's spine in half, and it fell motionless to rest at the base of the tower. Almost simultaneously, scorching flames cascaded from the end of Z'akke's staff to engulf another of the undead monsters, wrapping the creature in a melting embrace of yellow-orange fire. The zombie attempted to plod on, dead flesh and ligaments melting in the inferno before it collapsed to its knees and pitched forward to lie in the grass, still burning.

"Take them down!" Valletto yelled across to the salamander mage-priest as he conjured up a wall of whistling wind to slow the advance of the zombies across the little graveyard. "I'll hold them in place! You burn them!"

Z'akke nodded frantically and sent out another burst of fire to light up the dark skies above the chapel as Valletto saw a number of the zombies turn to head across the graveyard, away from the mages, and toward the slopes leading down to the town itself.

***

Metal thudded against wood in rapid, repetitive blows. Thesilar looked across to the northern gate as she approached with Ragran and saw a handful of town guards cowering by either side of the big, wooden doors. Perhaps ten guards, identifiable by their low-quality armor and rust-red tabards, manned the gatehouse – some shrinking against the walls by the gate itself, others crouching beneath the ramparts above it. The twin doors of the gatehouse continued to bang and thud, bulging out with the impact of the blows from the far side, some striking hard enough to momentarily bend the heavy oak timber barring the doors from the inside.

"We need to get those doors open," Ragran remarked as he headed purposefully across toward the gatehouse.

"What?" Thesilar exclaimed. "Don't be absurd! You want to let them in?"

"I can't fight them through a door," Ragran grunted, "and if I hold my ground in that gatehouse, I can't be outnumbered by much. I'll drop them, two at a time. Just like Clarion did at the White Pass."

"Just wait for a moment, would you?" Thesilar urged, sprinting ahead and vaulting up the steps leading to the meager, rudimentary battlements of the wooden stake perimeter wall. She encountered a trio of guards, practically on their hands and knees below the lip of the ramparts, indistinguishable from each other in their near identical tabards and wide-brimmed, kettle helmets.

"Who is in command here?" Thesilar demanded.

The sky lit up with a purple flare from the other side of the wall. Thesilar flung herself down below the rampart as a fiery bolt of magical energy hurtled up from the path to the north, slamming into the wooden battlements and setting them ablaze with unnatural flames. Thesilar risked a quick look over the wooden defenses. She saw thirty, perhaps even forty, skeletal soldiers crammed against the gatehouse, slamming their weapons into the wooden doors. Somewhere in the darkness ahead was the source of their guidance and the magical bolt that was hurled in her direction only moments before – a necromancer. Aided by her elven eyes – certainly superior to those of a human but not, contrary to common misconception, truly nocturnal – Thesilar made out the figure of a man on horseback by a copse of trees a little way down the path leading north. Three hulking, gargantuan figures standing taller even than the mounted man waited behind him. Thesilar's eyes widened as she recognized their distinctive, broad silhouettes. Trolls. She looked at the cowering guards and dropped down beneath the rampart again.

"Who has command of the defenses here?" she repeated as the entire gatehouse tremored with another heavy impact from the skeletons battering against the doors.

"Vendis!" a pale-faced youth stammered. "He told us to hold the gatehouse! We haven't heard anything since!"

Thesilar risked another peek over the ramparts at the skeletal horde below, and at the necromancer and his zombie trolls waiting further down the northern road. She knew undead and she knew how to fight. But she was also able to admit shortcomings in her own experiences – internally, at least – and what she did not know was military tactics. She had no idea how to mount a viable defense against a superior attacking force.

"Can any of you shoot? Do you have bows or crossbows?"

The frightened and silent exchanges between the trio of guards confirmed her suspicions. Thesilar nodded.

"Get to the south gate," she ordered. "Vendis is mounting the main defense there. Get every guard you can and head south. Go."

"But what about this gatehouse?" a second, older guard demanded.

"Those gates will break open," Thesilar replied, "nothing we have here can stop that. When they do, I do not think you will make any difference. Get all of your men together and head south; you might be able to make a difference there. Ragran and I will stay. Whatever makes it past us will be a lot worse off for it by the time it reaches you at the south gate."

The three guards needed no further encouragement. The armed men scrambled down the stairs, shouting to their compatriots to form by the gate. Thesilar paced down the stairs and over to where Ragran waited by the banging, trembling doors of the gatehouse as the guards ran off south to disappear into the dark streets of Torgias.

"That's your plan?" the hulking Northman said, his axe held at the ready. "Send away the only help we have?"

"You wanted a fight worthy of song, did you not?" Thesilar forced a grin. "Let them go to the south gate and bolster the numbers there. They were only watching a gate that will burst open at any moment. They are no use here."

"And when the gate does fall," Ragran queried, "what then?"

Thesilar took her bow from her back and drew an arrow from her quiver.

"We slow them down," she shrugged, "for as long as we can. I am not in the mood to die here, old friend. Not today. When this all turns to giant shit, I intend to run."

Ragran smiled and then let out a booming laugh at Thesilar's use of his own culture's somewhat vulgar phrase.

"Why not just open the doors now?" He grinned. "Let us start this thing on our own terms!"

Thesilar shook her head.

"There are about forty skeletons out there. That's enough to overrun the two of us with some ease. What concerns me more is the necromancer and his three zombified trolls waiting further down. Remember, Ragran, this is about us. This is all about us. They don't care about this town or the people here. It is all to draw us out."

"Right," Ragran grunted, "if they wanted to knock these doors down quickly, they'd be using those trolls. But we aren't supposed to know about them, are we? We're supposed to be surrounded and cut off by those skeletons first. Then those trolls will be sent in to finish us."

The doors continued to hammer, thud, and bang. A split appeared on the wooden cross beam tentatively holding them shut. Thesilar looked across to the doors and notched the arrow to her bowstring.

"Knock as many of them down as you can, big man," she said, "I have your back. I'll let you know when we need to run."

Ragran shot her a look and then paced across to take his place by the gatehouse doors. Thesilar watched him with growing unease. The simple look said more than any words. It told her that Ragran had no intention of running. That made no sense to Thesilar – the thought of fighting and dying for some backwater mining town in a nation that thought little of men of the north, and even less of elves. She did not have time to ponder the predicament any further. With a creak and a loud snap, the timber across the gatehouse entrance split in two, and the heavy, wooden doors swung open.

***

The scene at the south gate instantly brought memories of long forgotten wars flooding back to Aestelle's mind. Illuminated by the handful of flickering street lamps, miners and their families, traders, sailors, and farmers all huddled together along the wall in their masses. Groups of fours and fives clustered together, some with bags of possessions ready to escape the town to take their chances in the night countryside to the south. At least five hundred people, perhaps half the number made up of women and children, crouched or lay along the curve of the wooden palisade, some crying, some shouting at the handful of town guards in panic, others resigned to silence in acceptance of their fate. Two dozen guards manned the southern gatehouse, some frantically rushing through the groups of townsfolk in a futile attempt to instill calm, others standing atop the gatehouse itself and staring off to the south.

One of the guards rushed up to Vendis and Aestelle as they approached.

"Any news, Commander?" the blond-bearded guard asked eagerly.

Any answer from Vendis was cut off as Seeba growled threateningly at the young guard. The man looked down at the gur panther in terror and backed away quickly.

"Enough of that!" Aestelle snapped down at the powerful animal. "I have enough to think on without you eating the wrong people!"

Vendis rushed over to the gatehouse as half a dozen guards attempted to hold back a sudden surge from the crowd as the townsfolk who recognized the commander lunged forward to demand answers from him.

"Gregor!" Vendis shouted up to the top of the gatehouse. "What's out there?"

"Best you come up here for yourself, Commander!" a voice called down.

Aestelle turned to face the muscular gur panther at her side.

"You wait here," she ordered curtly. "Do not hurt anybody! Understood?"

The panther glowered up at her and let out a vicious roar that forced Aestelle to jump back defensively as a scream of terror was emitted from the nearest group of townsfolk. Gathering her courage to face the seething war animal, Aestelle paced back over toward her.

"Don't you give me that!" Aestelle snapped. "If you want me to take you home after this, you do as I bloody well say! Stay here, shut up, and don't kill anybody!"

The panther snarled again and turned her back on Aestelle, pacing back and forth in front of the gatehouse with a proud, petulant air. Content enough for now that she would behave, Aestelle left the creature and bounded up the stairs by the gatehouse to catch up with Vendis. The guard commander stood by two of his guards, staring off to the south. Four ranks of skeletons armed with swords and shields stood rigidly a few dozen yards from the gatehouse, their cream-brown bones illuminated by the rising moon.

"What are they doing?" Vendis thought aloud. "Why won't they attack?"

"They have not been ordered to," Aestelle exhaled. "My guess is that they are here to prevent anybody leaving. This is the stopper in the bottle. The main attack must be coming from the north gate."

Vendis turned to look up at the tall woman.

"So what do you suggest?"

Aestelle turned away.

"Well?"

"I'm thinking!" Aestelle growled. "I am afraid I am somewhat unaccustomed to finding myself trapped in a town surrounded by a small army of undead!"

Aestelle looked across at the waiting ranks of skeletons. It made sense. Any help for Torgias would come from the legion or the Sisterhood, and even if a messenger had already managed to bypass the surrounding undead – which had not happened – aid would not be forthcoming for a couple of days at least. Basilea, in all of its arrogance, assumed that any threats would come from outside her borders. Her huge, powerful military stood guard against the forces of the Abyss to the north and the conventional threats of mankind to the west whilst the navy protected the Hegemony across the seas to the south and east. Towns did not need guarding. Forty or fifty barely trained guards with spears and halberds were considered enough to maintain law and order.

Aestelle turned back to Vendis.

"We need to punch through these bastards and get everybody outside the town," she said, keeping her voice low. "If those skeletons are standing there to prevent escape, it is because our enemies want us to stay in Torgias. We have no idea how many are attacking from the north. It could be an entire army. These walls are not protecting the people; they are keeping them here in danger's way. We need to break out and flee south."

Vendis looked at Aestelle incredulously. His question was simple.

"How?"

Aestelle took a breath.

"Get every man you can who can raise a weapon. Get every miner and sailor who can swing a plank of wood and form them up into units. Give me your guards. I shall lead them, front and center."

Vendis nodded slowly.

"Right... right. That we can do. We have the numbers here. We can fight our way through a handful of skeletons."

Aestelle swallowed.

"It is not the skeletons that concern me most. It is whatever is controlling them. Vendis, get every guardsman you can assemble at the gates for me to lead against the undead. You follow with every fighting-age man and woman you can persuade to stand and fight. We shall drive a wedge through whatever is out there and get everybody out of the town."

Vendis quickly made his way back down the stairs and headed across to the scores of townsfolk waiting against the wooden walls. Aestelle looked to the south again. Unsheathing her greatsword, she headed down to the gates.

***

His bare, clawed feet struggling to find purchase on the slope, Z'akke stumbled down the incline toward the town. Behind him, the graveyard was lit up with the burning bodies of his fallen opponents; zombies returned to rest after his magical flames had eaten them away. Some, animated from an unseen force to the north, had still managed to rise a second and even a third time but were forcefully put back down by his own flames and the tornados of wind conjured up by Valletto.

"Over there!" Valletto called from beside him. "Down to the right, by that alleyway!"

Z'akke stared ahead and saw a pair of the stumbling corpses stagger off into the darkness, disappearing into the shadows of a narrow street that cut between two tall, wooden buildings. His sword and staff held ready, Z'akke reached the flat ground of the town and picked up his pace to dash after the pair of undead monsters. No sooner had he reached the entrance to the dark alleyway then a stinking corpse threw itself at him, yellow teeth bared with a hiss and gurgle of rotten vocal cords. Z'akke smashed a fist into the zombie's face, the stubby cross guard of his curved, notched sword slashing a vicious gash across the creature's cheek as it reeled back from the impact.

The second zombie was on him moments later, swinging a shovel down toward him. Z'akke reacted just a moment too slowly, but the metal shovel succeeded only in clanging loudly off the thick, boney carapace of Z'akke's shoulder. He reached out with his staff and conjured up a pillar of fire, sending the red-hot flames spewing out to engulf the zombie. The rotten mass of flesh was transformed into a silent, writhing torch that lit up the alleyway. The wall of the wooden building behind the undead creature simultaneously erupted in flames.

The first zombie hurled itself back in to attack Z'akke but was held at bay a moment later when Valletto appeared at the alleyway entrance and caught the creature with a burst of howling wind. Held safely away by the force of the arcane blast, the creature stood no chance when Z'akke leaned in and hacked it down with a trio of heavy cuts from his curved blade. The second, blazing zombie staggered in to attack again with the shovel, but Valletto's powers smashed into the creature and sent it tumbling through the air to disappear into the flaming wall of the building behind it.

Z'akke looked over to quickly nod and smile in gratitude to Valletto as he dashed over to catch up with the mage-priest.

"Thank you," Z'akke gasped quickly, "but I have... I have started a fire! This building! We must extinguish the flames before it burns down!"

Valletto looked across at the blazing building a few paces away. His eyes narrowed and a mischievous grin tugged at the corners of his lips.

"I wouldn't worry," he chuckled, "it's the town tax office. You've done these people a favor. In fact..."

Valletto held out a hand, and an invisible rush of air shot out and into the fire, fanning the flames and sending them rocketing skyward to engulf the roof of the building. He looked across at Z'akke and flashed an impish smile.

"Just in case," he shrugged.

Z'akke opened his fanged jaws to emit a hissing laugh, his eyes sparkling with excitement.

"Come on," Valletto urged, "I think that is the last of them from the graveyard. There are still both the north and south gates to defend."

"We should stay together," Z'akke suggested, "I do not think separating with all of this going on is a good idea."

"Agreed," Valletto breathed, moving quickly along the alleyway and away from the blazing tax office, "let's head to the south gate. The guard commander said the main defense would be staged there."

Z'akke nodded and picked up his pace to follow Valletto through the rapidly darkening, empty streets of Torgias.

***

With a yell, Ragran swung his heavy axe around again to cleave through the brittle ribcage of another skeleton warrior, cutting the undead soldier through and sending the corpse crumbling to the ground. A second warrior immediately tried to slip past him through the narrow opening of the gateway in the northern wall; Ragran slammed the haft of his axe into the undead warrior's face and forced it stumbling back into the endless wall of its compatriots. Piles of bones lay at Ragran's feet from the skeletal swordsmen he had cut down from his position in the open gateway; ahead of him a sea of dry bone, rictus grinning skeletons waited, seemingly almost patiently, to rush him two at a time to fill the small gap ahead of him in the wooden gateway.

Bones rattled and stirred by his feet. Ragran glanced down and saw the dull sparkle of dark energy as a ribcage, skull, and limb bones skittered across the ground to reform the dead bodies of one of the ancient warriors he had felled. Ragran stepped across and kicked the skull away, sending it hurtling back into the ranks of undead swordsmen ahead of him and breaking the spell before it could be completed. An arrow whistled through the open gateway, missing his head by only inches before slamming straight into the skull of one of the skeletons ahead of him, sending the ancient warrior crumpling down into the dirt.

Tirelessly, another two swordsmen charged at Ragran. With a roar, he hefted his heavy axe up and brought it crashing down to hack apart the first adversary. The second skeleton sliced a notched sword across his hip, drawing blood and sending a dart of pain shooting down his leg. Ragran turned and brought his own head crashing down into the boney forehead of his adversary, connecting with a loud crack and knocking the skeleton back a couple of paces. Freed again to move, Ragran swung his axe around and sliced through the skeleton's spine, severing it between the pelvis and the bottom of the ribcage, and sending the corpse tumbling earthward in two halves. Once again an arrow shot from behind him as Thesilar dispatched another skeleton with unerring precision. Relentlessly, another pair of skeleton warriors charged at him with swords and shields at the ready. Again, a burst of necromantic energy from the skeleton's unseen master hidden in the darkness to the north caused the bones at his feet to stir with unnatural movement.

"Ragran!" Thesilar called from behind him. "I'm moving up to the parapet! Keep them busy!"

Grunting from the pain of the latest attack against his flank, Ragran let out a bitter laugh. He held his ground as the skeletons advanced again and Thesilar dashed gracefully up the wooden steps to his left to take position on the ramparts above his head. Locked in combat with the endless horde of skeletons, Ragran nonetheless had the capacity to hear the whoosh of an arcane assault from somewhere ahead, and a moment later, the entire gatehouse trembled with the impact of a necromantic attack. Thesilar hurtled back down from the ramparts even quicker than she had mounted them.

"Ragran!" she gasped. "We need to go! We need to fall back! Those trolls are coming!"

Ragran punted another skeleton back into the waiting ranks of undead soldiers as a blade bit into his thigh. He let out a barely suppressed hiss of pain and cut down his assailant.

"No!" he grunted. "I'm holding this gatehouse! They can't surround me here!"

As if in answer, the wooden palisade wall to Ragran's right shook violently. Another thud signified a heavy impact, and then a third saw a rotten, green-gray fist the size of a man's torso bludgeon through the wall. They were coming through to either side.

"It turns out that they *can* surround you, after all!" Thesilar shouted, tugging on one of his arms. "Come on! We're falling back!"

***

"What have you got?" Aestelle called across as Vendis quickly made his way back over from the crowds of townsfolk huddled against the wooden wall. The guard commander picked up his pace until he was only a step away from Aestelle but then retreated again as the towering gur panther by Aestelle's side fixed him with a dangerous stare and growled threateningly.

"About thirty," Vendis muttered quietly.

"Is that it?" Aestelle exclaimed. "The entire population of the town is right there, and only thirty are willing to fight? This is for their families! For life and death itself!"

Vendis shook his head.

"If you take away children, the old, the sick, and lame... Look, this is all who volunteered, and I don't have the authority to force anybody to pick up a weapon and face the walking dead! My guards are back from the north gate. With forty of them, thirty men and women from the town, and those four adventurers over there, we outnumber the undead outside the gate by nearly two-to-one. We can fight our way through with that."

Aestelle swore and looked across at the quartet of adventurers Vendis pointed toward. She recognized them from the Trade Wind Inn; three men and a dwarf. All of them were young and without a single notch on their blades to speak of fighting experience. She shook her head. When she had faced undead, orcs, or the creatures of the Abyss before whilst standing in rank and file, it had been alongside blooded and expert fighters of the Sisterhood, legion, or the Paladin Order. One could accept being outnumbered a little when fighting in ranks of that caliber. However, she now faced the undead in a force where the most elite and dependable unit was forty members of the town guard – an amateur, peace keeping militia little better than an armed mob of peasants. Outnumbering their foes two-to-one might not be enough, and that was before even considering whatever awaited them in the darkness beyond the south wall that was controlling and orchestrating the lines of undead swordsmen.

Aestelle looked up at Vendis.

"I shall lead your guards," she declared, "you take the townsfolk around the left and tell those four would-be barrowers to hold the right. Do not let anything get on my flanks. I'll punch through these bastards. Let's get to it."

Aestelle jogged over toward the awaiting guardsmen. The gur panther dashed along next to her. She stopped and looked down at the panther.

"Look," she began, "I know you are not happy to be stuck with me, but I am not enamored of this arrangement either. As I told you, I am not a cat person. But I know your lot is favored by the Sisterhood because you know right from wrong. So just remember that as soon as we get outside that gate, you are fighting a perversion of nature to protect innocent people. Understood?"

The panther looked up at her silently and blinked.

"You don't know what a perversion of nature is, do you?"

The panther tilted its head.

"Just attack what I point at, alright?"

Aestelle reached the southern gatehouse. Some forty men in simple armor of leather and mail awaited her, identifiable by their red tunics and kettle helmets. Some of them she knew personally from her years spent in and out of Torgias. All of them, now more than ever, looked to her like pale, pathetic facsimiles of legion men-at-arms.

"Form up," she shouted, "four ranks of ten!"

The guards quickly did as she ordered them to. Aestelle took her place at the front of the unit and looked back at them. They stood shoulder to shoulder, their spears and halberds ready. None of them held shields. Aestelle had a little experience of fighting with a spear, certainly enough to know that moving and fighting as a disciplined unit was something that required training and skill that was currently notable in its complete absence. They needed space to fight.

"Guards," she shouted, "at one pace intervals! Open order… march!"

Pale and frightened faces, both young and haggard, looked to either side at their comrades in confusion.

"Spread out!" Aestelle explained. "Make sure there is enough room around you to fight! Quickly, now!"

The lines quickly and haphazardly opened up at her command. She checked left and right and saw that Vendis was ready with the townsfolk and the four amateur adventurers stood firm at her other flank. She looked forward as the gur panther paced restlessly back and forth ahead of her.

"Open the gate!"

Chapter Thirteen

From his vantage point atop the small hillock to the south of the palisade wall, Khirius saw the heavy doors of the gatehouse swing slowly open. Even from this distance, he could sense the crowd on the other side of the wall; hundreds of people crammed together in fear of the small hordes of skeletons that he and Cane had used to drive them into the town. The combined thrum of scores of hearts pumping blood along veins and arteries, all crammed together on the other side of the thin wall.

Khirius shook his head. Less than one hundred skeletons between them, and a town of five times that number of people. If they had any courage, they could have overpowered their attackers with numbers alone. But that was humans. No, that was Basileans. Completely and utterly incapable of accepting human loss. A single woman or child killed in this attack would mean disaster. Having every man and woman in the town charge from those very gates to attack with their bare hands would ensure victory, but the losses were unthinkable to the Basilean mind. Better to cower behind thin walls of wood and hope the problem outside would somehow magically disappear.

Ranks of armed men filed out of the walls and wheeled around to form a unit of spearmen, four ranks deep. Khirius was far from an expert on military matters, but even from this distance, he could tell that despite their uniform tabards and helmets, the men facing his skeletons had little experience in marching in ranks. The town guard, no doubt. Khirius narrowed his eyes when he saw Aestelle stood out in front of the guards. That complicated things.

To one side of the forty or so guards, Khirius noticed a slightly smaller collection of men and women, plainly dressed in the shirts, breeches, and skirts of every day townsfolk. Some carried improvised weapons such as wooden planks or kitchen knives. Khirius shook his head. This made things even worse. Khirius was, himself, in a delicate position balanced between the absolute need to stay on the right side of the Coven to ensure his own survival, but also by minimizing the loss of innocent lives in doing so. One did not become angry at a lion for eating to survive, and the same logic surely applied to vampires – killing for blood was necessary to exist and therefore could not be considered an act of evil. But attacking a town full of innocents just to drive out a handful of dangerous individuals? That needed to be done carefully.

A slow smile spread across Khirius' pale features as he saw a small band of armed men appear on the other side of the main force.

Four individuals – a dwarf and three humans – paced out into the night with weapons drawn. Khirius' smile broadened. They would do nicely. Khirius would never dream of attacking the townsfolk, men and women summoning their courage to fight for their families, whereas the town guard would be regrettable casualties but fair enough in his mind. They did, after all, accept payment in return for dangerous duties. But adventurers? Egotistical, greedy bastards who would hack down anything and anyone for a coin or two?

Khirius focused his gaze on the town guard and then formed a mental connection with what remained of the minds of the skeletal warriors waiting in the open ground to the south of the gatehouse. He implanted a single word in their collective consciousness. *Attack.* Satisfied that the skeletal swordsmen moved as one toward the town guards, he then looked back across at the quartet of adventurers. Three warriors and a magic user. Khirius advanced cautiously through the long grass, drawing his gold-hilted sword from his side. He picked up his pace, silently moving through the darkness and closing with his foes. The four adventurers moved forward as they saw the skeletal horde marching to face the town guards, no doubt looking to charge from the flanks or the rear to envelop their undead foes. They had not seen him. It would cost them.

The long blades of grass folded silently to either side as Khirius sprinted toward his targets, the balls of his booted feet light on the dry earth and his sword held up and ready to one side. He saw them all clearly now; a young but typical looking, bearded dwarven warrior with a heavy warhammer; two human warriors in mail shirts and armed with swords; and a tall, scholastic seeming mage in plain robes, carrying a staff whose arcane power Khirius could sense even from this distance. The vampire narrowed his eyes and focused. All four adventurers stared off toward the advancing skeletons, their focus dominated by the only threat they perceived. Khirius identified his main threat and leapt in to attack.

Propelling himself forward out of the darkness of the long grass, Khirius darted straight past the brown-bearded dwarf and lashed out with his sword. Driven forward by inhuman strength, Khirius' attack cut straight through the forearm of one of the human swordsman, severing the limb just below the elbow. As the blond man fell to his knees, screaming and clutching at the stump of his arm, Khirius rushed behind the drab-robed mage, reached around to clasp a hand across his face to hold him in place, and then sank his teeth into the shrieking sorcerer's jugular vein.

Blood sprayed into Khirius' mouth at volume, splattering onto the roof of his mouth with force like a scarlet waterfall. He swallowed all that he could desperately, feeling the warm, bitter liquid force itself down his parched esophagus and lubricating it, quenching his innards like rain cascading down into a desert. The force generated by the torn vein was too much for Khirius to manage and thick, crimson blood sprayed from his own mouth as he held the desperately writhing mage in place. In only the briefest of moments, he had succeeded in creating an injury horrific enough to shock the other adventurers into inactivity whilst he quenched his own thirst through killing off his greatest threat in their group. The mage's blood added to that of a miner Khirius had killed less than an hour before to sake his thirst.

The mage slipped from Khirius' grasp and crumpled to the ground. Khirius looked down and saw that in his thirst-driven desperation, he had half-severed the mage's head. The younger of the two human warriors darted over to drag the mutilated, one-armed warrior away from the deadly vampire. The young dwarf valiantly rushed at Khirius with an angry roar, swinging his heavy, two-handed warhammer at the suddenly rejuvenated vampire. Khirius stepped back to avoid the first blow and ducked beneath the second, marveling at the dwarf's skill at arms. It would be in vain; whilst the dwarf's martial skills were certainly greater than those of Khirius, his sheer speed was not. Khirius dodged and sidestepped a good half-dozen attacks before lashing out with his own blade. The dark-bearded dwarf expertly deflected his first attack, then his second, and Khirius found himself on the defensive again.

Dodging another hammer swing aimed at his head, Khirius ducked down and then drove himself forward into another attack. This time, his sword found its mark and plunged into the dwarf's neck, catching him just above the protection of his thick armor. The tip of his sword drove through the dwarf's throat and sent him gargling to the earth in a stream of blood. The vampire glanced around. The mage had already bled out and stared lifelessly at the night sky above. The two human warriors remained; the wounded man backing away from the vampire and crying out in pain whilst his comrade stood guard bravely in front of him, his sword held up and at the ready. His skills were nothing compared to his dwarven comrade; Khirius hacked down his final opponent with two heavy cuts to the chest. The first warrior looked up at him with pleading eyes, clutching at his bloodied stump, backing away pathetically.

The blond man said a word weakly to Khirius, his voice frail and terrified. Khirius closed his eyes. He hated that word beyond all others. When his victims said that word, they instantly transformed from mindless cattle into real people, with lives and emotions; a want and a need to live. It was too late to turn back now. Khirius brought his sword up over his head and flung the blade out to decapitate the final adventurer. He heard screams from behind him and turned to look over his shoulder. A handful of yards away, a few dozen townsfolk had idiotically decided to follow the guards out of the gates to watch the fighting from the wall. Others still had clambered up to regard the battle from the ramparts above. Some had already seen Khirius tear into the adventurers and were now pointing at him, screaming in alarm and terror. Whipping his dark cloak up around him, Khirius darted back into the shadows of the long grass to the south.

***

The four ranks of skeletal soldiers marched directly toward Aestelle and the town guards, the military discipline they once possessed in life still evident in their animated death. As one, the front rank brought up their circular shields and raised their swords. Aestelle heard somebody swear in fear from behind her. The last time she found herself commanding a body of troops in battle – at the head of ranks of Sisterhood soldiers over a decade before – Aestelle would have turned to harshly reprimand such a dangerously infectious display of cowardice. But these men were neither trained nor expected to stand against the terrors of the undead, and hollering at them would be unfair and do nothing good for their morale.

Aestelle raised her sword.

"Be ready!" she shouted back. "Do exactly what I told you! Keep it simple! Be ready!"

The lines of undead marched up the shallow incline toward the town gates, close enough now for Aestelle to make out individual patches of rust on their shields. She dropped to one knee with a creak of leather and looked across to the gur panther that waited by her side.

"You see them?" She pointed a gloved finger at the skeletal swordsmen ahead. "On my signal, you and I are going to punch a hole through the middle of them. Understood? On my signal, we carve a path so that the…"

The panther let out a huge bellow and pelted off toward the skeletons, plumes of dust kicked up in the wake of the colossal animal from her heavy paws.

"Shit." Aestelle shook her head before sprinting off after the bounding gur panther.

Behind her, the town guard yelled out as one and charged. The gur panther closed the gap in seconds, and with a guttural roar, propelled herself into the center of the front rank of skeletons. The first undead warrior was smashed apart, reduced to scattered bones as the heavy creature ploughed headlong into it before her jaws clamped around the skull of a second soldier. The ancient bone put up enough resistance against the vice like clamp for perhaps a second before the gur panther's fanged jaws snapped shut, crushing the skull spectacularly.

The panther continued on into the middle of the forty skeletons, a maelstrom of destruction as she lashed out with powerful, razor-taloned paws and a vicious bite capable of bisecting a man. Aestelle caught up moments later, hurtling through the gap made by the panther and into the second rank, swinging her greatsword around to cleave through the ribs and spine of a skeletal soldier and send it collapsing into the dirt. The surrounding undead responded immediately, turning in to face her and striking at her with rapid cuts from their notched swords.

Aestelle dropped a shoulder to dodge the first attack before bringing her long blade up to block a second, taking advantage of the briefest of lulls to plant a foot into her closest adversary and propel the walking corpse back into its dead comrades. She immediately capitalized on the opening she had created by swinging her sword out to strike at a skeleton in the first rank, but the creature quickly lifted its bronze shield, and the blow succeeded only in creating a dull clang on the ancient metal. A third skeleton to Aestelle's left moved in to attack her, sword held high. She quickly shifted her weight and drove the pommel of her weapon into the skeleton's face with a crunch of bone before striking out with the quillions of her sword, knocking a hole in the undead warrior's forehead.

With a series of shouts and screams, the town guard caught up with the fight and plummeted headlong into the stalled front rank of skeletons. With impeccable timing, Vendis and the volunteer townsfolk smashed into the skeletal horde's right flank only a second later, and the once neat lines of undead soldiers scattered as the battle descended into chaos. Aestelle ducked beneath a sword strike from a skeleton facing her but then let out a cry of pain as she felt a blade slice down across her back, easily cutting through her leather armor to draw blood. She turned in place and brought her blade up to defend herself, but her assailant was savagely knocked back as the gur panther leapt onto it and knocked it down before mauling it remorselessly.

To the left, two town guards planted their shoulders into a short line of skeletal swordsmen who had formed a shield wall and drove them back; to the right, a screaming, frenzied woman clubbed a skeleton down into the dirt with a fence post whilst next to her a young guard was hacked down bloodily by two undead soldiers. The battle opened up, lines scattered as isolated fights broke out between small groups of twos and threes.

Aestelle found herself alone, facing a trio of skeletal soldiers. All three darted in to attack her with swords held high. Always favoring speed as the best form of defense, Aestelle deftly side-stepped to avoid a first strike, swung her body to narrowly avoid a lunge from the second skeleton, and then angled her greatsword to deflect a vicious attack from the third. From not too far away, she heard shouting and cheering. She heard her name being called. Glancing behind her, Aestelle's jaw dropped in surprise as she saw a mob of townsfolk watching the battle from the ramparts of the palisade and the base of the wall itself. Perhaps a hundred men and women had crammed together to witness the fight, all shouting and screaming excitedly as they watched the battle turn in favor of their defenders, yelling encouragement as if watching a tournament event or gladiatorial arena.

Aestelle instantly knew it was wrong. She knew that many of them could have grabbed a weapon and joined those few brave men and women who had volunteered to march into the fight with Vendis; at the very least they should have remained inside the walls where there was some degree of safety. But Aestelle possessed enough self-awareness to know that her vanity outstripped her common sense by a country mile. She failed to suppress a growing smile and dived back in to attack the three skeletons.

The first fell to a strike to the neck that cleaved the skull straight off; the stylized spin Aestelle threw in before the attack was purely for show, and in reality, only succeeded in slowing the strike down. She followed up by twirling her sword theatrically up into the air and catching it by the blade before swinging it around to smash the cross guard into the face of a second opponent, knocking off the skeleton's jaw bone in a fountain of broken teeth. The third lashed out at her with its dented shield, but Aestelle was quicker, dropping to one knee and rolling beneath the shield before lunging up to strike an elbow into the skeleton's face with a loud crack of bone. Reveling in the cheers from the crowd and the shouts of encouragement from behind her, Aestelle traded blows with the two skeletons, adding flair to her moves whenever it was safe to do so before finding an opening and lunging forward to hack down with her blade and cut one of her opponents in half from shoulder to midriff.

A long stream of flame suddenly roared out from near the wall, the yellow fire wrapping around a skeletal warrior and charring it to ash. Aestelle looked across and saw Z'akke and Valletto leap into the fight, fire and storm winds smashing out to defeat yet more of the undead. Around her, guardsmen and frenzied townsfolk ganged up on the now outnumbered skeletons to beat and hack them into submission as the gur panther leapt from fight to fight, savaging undead warriors in a roaring frenzy. Aestelle looked back across at her final opponent as the skeleton attacked her again. She met the attack head on, slicing her long blade up to cut off the skeleton's sword arm before reversing the strike and hacking down to split open its skull. It slumped down to its knees and then pitched to one side.

An elated cry filled the night from the crowd at the foot of the wall and on the battlements. Aestelle looked around the small battlefield and saw that there were no undead remaining. The fight for the south gate was won. Breathing heavily with exertion, covered in a thin film of sweat and ignoring the pain racing across her back from her wound, Aestelle held her sword high above her head and turned slowly in place to accept the screams and shouts of praise from the crowd on the palisade wall. For a brief moment, her whole world seemed to slot neatly into place. She had done something good, something brave, something skillful that nobody else there could have done. She led the charge against evil to protect those who needed help, and they had won. She had risen again as a hero. The fact that she had done it with style before an adoring crowd only made the satisfaction of a job well done even more fulfilling. She closed her eyes and smiled, enjoying that moment.

Then she opened them and saw Vendis knelt over a dying guardsman, only a few paces away. Her smile instantly washing away, Aestelle sprinted over to the wounded guard and dropped to one knee. She looked down and saw the brutal wound to the young man's gut and the panic across his pale face. Summoning on the very essence of her soul, channeling her powers over the magic of divinity, Aestelle placed a hand over the wound and focused the flow of magic. A warm light emanated from her hand and the wound slowly began to close. The bleeding stopped. The injured guard let out a gasp.

"How many have we lost?" Aestelle asked, her head sagging forward with exertion from the use of divinity magic.

"Seven dead, at least," Vendis replied solemnly, "I don't know how many wounded. We need to get everybody out of the town and head south. My men said there was an attack at the north gate. That will break through and they will follow us. This isn't over."

Aestelle stood up and looked across the small battlefield. She counted at least ten dead, including some of the brave volunteer townsfolk. She looked across to the west and saw the four adventurers she remembered from the Trade Wind Inn. All four lay lifeless, torn to pieces bloodily by something far more ferocious than a skeletal swordsman. Z'akke and Valletto dashed over as the gur panther paced across, her head held high and proud.

"It's over," Aestelle said to Vendis, "for you, at least. Get everybody on the road south and keep going until dawn. We will make sure nothing follows you."

"What do you mean?" Vendis shot to his feet. "Ragran and Thesilar are dead by now if they haven't seen common sense and ran! Whatever they faced will be coming here any moment now!"

Aestelle looked across at Z'akke and Valletto. The salamander grinned and nodded. Valletto raised his eyebrows and exhaled, then nodded too in agreement.

"We are going back into the town," Aestelle declared, "whatever is coming this way, we will stop it."

Vendis shook his head.

"There are three of you!" he exclaimed. "Three of you and a panther! Stay with us! We'll hide in the dark! These things can't follow us forever! By dawn, this will be over and we can come back to..."

Aestelle shook her head.

"Take them south, Vendis. Do not stop for anything."

Tucking a lock of blonde hair behind one ear and throwing a wink of gratitude down to the gur panther that walked by her side, Aestelle headed back toward the town gatehouse. The crowds of townsfolk lined the road leading up to the gate, shouting and cheering in jubilation as Aestelle, Z'akke, and Valletto walked wordlessly along the road, through the gate, and back toward the center of Torgias to resume their fight.

***

The second arrow shot true, along the same path as the first. The deadly projectile impacted into the dead flesh of the zombie troll with a dull thud, less than an inch from where the first arrow protruded from the green-gray skin. Neither shot seemed to have any effect on the lumbering monstrosity as it bounded down the cobbled road, its white, dead eyes fixed on Thesilar. Holding her position, Thesilar grabbed a third arrow from the quiver on her back and notched it to her bow, drawing the string back across her chest. The zombified troll let out a rasping, hoarse cry, and then Thesilar let fly. The arrow shot straight down toward her point of aim, hurtling along the darkened, narrow street to find its mark. It slammed deep into the zombie troll's throat.

The towering monster stopped dead in its tracks. It tried to look down at the source of its discomfort, its rotten chin prodding almost comically against the protruding arrow lodged into its neck. The troll reached up and grabbed the wooden stem of the arrow, breaking it off and throwing it aside. Eyes wide, Thesilar gasped a word she was not proud of using, and turned on her heel to flee. The troll hurtled after her, huge feet crashing down clumsily on the cobbles below, arms flailing to either side to smash fists arbitrarily into the wooden buildings of the street to turn walls into a storm of twirling matchwood.

Thesilar rounded a corner and sprinted down a dark, narrow alleyway. She almost immediately saw a pair of the surviving skeletal swordsmen from the fight at the north gatehouse only a few paces ahead. Using her momentum and elven agility to its upmost, she jumped high and planted one foot against the alley wall to the side of the skeletons, shoving herself off the wall to jump clean over their heads and land a yard on the other side, still sprinting. The alleyway behind her exploded into a thunderous crash of breaking wood as the zombie troll continued to pursue her; she risked a glance over her shoulder and saw the troll charge straight through the two skeletons, crushing one of them underfoot.

Emerging out of the end of the alleyway, her bearings completely lost, Thesilar found herself in the open main town square of Torgias. She let out a gasp of surprise when she saw Ragran up ahead – after fleeing from the troll onslaught at the north gatehouse, they had quickly become separated. Ragran stood stoically before the second of the three zombie trolls, his heavy axe raised, his body battered, bruised, and bleeding from a dozen wounds. The zombie troll facing him fared no better, with great gouges and chunks torn from its flesh as evidence of the ferocity of Ragran's attacks.

The northern barbarian turned his head to regard her as she hurtled toward him, relief washing over his tired eyes at the sight of his ally.

"Thes, help me with..."

His plea was cut off as the zombie troll pursuing Thesilar smashed through the alleyway behind her with a dry roar of anger. Ragran's relieved expression instantly turned to weary anguish at the sight of the second troll pursuing Thesilar.

"Thes! You f..."

His insult was cut off as the troll facing him grabbed him by the ankle, lifted him off his feet, and then slammed him down into the cobbles below him. With a snarl, the troll flung Ragran across the town square to plunge straight through the wooden and plaster wall of the town hall with a crash of broken planks and splintered wood. Alone, facing two wounded and raging zombie trolls, Thesilar looked in desperation around the town square for a means of escape.

On the far side of the square, only a few paces from the hole in the wall that Ragran had plummeted through only moments before, a horse wagon lay abandoned against the town hall. Seizing her opportunity, Thesilar sprinted headlong toward the wagon, swerving quickly to avoid a clumsy punch thrown in her direction by the troll in the middle of the square, before jumping onto the wooden carriage and leaping up to grab the lip of the town hall's roof. Gritting her teeth, she quickly dragged herself up onto the roof and looked down at the two zombie trolls below. Gasping for air, her hands planted on her knees, she watched as the trolls paced slowly toward her. To the west, she could see a single building blazing furiously. From the south, inexplicably, she could hear hundreds of voices cheering enthusiastically. Below her, the shattered wood of the wall split and snapped as Ragran tore his way through and staggered back out into the town square. He looked up at Thesilar. She forced a smile down and then nodded in the direction of the enormous zombie trolls.

"One each, then, or do you want to get your breath back whilst I take both of them?" Thesilar called down.

As if in answer, a series of slow thuds echoed from the road leading from the town square to the north gatehouse. Thesilar looked across and felt what little optimism still remained suddenly dashed when the third zombified troll dragged its feet forward to stomp into the town square. Thesilar stood up straight again and stretched out her back. The initiative lay firmly with her; given her speed, agility, and commanding position on the rooftop of the town hall, she could easily turn and run, disappearing into the darkness of the thin streets below and escaping the town. But Ragran did not have that luxury. The wounded barbarian looked wearily across at the trio of trolls lumbering toward him, his hands tightening their grip on his trusty axe. If left alone, he would not stand a chance. Then again, even with Thesilar's help, the two of them did not stand any viable hope of survival.

Thesilar snorted out a brief laugh as she suddenly remembered her first meeting with Ragran over a decade ago. A drunken, lecherous oaf in a tavern, filled with boastful ambition and egotism. In his mind, at their first meeting, he was paying her the highest of compliments by staggering across the tavern, grabbing her posterior and offering to buy her a drink. Naturally, she had done the right thing and punched him in the face. Thirteen years ago, based on that meeting, she would have turned and run. But now, looking down at the middle-aged, graying warrior in the square beneath her, she saw a man who had her back at every encounter. Although sometimes a year or two would drift by without their meeting, whenever they did cross paths again, it was as if they had never been apart. He was like kin, now. Like a cousin. Family.

"Take the one on the right!" Thesilar shouted down, grabbing an arrow from her quiver and notching it to her bow.

Ragran sprinted off toward the northern end of the square with a yell, his axe held high. Thesilar aimed her bow and let fly, sending an arrow slamming into the chest of the central of the three zombie trolls. She followed up with a second, third, and then a fourth arrow, all deadly accurate into the same target. The troll stopped dead, head lolling groggily. It dropped to one knee. Then the third troll reached the town hall.

Putrid, rotting fists smashed into the wooden walls beneath Thesilar. The roof shook and buckled, knocking her off balance. She quickly sprinted away, only a moment before the section of roof where she had stood collapsed entirely. Wooden planks fell away behind her as she ran, the troll clumsily sprinting after her a floor below, pummeling the walls frenziedly with two clenched fists. Thesilar reached over her shoulder and grabbed another arrow; still sprinting, she raised her bow and shot out another deadly projectile as she ran, hitting the wounded troll in the center of the square in the gut, just as it was struggling back up to its feet. Ahead of her, the roof abruptly ended and she jumped for all she was worth, leaping across the gap of the alleyway below to land on the next roof as the town hall was decimated behind her.

Running ahead, Thesilar reached back to grab another arrow, cognizant of how few remained in her quiver. It would soon be time to rely on her sword. She winced at the thought. As Thesilar reached the end of the next roof and the corner of the town square, she turned to jump onto the slanted roof of the town's main church. Hitting the steep roof with a crash, she scrambled up toward the top of the building as she saw Ragran trading blows with one of the trolls below her. Wide-eyed, she watched astounded as the battered, bloodied warrior swung his axe around to connect with the zombie troll, hewing open a great wound in its chest and knocking it staggering back. She had no time to see anymore; scrambling up the slope, she reached the top and nimbly vaulted over to slide down the other side, picking up speed before propelling herself clear of the roof to land atop Torgias' town exchange office. She turned and rapidly loosed an arrow after the pursuing troll, catching it in the gut.

In the center of the town square, the troll she had badly wounded previously now staggered back to its feet, the legendary regenerative qualities of its species having carried across into its existence in undeath. Wounds closed over as the troll flung its arms out and let out an almighty bellow. Three against two again. And Thesilar had only four arrows left. She grabbed at one of her final projectiles and wearily raised her bow to aim at the troll hurtling in pursuit of her. Then she saw a rapid blur moving out of the corner of her eye.

The muscular form of a gur panther bounded out from the road south of the town square and across the cobblestones. The creature pelted rapidly to the middle of the square and propelled herself up from her hind paws to hurtle into the wounded zombie troll. With a sickening crunch, the gur panther closed her jaws around the troll's lower jaw and hung from the undead monster, violently shaking and swinging her entire body until the jaw ripped clear and the panther fell to the ground. The gur panther's head shook as its own jaws clamped together, the resistance of the bone failing after a few moments. With a sickening crunch, the troll's lower jawbone was snapped in half by the force of the panther's bite and fell to the ground in two parts. The panther leapt back in to attack as an arrow whistled through the air and thudded into the side of the troll's head. Thesilar looked across and saw Aestelle, Z'akke, and Valletto rush into the town square.

***

Valletto stared up, wide-eyed at the trio of rotting, revolting, undead monstrosities in the town square. All three zombie trolls still maintained their powerful, broad frames from life – their muscular shoulders hunched, their squinting eyes set below heavy brows on heads that seemed too small for their bodies, their legs powerful if, again, seemingly tiny compared to their thick arms and barrel chests. The green skin associated with trolls in life was replaced with an almost leathery gray-brown on each of the three zombies, each with jagged holes showing dead flesh and yellow bone beneath, each ugly wound lined with a gangrenous green. One troll was locked in a fight with Ragran at the far end of the square; a second chased after Thesilar who sprinted and vaulted lightly from rooftop to rooftop whilst her gargantuan pursuer smashed and pulverized buildings beneath her with clenched fists; the third stood in the middle of the square, torso bristling with arrows and its lower jaw torn off by the gur panther. Aestelle was already sprinting toward the center of the area, sword in hand to join the fight alongside the panther. Valletto looked across at Z'akke.

"Let's help Thesilar!" he shouted.

The salamander mage-priest nodded and dashed off after the zombie troll stood below the elf ranger. Valletto followed the burly salamander as the zombie troll let out a dry, deep, and warbling roar, smashing another fist into the plaster wall of the shaking building Thesilar stood atop. Valletto held out a hand and summoned a torrent of wind around the gargantuan undead troll. Dust and dead leaves swirled rapidly around the troll's feet for a few brief moments until the spell grew to its apex. An unseen hammer blow of wind smashed into the troll, knocking the creature off its feet and sending it piling through the battered wall next to it, disappearing inside the darkness of the devastated building.

Thesilar took advantage of the lull in the troll's onslaught to jump down nimbly from the roof above, landing gracefully in a light roll before dashing over to join the two mages.

"Can you kill this thing without me?" she gasped breathlessly.

"I... I... err..." Z'akke stammered.

"Good," Thesilar nodded, drawing her sword and running off to where Ragran stood alone against another of the huge trolls.

Z'akke looked across at Valletto nervously. Valletto looked up at the blue-eyed salamander. With a low, threatening grumble, the troll clambered back up to its feet and stepped out of the debris of the crumpled plaster wall Valletto had propelled it through. It stared down at the two sorcerers with a surprising amount of feeling and malice evident in its white, dead eyes.

"If you have any more of those energy crystals," Valletto swallowed, "perhaps one really, *really* good one... I suggest you use it now."

***

Aestelle dived to one side and rolled across the cobbles, narrowly avoiding the flailing fist of the zombified monster towering above her. She looked up and saw the hideous creature illuminated in the moonlight; rusted, ill-fitting plates of improvised armor hanging from its shoulders, combined with hastily stitched together scraps of rotten leather and shredded animal skins. She darted into attack, slicing her greatsword across the outside of the creature's knee as she stepped past in an attempt to encircle it. The gur panther lunged forward to strike, saw a fist crashing down toward it, quickly thought better of it, and backed away rapidly to avoid a killing blow.

Emanating a grating noise somewhere between a hiss and a wheeze – due, no doubt, to lacking an entire lower jaw – the troll pivoted in place and looked down at the debris remaining from one of the half-collapsed buildings left in the wake of its undead comrade's destructive sprint after Thesilar. The troll leaned over and picked up a long, thick beam of wood from the building's wreckage. The panther immediately leapt onto its back and sunk her teeth around its spine, clawing viciously at the dead flesh as she hung in place. The troll shifted and swung, lashing out blindly at the creature on its back with fist and improvised club alike. Aestelle saw her moment and shot in for another attack, cleaving up to hack a great wound across one of the zombie troll's forearms before swinging down to slash through the leather armor across its belly. Her flashing blade sliced neatly through leather, skin, and flesh alike and a dry, stinking length of entrails spilled out on the cobblestones before her.

Before she knew what had happened, pain raged across the entire left side of Aestelle's body, and she was spinning through the air. She let out a cry as she landed heavily on the cobblestones, her sword bouncing away from her with an almost musical succession of chimes. Her vision was blurred, her hearing replaced with an endless high-pitched whine, and the horizon refused to sit properly level. Fighting back a sudden urge to vomit, she tried to force herself up onto one arm but let out a cry of pain when that arm gave way beneath her as she crumpled back down to the ground. The light of the moon was blocked out as the black silhouette of her destroyer limped to stand over her. The troll stared down at her prone form, the huge length of timber held high over its head in both hands.

The panther appeared from nowhere, its powerful jaws clamping around the back of the troll's leg as her claws ripped at the dead flesh. Aestelle watched in awe as the entire calf detached from the back of the shin and the troll collapsed to one knee. The panther pelted across and stood protectively in front of Aestelle, roaring up at the maimed zombie troll. Fighting to focus the thoughts in her dull, aching head, Aestelle quickly planted her right hand against her wounded left arm and sent out a wave of healing magic. The pain in her side was replaced with the exhaustion that followed using divinity magic, but her arm responded, and she was able to stagger back up to one knee and grab her sword before wearily standing again to face the troll.

***

His breathing labored, Z'akke looked down at the glimmering energy crystal in his hand. The lower powered examples – the blue and green crystals – were certainly useful and common enough; he had even created many himself when he had the components to hand. But the crystal that sat in his scaly palm was more than that. Rarer. A purple crystal. One of the few he had ever encountered and one he had saved for nearly a year for the right time. This moment was that time. Z'akke looked up at the towering zombie troll ahead of him as Valletto tried in vain to stop the gargantuan creature advancing toward them. The aeromancer stood braced next to Z'akke, both arms extended, a howling gale of wind shooting from his palms and into the deadly creature only a few paces ahead.

"Z'akke!" Valletto yelled over the whistle of the magical winds as the troll slowly struggled to move one leg forward, then the other, fighting its way through the arcane tornado. "Burn it, Z'akke! Burn it!"

Z'akke closed his hand around the purple crystal. He tossed his flaming staff to one side and held out his free hand, staring at the space between his outstretched claws. He took in a few deep breaths to calm himself and then allowed a spark, an essence of fire, to illuminate from the skin of his palm. Focusing to channel his energies into that point, Z'akke concentrated until the spark erupted into a small, white-hot fire. At that point, he squeezed his other hand shut and crushed the purple crystal.

Energy exploded in his clenched fist, shooting up his arm and into his very core. Z'akke's eyes opened wide as his body tremored, his mouth forced open as a long breath flooded out of his heaving lungs. Focusing again to force a mastery over the invasion of magical power in his body, Z'akke pushed the essence of the crystal down his outstretched arm. The white fire in his hand flared up instantly to a blinding light, illuminating the entire town square and forcing Z'akke to turn his face away from the intense heat he had created. Quickly, before the moment was gone, Z'akke rushed forward and planted his burning hand against the zombie troll's belly.

The undead monster's gut was instantly incinerated, flames shooting through its body to punch a hole in its back. Z'akke angled his hand to face up toward the heavens, and the flames moved in turn to scorch through the troll's innards. Its eyeballs melted instantly, and white fire shot out of the vacant eye sockets as well as the troll's open mouth. The towering creature remained upright for a moment until the entire contents of its body were incinerated to ash. What was left of the creature collapsed in a heap like a smoking, stench-filled blanket of blackened skin, the oddly intact arms and legs still attached to the smoking remains of the body.

Z'akke collapsed to one knee, his skin clammy and his body exhausted. Valletto rushed over to him, grabbing him by one arm and helping him back to his feet.

"Windy man," Z'akke gasped, "I... I want to say something witty... about what I just did to that troll... but I am afraid... I'm just not funny..."

Valletto forced a smile and picked up Z'akke's staff, handing it back to him.

"Come on!" he urged. "Let's help the others! This is not over yet!"

***

The bone was not broken, Ragran was fairly sure of that, but whatever the blow from the troll had done to his battered, aching body left him unable to lift his right arm above head height. Not the best situation to be in when facing an adversary twice your size. Thesilar deftly avoided a fist aimed at her head, sidestepping to the creature's left to then deliver a sword strike up into the troll's torso, lancing her blade up beneath the bottom of the monster's protruding ribcage. Blood running from his many wounds, his limbs protesting at the work demanded of them, Ragran flung himself into an attack and brought his axe around in a wide arc as if chopping down a tree at its base.

His axe bit deeply into the troll's ankle, slicing through the flesh and lodging in the bone. Before the troll could respond, a roaring wind swirled up from beneath it and knocked the creature staggering back away from Ragran and Thesilar. A few years before, Ragran would have taken advantage of the opening to rush in and lop off the creature's head; now he was just glad of a moment's respite to lean over and take in a few long breaths. He looked up and saw Valletto rushing over to their aid. That could only mean that the battle was going their way – Ragran glanced over to the far side of the square for confirmation and saw the charred remains of one of the zombie trolls where he had seen the blinding flare of light a few moments before.

"Thes!" Ragran gasped, pointing at the corpse. "Look! We're winning!"

Before the elf ranger could reply, the sound of feet and hooves clipping over the cobblestones drifted across the dark town square from the west. Ragran turned to face the sound. A line of ten skeletal swordsmen marched into the town square with their swords and shields held ready; no doubt some of those who had survived Ragran and Thesilar's defense of the north gatehouse. Behind them, mounted on a powerful looking black horse was a stern looking man with a neat beard of black, wearing a dark tunic and breeches. Even from this distance, Ragran could tell he was of the living, which marked him out as the necromancer that had orchestrated every attack they had faced that night. Ragran gritted his teeth as he eyed the rider. Thesilar looked over at the new arrivals, let out a groan, and then flashed a scornful look at Ragran.

"*Thes! Look! We're winning!*" she boomed at him, imitating his accent perfectly. "That's your fault for saying something so stupid!"

From the center of the town square, Ragran saw Aestelle jump back to avoid a lumbering attack from the second zombie troll as Z'akke rushed across to help her. She looked over at the skeletons and their necromantic master to the west and then shouted out a command to the gur panther. The snarling creature broke off her attack against the troll and pelted off across the cobblestones, eyes fixed on the row of armed skeletons. With a roar, the panther leapt into them, knocking a first to the ground and pinning it down whilst her powerful jaws clamped around its skull and wrenched it clear of the body.

"Can you... kill this thing?" Valletto shouted from Ragran's side, blasts of wind still shooting from his hands to slow the advance of the troll only paces away. "This isn't... as easy as it looks!"

"Aestelle!" Thesilar yelled across the square. "Arrows! Throw me your quiver!"

The row of skeletons wheeled around with an almost elegant discipline, maintaining a line to form a barrier between the rampaging gur panther and the necromancer. The necromancer looked across at Ragran and Thesilar and held up a hand. A crackling purple sphere appeared, growing in both size and intensity. The wind holding the troll at bay from Ragran immediately faded away to nothing as Valletto turned to face the necromancer and held up a hand. The necromancer's purple sphere of arcane energy immediately died away. Again, the dark sorcerer held out a hand, and the crackling, spherical purple flames blossomed up in an unholy light to illuminate the far corner of the town square. From his other side, Z'akke held out a hand, and for a second time, the necromancer's magic was nullified into nothingness.

***

Aestelle jumped back away from the troll's flailing attacks, hurriedly tearing her quiver of arrows from her back before flinging it across the square to land near Thesilar. She did not have time to see if Thesilar managed to make it across to the arrows; forced back from a series of thunderous attacks now that she faced the troll alone, Aestelle ducked and jumped away from each strike in turn. Constantly on the defensive, never freed for a moment to contemplate an attack of her own, Aestelle rolled away from another strike and then thought better of her predicament before turning to run from her gigantic assailant.

The troll immediately pursued her but stopped dead in its tracks after only a few paces when a fireball slammed into the side of its face and set its head ablaze. Aestelle looked around her and saw that the skeletal swordsmen had formed a semi-circle around the gur panther and stabbed and hacked down at her whilst she ferociously defended herself. Ragran swung his axe around into an already gaping wound on the other troll, slicing in with enough force for his blade to emerge out of the other side, severing the troll's foot entirely. The undead beast toppled over and crumpled down onto its back with a thud. The necromancer attempted yet again to conjure up a sorcerous attack but was again foiled when Valletto held up a hand to cancel out his powers. With a cry, Aestelle sprinted over to the line of skeletons attacking the panther and brutally hacked one down with an overhead strike to split apart its bony chest.

The necromancer looked frantically from one side of the town square to the other. One wounded troll, its face still ablaze with magical fire, lumbered after Aestelle whilst she cut down a second skeleton; the other tried to drag itself away as Ragran stood roaring victoriously above it, hacking his axe down into its back again and again. Dragging his black horse's head about by the reigns, the necromancer dug his heels into his steed's flanks and galloped away along the road leading to the north gate. Out of the corner of her eye, Aestelle saw Thesilar notch an arrow to her bow, draw back the string, and remain gracefully poised to release the deadly projectile as she stared to the north at the fleeing necromancer. At that range, against a rapidly moving target in the dark, Aestelle dismissed any chance of even Thesilar hitting her mark. The elf let fly.

The arrow disappeared into the darkness. A second later, the necromancer braced up in his saddle and then toppled from the speeding horse. His body lay still in the gutter by the roadside. Instantly, the zombie troll charging at Aestelle slowed to a plod and then stood still, staring vacantly at its feet. Likewise, the skeletons ceased to fight and stood all but motionless, their heads turning idly as their bodies swayed to-and-fro in the breeze. The gur panther wasted no time in leaping on another of the skeletal soldiers and mauling it violently. Tucking a strand of sweat-soaked hair behind her ear, Aestelle let out a sigh and looked around the decimated town square as the pain of her wounds suddenly became apparent. The last zombie troll sagged down to its knees and then fell lifelessly forward on what was left of its hideously burned, maimed face.

An absolute silence descended on the town square, save for the quiet crackling of flames from the two smoldering trolls and the crunching of bones as the gur panther lay calmly on her belly, gnawing on the skull of one of her victims. Thesilar lowered her bow and winked cockily in the direction of the dead necromancer. Valletto raised one hand to his head and collapsed back to sit on the debris of a destroyed building. Ragran grunted something and nodded in satisfaction. Z'akke was the first of them to smile.

Chapter Fourteen

There were still a few scant hours of darkness left before dawn by the time Khirius reached the village of Aphos. The small settlement slept silently; not a single light illuminated a window in any of the little collection of simple buildings, with only the gentle blow of the breeze and hoots of owls breaking the silence. There was not time enough to return to Torgias before sunrise, leaving Khirius at the mercy of the Coven for shelter from the sunlight during the day. Only now did he stop and think on his loyal servants; he did not recall seeing them at any point during the attack on the southern gatehouse or when he loitered afterward to watch Cane's death in the town square after his botched attempt to kill the five adventurers. Still, casualties amongst the townsfolk were so low they were as good as non-existent. Khirius had made sure of that.

Sensing the familiar, dark aura, Khirius turned in place by the edge of the trees surrounding the village. He saw a lithe, shadowy figure in the woods ahead. The hooded shape held up a hand.

"Come no closer," she whispered.

Khirius obeyed.

An owl hooted a few branches away from where the two vampires stared at each other.

"Where is Cane?" Annaxa demanded, her hoarse voice hushed.

"Dead."

"I am surprised. I do not like to be surprised."

"I'm not sure what happened," Khirius lied. "I attacked the south gate and Cane attacked the north, just as we discussed. I achieved the task you gave to me. I sensed Cane working to the north, and then... I sensed him no longer. He fell. He failed to achieve the task."

The hooded vampire stared at him, eyes hidden beneath the dark hood but still powerful in their invisible stare. Khirius felt the glare bore into him, probing at his intentions, just as he often did with mortals. He met the stare evenly. To turn away would be to admit to his dishonesty.

"What exactly did you achieve?" the female vampire whispered.

"You said to kill the adventurers," Khirius replied. "My instructions said there were five. I found four and killed them myself. Which one escaped, I do not know. Perhaps Cane killed the fifth before he fell."

"The four," Annaxa said, her tone severe, "describe them to me."

"Three men," Khirius recalled honestly if relying heavily on equivocation, "a mage and two swordsmen. And a dwarven warrior."

Again, the invisible eyes bored into him.

"They were not the ones I wanted dead."

Khirius continued to meet the icy glare.

"I never once told you that I was an assassin or a military leader," he said. "One adventurer is the same as any other to me. I had never heard of any of these apparently famous mercenaries before. I saw a group of them in the area of the attack that I had been charged with carrying out. I successfully eliminated them. I did the job. Your problem is with Cane, not me. Perhaps you could raise him and tell him that."

The use of aggressive humor seemed like a poor idea the very moment it escaped Khirius' dead lips. The intention was to demonstrate to Annaxa that he was not afraid of her, nor was he to be bullied or trifled with like a sycophantic serving boy. In actuality, the words sounded like a challenge, even to Khirius once he had spoken them. The icy glare from Annaxa continued to probe him.

"They were not the ones I wanted dead," she repeated, "and I rather think that you knew that."

Khirius narrowed his eyes. Even though Annaxa was entirely correct and justified in issuing the accusation, he found himself unaccustomed to confrontation. Anybody who knew who and what he was did not dare. He used that feeling of having his honor affronted to fuel his retort.

"And that is a different accusation entirely! I have carried out your dirty work for you despite being neither a soldier nor a murderer! I have carried it out to a high standard! You now stand before me and first accuse me of incompetence! And now of dishonesty!"

Annaxa took one step forward, gliding silently across the wet grass at the foot of the ancient trees. He could still feel her invisible eyes, hidden beneath the dark hood, fixed on his.

"You are without a home, without significant wealth and resources, and without political influence in this place," Annaxa warned in a hoarse whisper. "Don't push your luck."

Khirius recoiled, wincing at a faraway recollection triggered by her choice of words. He quickly dismissed it; now was not the time to reminisce on events of decades ago.

"Precisely! I have nothing! Absolutely nothing! This Coven is the only security I have, the only choice open to me if I wish to continue to exist! On the one hand, the Coven is my only way ahead, and I would risk my entire existence by betraying it! On the other, you have already explained in rather vulgar terms that I have lost everything, so that leaves me with nothing left to lose! Why would a man with nothing take a risk on his only path to a decent future?"

The owl suddenly shot into the dark sky and fluttered away. Silence then descended on the edge of the woods for a brief moment. A hiss emanated from Annaxa's hood. Khirius narrowed his eyes again. It was not a hiss. She was laughing.

"Everybody has something to lose," the vampire chuckled, "everybody. Even you. I assure you. You have something to lose. Now, go and rest in the village. I will think on whether I believe your version of events and whether I still trust you."

Khirius thought on a response but shook his head and turned to storm away from the other vampire. He took only a few paces before stopping and turning again to face her. She remained fixed in the same place, still staring at him.

"How will I know when you have made up your mind?" he demanded.

The lithe vampire folded her arms across her chest.

"You will know," she whispered.

***

The upper rim of the dawn sun sat perhaps an inch above the horizon, slowly chasing away the blues and blacks of the night to replace them with the dull, earthy colors of Torgias. The five adventurers and the gur panther lay in the silent, deserted courtyard of the Trade Wind Inn. Valletto lay sprawled out on top of one of the outdoor tables, quietly snoring. Aestelle sat at the next table along, silently flicking through the pages of what looked like a holy book whilst gently tousling the fur of the enormous panther that had fallen asleep on her feet. Z'akke tottered back and forth from inside the inn, bringing out armfuls of chopped wood to prepare a fire in the center of the courtyard. Ragran paced up and down, a perpetual grin plastered across his face as his eyes darted about manically, replaying the night's battle in his head.

Thesilar leaned against the edge of the inn's doorway, her hand clasped around the green stone hanging from her neck. It grew warmer. She smiled.

"Hurry up with that fire!" Ragran beamed. "I am now hungry!"

"This was my idea anyway!" Z'akke countered as he dropped another armful of quarter cut logs. "I thought it would be nice to have a dawn breakfast out here after we all survived such an odd night."

"Then hurry up and light it!" Ragran nodded frantically. "Do something useful with those flame powers of yours!"

Z'akke looked across at the battered, bandaged barbarian and narrowed his eyes.

"Where I am from, fire is sacred," the salamander said seriously. "It is at the core of the Three Kings as it is in the core of every salamander. To wield it is a gift and an honor. It most often comes with the sacred responsibility of taking the vows of priesthood, to use that power for worship and to slay evil. What you call pyromancy is a hallowed part of my people's culture. And you would reduce it to saving some time to prepare your breakfast?"

Ragran's shoulders slumped as he looked across the courtyard at the salamander mage-priest with utter disdain.

"Just shut up and light the fire, fool, I am hungry!"

Z'akke hissed and spat out an insult in his native tongue as he knelt down to arrange the logs. Surprised at the ferocity of his words, Thesilar let out a laugh. Ragran's head span around to face Thesilar.

"What?" he demanded. "What did the little gecko say? Z'akke, if you have dared…"

"Dared to what," Thesilar smirked, "insult Ragran the Mighty? Were you not there when he burnt the insides out of a zombie troll with a single touch? Z'akke can say whatever he wants, Ragran. You might beat him in an arm wrestle or a fistfight, but he can turn your entire innards into ash. So I would recommend less of the tough talk from you."

A huge, toothy smile lit up Z'akke's face as Ragran grumbled under his breath. The salamander held out a hand and the pile of logs burst into flames. Valletto sprang up from his slumber and looked around in alarm.

"We're making breakfast!" Z'akke greeted him cheerily.

Still grumbling, Ragran walked over to sit down next to Aestelle. The gur panther's eyes shot open and she raised herself to her feet, fixing him with a threatening stare and growling. Ragran jumped up and stepped slowly away.

"Alright… Panthra, no need to get upset."

"Seeba," Aestelle corrected, "her name is Seeba. I think that after the help she provided last night, the least we could do would be to call her by her name."

Seeba slowly settled to lie down again, her eyes still fixed on Ragran as Z'akke wandered back inside the inn to find some food to cook.

"What now?" Ragran exclaimed. "What's its problem with me?"

"Well," Aestelle said, carefully closing her book, "she doesn't like you. It's not personal. In the same way that mages can sense magical powers being used, gur panthers can sense divinity. They sense holy magic. It is one of the reasons why they permit members of the Sisterhood to be near them. The other is that... well, the bigger, fighty ones are the females, and to put it bluntly, they tend to hate men. You are both male and also don't have a single shred of a holy aura about you."

Ragran's face twisted into a scowl.

"That thing hates me because I'm a man! What about Valletto? Why isn't it growling at him?"

"She probably would if you weren't here," Aestelle said, "but she has picked you to... hate more, I suppose."

Ragran's scowl eased and then transformed into a smug smile. He looked across at Valletto, grinned, and nodded.

"It is alright, little man!" Ragran smirked. "The big cat hates me more because I am more of a man! These things can sense it, you see! More manly! Don't feel bad, wizard. Between the two of us, it was always going to be me."

Valletto wiped sleepily at his eyes and looked down at Seeba.

"Quite alright," he said, "you are more than welcome to that thing's attention."

Thesilar pushed herself off from the doorway and walked across to the fire, still careful to keep her distance from the gur panther.

"Learned elves that study animals have written volumes on creatures such as these," she said. "It is not my specialty, so my knowledge is somewhat limited. However, there are a fair few legends and tales floating around about men trying to tame these things. If the legends are true, and a mighty warrior is single-mindedly fixated with the notion of riding a gur panther into battle, there is but one way to remove that manly aura."

She pointed at Ragran's groin and made a chopping motion with her fingers. Ragran stared at her in disgust, his jaw open.

"Nothing is worth that," he finally managed, "nothing."

Z'akke returned to sit down next to the fire, producing a thin, metal stick from his pack, and after skewering a few hunks of meat, set about roasting them on the fire. Ragran found a skewer of his own and sat next to Z'akke, roasting his own chunks of food. Aestelle returned to her book. Thesilar walked across and sat on the bench next to where Valletto sat on the tabletop. The mage looked across at her, the barely perceptible wince in one eye betraying his suspicion of her motives to join him.

"What will you do now?" Thesilar asked him, her voice low to keep the conversation from the others. "You could easily go home. You have done far more than you set out to do."

Valletto hopped down from the table and sat on the bench opposite to Thesilar, planting his elbows on the tabletop and resting his chin in his hands.

"I don't think I can," he finally said, "not with all that happened last night. You see, the man I work for, he sent me here to investigate this cry of alarm over necromancy in Tarkis. From what you told me last night before it all became rather exciting and violent, there is a chance that Arteri the Plague is up that mountain. I need to send that information back to the capital and see what my orders are. It's a formality, really. I already know that I will be expected to carry on until Arteri's presence is confirmed as real or not."

"Are you sending that message today?" Thesilar asked.

Valletto nodded.

"I'll give it another hour or so. I am told that sending a message across the arcane plains is a complicated endeavor at the best of times but is made even more difficult if the recipient of the message is asleep."

Thesilar nodded. She looked across at where Aestelle read slowly through her Eloicon, her face a picture of concentration. The gur panther at her feet lay slumped with her head on her front paws, staring forlornly off into the distance. Ragran and Z'akke argued over the finer points of cooking meat over an open fire.

"It may not seem it," Thesilar said, half to herself, half in a hushed voice for only Valletto to hear, "but moments like these are what it is all about. For me, at least."

Valletto looked across quizzically.

"What do you mean?"

"This," Thesilar nodded at the others, "this... feeling, I suppose. When you are tired after a day of wasted energy – a long journey to nowhere, perhaps – then that feeling of exhaustion makes the whole world seem worse. I don't need to tell you that, you are a parent, after all. But... right now I am utterly, utterly exhausted. We have been up all night after a rather colossal battle for life and death. My eyes hurt, my limbs are heavy, but..."

Thesilar tailed off for a moment as she searched for the words to try to explain the feeling of contentment she currently enjoyed.

"We all survived," she continued. "From what Aestelle said about the fighting at the south gatehouse, the loss of life was remarkably small. We sit here, outside this temporary home of ours, alive and well having done something... fantastic. Something truly incredible. Something... good. And to be here at this moment, exhausted, battered, and bruised, with these people who all mean so much to me... moments like this are rare. Moments like this when one can revel in the utter exhaustion having all survived together to overcome evil... I am truly happy."

Valletto issued a small but sincere seeming smile at her words.

"Have you told them that?" he asked.

Thesilar raised an eyebrow quizzically.

"You said that these people here with you, they mean a lot to you. Have you told them that?"

Thesilar let out a short, quiet laugh. She suppressed her reactive response to tell him not to be ridiculous. She then thought on his words. These were all impressive people. She had known Ragran for the longest, and in many ways, it was sad to see him growing older before her very eyes, slowly fading from the legend of the Howling Peaks that he had become over the years. Seeing him now, so animated and full of life after the battle, was like a look back at the man he was in his youth. It made her equally happy to see Z'akke growing in confidence, standing up to the boisterous barbarian as they argued next to the fire. Of course, she had always known he had the potential to become a powerful sorcerer. She had never expected to see him destroy a zombie troll with a single attack, even with the aid of a potent energy crystal. Then there was Aestelle, a woman who had once been something between her apprentice and the younger sister she never had. It pained her to admit that Aestelle was fully capable in her own right now, beyond needing Thesilar's counsel and guidance.

"Yes," Thesilar agreed quietly. "Yes, perhaps I should tell them. That is rather overdue."

Valletto stood up and dusted down his dark tunic.

"Well," he said to the others, "I have managed to ruin our plans by sleeping through our sunrise together, so I might as well go and get an hour's sleep before I report in to my superior at the Duma."

"You're not having breakfast with us?" Z'akke asked from where he perched next to the fire, waiving a meat-covered stick in Valletto's direction in what Thesilar could only assume was supposed to be an appetizing gesture.

Valletto shook his head.

"Is it because of all the burnt bits of troll you saw in the town square?" Z'akke asked.

"It wasn't," Valletto said, "but I think that perhaps it is now."

"I think I shall get some sleep, too." Aestelle stood up. "A couple of hours and then I will be leaving to take this girl back to her home at the abbey."

Seeba looked up at Aestelle dolefully. Aestelle smiled.

"Half an hour," Thesilar said, walking over to crouch next to Ragran by the fire, "just half an hour. Let's all have something to eat and then we can go and get some sleep. We will all be able to figure out how best to proceed after food and rest."

Valletto looked across at Aestelle. Aestelle shrugged. The two walked over to sit around the fire as Z'akke let out a happy hiss and a stream of smoke from his nostrils to see the whole group together. Seeba crawled across and flopped down between Aestelle and Z'akke, eyeing Ragran suspiciously as the first round of food was passed around.

***

Aestelle woke with a start, one hand reaching for the knife beneath her pillow. She sensed that same dark presence again. She sat bolt upright in bed and cast her eyes around the room. The fire still glowed a warm orange and her greatsword sat propped up against the side of the four-poster bed, within easy reach. The sensation, if it had in fact ever been there and was not any more than a bad dream, was gone. Aestelle walked across to the bay windows, stepping silently and carefully past where Seeba lay asleep at the foot of the bed. She peeled the heavy curtains back by an inch to peer outside. Her plan of catching a brief couple of hours of sleep had not worked at all; the setting sun marked the time out as evening, signifying that she had in fact slept through the entire day. The courtyard outside was still empty; the hanging lights from the walls and the path leading to the inn remained unlit. Torgias was still deserted.

Deducing that the others may be awake and looking for an evening meal, Aestelle hauled on her clothes with the intention of heading down to the inn's main rooms. She picked up her leather vest, saw the deep cut down the back from the previous night's battles, and elected to wear a silk shirt from her wardrobe in its stead. Thanks to her oft-used healing magic, she was left with only a few superficial cuts and some ugly bruises; her divinity healing had been used mainly on herself and Seeba. Thesilar and Z'akke, as always it seemed, escaped without any significant injuries. Valletto used some healing potions of his own. Ragran insisted on having his wounds stitched – he wanted the scars. Aestelle was about to leave the room when she saw her reflection in the mirror.

"Good gosh, no," she inhaled deeply, "that will not do."

After washing her face, she set about the long, painstaking process of arranging every last strand of hair perfectly and applying her various powder and salve makeups. She suppressed a laugh as the enormous panther rolled over in her sleep and let out a human sounding snore. Then she saw the letter that had been slid beneath her door. Picking it up, she immediately noted the high-quality paper. Unfolding it, she read the simple note.

Meet me in the stables. K.

Aestelle placed the letter down on her dresser. Strange notes sent by admirers, requesting secluded nocturnal meetings, had been a regular part of her life ever since leaving the Sisterhood; but something about the note left her uncomfortable. She buckled her belt around her leather leggings and slid her two throwing knives into their sheaths at the small of her back before grabbing her sword and scabbard. Holding the sheathed weapon by one side, she made her way out of the master bedchamber block and toward the stables.

The agitated sound of horses left alone, unattended and unfed in the stables, somehow left her slightly more comforted. The red sun disappeared beneath the horizon, dulling the colors of the day and leaving the cold, silent world in a lifeless palette of dull, half color. Aestelle sensed the dark aura before she even reached the stable doors. She opened them and peered inside, her right hand moving to the handle of her sword whilst her left clutched the scabbard tightly.

"There will be no need for that," a familiar voice said quietly from the shadows.

Aestelle turned to regard a tall figure in the corner of the stable. The vampire was clad in the same attire as on the night he had broken into her room; a rich tunic and a long cloak, both in black. Yet, despite the clothing, he looked entirely different. The thin, aging monster was replaced with a tall, broad-shouldered man of perhaps twenty-five years of age. His skin – what little she could see of it in the near darkness – was smooth white and without flaw. His black hair was neatly arranged. His features were well-defined and handsome.

"You look… better," Aestelle said, one foot holding the door open and her hand still on her sword.

The vampire took a pace toward her. Aestelle drew her sword an inch from its scabbard.

"As I said, there is no need for that," the vampire said passively. "In two hundred years, I have only ever killed one woman. And I assure you, she deserved it."

"Well!" Aestelle let out a brief laugh. "And they say in the capital that the age of the gentleman is dead and gone! A vampire that does not kill women! Not unless he decides they *really* deserve it."

"There is no need to be facetious," the vampire said as he drifted closer. "We are allies, after all. Could you put the sword down? You are making me… uneasy."

Aestelle stared at the vampire as he paced closer. Remembering their ability to hypnotize their prey, she quickly diverted her gaze.

"Allies? I do not know much of the undead. But I do know a little. Tell me – are you now seemingly four decades younger than on our last encounter because you have dined on the blood of the living? And ended somebody's life by doing so?"

The vampire stopped, only two or three paces away from her.

"Would you become angry with any predator for killing merely to live themselves? I kill because I have to. You seem perfectly comfortable in the company of those who kill for money. The moral pulpit you preach from is built on rather unsteady foundations."

"I kill monsters!" Aestelle snapped. "You kill miners defending their homes and families! Don't you dare judge me!"

Aestelle immediately regretted her confrontational words. This creature could end her life in the blink of an eye. She reminded herself that she would do better not to antagonize him.

"I killed one miner," the vampire shrugged, taking a pace closer again, "and... a few amateur adventurers. I am genuinely sorry for the miner, and for the handful of his companions that were killed by the skeletons I commanded. But this was a simple and obvious case of inflicting a minor sacrifice – if you pardon the pun – for a greater good. I needed the attack at the south gate to look convincing until I threw it away so that the townsfolk could escape. As for those adventurers... no, they take gold to kill. They knew the dangers of the life they chose. I feel no pity for them."

Aestelle took in a breath. She slid her sword back into its scabbard but kept her right hand on the handle.

"Why have you summoned me down here?" she demanded.

The vampire took another pace, now only inches away. She could make out the perfection of his white skin, lacking even visible pores. Worse, she was close enough to see that he did not breath. The realization brought goose bumps to her skin. She shuddered when he placed a hand across hers and gently moved it off her sword handle.

"To see you again," he replied, "to talk to you. To make sure you understood why I did what I did at the south gate. And to tell you what I know about the events of the past few hours. So that you know I am on your side."

The vampire took a step back. Aestelle carefully moved one hand behind her back and onto the handle of one of her throwing knives.

"And what do you know?" Aestelle asked.

"The population of this town is already on its way back," the vampire said. "As providence would have it, a detachment of legion soldiers on route from Tmoskai to the City of the Golden Horn were diverted due to flooded roads. They encountered the fleeing people of Torgias and are escorting them back as we speak."

"They would have been back here soon enough, regardless," Aestelle replied. "How is this information going to assist me in stopping Arteri from rising from his tomb?"

The vampire tilted his head to one side.

"I doubt very much that it will," he said, "but given how precarious my position within the Coven is at the moment after assisting you and your friends, I am afraid that is all I know. Besides, you cannot blame me for wanting to see you again."

Aestelle leaned against the doorway, one hand clutching the center of her sword scabbard, the other ready with the throwing knife behind her back.

"You seem a little confused," she sneered, "about comparing reality to those rather turgid and puerile plays that are performed on the stages of theaters in the capital for the benefit of the rich, overly romantic, and stupid. Let me assure you that there is absolutely nothing romantic about waking up in the middle of the night to find that a two-hundred-year-old undead killer is watching you sleep."

The vampire smiled.

"Shall I just bring flowers next time?"

Aestelle exhaled and shook her head. She had attracted an army of admirers over the last ten years – rich, powerful men with titles; famous and deadly adventurers – but never something so sinister and intimidating as what stood before her.

"Next time, prove whose side you are on by coming here with some information I can actually use," she said, taking a step out of the barn. "Next time, tell me something that will help me stop your Coven resurrecting that evil bastard in the mountains. Now if you will excuse me, I think that concludes this meeting."

"Of course. Good night."

The vampire bowed graciously as Aestelle closed the door to the stables. She walked briskly away, afraid to look back in case the deadly creature was following her. However, the dark feeling very soon receded. Nonetheless, Aestelle headed straight to the inn's bar, where she was relieved to find Ragran and Valletto. She headed straight past them to retrieve a bottle of wine from behind the bar and poured herself a glass.

"You expecting trouble?" Ragran remarked, nodding at her sword.

"Nothing I cannot handle," Aestelle replied.

***

The town square was already looking remarkably better by the time Valletto and Z'akke arrived at the entrance to the town hall. The population of Torgias had drifted back in through the southern gates and by boat to the docks in small groups over the past two days and, aside from the burnt tax office and the demolished town square, life almost immediately returned to normal. Valletto had at least succeeded in contacting Saffus at the Duma – a simple transmitted message of *'possible return of Arteri, Tarkis.'* The answer was predictable: *'investigate further. Find confirmation.'* However, the threat by itself would be enough to concern Saffus, Valletto was sure of that. He would be very surprised if a military force of some description had not already been mobilized and dispatched to lend them aid.

Little else had occurred since then. Aestelle departed to return the gur panther to the Sisterhood. Thesilar left to head back to the mountains, keen to explore the area around Mount Ekansu to discover more about the threat they faced. Naturally, Valletto, Ragran, and Z'akke had all offered to accompany her. Quite rightly, she said that considering she was merely scouting the area in secret and not entering the mountain again, she would work better alone. That left Valletto, Ragran, and Z'akke alone for a day or so, until they were summoned to the town hall. The summons came in the form of a messenger who appeared at the Trade Wind Inn, solemnly declaring that the mayor of Torgias wished to speak to the adventurers involved in the fight in the town square. Ragran had refused to answer the summons.

"Do you think this is about a reward?" Z'akke smiled eagerly as they crossed the square, raising his voice over the banging of hammers and sawing of wood as carpenters, joiners, and builders set about repairing the damage to the surrounding buildings.

"Somehow I doubt it," Valletto remarked dryly.

It seemed nothing short of a miracle that the town hall still stood. The top two floors had escaped relatively intact, but the ground floor was missing its entire front wall where one of the frenzied trolls had smashed through it in a bid to chase down Thesilar, causing parts of the floors above and even the roof to collapse. Under a cool, gray sky, perhaps a dozen builders worked away at shoring up the damage with wooden posts to prevent the entire building from collapsing whilst a more permanent solution was carried out. Horses and carts came to and fro from the town square, dropping off logs and planks for the surrounding buildings. A few men-at-arms – professional soldiers of the Hegemon's legion – were visible dotted around the square. They had, no doubt, come in when escorting the population back from their brief, rural exodus to the south.

"You there!"

Valletto turned and saw two figures standing by the stone steps leading up to the town hall. One was a tall, thin man in dark robes and a black, wide-brimmed hat that starkly contrasted his icy, white hair. His stoop marked him out as elderly, in poor health, or both. The second man was a little shorter, a lot fatter, and with a white-gray moustache that extended past his ruddy cheeks to join his short hair. He wore a long coat of red and tall boots over his pale leggings.

"You!" the man in the red coat repeated. "Come over here!"

Valletto and Z'akke made their way over to the two men by the town hall.

"Are you the ones responsible for all of this mess? This catastrophe?" the whiskered man demanded.

"Well, of course not," Z'akke replied, his scaly face twisted in confusion, "this was done by zombie trolls. Everybody knows that. We are neither undead, nor are we trolls. I'm a salamander. Trolls are much bigger."

Valletto choked on a barely suppressed laugh.

"Don't play funny with me!" the rotund man growled. "I have it on good authority that this... calamity was caused by a fight between undead and a band of barrowers! Adventurers staying at the Trade Wind Inn! Are you responding to my summons?"

"Yes, that's right." Valletto cleared his throat. "Am I to assume that you are the mayor?"

Valletto noted two town guards walk over from the side of the town hall, their halberds held ready.

"You are damned right I'm the mayor!" the tubby man exploded. "I am out of town on business for four days, and I come back to this? I am well aware that the barrowing industry brings in adventurers such as yourselves to this region, and I am aware of the profit it once generated some years ago! But whilst barrowing is legal, it has never once resulted in characters such as yourselves bringing monsters back from the tombs and barrows to destroy half a town!"

Valletto glanced across at Z'akke. When their escapades were described in those terms, it sounded a lot worse than it had felt in the moments after their victory in that very square. Valletto let out a sigh. Sadly, there was some truth in the mayor's words.

"The locals seem to think that you are some sort of heroes for slaying monsters and keeping the loss of life to an absolute minimum. Let me be perfectly clear in spelling out to you that my opinion on the matter is somewhat contrary! This place was perfectly peaceful and intact when I left it! And all evidence I've heard seems to point to this whole misadventure having never occurred if you were not here! If you have brought danger to innocent people that has resulted in loss of life, you will both be facing a long term in prison! At best!"

Valletto nodded grimly and winced. The mayor was entirely correct. From what Thesilar had told him prior to the battle, this was all about drawing them out. *They* had brought the danger to Torgias. Their presence had led to the loss of innocent lives. But Valletto was firmly of the opinion that none of that was their fault, and he would be damned if he would swing for it. He reached inside his tunic and produced his written orders from Saffus.

"My name is Captain Valletto of Auron, Deputy Senior Battle Mage of the 2nd Legion," Valletto said formally. "I am here under the orders of Grand Mage Saffus of Aigina, Advisor Primus of the Arcane to the Duma. I am not a barrower or amateur adventurer. I am here as an agent of the Duma, carrying out an official investigation. Here is my written authority."

The mayor snatched the letter, his eyes still fixed on Valletto's for a moment until he read through the words on the yellowed parchment. His lips curled up into a sneer. He passed the letter wordlessly on to the tall, thin man in black stood next to him.

"So you are claiming that this is a military matter, Captain?" the mayor demanded.

"No, not at all. It is an investigation ordered by a senior official representing the Duma's authority on matters of internal security. The loss of life here is regrettable, truly regrettable. As is the damage to property. But all of this comes at the behest of the Duma. This is nothing to do with private profiteering from looting barrows. There can be no accusation of law breaking or accountability for loss."

The mayor looked up at the tall man in the wide-brimmed hat. He raised an eyebrow and nodded. The mayor's nose wrinkled in frustration.

"And what about... *that*?" the mayor pointed at Z'akke.

"I'm Z'akke!" the salamander smiled a friendly greeting.

"Are you telling me that... *that* is an official representative of the Duma?!" the mayor demanded. "And you, sir, you address me as 'my lord!'"

"Thank you, but no," Z'akke replied. "You don't have to call me sir, but you are not my lord, so I won't call you 'my lord.'"

"*You*," the mayor snapped, "are as good as nothing here! Lower than common peasantry! You will..."

"This individual," Valletto interjected, "is Z'akke, a mage-priest from the Three Kings. His religion is officially recognized by the Hegemon, which means that he is not a peasant. He is a foreign religious official. He does not have to address you by your recognized marks of respect as a Basilean official."

The portly mayor opened and closed his mouth several times before he managed to string together another sentence.

"You expect me to believe that he is a priest?!"

"I can prove it to you, if you want." Z'akke shrugged, holding out a clawed hand as a small, yellow flame flickered in his palm.

"That won't be necessary." The tall, thin man in the black hat smiled a predatory grin. "Mayor Grennias, if you would be so kind as to give me a moment or two with our friends here."

The mayor looked across at the tall man and then turned to walk quickly down the town hall steps, muttering obscenities to himself. The white-haired man fixed his smile on Valletto and Z'akke.

"Captain," he began, "that was an impressive display of legal knowledge. It was even accurate in a few parts. My name is Turius, I am the magistrate of this area and the Duma's official representative for the Tarkis region."

Valletto physically felt the color draining from his face.

"Your letter of authority and your mitigation for your actions here actually hold some water," the aging man continued, pausing to cough into a handkerchief, "and knowing the political power your master Saffus holds, I would imagine that you are on fairly safe ground. However, perhaps not so much for one or two of your friends. Now, the two of you I am not familiar with. The famed Ragran and Thesilar are familiar to me, and the lovely Aestelle I know really rather well. So... given that you have played your legal card in a rather clumsy manner, allow me to do the same but with a comprehensive knowledge of the law of the land behind me. As is my legal right as magistrate to know, the two of you are going to tell me everything – and I do mean *everything* – about what has happened here in the last few days."

Chapter Fifteen

Her black cloak billowing out in the wind, Aestelle stared silently down the rocky path at the cold, gray complex of buildings that had been her home for nearly twenty years. The abbey of the Order of the Penitent and the Devoted sat at the bottom of the River Naxi valley, winding in between the peaks near the eastern extremities of the Mountains of Tarkis, some way west of north from Torgias. Being situated in low ground made it in many ways less than ideal as a military installation; the view of the surrounding lands was severely limited so lookout posts high up in the surrounding peaks provided any warning of a potential threat. However, the sheer slope of the peaks was so aggressive that an attack from the higher ground was absolutely impossible, which did at least provide protection to the abbey's northern and southern sides.

The reason for the abbey's poor choice of defensive position lay in the fact that it did not start its existence as a military site. When the abbey was first built some three hundred years before, its purpose was to provide shelter for pilgrims heading to the base of Mount Kolosu and to train sisters in divinity magic to lend assistance to the region by curing the sick and injured. Those noble beginnings were still evident in the smooth, elegant architecture of the abbey's white stone main building and the double spires blossoming up from the abbey's east and west sides. The beauty of the old building was ruined by the more recent additions around it; blocks of dormitory cells made up of simple, gray stone for the hundreds of aspirants, novices, and confirmed sisters were arranged haphazardly around the site to take advantage of areas of flat ground in the valley. A curved wall ran around the perimeter of the entire site, dominated by a heavily fortified gatehouse and guardroom, and punctuated at intervals with circular guard towers.

"Welcome home," Aestelle remarked quietly, half to Seeba and half to herself.

The gur panther looked up at her silently. Aestelle tried to smile down to the animal but managed only a grim smirk from one side of her mouth. Their journey together over the past two days had been mainly in silence, with Aestelle voicing her thoughts aloud to the powerful creature whenever she stopped to think about Joselin and remembered the strong bond that Seeba no doubt shared with her former master. The bond whose loss the deadly creature no doubt mourned, in her own way.

Aestelle walked down the winding path threading through the jagged rocks toward the abbey. The River Naxi threaded in from the south; the supply of fresh water for the abbey and, for some of each winter, a near freezing source of opportunities for both harsh training and punishments. The rocky plains to either side of the path slowly morphed into more gentle fields; the training grounds she had spent years in, learning to fight, track, ride, and navigate. The fields now were empty; a sure sign that a significant part of the order was away on campaign, fighting the Hegemon's enemies in some far-flung corner of Pannithor.

The gatehouse loomed toward Aestelle as she walked closer, Seeba padding along the path next to her.

"You were a good companion," Aestelle remarked as they approached. "You are very good in a fight and you don't talk much. I shall be sorry to see you go."

Up ahead, Aestelle saw the open doors of the gatehouse and the fork in the road leading up to it; one path heading straight inside whilst the other squeezed through a narrow tunnel built around the southern tip of the perimeter wall. Two sisters, resplendent in their blue surcoats worn atop their white tunics and leggings, watched as Aestelle approached with Seeba. Both held long-bladed spears. Aestelle saw one of the women turn and shout something through the short tunnel leading through the gatehouse. She could not blame them in being alarmed. An armed woman, clad in black leather, was at their doorstep with an animal that was clearly identifiable as one of their own war panthers.

"Halt!" the taller of the two sisters called as Aestelle arrived within a few paces. "Identify yourself!"

Aestelle tutted and looked down at the woman. Broad-shouldered, her hair hidden behind a hood of blue – a rather traditional, even outdated choice of garb for sisters that stemmed from a time when a woman openly displaying her hair was considered sensual and provocative – her smooth face looked barely out of its infancy.

"Go and fetch a grown up, girl," Aestelle sighed, "I don't have time for your shit."

The shorter sister, a stockier woman with flame-colored hair, took a pace out and glowered up at Aestelle.

"You explain to me why you have turned up at our gates with one of our panthers, and I shall decide whether you warrant an audience with a higher ranking sister or the butt of my spear."

"Is that right?" Aestelle shook her head in derision. "I find it very hard to believe that you would openly spurn the twelfth rule of your Order's charter which, unless things have changed a great deal around here, is also the second rule of standing guard at these gates. Something about hospitality to all visitors? Never drawing a weapon without good cause? Or do you need re-educating on your own damn rules?"

Before the astounded sister could reply, a familiar voice from Aestelle's past rang out from the short tunnel beneath the gatehouse.

"Aestelle?!"

Aestelle looked across. She saw a thin figure cloaked in blue approach from beneath the gate, her brown-blonde hair crowning a round, kindly face. Aestelle's eyes widened in amazement as she recognized the approaching woman.

"Claudia?!"

"Senior Sister!" the shorter of the two guards stood rigidly to attention. "This woman has approached us in a hostile..."

Claudia held up a hand.

"Hush," she commanded, before walking over to Aestelle with a rapidly growing smile. "You... you have not aged a single day! You are exactly as you were when you left!"

Aestelle wished she could repay that same compliment to Claudia, but the lines around the woman's eyes spoke of years of hardship since they last crossed paths. Since the day Aestelle flung down her blue surcoat and stormed out of the very gate they now stood beneath.

"You... look well, Claudia." Aestelle smiled sincerely. "I have sort of... blinked and missed ten years, it seems."

Claudia gave Aestelle a warm embrace that she tentatively and awkwardly reciprocated.

"What brings you here?" Claudia beamed, stepping back. "It must be something important to drag you all the way back to this place!"

Aestelle glanced down at Seeba, who flopped down to lie next to her feet and rested her chin on her front paws. Claudia looked down at the panther. Her smile faded away almost instantly.

"That's... that's Sister Superior Joselin's panther."

Aestelle took Claudia by the arm and guided her a few paces away from the two guards.

"There is something going on in Mount Ekansu, Claudia," Aestelle explained in a hushed voice, "something important. I need to speak to the abbess."

Claudia looked up at Aestelle with a grim resolve.

"Did you find Joselin?" she demanded. "What happened?"

"I was... with her when she passed," Aestelle exhaled. "The others with her were already dead. Joselin did not have long left. She told me to bring Seeba back here and alert the abbess about what she found."

"Then there is no time to lose." Claudia swallowed. "Follow me. Leave the panther at the guardroom for now."

Aestelle followed Claudia through the gates and into the abbey's courtyard. She removed her bow, quiver, and cloak, and threw them across to one of the sisters by the guardroom before striding along the familiar stone pathway threading through the interior training grounds and dormitory buildings. Responding to a snapped command from Claudia, Seeba ambled grumpily off to wait by the doorway to the guardroom. The path continued up a shallow incline, past where the River Naxi cut through the complex itself. Aestelle let out a short laugh and shook her head when she saw one young sister stood up to her waist in the freezing water, shivering and gritting her teeth as she held a heavy iron bar high above her head. Aestelle remembered that punishment well.

A group of ten adolescent novices practiced swordplay in a small field to the right of the path; further along to the left, a younger group of girls ran lengths of another field, stopping at each end to endure press ups and sit ups as directed by the yells of a supervising Senior Sister. Curious eyes from the young novices and the experienced instructors alike stopped to watch Aestelle as she walked purposefully past with Claudia.

"I would imagine it is more than a little strange being back here," Claudia commented.

"Nothing I cannot cope with," Aestelle replied.

"You look well. Sort of... how I imagined you would end up looking once you left."

"I suppose that is a compliment?" Aestelle asked warily.

Claudia flashed a friendly smile. The pair arrived at the main gates to the old abbey, which Claudia pushed open. The immaculately cut grass of the central square practically glowed green in the afternoon sunshine whilst long shadows were cast on the cloisters running to either side by the tall, smooth pillars holding up the ceiling running around the central square. A group of novices, barely ten years old, stopped midway along one of the arched corridors to stand aside for Aestelle, looking nervously up at her in silence as she paced past them, towering over them. She followed Claudia along the familiar, well-trodden path of any sister with a history of discipline problems that led to one inevitable end at the northern tip of the top floor: the abbess' office.

"Best you wait here for a moment," Claudia nodded before knocking on the door and awaiting permission to enter the office.

Aestelle stood silently in the corridor, her toned arms folded. Sunlight poured in through the windows along one side of the long corridor, illuminating the stone floor with pools of light at regular intervals. She remembered standing at this very spot, several times before. Most importantly, she stood here awaiting judgment after the accusations against her that led to her being ordered to carry out the painful, degrading and humiliating Fourth and Fifth Steps. Aestelle found her heart pounding. She remembered standing here in silence, facing her accuser on the other side of the corridor as they waited to be summoned to present their arguments before the stern face of Abbess Vita. Her accuser on both occasions had been Joselin. Aestelle smiled bitterly as she recalled Joselin's words.

"I never hated you."

"Lying bitch," Aestelle murmured under her breath, mentally calculating how old Abbess Vita must be by now. She would definitely remember Aestelle, of that she was sure.

The door swung open again. Aestelle suddenly felt nauseous with anxiety.

"Come in," a voice commanded.

Aestelle walked into the same simple, sparse office she had been ushered into by the kindly Prioress Marilla when she was but five years old. Somehow, she still vaguely remembered a few details of that evening. In broad daylight, however, the office somehow seemed even colder. The same featureless, wooden desk sat facing the door, sunlight shining through the window behind almost as if by design to force visitors to the office to wince and turn away from the glory of the heavens as it assaulted their vision.

The abbess looked up from behind her desk. It was not Vita. Aestelle froze in place as she recognized Decima. Wrinkles now regularly punctuated the dark-skinned woman's unyielding face, and a few wisps of gray hair escaped from the rim of the white shawl wrapped around her head. Conditioned by years of training, Aestelle moved to instinctively bow in respect to the abbess. Then she remembered who she was and why she left.

"Hello, Decima." Aestelle flashed a cocksure grin, deliberately avoiding using the formalities of her lofty title. "I'm back."

"Senior Sister Aestelle," the iron-tough, veteran sister leaned forward across her desk, "what in the Seven Circles of the Abyss are you wearing?"

Aestelle glanced down at her salacious attire. She forced a broader grin, despite her rising discomfort and queasiness at her situation.

"This? It actually provides more protection than what little armor this place ever gave me. But more importantly, it shows off my curves."

"You haven't changed at all," Decima sneered, "not one bit. All right, Claudia. You can leave us."

The shorter woman flashed a brief, encouraging smile to Aestelle and then left the office, carefully closing the door behind her.

"Be seated." The abbess gestured to the chair in front of her desk.

"You sure?" Aestelle planted her hands on her hips. "You don't want me to stand to attention so that you can yell at me?"

"Just pack away your petulant attitude for five minutes, act your age, and sit down!" Decima snapped. "We have important things to talk about. I would have thought that by now you would have grown out of the adolescent rebellion phase of childhood. What are you now? Thirty? Thirty-one?"

Gritting her teeth, Aestelle obediently sat down but took the time to take her extravagant sword scabbard from her back, dump it on Decima's desk with a loud clatter, and then sprawl back lazily in the chair and cross her legs.

"Where is Abbess Vita?" Aestelle sneered. "Did she get bored of bullying children?"

"She died," Decima said seriously, "three years ago."

Aestelle let out a gasp. She sat up straight in her chair, the smile wiped from her face.

"I... I am sorry..." she stammered.

"I know you are, Aestelle. You always had a good heart, but it appears you still have a gift for speaking before thinking. Am I to assume that your presence here with Sister Superior Joselin's gur panther means that the Sister Superior is now dead?"

"Yes," Aestelle replied quietly, the clawing at her gut intensifying, "she was killed along with her sisters fighting against the undead in Mount Ekansu. I... I could not have stopped that. I could not save her."

The abbess raised one eyebrow.

"I never implied that you could."

"Well shit, Decima! It sodding well feels like you are!" Aestelle found herself growling uncontrollably.

Decima shrugged apathetically.

"Is swearing supposed to... shock me somehow? Am I supposed to be impressed by your complete lack of manners and propriety? Is the hardened mercenary woman of war sat before me meant to have me quaking, or perhaps thinking 'heavens, Decima! Aestelle turned out as tough as old boots after all! Perhaps we were all wrong about her!'"

For a second time, Aestelle found herself disarmed by the older woman's words and sank back into her chair, folding her arms.

"Then let us move on," the abbess continued, "we need to discuss what Sister Superior Joselin was investigating and what the next step will be."

Aestelle blinked in surprise.

"That's it?" she demanded. "Joselin is dead and we shall just... move past that without so much as a second thought?"

"Is this the part where you will pretend that she was a close friend to you? That you are deeply wounded by her passing?"

"Well you damned well should be!" Aestelle snarled, leaping to her feet and planting her hands on the abbess' desk to lean across. "She gave her entire life for this Order! That should be worth a moment to you, if you can manage it!"

Decima met Aestelle's stare without flinching.

"There will be time to mourn her passing and pay respect later."

"Because callously skipping five minutes of sentiment will make *all* the difference in saving the world from evil!" Aestelle drawled sarcastically.

Decima shot to her feet.

"Senior Sister Aestelle! You seem to have forgotten yourself! Sit down and shut up!"

Instinctively, despite the passage of so many years, Aestelle moved to sit, as commanded. She stopped herself halfway and stood to fold her arms.

"Piss off, Decima!" she snapped. "I left this Order for a reason! So that narrow-minded idiots like you would not be able to tell me what to do! And that is twice you have referred to me by a rank that I do not hold!"

Decima's eyes narrowed, and the slightest of smiles tugged at her lips.

"Oh, but you do. You see, when you stormed off in your petulant display of angst and attention seeking, you did not follow proper procedure. You are still listed as a sister of this Order. You never left."

Aestelle's jaw dropped. She shrunk back, an instant pain rising in her gut. She opened her mouth to speak but only managed to let out a gasp of surprise. Sinking back into the chair, she stared straight ahead through the window behind Decima.

"Back to the task in hand, then," the abbess continued. "You will no doubt..."

"Wait," Aestelle held up a hand, "that is absolute nonsense! I voiced my intentions perfectly clearly the day I left! There was absolutely no room for ambiguity! I told you all quite, quite clearly that I was done! I even tore off the bloody colors and threw them at somebody! So no, I am not still a part of this Order! And even if I were, as I recall, you lot demoted me from Senior Sister! Twice!"

The middle-aged nun sat down opposite Aestelle and eyed her coolly. Aestelle attempted to meet the icy stare but failed. What if Decima was right? She could not be! Aestelle could choose to leave the Order, surely? Others had in the past.

"Aestelle," Decima spoke calmly, "you were promoted to Senior Sister the day you took command of my unit after I was wounded and led them in battle. You were then demoted after disgracing yourself and the Order as part of being sentenced to endure the Fourth Step..."

"Disgraced?!" Aestelle growled. "Joselin came crying in here to Abbess Vita to tell tales on me for what? Sharing a table with three legion soldiers who were having a harmless drink?"

"Oh, this again!" Decima gesticulated with both of her arms. "Aestelle! You were guilty! And you were not given the Fourth Step for one isolated incident! You had a long history of ill-discipline and insubordination! You were then, as a final, *final* act of poor judgment, caught drinking with men in an alehouse whilst disgracing your uniform!"

"I was drinking water!" Aestelle jumped back to her feet and pointed in accusation at the abbess. "And I was not disgracing my uniform! I made a mistake in my interpretation of the regulations!"

"You were flashing your thighs around like a common harlot!"

"I thought the rules said that in hot weather, uniform could be removed from the upper *limbs...*"

"The clothing regulations *clearly* state that in summer, under a Sister Superior's direction, uniform may be relaxed from the upper *arms!* You *knew* that!"

Again, Aestelle slumped back into her chair, defeated. She remembered the incident well. She was telling the truth; when Joselin caught her drinking with the soldiers, she did have water in her tankard. But Decima was entirely correct about her deliberately choosing to misinterpret the clothing regulations. But she was nineteen, momentarily free from the abbey, and enjoyed the rare opportunity for attention.

"After you were promoted back to Senior Sister for a second time," Decima continued, "when your actions then resulted in being sentenced to the Fifth Step, you know full well I tried to defend you. And I still do believe that you did the right thing. But I was overruled. But the Fifth Step is different. It is all or nothing. If a sister survives the

Fifth Step to return to the Order, the accusation is dropped and she is proven innocent. If you had stayed around long enough instead of stomping off like a sulking child, you would have heard that your rank had been restored."

Aestelle shook her head in frustration before turning away to stare into the far corner of the austere chamber.

"You are completely missing the point," she hissed. "This is nothing to do with rank! You have decided that I am still a part of this Order! That is *my* choice to make!"

"Abbess Vita decided that," Decima replied, "and if I were you, I would take that as a great compliment. After you turned your back on everything this Order did for you, she still gave you the option of coming home. She entered you in the Order's records as an auxiliary. You are on indefinite leave of absence from the Order, but you still retain your rank. That way, whatever debaucherous existence you have chosen for yourself in the last decade cannot be held against you. To a point, at least. You are effectively in reserve. If you choose, you could put on the uniform right now and pick up exactly where you left off."

"What, a whipping girl being terrorized by the likes of you?" Aestelle sneered.

Decima raised her hands to her face for a moment and took in a deep breath. Aestelle shook her head, the sickness in her stomach still gnawing away. The surrealness of being in the abbey for real rather than as part of one of many nightmares she had suffered over the years was bad enough, but now came the realization that, in a horrifically misplaced gesture of what was supposed to be kindness, she was actually still technically a part of the Order of the Penitent and the Devoted. It was a questionable decision by the previous abbess. Aestelle bit her lip. Abbess Vita being dead and gone seemed to be just another part of the waking nightmare.

"This is a conversation for another day," Decima finally said. "I am not wasting any more time going over old ground with you. A decade, Aestelle, an entire decade apart, and it has taken about five minutes for you to remind me why everybody here couldn't stand you and your petulant attitude! Now put all of that to one side! We need to discuss Mount Ekansu."

Aestelle turned to snap an angry retort, content that she did not need to fear any reprisals for insulting or swearing at the abbess, but stopped herself. This could go on all day. It would achieve nothing.

"There is an organization," Decima began, "the Coven."

"Yes, I know all about that," Aestelle folded her arms and stared up into the far corner of the chamber again. "Joselin told me before she died. And I have... a contact within the organization."

The abbess narrowed her eyes.

"Oh?"

"He claims that an individual of immense power has been awoken within an ancient tomb secreted within Mount Ekansu. I know that somebody has been awoken there – that much is true as I was the one who did it, inadvertently, whilst attempting to guide a Duma-sanctioned expedition through Tarkis. But my contact claims the individual is Arteri the Plague."

If the mention of the cursed name generated any emotion in the abbess, Aestelle failed to detect it.

"And your… contact. How reliable is his information?"

Aestelle stopped to think upon her recently acquired undead admirer.

"I am not sure. He has proven himself to be neither reliable nor a liar. He also claims that the Coven's coordination of necromantic activities in the Tarkis region is governed by a vampire named Lord Annaxa."

Decima nodded.

"That name we have encountered before. He…"

"*She*," Aestelle corrected, "he tells me that Annaxa is actually a woman."

"Interesting." Decima tapped a finger pensively atop the desk. "And the tomb? Are you planning to return to Ekansu?"

"Yes, I have with me a legion battle mage, acting on behalf of the Duma. He has sent a message back to his superiors, so I think we can expect a bolstered military force to be on the way to us. But that will take days, and we do not have time."

"Then we will take the tomb by force," Decima declared. "The majority of my fighting strength may be away on campaign, but still I have a good number of sisters at this abbey who are not."

Aestelle shook her head.

"This is my problem. I need to solve it. I shall go in, with my companions. We have tried stealth – twice – it has not worked. We need to kick the doors down and kill everything we see. We need to make a proper mess of the whole place and panic them into action. But… if that is the way ahead, then yes. Yes, I think having some support from this Order would be invaluable."

Decima stood up and turned to look out of the window across the training fields below her chamber. Aestelle's eyes fell back on her greatsword, dumped unceremoniously on the abbess' desk. The decorative, black scabbard and richly jeweled hilt no longer seemed the symbol of status Aestelle had hoped to boast by barging back into the abbey. She remembered the sordid story behind her acquiring of the valuable weapon, and now it seemed to exemplify the woman she had become after turning her back on the Order. She looked up at Decima as the older woman turned again to face her.

"Tell me what you need," the abbess said.

***

It was not so much the hours of inactivity spent wedged in a small, rocky crevice, occasionally blasted by gusts of freezing mountain winds that bothered Thesilar. It was the hours spent alone with her thoughts. A few dozen yards ahead of her was a cave, yawning out from the depths of the cavernous network mined into the bowels of Mount Ekansu. It was the fourth opening she was aware of; the first was the entrance they had used to initially gain access to the catacombs whilst the second was the opening to the surface she had discovered with Ragran after the cave in. The third was marked on Thesilar's map by Aestelle; a larger opening she had escaped from after being guided by one of the dying Sisterhood warriors. But this fourth opening was entirely new to Thesilar, located after the better part of two days searching.

Another blast of wind howled across the jagged peaks, whipping through the rocky crevice Thesilar crouched within, chilling her to the core. Other adventurers who had worked alongside her in the past had made several misassumptions about her, based on being an elf and a ranger. In the minds of many, an elf ranger was a skilled scout with centuries of experience in every climate across Pannithor. In actual fact, Thesilar had only a handful of years' experience as a ranger, and that had been spent exclusively in a woodland environment. Certainly, the decades that followed allowed her to take those core principles and adapt them to many other environments, but even now she was far from an expert tracker and survivalist in the mountains.

Shrugging off a shiver, Thesilar kept her eyes fixed on the cave opening ahead. She hoped for something she knew to be less than likely; for someone or something connected to the Coven coming into or out from that cave at some point overnight. Animated dead workers were all well and good for needing little support, but by and large, the necromancers that commanded them still needed basic provisions such as food and water. She only hoped that storing provisions for the long term, with a siege mentality, was something that had not occurred to them.

The sun dipped down to fade from yellow to orange as it slunk beneath the horizon. An hour drifted by with only a long-distance sighting of a mountain goat to punctuate the boredom. Her mind wandered, back to her conversations with this latest band of comrades. She thought on Valletto's words, his questioning her need to tell them that they meant something to her. A thoroughly... Basilean mindset. She also thought on her final conversation alone with Aestelle, and that point where she very nearly told her the reason why she left her home and turned to a life of adventuring. That would have been a mistake. Nobody needed to know. They would look upon her differently if they found out...

Rain drove down from the dark heavens above, pelting the green leaves of the dense line of foliage surrounding the castle. The building was, at least officially, designated a castle but more from the point of view of the owner's vanity rather than a legitimate claim to being a fortified site. The castle, whilst impressive enough, was little more than a squat, angular manor house of beige stone with a single turret and a tall perimeter wall. A solitary track led up the shallow hill to the gatehouse where two guards stood beneath the shelter of a small, wooden roof. The guards, illuminated by torches along the walls, were young, bored looking, and wore the most basic of armor. They did not pose much of a threat, but mortal danger was not the issue. Getting inside the castle, carrying out the task, and then escaping undetected was the challenge at hand.

Thesilar turned to face Torhile. The pale half-elf looked across at her, her features half-hidden beneath her dark, soaking wet hood.

"Last chance, cousin," Thesilar said, "are you sure that this is what you want?"

The tall woman issued a grim, single nod of her head. Thesilar looked back at the guards. From their vantage point in the bushes, they had seen nothing for an hour now, save the two guards changing over at midnight and a third sentry slowly walking around the perimeter wall.

"The south wall," Thesilar whispered, "I shall climb over and secure a rope for you. Then I shall go inside the main building. Watch for the west face of the main block, second floor. Once inside, I shall find the quietest room I can, open a window, and throw another rope down. Only when you have seen that rope are you to move, understood?"

Torhile nodded again, her eyes set grimly on the building ahead.

"It will be up to you to time it so that you do not encounter that guard." Thesilar pointed at the single sentry walking around the castle. "You are alone there. If the alarm is raised, then get away. I am able to take care of myself."

The half-elf looked across at Thesilar again. For the briefest of moments, there was a glimmer of warmth, compassion, even vulnerability in her normally stern, unyielding eyes.

"You do not... have to do this, Thesilar," Torhile whispered. "Now

that I have seen the place for myself, I think I can get in alone."

"I think you might, yes," Thesilar replied quietly, "but I know I can. I shall secure a path for you so you can do what needs to be done. We are in this together. This is what family is for."

"And once it is done," Torhile exhaled, "our lives will never be the same. This is your last chance to back out, Thesilar. In less than an hour, you will be an accomplice to murder."

The word caused Thesilar to shiver. Of course they had discussed it before, but the impact of the implication even now did nothing to lessen the feeling of dread in her heavy heart.

"I know what we are doing here," Thesilar replied, "but we do it as we agreed. One life. The magistrate will call it murder, but we both know this is a deserved vengeance for one who cannot stand to represent himself. But it is to be one life alone. Nobody else is to be hurt. If the alarm is raised, or if you or I are seen by a guard or servant, then we abandon this and run. Only one life is to be lost tonight."

Torhile nodded slowly.

"Agreed."

Thesilar flashed a brief, forced, and insincere smile to her cousin.

"Watch for me by the windows on the second floor."

With that, she hauled the two coils of rope over her shoulder, checked her dagger was secure in its sheath, and then silently emerged from the foliage to dash off across the dark field toward the castle wall.

Thesilar felt a sickness in her throat as she recalled that night, silently hauling her cousin in through the open window of the castle and standing guard for minutes that seemed like decades before Torhile returned, signifying what had been done with a slow, single nod. They had discussed it many times in the years that followed, and the subject of regret always seemed to burst to the fore. Thesilar did not regret assisting her cousin in murdering her own grandfather. At least, not in the few years that followed.

Now, freezing in a rocky fissure, watching a silent cave as twilight descended upon the Mountains of Tarkis, she was not as sure. First, on a purely selfish note, an entire lifetime spent in exile was a long time indeed after the actions of but half an hour; especially when that lifetime was of elven duration. Then there was the moral issue. The philosopher Kennarten said, 'to assume godhood for the perception of justice is to forsake morality itself.' Only the gods above should choose when a life could be taken in the name of vengeance. Then again, Kennarten's outlook on life was never realistic or achievable, even by a pacifistic elven philosopher's standards, Thesilar mused grimly to herself as she continued to stare at the cave entrance in a cold, gloomy silence.

***

The resilience of mankind still surprised Khirius after so many years of observing it from the shadows. He had seen men and women build up their lives and fortunes again after losing everything to ill-providence or calamity; likewise, he had witnessed quiet, resolute courage after the most tragic personal losses of family and friends. As he sat alone, in a corner booth in the Trade Wind Inn, he saw mirth and merriment from men and women who only two days ago were limping and scrambling through the cold darkness of the fields to the south of Torgias, cast out of their homes by walking nightmares conjured into being by the dark powers of necromancy.

The landlord's wife smiled as she carried a tray of tankards over to a table of sailors; four wealthy mine owners joked loudly as they drank and played cards together; a group of affluent merchants in another booth toasted and sang to celebrate the birthday of one of their party. The scene was almost enough to make Khirius smile. Despite the distractions, he kept his eyes on a booth near the main door. A trio of now familiar figures – a salamander and two humans – sat quietly with their own drinks.

Khirius would be the first to admit that Annaxa's words in the woods outside Aphos had left him thoughtful, wary, and even intimidated. Did he have so much to lose? Was tricking the Coven with his deceitful actions so unwise? It was a well thought out plan, and one he thought to be believable in its deceit. Yet Annaxa apparently remained wholly unconvinced, leaving him spending the last two nights mulling over the few options left open to him if he intended to carry on existing, even in the nightmarish form of an undead monster who prevailed only by killing others. Khirius found himself straying toward no longer believing that he had the luxury of morality. Attempting some sort of ethical existence would inevitably lead to his demise at the hands of the Basilean authorities if he was discovered, or the Coven even if he remained undetected. He needed aid, support, and a pathway ahead. That was why he had decided to kill Ragran.

Killing the lumbering barbarian warrior would, no doubt, prove some degree of both loyalty and competence to the Coven. Of the five adventurers that concerned Annaxa, Ragran and Thesilar were the most famed and dangerous. Thesilar was not an option to Khirius – the only woman he had ever killed was the one who made him what he was – and that left Ragran, the salamander, and the mage. Having capitalized on his augmented senses to eavesdrop on their conversations for the past two hours, Khirius had learned that the mage was a father of two. To Khirius, taking a child's parents away was as unforgiveable as killing a woman, and so that ceased to be an option. He would not kill the salamander – for one, the salamander also had children at home, but Khirius also had a deep respect for that entire race and their customs. But Ragran? Nobody would miss him. No family, no real morals, a half-forgotten mercenary past his prime. Khirius watched him in silence, wondering what the big man would think if he knew he would not live to see dawn.

The barbarian downed another ale and burst out laughing as the mage shared a joke with him and the salamander. Khirius had stopped listening to their exact words some time ago; the decision was made now, so it was merely a case of waiting until his prey turned in for the night. Khirius winced. He felt a slight darkness, a mildly claustrophobic presence drift by somewhere close. It seemed familiar. Then again, so many things did after spending two centuries only occasionally relocating within the same couple of hundred leagues of Basilea and Primovantor. The landlord's wife brought over another tray of drinks to Ragran and his two comrades. Khirius let out a disgruntled curse and sank lower in his booth seat.

The presence was still there. Khirius fidgeted uncomfortably in his seat, unable to concentrate on his self-assigned task or shake that uneasy feeling that the familiarity he sensed was real and tangible. He turned his attention away from the booth by the door, focusing his unnatural senses on the other occupants of the room. Even taking a few moments to pierce the mesh of noise made by laughter and song, he found nothing out of the ordinary. Khirius stood and made his way slowly across the room. He reached the door leading up to the accommodation rooms. He slowly clambered up the rickety, creaking staircase as the mirth of the main bar grew quieter behind him.

On the floor above, Khirius could sense pounding pulses in some of the rooms. Life carried on as normal, each doorway marking out a room where within a mortal man or woman carried on addressing their daily challenges, goals, loves, and fears. The dark presence receded. Khirius felt the pressure on his chest ease off. He could still sense something; as if an intruder had been and gone but left a trail behind that was slowly dissipating. The wooden boards of the corridor beneath Khirius' feet stopped creaking as he froze in place. He was next to his own room. He slowly turned his head to face the oaken door. It was half-open.

Clenching his fists, Khirius darted inside his room. He froze only a pace inside, held in place by the sheer shock of the horrific sight presented to him. Four dead bodies littered the room. Tonnen lay crumpled on the floor before him, his hands rigidly frozen in place ahead of his chest as if trying in vain to push off an assailant. Peggi and Fiana lay discarded and motionless on his bed. His beloved, loyal Hanna lay slumped over his dressing table, her dead eyes frozen forever in the picture of absolute, abject terror that dominated the final, awful moments of her short life. All were colorless, drained of blood, with puncture wounds on their necks.

Khirius let out a stifled cry of misery for their loss. The cry became something closer to a dry retch when he looked up and saw the far wall of his inn room. His chest burning with the physical pain he felt from the desolation and despair of losing his loyal servants, he let out another gasp as that pain escalated into a stab through his cold, inert heart at the vision ahead of him. Written neatly, carefully, and callously in blood on the wall ahead was a simply phrase.

We all have something to lose.

Khirius took a step back, a quiet, hollow howl of agony escaping his lips as his hands clutched in desperation at his temples.

"I would like to know your Lord Annaxa's true identity first."

"Don't push your luck."

He recalled the phrase from that first meeting, the only thing Annaxa had said to him. Then he remembered the uneasy feeling in their encounter at the woods and everything fell into a hellish, painfully logical place in his mind.

"You are without a home, without significant wealth and resources, and without political influence in this place. Don't push your luck."

Khirius sank to his knees next to Tonnen's body as his mind was wrenched back to a different time, a different world, and a different existence...

Khirius knew very little about music. The quartet of minstrels all played stringed instruments that looked like lutes, but the different sizes apparently equated to different pitches, sounds, or noises, or something he had little interest in. The minstrels' gallery was set up just to one side of the enormous, marble fireplace, the flames seeming to flicker and dance in time with their music. The tables and chairs of the main hall were all pushed against the walls to open up a large space for dancing, and some seven or eight couples were already engaged in the rather complex footwork of the Genezan Three Step.

Draining his glass of red wine, Khirius leaned back against the rough, white wall of the castle's main hall. Perhaps fifty people were in the room — not including the servants — all dressed in their finest evening wear to celebrate the Autumnal Passing. His uncle, who played their host, had provided excellent food and wine to accompany the annual event that would, no doubt, run on into the early hours. He had also, Khirius noted, provided excellent company.

Lady Tansia of Halli had arrived in the area only two weeks before but had turned the worlds of the region's rich, eligible bachelors upside-down. Although perhaps approaching thirty years of age, she was somehow still single, which, considering her beauty, wealth, and intellect seemed utterly implausible. Khirius watched as the tall, youthful Baron of Dommeni stood over her, frantically attempting to regale her with amusing anecdotes. The white-skinned, raven-haired beauty simply flashed him a polite but unimpressed smile, one hand idly fluttering away with a fan of black lace that complimented the dark trim of her satin red evening gown.

After a few moments, the blond baron bowed and walked away, his face a picture of disappointment. The third man she had rejected in the last half hour. Khirius sprang from the wall and paced quickly over, threading his way nimbly through elderly relatives and serving staff carrying silver trays, delicately balancing crystal wine glasses. He was raised and educated well by his tutors; he knew that formalities dictated a formal introduction and certainly an escort if he intended to leave the room with her. But that did not fit his plan. Tansia looked up as he approached, flashing a dazzling smile his way. Having only watched her from afar, he found himself taken aback by her beauty when up close; the impeccable lines of her figure, her smooth, perfect skin lacking even a single blemish. He held out a hand.

"Would you care to dance?"

Tansia's dark eyes narrowed, but the smile remained.

"With a complete stranger who has not even introduced himself properly? Think of the scandal, sir! We would both burn in the fires of the Abyss!"

Khirius found himself laughing at the unexpected response, perhaps a little too much. He quickly checked his laughter for fear of appearing too eager but kept his arm outstretched.

"It is a risk I am willing to take," he issued a charming smile, "if you would but accompany me to the floor."

"You have been watching me for the better part of an hour," Tansia replied, "you have seen me decline the advances of a number of young men. What makes you think that you would succeed where other men have failed?"

Khirius paused for only the briefest of moments before responding.

"Because I am more handsome and more entertaining company than any of the others."

Tansia raised an eyebrow.

"And more confident," she said coolly.

"I am told that confidence is attractive, my lady."

The black-haired woman shrugged in agreement and accepted his hand. Khirius led his prize to the dance floor, reveling in the astounded looks and muttered remarks from the rejected suitors that littered the pathway to his symbolic podium. Khirius led the older woman confidently through dance after dance, displaying his expertise in footwork both fast and intricate, and slow and measured. An hour passed in blissful silence as she matched his every step, the musicians playing song after song from every region of Upper Mantica. When the floor was more packed and the glamorous couple was lost amidst the crowd, Khirius dared to allow his hands to roam across her body. Tansia shot him a warning look.

"Don't push your luck."

But push his luck he did. An hour later, he led her up to his bedchamber. Half an hour after that, she sank her teeth into his neck, drained him of his blood, and transformed him into a vampire.

Chapter Sixteen

Pondering over just how quickly life had somehow returned to normal in Torgias, Z'akke sat on the edge of one of the tables in the courtyard of the Trade Wind Inn. He watched as a merchant's wagon was hauled across the cobbled stones toward the northern end of the complex, where Fran, the landlady, waited impatiently. Only days before, the entire town had been evacuated after an undead attack. Now, with the town's defenses bolstered by legion men-at-arms, the same people who ran screaming through the night from skeletons and zombies carried on with their business as if such a catastrophe was a daily occurrence. Z'akke smiled grimly at the thought.

Humans were a resilient folk. That much, Z'akke had ascertained from his years of travel. The dwarfs had that reputation for stoic sturdiness, but Z'akke saw it more in humans. They dealt with things with a more understated dignity. If a dwarf settlement had been attacked by the undead, there would already be an endless succession of bitter oaths, raging little folk screaming and ranting about insults to their ancestral homes, councils assembled where iron-clad midgets with beards would attempt to out-do each other with coarse tales of manliness so that they would be selected to lead the inevitable counter attack... Z'akke found the dwarfs to be difficult people. He tilted his head from side to side as he mused over that thought. It was very unfair to judge an entire race on his limited experiences. It would be more accurate to say that the tiny number of dwarfs he had met and worked alongside were all complete arseholes. But he was confident that the rest of them were probably much nicer.

"Morning," Valletto greeted wearily as he walked over from the doors to the main inn building, rubbing his dark eyes.

Z'akke looked at the mage as he wandered across, his dark tunic left undone despite the biting autumnal chill. The human mage sat down opposite the salamander, lowering himself slowly and raising one hand to the short, slightly graying hair at his temple.

"Do you think, maybe," Z'akke started tentatively, "you should not try to keep up with Ragran in drinking?"

Valletto nodded slowly.

"Yes. Yes, I do think that."

Z'akke hopped down from the edge of the table.

"I'll go and get some water for you," he offered.

Valletto held a hand up.

"I'll... I'll work up to that."

Z'akke resumed his perch and looked down uneasily at his fellow mage as Valletto placed both hands to his temples and took in a succession of long, slow breaths.

"Why do people do this to themselves?" Z'akke asked. "You are literally poisoning your own body. Why do you do it?"

"It's one of life's great mysteries," Valletto replied with a forced smile. "It always seems like a good idea at the time. But the older one gets – and I am starting to feel the passage of years, now – the more it hurts the next day."

"It never seems to hurt Ragran," Z'akke replied.

"Yes, but there's two reasons for that. First, Ragran is tavern-fit; that means he is in regular practice of poisoning himself with ale so his body weathers it far better than somebody well out of practice. Somebody like me. Second... well, Ragran's an idiot."

Z'akke chuckled lightly but quickly stopped himself; not because he thought he was being unpleasant, but more from years of funny looks from other races who heard the clicking, chittering laugh of a salamander and made unkind comments about the sound.

"Ragran is not nearly so bad as some people say," Z'akke said. "He has not chosen the path of the academic, but he has a worldly wisdom that comes with years spent traveling the world. And as for your lack of... tavern fitness... I think that is because you no longer drink due to your commitment to your wife and children. The fact that you are in pain now is proof that you have chosen the right things to dedicate your life to. To being a husband and father. In a strange sort of way, I think you should be proud of being in tatters at the moment, if you'll allow me to say so."

Valletto looked up, his eyes still narrowed in pain, but with a slight and genuine smile across his lips.

"You always find kind words to say about people," he remarked. "It leaves me wondering why Thesilar and Ragran are so unpleasant to you."

"That's easy enough to explain." Z'akke shrugged. "I told you about my father. He told me that being in the navy was like being in a colony of ants. Everybody knows their job and everybody has to pull together and do their part to keep the ship safe. From what I've learned, being an adventurer is like being in a pack of wolves. You live and fight together, but the moment any threat has gone, the infighting starts. Everybody wants to be the top dog, the one in charge. Thesilar and Ragran... and Aestelle, when I think about it, they all want to be seen as the strongest."

"Bullying isn't strength," Valletto said, "not where I come from. We spoke about this before. I've spent years in the legion. Not as a soldier, but still in military service. Of course I've seen bullying, but in most cases, it's been stamped down pretty quickly. It's not even about kindness. It's about impairing fighting ability. But I digress. My point is that it makes me sad to see. And I still don't know why they do it. They ridicule you for being obsessed with gold and treasure."

A chill cut through Z'akke's chest at Valletto's last few words. He felt his smile fade instantly. He stepped down from his seat on the edge of the table and turned away. Of course he knew what the others said about him. But he was bound to secrecy. He had given his word. He could say nothing. The honor of his clan was at stake.

"Are you alright?" Valletto asked.

Z'akke turned back around and forced a smile. He considered passing off his reaction by diverting the conversation elsewhere but found himself stopping before he did so. He looked down at Valletto. Everything from Z'akke's education within the hallowed ranks of the priesthood told him that he should be suspicious of the human mage. The salamander mage-priests saw magic as sacred, wondrous, spiritual, a gift bestowed from the lineage of The Deliverer herself. But throughout that long and arduous training, Basileans were always mentioned as the polar opposite; seeing magic as an arcane science, devoid of any spirituality or soul.

Yet, when Z'akke looked down at where Valletto sat, he did not see a confrontational cultural opposite. He saw a friend; a kindred spirit, a fellow husband and father who prioritized his family and basic morality above all else. For years, it had been so difficult and so wearing to keep his clan's secret. So many times he had questioned whether it needed to be a secret at all – was a need for external help so bad? Was it even a weakness? Would other clans really see it that way, or would they be sympathetic, lest it happen to them?

"The gold isn't for me," Z'akke found himself stammering. "It... never has been. I need it to pay for something... noble. It is why I am here. It is why I have been out here for years now."

Valletto slowly raised himself to his feet.

"What happened?" he asked quietly.

Z'akke shook his head.

"I've already said far too much! We were sworn to secrecy before we left. We were instructed that we could never say a thing! Not even hint at why we were sent out. I... can't say anything. I shouldn't have even said this much. Please do not tell anybody."

Valletto nodded slowly.

"Look... I won't say anything. To anybody. I have no idea what is going on with you, but one would think that anybody who spends even a single day in your company should have the intellect to deduce that your hunt for treasures never had anything to do with personal wealth or greed. Please do not for a moment think that there is even a shred of pressure from me to talk about this. This is your business, not mine. Just know that if anything changes and you are able to talk about this, you have my word that I will keep your secret safe and that I will do all I can to help you."

Z'akke felt some of the tension across his chest ease. Some, but not all. He had most certainly said too much.

"Thank you," he nodded his head respectfully.

"Now if you'll excuse me for a brief moment," Valletto winced as he slowly turned to face the doors to the inn, "I think it is time for me to brave some water."

"I'll get that for you," Z'akke offered.

"Quite alright," Valletto said before slowly walking off toward the doors, his shoulders hunched and his head drooped.

Z'akke sank down to one of the bench seats and looked across the courtyard, toward the south and where his home waited for him hundreds of leagues away. He remembered that curious mixture of apprehension and excitement when he had first left, years ago now, on this sacred quest across the seas to find the cure that would finally end his clan's plight. To begin with, every dawn felt like a failure as success in his quest eluded him. Now, four years later and not knowing if his fellow mage-priests who were sent out with him were even still alive, the pressure of his clan's fate had faded into normality; a chronic unease that never truly allowed him to relax and enjoy the marvelous spectacle of new lands and incredible people. His mind drifted back to the very day the four of them were sent out with their mission.

The lava pool filled the cave with a close, comfortable heat, despite most of its rich smoke pouring out of the cave mouth in pulses of gray cloud. The cave floor beneath Z'akke's feet was smooth, polished into a slight shine by decades of temple acolytes. The temple-city of Triass itself lay sprawling out at the foot of the mountain, its neat buildings of light wood and yellow stone seemingly woven into the living tapestry of the great jungles of the island of Ghekk; the smallest of the Three Kings. Whilst the temple-city was in itself a seat of worship to Kthorlaq the Deliverer, the true spiritual center of worship for the Lava Tail Clan was up in the mountain itself, in the very temple Z'akke now stood alongside his brother and sister mage-priests.

A great effigy of the Deliverer, cast out of solid bronze, stood maternally over the sacred lava pits of the clan, her arms outstretched lovingly as if to embrace the stone and gold altar at the edge of the pool. The cave housing the sacred site lay open along one side, giving a clear view of the blue sky above and the jungle city stretched out amidst the vivid green trees below.

Z'akke stood in line next to three of his fellow mage-priests as D'rokna, the high priest of the clan, stood before them flanked by two incense-burner bearing acolytes clothed in robes of red. The ancient priest looked down at the quartet of younger salamanders before him, his long, thin snout twisted into a broken-toothed smile of avuncular pride.

"Today is the day, brothers, sister," D'rokna began, "I have been granted authority by Tz'Arak himself to send you out into the world to find a solution to our clan's ongoing problem."

Z'akke stood upright, the air whistling past the gaping mouth of the cave tugging at his red, ceremonial robes as he listened attentively to his master.

"The task ahead of you is not easy. It will not be quick. It will not be safe. It pains my heart to send you out, but that pain is opposed by the pride and love I feel for the four of you for volunteering for this undertaking. I know you have homes here. I know you have family. I know all four of you are loved, deeply. But the sickness within our clan grows worse with each hatching season. This season is the very first which sees our population begin to dwindle."

Z'akke hung his head in sorrow at the thought. He had been so lucky. His mate's eggs had hatched without any problems, granting them three beautiful hatchlings. But so many others had not enjoyed that luck and were left devastated during the hatching season after finding their eggs unfertilized. The clan's secret sickness was spreading with every passing year.

"Every attempt we have made to remedy this terrible affliction has failed," the aging priest continued, "and as you all know, Tz'Arak and his council have decreed that we must look farther afield. We must look outside our own borders for a cure. We must look to the wise men and women of the noble races to heal the illness in our clan. You are to go out to find a cure, and return here before it is too late."

The four mage-priests listened intently, their high priest only confirming the plan they volunteered for days earlier. Z'akke swallowed uncomfortably. He knew that leaving his mate and children would leave them distraught. But he had to volunteer. He had never known the pain of an unsuccessful hatching. He owed it to all of those who had suffered such a terrible loss. He owed it to the clan to head out and face the dangers of the world, to leave his own young behind without their father so that the suffering would one day end. But the thought of their faces left tears in his eyes as he listened to the high priest's words.

"The Clan Lord has decreed that you must tell nobody of our plight, save those will the knowledge to help us," D'rokna continued. "Not a word of our sickness must leave our clan, unless it is spoken to mages or healers who you believe can help us. Every effort must be made to keep our shame a secret! The council has decreed this to be a priority! You must all swear that you will honor their wishes."

Each mage-priest in turn muttered a quiet oath of acknowledgement as they stood in line, heads bowed, claws wrapped around their staffs. D'rokna gestured to another young acolyte who waited by the altar. The adolescent salamander made her way over with a bowl of oil. D'rokna walked across to stand in front of Z'akke as the oil bearer and incense burners followed the high priest.

"Brother Z'akke," the ancient priest smiled, laying a hand on the burly salamander's shoulder, "the first to volunteer for such a task. Always the first to volunteer, Z'akke! The clan will miss your optimism, your heart, your compassion, and your laughter."

D'rokna reached a claw down into the bowl of oil and smeared a symbolic circle across Z'akke's head.

"Brother Z'akke," he continued more formally, "the Council of the Clan Lava Tail has authorized you to leave our borders. You are to search for a cure for our illness. You have been ordered to travel to the land of Ophidia to find help in this, most grim time…"

***

His footsteps echoing along the ancient passageway, Khirius paced toward the age-old burial chamber with grim determination. His cold, gray fingers were curled into tight fists by his side, his eyes fixed on the doorway at the end of the dimly lit corridor. Two undead guards stood rigidly to attention to either side of the entrance; the style of their rusted armor and their imposing height marking them out as elves when they had once lived. The various guard rooms along the way through the mountain tunnels were almost exclusively protected by undead humans; the presence of elves around the area of the burial chamber itself was yet more evidence that the corpse within the forbidden chambers was exactly who the Coven claimed it was.

Khirius stopped by the skeletal elven soldiers. Both silently extended an arm to cross their glaives ahead of him, barring his way. Taking a moment to quell his raging anger, Khirius focused his senses on the two dead guards. The necromancy animating them was ancient; nothing more than the original incantations from centuries before that left the two corpses waiting at that very door for countless years. If they had been animated and controlled directly by another necromancer in the last few days, this would be more problematic. But using his own necromantic powers to oppose an automatic reaction rather than the will of another necromancer was simple enough. Khirius held out a hand and cast a simple incantation. Both skeletal elves stood back to attention, their weapons pulled smartly to their sides to allow him to proceed.

Flinging the doors open, Khirius barged into the next chamber. The adjoining room was square; its walls smoother than the roughly cut corridor leading to it. Two doorways were hewn into the opposite wall, whilst the other walls were covered by tall bookcases of relatively new looking wood, each shelf crammed with tomes, scrolls, or jars of components. A single table with a collection of mismatched chairs took up the middle of the room. A robed figure – a man of perhaps thirty years, looked up from the assortment of parchments spread out across the table, his pale, rotund face and piggy eyes screwed up in frustration by Khirius' arrival.

"Who are you?" the short man demanded. "You're not supposed to be in here!"

"Tell me where Annaxa is," Khirius hissed, pacing over toward the robed figure.

"I will tell you no such thing!" the academic babbled, staring down awkwardly at Khirius' feet as he approached. "I don't know how you got in here, but you are not supposed to…"

Khirius grabbed the man by his throat and hauled him up into the air before slamming him down onto the table, the force of the blow scattering parchments in every direction. His teeth bared, Khirius leant in.

"Tell me where she is! Or as the Ones above are my witness, I'll give you a death more painful than you thought possible!"

The young scholar looked up at Khirius with terrified eyes, his hands desperately and pathetically scratching at the vampire's iron grip around his throat. Khirius sensed a flare of magical power building in the scholar as he choked on the table beneath him. To re-emphasize his point, Khirius lifted the man up into the air and slammed him down a second time, with significantly more force. He heard a bone crack. The scholar's face flushed a deep red as spittle speckled his quivering lips. Terror dominated his bulging eyes.

"Opposing me isn't the answer, you worm!" Khirius yelled. "Now, tell me where Annaxa is or I'll tear one of your hands off!"

Khirius relaxed his grip to allow the man to speak. The diminutive scholar choked out a series of hoarse coughs, fighting to catch his breath before he spoke.

"I… I can't!" he pleaded, looking back at the doors behind him. "I… the things… she would do to me…"

Rage flared up to fog Khirius' mind in scarlet. He thought on that awful, bloody image of his loyal servants disrespectfully piled up in the inn room, lifeless and drained of blood, terror in their dead eyes.

"What *she* would do?!" he screamed. "It appears to me that you are not taking me seriously! Let me help you understand the severity of your situation!"

Khirius clamped one hand on the writhing man's wrist, and with his other, twisted the man's hand around until bone snapped. Numb to the screams and pleas for mercy, wrenching the fragile, mortal wrist with the ease of a giant breaking a child's toy, the vampire turned the quivering hand in place until bone, flesh, and sinew gave up the fight and it detached completely in a pulsing wave of blood. Khirius' eyes opened wide as he saw the crimson fountain. The thirst raged within him. He lunged forward. No. He needed answers far more than he needed to feed.

Before he could speak again, the left hand door on the far wall opened. Khirius looked up. The passageway beyond it was empty. He sensed the most vague aura of magical energy. His grip on the sobbing, bleeding scholar relaxed, and the mutilated little man crawled quickly away, clutching at the bleeding stump of his wrist. Khirius walked over to the door. A long, dark corridor waited for him beyond it.

His wrath morphing slowly into trepidation, Khirius tentatively stepped into the corridor. The rough walls were narrow. The ceiling was low. The lack of torches forced him to rely on his unnaturally augmented eyesight as he walked further along the corridor. Despite the visual appearances of a dead straight pathway ahead, Khirius found his legs suddenly heavy as if walking up a steep slope. Only paces later, he flung one arm instinctively to press against a wall as the floor beneath him felt as though it was twisting steeply to one side with each step. The single doorway up ahead loomed closer. The stale, musty air felt hot and close. For the first time in two centuries, he fully remembered the sensation of needing to breath. The doorway ahead opened on its own accord.

One cold, pale hand pressed against the rough stone wall to his side, Khirius staggered on toward the door. The doorway was black, completely devoid of any light or color. Silence waited as he approached. Khirius heard a heartbeat pounding in his ears. It made no sense. His own heart had not beaten a single pulse for centuries. He reached the doorway. Even only a single pace away, he could see nothing through the darkness ahead. He reached out a hand. The door seemed to pull him in. Khirius gathered his resolve and stepped forward.

Khirius' senses focused sharply as he found himself at one end of a long, rectangular chamber. Pillars of orange-brown stone lined both sides of the chamber to form arches that were left plunged in shadow. In between the arches, one on either side, a tall, impressive door twice the height of a man and nearly as wide stood shut in the shadows. In the center of the chamber, on a raised circular platform lit by candlelight, lay a stone tomb edged in gold and decorated with ornate, beautifully carved symbols. A lone figure clothed in black robes stood before the tomb. Despite the raised hood hiding her features, Khirius knew exactly who she was.

Letting out a yell of curses, Khirius sprinted forward toward the hooded figure. The short woman held out a hand. Instantly, four skeletal guards emerged from the shadowy alcoves, their bony forms adorned in ancient, bronze elven armor and their dead fingers holding tall, curved shields and long glaives at the ready. Khirius' violent curses transformed into a long yell of rage as he accelerated through the chamber, hurtling toward the ancient undead guards.

The first armored skeleton lunged forward with a superbly aimed strike, demonstrating a clinical precision of attack that could only have come from years of training and experience in a long forgotten life. But it was not nearly enough to defeat Khirius' unnaturally augmented senses; he ducked beneath the blow and lashed out with a fist, connecting his knuckles into the undead elf's face with enough force to plunge straight through the skull, transforming bone into dust.

The vampire quickly drew his ornate sword and deftly avoided a strike from the next undead guard before batting a shield aside and then cutting the warrior in half just below its ribcage. The final two guards stood together in front of the robed figure, their shields locked in place to form a small wall with their glaives jutting out above.

"Stop this," the hooded figure said, "let us talk."

The undead woman's manner gave away nothing. The words alone may have betrayed fear, but there was none of that woven into her tone. The skeletal guards backed around slowly, their shields and glaives pointed at Khirius as he paced around to one side, his eyes locked on the hooded figure behind them.

"Why did you kill them, Tansia?" Khirius growled.

The hooded vampire folded her arms.

"It took you a long time to deduce who I am, Khirius," she chuckled lightly.

"They did nothing to you!" Khirius yelled, his hatred echoing around the chamber. "Why did you do it?"

A moment's silence passed. The candles surrounding the stone tomb flickered.

"Why did I do it."

It was not stated as a question. The woman simply repeated his words, openly mocking him. She reached up and slowly pulled down her hood. The woman Khirius remembered was long gone. Where there had once been a near peerless beauty augmented by the unholy grace of vampirehood, a shocking disfigurement now stood. Rotten flesh clung to bone; clumps of hair hung from wrinkled, yellowed skin.

Dead eyes of milky white, punctuated only with pupils of pale gray, stared out. Thin, dry lips receded to reveal long, broken, and stained teeth.

"Why did I do it?" Tansia asked. "Why do you think? Look what you did to me."

Khirius stopped, frozen in place. The disheveled crone before him bore no resemblance at all to the beautiful woman who had murdered him in life and cruelly dominated him in the first few years of his undeath. Only her voice remained familiar. Still dripping with malice.

"Look what you did to me!" she screamed, her thin fists clenched. "By the depths of the Abyss, you bastard! If you were going to kill me, then you should have done the job properly! Not left me like this!"

Khirius let out a gasp. He took a step back, shaking his head. It made no sense! He remembered the ambush, all those decades ago. Everything was in place: divinity magic, rites of binding, holy water... He even personally removed her head from her body. No vampire could have survived it.

"How..."

"How?" Tansia thundered. "It does not matter how! It took me one hundred years to recover enough strength to even walk after what you did!"

"Am I supposed to feel sympathy?" Khirius growled, his resolve growing to push aside his shock. "Am I supposed to feel even a shred of remorse? You murdered me! You took my life!"

"You deserved it, you whimpering shit!" the haggard vampire snapped. "I watched you that night! A pretty, pampered noble with nothing on his mind other than bedding women only to discard them like refuse the next morning! You were lucky I made you what you are! Blessed! I didn't murder you, you pathetic fool! I elevated you! And this is how you repaid me?"

"This?!" Khirius snarled, gesturing to himself. "This?! This is no blessing! Cutting off your damned head was the only blessing! This is no way to exist!"

"Not now, no," Tansia seethed, "but it was! So now I carve out a new path. As Lord Annaxa. Rising steadily through the ranks of the Coven, with power enough to make this existence worthwhile. Interesting. Occasionally even... entertaining. Killing your servants and knowing what it would do to you. That was entertaining. By the Ones, Khirius, it took me one hundred years to track you down once I regained my strength. One hundred years to think up what I would do to you. You hid well up until you made that one error. Such a simple, stupid thing."

Khirius paced to his left, staring at the accursed wretch before him, planning his attack around the two undead elven soldiers as she continued.

"When they find us, Khirius, we have to move on. We have to start again. I taught you that. I also taught you to never, ever, no matter how many years have passed by, use the same name again. I didn't think I needed to tell you that you never to use the name you had in mortal life! You imbecile! It made my decade, when word reached me of a handsome, reclusive nobleman locked away in a manor, going by the name of Khirius! It took barely a month to plant enough evidence to bring the Brotherhood's eyes on you!"

Khirius' own eyes opened wide. His sword fell from his limp fingers and clattered nosily on the stone floor by his feet.

"You... you sent the Brotherhood after me?"

"I invited you here to the Coven first." Tansia grinned. "But when you were so rude as to leave my letter unanswered, I felt myself forced to do something a little bit more drastic."

His red eyes narrowed in fury, his fingernails digging into the palms of his own hands, Khirius stared at his former mistress with unbridled hatred.

"So here we are again," Tansia chirped merrily, "with me in power and you being my slave."

"You mistake this situation!" Khirius grunted, dropping to one knee to recover his blade and then slowly rising. "You have no power over me! You have nothing!"

"Oh, Khirius," Tansia shook her head, "always easy on the eye but quick with neither intellect nor wisdom. Even now. I have everything. You have nothing. Don't you see? I have taken your home. I have killed everybody who was loyal to you. That family fortune you sneaked away in the carts? All that treasure amassed by your ancestors for generations? It's mine now. I have everything. All you have is the shirt on your back. Your title, lands, money, friends... all gone. I've taken everything from you. And the best part? I've even taken your security. You have nowhere to hide. Without me and the safety provided by the Coven, you will be destroyed within days. You are my slave, Khirius, just as you were in the beginning. Only now... well, now it is worse. Because now you have made me angry, too."

His hands shaking, Khirius slowly raised his blade. Whilst his connections with his mortal life had faded with every passing decade, he had always aspired to do something good, something noble with the money from his long lost family estate. But more than that, there were those people who had remained loyal to him. Those who had protected him when he was at his most vulnerable. Those who hid him away and kept him safe, even knowing exactly what he was, when it would have been so much easier to end his existence. He closed his eyes and remembered Tonnen and Hanna, discarded and lifeless in the inn. He looked up at Tansia.

"You have miscalculated," Khirius hissed, "badly. You see, whilst you were rotting away in pieces for a hundred years, I was growing stronger. Whilst you were limping and plotting your revenge for a second hundred years, again I grew stronger still. I am not the new-blood vampire you remember. I am…"

"Khirius, shut up!" Tansia sighed. "I know exactly what you are. But I'll tell you what you are not. You're not a soldier. You're not a vampire lord, master of the battlefield. You barely know how to hold a sword. It's only your vampiric speed and strength that give you that edge. You don't actually have any skill. So save me your pathetic speech!"

"No," Khirius took a pace forward, "I may be no vampire lord, no master of the field of battle… but I am your better. You are nothing compared to what you were. You are a broken, haggard wretch now. Do you really think that two undead elves will give you the edge you need to defeat me in battle?"

The small, hideously disfigured vampire clasped her hands at the small of her back. She took a few paces, her eyes casually taking in the detail of the ancient ceiling above her. She let out a small chuckle. It grew into a laugh. She looked back at Khirius with her lifeless, white eyes.

"No," she replied, "no, I don't think these two are much of an edge. I do, however, think that I am more powerful than you give me credit for. I fancy that if you and I were to go head to head, the odds would be in my favor. But you know me, dear Khirius! I would *never*, *ever* play my hand if I thought that the odds were merely in my favor. No! I only ever play my hand if I know categorically, with absolutely certainty, that victory is on my side of the table. That's why I've got something extra to slant the odds in my favor. Hugely in my favor."

Khirius stopped. He met Tansia's stare evenly. Was this a bluff? Out of his line of sight, he heard one of the tall doors he had seen through the alcoves slide open. Khirius heard a clicking, and then a thump behind him. The stone tiles beneath his feet tremored. His anger and confidence slowly eroding, he turned in place, his eyes tracking up in horror to the twin terrors looming high above him.

***

Dragging his feet wearily down the creaking staircase leading from the accommodation rooms to the main tavern bar, Valletto suppressed a weary yawn. The row of neat little rooms the floor above had become all the more quiet when a visiting nobleman's handful of servants – generously accommodated in rooms that could easily be considered somewhat above their status – had suddenly departed from the Trade Wind Inn. However, despite the empty rooms around his, Valletto now found himself half-awake and certainly unable to return to his slumber after a large seabird had defied the laws of nature and decided, before sunrise, to pick through the remains of discarded, leftover food behind the inn's kitchens, cawing at a deafening volume whilst it did so.

The bar was all but empty, with only a young man and woman from the inn's serving staff slowly and half-heartedly preparing the room for breakfast whilst the pre-dawn glow of sunlight began to enrich the palette of the sky outside. Yawning again, Valletto rubbed at his eyes as he plodded through the bar and to the main entrance, opening the door to be greeted with a waft of cold, refreshing air before he wandered out into the courtyard.

The cobblestones beneath his feet were slippery from the morning dew as he paced wearily past the tables and bench seats lining the inn's walls and out toward the perimeter of the inn complex. Out to the east, fishermen would already be leaving the small port in the day's first rays of light, whilst miners would no doubt have left their homes outside the town walls to file toward another day spent deep underground, braving the hazards of cave ins for meager wages.

"Excuse me?"

Valletto stiffened up in surprise, taken completely unaware by the voice to his side. He turned and looked across to see a soldier of the legion, identifiable by the white and blue tabard neatly draped over his platemail armor, helmet carried at one side, and broad-bladed daga sword worn at the other. The soldier looked young, still in his teens, his dark hair cropped short and accentuating an angular face and square jaw.

"I'm sorry, sir," the soldier said, "the serving staff directed me toward you. I'm looking for the group of mercenaries that defended this town a few days ago, during the undead attack."

"Yes," Valletto nodded, wincing as he heard the grating caw of that same damned seabird responsible for waking him up as it continued to pick away near the kitchens, "you'd probably want Aestelle. She's sort of in charge of this one. She's been away for a couple of days now."

"It was actually Captain Valletto of Auron I was sent to find, sir," the man-at-arms replied.

Valletto's eyes narrowed in confusion.

"Yes... that's me."

The soldier reached down to his belt and produced a small bundle, tied neatly but austerely in string.

"A dispatch rider arrived from the capital with orders for our garrison, sir," the soldier said. "He also had these two letters addressed to you. I was sent to find you."

Valletto accepted the parcel, the seal of Grand Mage Saffus of Aigina practically leaping off the envelope of the upper letter. Valletto untied the knot and discarded the string, revealing the second letter as he did so. His heart immediately grew heavy as he recognized his wife's handwriting on that second letter. He stared down at it in silence for some time. He was vaguely aware of the soldier saying something and then walking away.

"Thank you," Valletto called after the messenger before his eyes fell back down to the two letters.

He walked slowly over toward the perimeter wall, away from the inn's main building and the incessant cawing of the damned seabird. His hands shook. Telling himself that orders from the capital were his top priority and suppressing the voice inside his head that accused him of cowardice for delaying the opening of the letter from his wife, Valletto broke the wax seal of the envelope from Saffus. He unfolded the letter and cast his eyes quickly over the words.

"Valletto,

Whilst our infrequent exchanges across the plains have given me an overview of your progression in and around Torgias, I felt it necessary to give you more detail regarding the general situation. Word has reached the Duma of the undead attack on Torgias, but given the early reports that the attack was successfully fended off with minimal force and negligible casualties, the incident is regarded as isolated and of very little importance – despite the decision being made to evacuate the entire town for a brief period. The legion force sent to bolster the town has very clear orders: defense of the civilian population is the absolute priority.

However, the threat in the mountains that you were originally sent to investigate still remains at large. Without a positive affirmation of what this threat is, the Duma will not divert any further military resources, given the clearly defined and greater needs in other areas. Therefore, your orders are to positively identify this threat and report back to me as a matter of urgency. With legion resources in the area being engaged in the defense of Torgias, I have written to the Abbess of the Order of the Penitent and the Devoted to request military aid for you.

Whilst I appreciate the severity of the strategic situation the Hegemony finds itself in, I fear that the threat you are uncovering is not being taken as seriously as it should. I am relying on you to provide the evidence required to force the Duma into action and dispatch a significant military force to address this threat; this enemy lying in wait within our very borders. I have confidence in your ability, determination, and integrity in ensuring this is done.

Saffus"

Valletto folded the letter again and looked up at the slowly but steadily illuminating sky above. He let out a breath through his nostrils and thought on the words. After a few moments, he opened the letter and read it through a second time. Nothing changed. Whilst he appreciated the words from Saffus, the contents of the letter could perhaps have easily been summed up in very few words. 'The Duma is not taking this seriously. Whatever you are doing up there, do it faster.'

Exhaling slowly, he considered reading the letter yet again. The nagging voice at the back of his mind told him that doing so would be nothing more than a delaying tactic. Knowing what he needed to face, Valletto put away the first letter and opened the second. Two sheets of parchment were sealed inside. Valletto skim read the first. He was not sure why the thought of reading it properly, word for word, was so terrifying.

"...so sorry that you are away from us... we are all praying for your safety, and also your happiness... the children miss you dearly and check the road every morning and night to see if you are coming home... whatever it is that I said or did to make you volunteer to go, I am eternally sorry and will do anything I can to remedy it when you get home... we will always love you, unconditionally..."

The tears that slowly formed in Valletto's eyes from the sheer guilt caused by his wife's words were pushed to overflowing when he saw the second parchment – a childishly scrawled picture of a stick man casting spells to defeat a monster and then going home to be cheered by two stick children. Below it was a series of incomprehensible scribbles and scrawls clearly drawn by a child barely old enough to hold a quill pen. Tucked away in the corner of the envelope was a tiny, toy wooden soldier painted simply in chipped, Basilean blue. It was one of the toy soldiers Valletto had made for his son on his last birthday.

It was at least an hour until Valletto managed to compose himself. Wiping his eyes and taking a few long, deep breaths, his shaking hands folded the letter from his wife and the pictures from his children. Storming off and leaving them behind was truly the single most stupid thing he had ever done in his life. Rapidly approaching middle-age,

Valletto had enough worldly experience to know that the overwhelming majority of arguments and confrontations were caused by both involved parties; there were very few truly malicious people, and in most cases, altercations were simply a result of miscommunication. But not in this case. His wife had written to him to accept blame for pushing him away. She was wrong. It was his fault; his fault entirely. There was no compromise, no miscommunication. He was wholly to blame. Placing the letters in the pocket of his tunic, Valletto strode purposefully back into the inn.

As if magicked up to begin the series of events that could solve his problems, Valletto saw both Aestelle and Thesilar stood over a table in the group's familiar corner booth. Thesilar wore her normal lose, ruddy green garb, her hair hastily scrapped back in a ponytail. Aestelle was clothed in her form-fitting armor of black leather, her greatsword and a quiver of arrows worn over her bare shoulders. A map was spread out before them, and equipment pouches were piled up on the floor by their feet. Both women looked up as he approached.

"You're both back," Valletto observed.

"So it appears," Thesilar remarked dryly.

Aestelle narrowed her eyes.

"Are you alright?" she asked.

Valletto paused. He considered telling them about the letters but stopped himself. Neither of them were truly his friends.

"I've received a letter from the capital," Valletto replied. "My orders are to positively confirm exactly who or what is in that burial chamber. I need to go in. My orders also suggested we seek military assistance from the Order of the Penitent and the Devoted, as there will be nothing forthcoming from the legion."

"Then as the old saying goes, we are definitely on the same hymn sheet," Aestelle smiled grimly, "as we already have aid from the Sisterhood. And we are going into that chamber to finish this."

"When?" Valletto asked.

"Now," Thesilar said. "I've sent Z'akke to go and fetch Ragran. As soon as they are ready, we are leaving."

"Good," Valletto nodded slowly, "because I need to get back to the capital. So, whatever is in there, even if it is Mhorgoth himself... I'll strangle the bastard with my bare hands. I'm ready to go as soon as you are."

Chapter Seventeen

Mount Ekansu loomed up from the evening mist drifting across the surrounding lower peaks, a solitary blade of gray-black rock punching up toward the darkening, iron skies above. Despite its snow-capped majesty and the spectacle of the entire range of Tarkis, Ragran found himself uninspired. Deflated. Even bored. It was that same tired trudge across the foothills and surrounding peaks to reach that same mountain that had yielded nothing for them in the last two visits, with the same group of people who were beginning to grate on his nerves. Z'akke's annoyingly chirpy optimism, Valletto's pathetic whining about his family, and Aestelle's ceaseless arrogance and vanity. At least Thesilar was solid and dependable. As was that enormous gur panther Aestelle had brought back from the abbey again. As much as Ragran tired of keeping his hand near a weapon at all times just in case the huge animal decided to lunge for him, he knew it would be useful in the fight ahead.

But those differing sources of irritation from each of his companions led on to another thought; that most of them had some sort of source of inspiration for what they did, for why they were there, trudging up that mountainside. Aestelle wanted to be a hero, to be loved and worshipped. Even Ragran could see that. Whatever happened between her and that Sisterhood was left unresolved, a gaping wound that Aestelle had somehow decided that glory and fame would heal. Perhaps she believed that being adored as a hero would somehow 'show them' they were wrong about her. Ragran's internal musings took him no further than that.

Then there was Valletto and Z'akke; two kindred spirits in their passion over magic, obsessive loyalty to their families, and… lack of resolve. Ragran grunted a brief laugh. At least he had some understanding over Z'akke's predicament, being a stranger in a foreign land, many days travel from his loved ones. Valletto was within the borders of his own nation and could walk home within a few days. Ragran honestly had no idea why the man was always so sullen and miserable. Perhaps this was why he found Thesilar's company the most bearable of the group. She did not have some theatrical 'purpose.' She just existed. She just got the job done. Like Ragran.

The path ahead meandered around to the left, up a steep incline made of a stony surface through which a few, isolated pine trees had still managed to take root. The now familiar rocky peak loomed ahead. Ragran looked up across the darkening sky. He felt something unfamiliar, a premonition. He muttered under his breath and pushed the feeling to one side. He knew himself well enough to know better than descending into hysteria over something as trivial as a mere feeling of impending doom.

At the head of the adventurer's small column, Aestelle held up a hand to signal the others to stop and then immediately moved that hand to her greatsword. Ragran hefted his heavy battleaxe from his own back and cast his gaze through the surrounding trees. His concentration and readiness for battle immediately eased off as he saw the gur panther amble off merrily toward four cloaked figures who emerged from the trees ahead. All were of slim build, their cloaks colored in a blue-gray that nearly matched the rocks of the mountains. Her hand dropping from the handle of her greatsword, Aestelle walked out to meet them. Ragran jogged to catch up with the others as they, too, quickened their pace to meet the new arrivals.

The first cloaked figure lowered her hood to reveal the features of a dark-haired woman in her twenties with olive skin and hazel eyes. She issued a greeting in a language Ragran did not understand. Aestelle replied in the same tongue.

"Sisterhood," Ragran said quietly as he approached, much to himself.

"Sisterhood Scouts, to be specific," Thesilar said quietly.

Meeting the Sisterhood warriors outside the mountain was the next stage in the plan Aestelle had described back at the inn; a plan that Thesilar had opposed by highlighting some very real flaws. The support from the Sisterhood did not stop only with soldiers; each of the adventurers carried a satchel of healing potions, provided by the Order.

"The main entrance is just up ahead," the dark-haired scout said to Aestelle, "but once you are in and cause anybody to try to leave, it will most likely be through one of the more secluded entrances."

"Of which there are another three," Thesilar interrupted, looking down her thin nose at the human scout, "and one is sealed by a cave in."

The dark-haired sister looked up at the elf.

"Five," she corrected with a mostly concealed smirk. "We found five. And they've re-opened the cave in already. But well done with the three you managed to stumble across."

Z'akke let out a series of chittering, clicking laughs and pointed a clawed finger at Thesilar's face.

"They're better than you!" the salamander beamed. "And this is supposed to be your main talent!"

"Regardless," Aestelle interjected, "are your scouts in position? The plan remains the same. We are going straight in through the main entrance that Sister Superior Joselin discovered. It's how I got out last time, and it is by far the quickest way to the main burial chamber. As soon as we start dropping these bastards, I would bet they will try to get Arteri out of there."

"Why?" Thesilar demanded, her lithe arms folded. "We've been in twice already and they were not worried by our presence. Why will they panic now?"

Aestelle turned in place and glowered at the elf ranger.

"Because," she sneered, "just as I told you when we debated this, at length, in the inn, this time we will not be relying on stealth. We are going to kick the front doors down and kill everything we see."

"And activate every trap we do not see," Thesilar winced, "because as I recall, the first time we went in there we *were* relying on stealth and we still nearly ended up with one dead. From a trap."

Aestelle paced over to Thesilar, her teeth gritted. Remembering the bloody, one-sided fight that had erupted last time Aestelle lost her temper with her former mentor, Ragran stepped in and stood next to Thesilar.

"Look!" Aestelle growled regardless. "We have a plan! I have agreed this with the abbess! Sisterhood scouts will secure every way in or out of that mountain. We go in and tear the place apart. We either fight our way to the tomb and burn whatever is in there, or we cause enough panic that they try to flee – straight into a line of a dozen bows at every exit."

"If you want to tear the place down, then we should all go in together," Thesilar argued. "We should punch through every entrance simultaneously rather than wait outside and waste our resources."

"I am not arguing about this again!" Aestelle pointed a gloved finger in accusation at the elf. "If we all go in, we cannot support each other! If they try to fight their way out of just one of the entrances, then at least two other units of sisters will be close enough to support the exit that is contested! If we all go in, every group is on their own! If you do not agree with the plan, Thesilar, then sod off home! But I am going in there! Imminently!"

Ragran cast his eyes around the assembled warriors. The Sisterhood scouts watched the infighting amidst the adventurers with nonchalance. Valletto eyed the mountain ahead anxiously. Z'akke's head swiveled from side to side to follow the argument before him, his fanged snout curled into an inane grin. Thesilar shook her head in disappointment, her pale face serious in concentration. Aestelle stared at the elf through narrowed eyes, her perfect features darkened in anger.

"I don't see how this will be so easy for the five of us," Ragran folded his arms, looking down at Aestelle, "or six, if you want to include that war cat. We did well defending the town a few nights ago. But don't let that go to your head, Aestelle. What waits for us in there will be a far greater threat."

"No! It will not!" Aestelle snapped. "In all of your years of fighting, have you learned nothing of necromancy? Do you still not see? They wanted to kill us when they assaulted Torgias! They sent everything they could! Undead armies depend on the control of necromancers, not how many bodies they have lying around and ready! Any individual necromancer can only control a finite number of undead. Yes, there will be a whole heap of dead soldiers in that mountain! Too many for us to face! But that does not mean for a second that they can all be animated and controlled at the same time!"

"She is correct," Z'akke nodded sagely, "it is not about the number of skeletons or corpses in there, it is about the number of necromancers and their power. And if they had more to spare, we would surely have faced more when Torgias was attacked."

"Do you both hear yourselves?!" Thesilar exclaimed. "I know how necromancy works! Aestelle, I was the one who taught you about it! I do not care if only twenty skeleton warriors in there can be raised at once! I care about the fact that every time we fell one, another will be raised from their near infinite supply of corpses! If you want to defeat an undead army, you use an army! We are not an army! Ragran and I have been doing this for a lot longer than you. We cannot win with brute force!"

Aestelle leaned forward to shove her face only an inch from Thesilar's.

"Then hit them harder!" she said slowly and venomously. "So they cannot get back up!"

"Enough of this!" Valletto shouted. "We have a plan and a decision has been made! Enough bickering! We commit to the plan, now! Are you in?"

Ragran again looked at the assembled warriors. The scouts continued to watch the argument impassively. Z'akke bowed his head and muttered what Ragran assumed was a brief prayer to his people's Deliverer. Aestelle turned away, drew her sword, and rotated her shoulders and neck to limber up for the fight. The gur panther stared up at the mountain, its eyes narrowed with an almost human display of anger and sadness.

"Alright," Thesilar nodded, "alright. Let's go and save Basilea."

***

The shallow slope leading up to the tomb complex entrance broadened out, enough for the five warriors and the lethal gur panther to approach in a line, side-by-side. A sheer drop plummeted down to either side of the arched, rocky path, the jagged stones far below hidden in the darkness of the evening shadows. Her greatsword held in one hand and resting across her shoulders, Aestelle looked ahead at the entrance; a dark, narrow cave hidden behind drooping pine tree roots, damp moss, and green lichen. It was the same cave she had escaped by after leaving Joselin and her comrades' bodies behind. Aestelle shuddered at the thought of facing them in combat, should the tomb's occupants have found a way to raise the sisters as undead warriors. She looked to either side.

Ragran carried his axe across his barrel chest, his eyes fixed ahead. Z'akke walked calmly, a slight smile on his face, as if out for a gentle walk somewhere scenic. Thesilar's eyes flitted up, down, and from side to side, constantly searching for any potential threats, an arrow already notched to her bow. Valletto looked dead ahead at the cave, one hand clutching tightly to his staff, his eyes narrowed in concentration. Seeba padded along the rocky surface by Aestelle's side, her own eyes telling her story of loss as she looked ahead at the cave where she had watched her former mistress fall.

Aestelle was the first into the cave. The cavernous opening towered up above them, sloping up quickly to the extent that the natural ceiling above was beyond even the flickering light created by the flames atop Z'akke's staff. Stalagmites and stalactites jutted out from above and below, lining the cave like hideously misshapen teeth of a terrible creature from legend as they advanced through its mouth and toward its heart. Up ahead, the ancient entrance to the tomb complex lay carved in the jagged rock face; two grand pillars supporting a triangular cross beam, etched with dust-covered symbols. The stone double doors were already open. Aestelle saw a long corridor stretching out on the other side, its walls lit with flaming torches.

"Here they come," Thesilar warned, raising her bow and drawing back on the string.

Aestelle heard the clicking and clacking of dry bones from the dimly lit corridor ahead. She paced forward wordlessly, Ragran by her side, ready to take on the brunt of the advancing undead whilst the bow and magic from behind would do their work. She could see the front rank of the advancing undead guards now; skeletal soldiers clothed in faded rags and torn coats of mail, carrying heavily pitted blades in their boney fists, packed shoulder to shoulder in the narrow corridor as they advanced in pairs. An involuntary smile spread across Aestelle's lips. Where fear should have been, she felt only excitement and exhilaration. She looked across at Ragran. The huge man nodded. Seeba forced her way between the two warriors, pushing them apart with her bulk before standing a pace ahead of Aestelle and looking back. Aestelle smirked cockily down at the gur panther.

"Go."

Seeba pelted down the corridor, rapidly accelerating to a full sprint that seemed impossibly fast for such a large creature. Aestelle and Ragran ran after her, their two-handed blades held high and ready to strike. An arrow was loosed from behind, whistling past Aestelle's shoulder and over the top of Seeba to plant directly into the chest of one of the skeletons, returning the undead warrior to the grave. A fireball hurtled past a moment later, engulfing the front rank of the skeletons in roaring flames and sending an undead warrior staggering blindly to one side for a few paces until it clattered down to burn on the rocky floor.

Seeba leapt up to attack the front rank of two skeletons, hurtling into the first animated corpse with enough force to knock it to the ground, where she quickly clamped her jaws around the dead warrior's skull and pulled it free from the body. A skeletal swordsman from the rank behind immediately stepped up to attack but was felled by a powerful swipe across the ribs from the roaring gur panther. As far as Aestelle's eyes could make out in the dimness, ranks of skeletal soldiers waited crammed in the corridor, side-by-side in long precessions of ranks of two, nudging forward whilst the raging gur panther tore into the head of their deathly column.

Aestelle caught up with Seeba, initiating her first attack with a powerful, overhead swipe that hacked down to cleave through her undead opponent. Leaping across to plant her back against the huge gur panther, Aestelle rolled over the creature into a follow up attack, lashing out with her long blade to slice across the chest of a second undead warrior. Ragran smashed into the fight like a hurricane, his heavy blade decapitating a skeleton and smashing open the guard of a second.

"Force them back!" Aestelle growled as she ducked beneath an attack from an axe-wielding skeleton. "Get them out of this corridor!"

Aestelle and Ragran stood shoulder-to-shoulder, hacking and slicing at the wall of skeletons as Seeba ran violently amok through the undead column. Aestelle parried a blow from a skeleton armed with an ancient bronze sword, batting the attack aside before grabbing her own sword by the blade and swinging the heavy cross guard around to smash the undead warrior's skull apart. With a brief respite until the next warrior stepped forward, Aestelle looked across and saw Ragran lunge in to headbutt a warhammer-wielding skeleton opposite him. The skeleton staggered back from the force of the blow, giving Aestelle time to lop its head off before she was forced to resume her guard when the next undead warrior stepped forward.

***

Up ahead, the fight spilled out into a dimly lit room with a low ceiling as Ragran led the charge against the undead. With a roar, Seeba leapt out of the corridor and into the room, knocking down a skeleton that Z'akke sensed was just being re-animated. Aestelle was next through the doorway, linking a series of stylized and over-embellished blocks and parries until her cockiness was punished with a slice across the arm. Thesilar let loose an arrow to dispatch her assailant, and Aestelle charged back into the fight.

"Idiots!" Thesilar snarled as she snatched another arrow from her quiver. "They are taking the fight into the open, where the enemy can use their numbers against us!"

"I don't know!" Z'akke beamed, edging forward. "I think this is all going rather well!"

Already feeling the effects of continued use of his pyromantic powers, Z'akke unsheathed his sword and flung himself through the doorway into the packed room. Seeba continued to fight ferociously in the center, flanked on either side by Ragran and Aestelle. Z'akke dashed off to the left, taking position at Ragran's side just as a skeletal spearman attempted to move around to flank the giant human warrior. Z'akke hurtled across to cut off the advance of the skeletal soldier, swinging out a heavy but well-timed blow with his sword to cut off the end of the undead warrior's spear before reversing the blow and hacking off the top of its cranium. A second skeleton jumped in to attack the salamander mage-priest, but Z'akke was faster. He slammed a fist heavily into the skeleton's face, knocking its head back with a clicking of bone before a powerful sword strike cut the undead warrior down. Z'akke allowed himself a broad grin. He ought to use his sword more often, he thought to himself.

Z'akke sensed the flare of magical power as a spell was cast on the other side of the room. He looked across and saw Valletto strike his staff against the tiled floor whilst holding out his forearm. A deafening rush of wind whipped up around the sorcerer and then smashed into an advancing rank of three skeletons, tearing the first undead soldier limb from limb and sending the second two scattering back against the wall behind them, where one was quickly beheaded by Thesilar's sword. The six warriors formed a rough arrowhead as they continued to advance into the chamber, fighting their way forward step by step as they faced skeletal warriors ahead, and from directly behind as unseen necromancers continued to re-raise those few battered bodies that were still in a position to be animated and flung back into the battle.

***

Aestelle brought her blade back over one shoulder to block the attack, feeling the cold steel press against her with the force of the blow. Quickly bringing her sword across to her left in time to deflect another attack, she then saw an opening in the skeleton's guard and brought one foot up to plant a kick against the dead warrior's ribcage. The undead soldier stumbled back and Aestelle advanced, planting a shoulder against her adversary to barge it back again to create enough space before lancing the tip of her blade through its ribcage and severing the spine. The skeleton dropped down to her feet in two uneven parts. The room fell silent. Pain flared up from Aestelle's wounded arm. She glanced around and saw her comrades stood ready for another attack from the seemingly endless precession of undead. Thesilar let out a contemplative breath, half-closed her eyes, and then spoke.

"D'you know, I rather think they know we are here now."

Aestelle pressed a hand against her wounded arm and allowed a wave of divinity magic to transform the open wound into a long bruise. Ragran likewise treated a wound across his bare chest by pouring half of a healing potion across it and then downing the rest. Z'akke tapped his staff against one open hand pensively, watching the twenty or so motionless skeletons piled around them. Valletto took a step back toward the center of the room whilst he looked up at the ceiling above, but he drew too close to Seeba and elicited an unfriendly growl that made him instinctively jump away again. Thesilar nudged a skeletal corpse with one foot and peered down at the body.

"Bloody bone idle, this lot," she remarked.

The room remained silent. Thesilar looked up at her fellow adventurers with an expectant grin.

"Nothing? Anybody? Bone idle?"

Z'akke suddenly burst into a clicking, chitterous laugh.

"I just got it!" the salamander beamed.

"Two dozen skeletons," Valletto exhaled, lowering his staff and sword. "I might be new to your world of adventuring, but I'm willing to bet that this was nothing more than fodder to slow us down whilst they mobilized the main defense."

Ragran let out a brief chuckle.

"Good of them to do so. Good warm up."

Aestelle looked at the far end of the room where a solitary doorway waited. She remembered leaving via that doorway after her fateful encounter with Joselin and Seeba.

"Through there," she nodded to the others, "there is another corridor that splits into two. We need to head right. Left goes deeper down, which is normally indicative of a more important part of a tomb complex, but not in this case. Left leads... well, we need to head right."

Thesilar walked across to Aestelle, slinging her bow over one shoulder.

"Interesting place," she said quietly.

"You would know more than I do about that," Aestelle folded her arms.

"Yes, I would. And I do. You see, this entrance we have just taken was built very much with the future in mind. Whoever planned this tomb clearly thought that one day it would be a very overt and well-known place of worship. But not at the time of construction. Back then it was all a secret."

Aestelle frowned.

"How do you know that?"

"The entrance we just used," Thesilar gestured behind her, "it is really rather grand. But it is also hidden away inside a natural cave. It was built thus so that one day, when whomever built this place had won a war or whatever was planned and was able to publically declare their politics in this region, that cave could be made into the main entrance for the entire tomb network. So that worshippers might come here, straight to the main level, and sing their praises to whoever lay here, or whoever once lay here. But last time we were here, we came in through an old airway for the builders way, way up there."

Aestelle looked pensively up toward the area of their last expedition and thought on just how long it took to fight down to this level, where Joselin and her sisters had barged their way directly into. The history and the make up of the tomb complex made a lot more sense once Thesilar voiced her thoughts; a secret, multi-leveled, complex and well-defended network of tunnels and catacombs leading to the main burial chamber that, one day, Mhorgoth's disciples hoped to open up to worshippers. Aestelle looked across at Thesilar. She may have been the better of the two with blades and fists – and certainly when it came to beauty, Aestelle mentally asserted – but her old mentor was still years ahead in understanding the complexities of tombs and the undead.

"What you told me, last time we were alone," Aestelle said quietly, careful that none of the others could overhear, "about your cousin. I am... sorry that we have not had another chance to discuss it."

Thesilar's features hardened a little, momentarily transforming from excitement and interest in their surroundings to an almost melancholy regret. She quickly hid it with a smile.

"And I am sorry that we still have not spoke about this man of yours," she said in a hushed tone.

"Which one?" Aestelle flashed a cocky smile.

"*The* one," Thesilar replied seriously. "The only one that clearly has ever meant anything to you instead of some meaningless, isolated encounter."

Aestelle's smile faded away. She felt her features darken as she exhaled quietly, recalling their final meeting.

The late afternoon breeze wafting across the cliffs from the south brought the slightest, refreshing respite from the fierce sun in the cloudless sky. To the south, the sunlight picked out the peaks of the small waves rippling across the Sea of Eriskos as fishing boats, small merchantmen, and a pair of naval sloops gently drifted along the coastal sea-lane. Her fingers clutching the reins of her horse, Aestelle looked up at the tall paladin stood with her at the crossroad by the extravagant inn. Orion glanced across uneasily, the low sun causing his flawlessly handsome features to twist in a wince. He wore the extravagant garb of a freshly promoted Paladin Defender, complete with a cloak of dazzling blue worn across one shoulder of his highly polished plate armor. That was his reward for his part in saving the Hegemony from an Abyssal invasion at the Battle of Andro. Aestelle's prize was far simpler and more reflective of her standing in the Hegemony. She had been given a lot of money, and nothing else.

"I really could not think of anything as sentimental or impressive to give you in return for your Eloicon," Orion stumbled over his words, his eyes now fixed clearly at his feet. "I am afraid this was the best I could do. Its color is the same shade as that of my Order. So you can remember us. Fondly, I hope."

Aestelle accepted the gift the burly knight offered; a brightly colored sapphire of blue. She noticed that it had already been drilled through so that she could wear it in her hair. She felt a smile light up her face. It was beautiful, clearly expensive, but more important than all of that, it was personal. Thoughtful. She had received so many gifts from men attempting to woo her that they all merged into one tedious recollection of dreary flowers and glasses of wine. This was the first gift she ever received that made her feel warm inside.

"Thank you, Ri."

"Do you have to go?" the blond paladin suddenly looked up and met her gaze.

Aestelle let out a short breath. There it was. The resolve was crumbling. She suppressed a smile. Many men before had failed to control their feelings before now. Finally, after fighting back-to-back in small skirmishes and a major battle, after the bickering and the jokes, the stolen glances and the unsaid words, he was finally going to admit his feelings for her.

"It's what I do." Aestelle shrugged, daring him to press her further. "What else is there?"

"You could stay. You could... I do not know... rejoin the Sisterhood. They would take you back in an instant. Or... you could become a paladin. You can fight better than anybody I know! You can ride a horse in battle! Tancred could put in a word for you. You would only have to learn to fight in armor, and that is not so difficult."

No, no, no! The idiot did not get it! This was not about war! It was not about who to join, or belonging! It was about them! The two of them!

"I don't take orders well, Ri." Aestelle looked him dead in the eye, forcing him to glance down at his feet again. "I never did. That is why I left the Sisterhood. I don't want to go through all of that again."

Orion looked up. He met her gaze. She saw a flicker of confidence return to his eyes. Her optimism grew once more.

"I wish you would not go," he said softly.

Aestelle stepped in, close, too close for mere friends, just as she had several times when they had been on the road together. This time, he surely had to pick up on the signs.

"Then give me a reason to stay," she said.

Just kiss me, you bloody fool! Aestelle's mind raced. Mere seconds dragged on like years. Orion's eyes slowly sank back down to his feet. He took a step back, his shoulders slumped in resignation.

"You are right," he said quietly, "it would never work. I have to respect who you are and what makes you happy."

No! No, no! You bloody idiot!

"You are best living your life of adventure on the open road," the knight concluded, "I have to respect that."

Her heart heavy with despair, Aestelle closed her eyes and shook her head. She too stepped back. The moment was gone. Lost. Was he rejecting her? Surely not. For all his courage in facing mortal peril, he just did not have the backbone to make his move. And given her endless reserve of perfect qualities, she would be damned if that move would come from her first. Some might call that arrogance, but to Aestelle, it was simply knowing one's own worth. Looking up at him now, the dynamic, daring, dangerous man she had found herself falling for was replaced with a simpering, broken coward who would not make that move. She was better off without him. Yes. Better off. Her mind fogged by anger, confusion, and disappointment, she looked up and forced the most false smile she had ever mustered, before flashing him a wink and pressing a friendly fist against his shoulder.

"Take care, Ogre. You're a good friend."

Her stomach turning over and over, her heart hammering in her chest, Aestelle continued her veneer of coolness and vaulted up onto her horse. She immediately regretted her choice of last words. She had stressed the word *'friend' to punish him for his lack of resolve. He did not deserve that.*

"You're a good man, Ri," she said sincerely, her voice choked. "Don't ever let anybody tell you otherwise."

Dragging the reins of her horse around, Aestelle brought her steed onto the north road and spurred the animal into a canter, tears rolling down her cheeks for the first time in years as soon as her back was turned on the forlorn paladin.

"I don't know which one you mean." Aestelle shrugged nonchalantly, suddenly hugely self-conscious of the blue sapphire worn separate from the other precious stones, in that special place to one side of her face. "One would assume you are back on the trail of your fictitious love story which you appear to have plucked straight from the lyrics of these ludicrous bard songs about me. Thesilar, there is nothing to see. I do not do… romance."

The slender elf's face slowly grew grim, her delicate features hardening as she leaned closer in toward Aestelle.

"For all of your posturing," Thesilar said quietly, "for all of your bravado, your swagger, your strutting arrogance… you really are an absolute, unpardonable coward sometimes."

Thesilar turned her back, whipping her ponytail out behind her before striding off to the far end of the room. Her face reddening, Aestelle watched her go. What absolute nonsense! She knew exactly what Thesilar was referring to. She could have voiced her feelings at any point, if she so chose. But why should she? There was no one who held parity with Aestelle. Any man would be lucky to hold her attention, let alone something longer term and more meaningful. It was not cowardice that stopped her from speaking out on the cliff top that day. It was rightful and justified pride. She did not chase. She was chased. That was how it was. Her jaw set grimly, she paced off after Thesilar. Before she could open her mouth, Valletto suddenly turned to Z'akke.

"Z'akke!" the sorcerer called. "Do you sense that?"

The muscular salamander mage-priest nodded slowly and looked across at the door at the far side of the room.

"They're coming," he smiled grimly.

Chapter Eighteen

Thesilar swore as a salvo of arrows thumped into the makeshift wooded barricade. She peered cautiously over the top of the upturned table and across the cavernous hallway where a rank of gray-fleshed, animated corpses of her long dead kindred lined the raised platform at the far side of the room, dead hands grabbing arrows from quivers on their back. She shot to her feet, drew back her bowstring, and quickly loosed off an arrow into one of the skeletal elven archers, catching the abomination square in the chest. To her right, Aestelle leant around the side of a crumbled pillar and loosed off an arrow from her own bow but succeeded only in catching one of the undead kindred archers in the leg.

The fighting had raged to and fro through the catacombs for over two hours now. A trail of corpses returned to death punctuated the adventurers' meandering advance that had now led up to the next floor and a large, open chamber that was littered with broken furniture of stout wood. Thesilar and Ragran crouched behind one upturned table whilst Z'akke and Valletto took cover behind a second, leaving Aestelle isolated on one side of the room behind a pillar of gray stone, struggling to keep Seeba under control and from dashing off into danger. Ahead of them were ten skeletal kindred archers – somehow more offensive to Thesilar, who was well used to facing undead who were once human, but not as accustomed to seeing the dead of her own kin's sanctity insulted by dark magic. Two groups of elven zombies, clad in ancient but stout armor and carrying tall spears, maneuvered themselves to the flanks of the large room as their archer brethren continued to target the tomb's invaders.

"Now what?" Ragran grumbled, yanking an arrow out of one arm and downing yet another healing potion.

"I could try talking to them?" Thesilar shrugged. "They were once elves, after all. We might find some common ground."

"I'm glad you think this is funny, Thes!" the northern giant boomed.

A blast of fire erupted amidst one of the groups of five zombie tallspears, swallowing up an undead warrior in a ball of orange flame. Thesilar felt a pang of sympathy as she saw the violence of Z'akke's magic, even though it was one of her ancestors being returned to a holy rest. She felt an anger grow within her at the thought of her own kin, supposedly wiser and above the petty meddlings in dark magic that one would expect from mere humans, duped into following one of their own along the forbidden pathway of necromancy. She then mentally chastised herself for allowing her concentration to drift in the midst of battle. She looked across at Ragran. The barbarian looked back. He winced as another salvo of arrows thunked against the table.

"What's wrong with you?" Thesilar demanded.

"I... I'm..."

"What?" Thesilar insisted, risking another glance over the barricade.

Ragran shook his head.

"I think this is it."

Thesilar stared down, wide-eyed at her old comrade.

"What do you mean?"

"I'm not getting any younger, Thes. I have to run out of luck sooner or later. I... I've had a feeling about this since we got here. I think this is it."

Thesilar leaned around the edge of the table and shot an arrow straight into the forehead of one of the advancing tallspears, dropping the zombie in its place.

"Don't talk nonsense, you oaf!" she snapped. "We've faced worse than this! Now come on, they'll be on us in seconds and we need you!"

Ragran's brow lowered. He nodded in quiet acceptance, somehow looking older than ever. For not the first time, Thesilar felt that awful twist in her gut, the pain of knowing that she would outlive each and every one of her human friends. She quickly repressed it.

On the far right of the room, Aestelle and Seeba charged out of cover and into the advancing tallspears. Z'akke and Valletto left the cover of their own barricade and rushed forward to assist, wind and fire blasting from their staffs. A hail of arrows shot into them. A projectile slammed into Z'akke's armored chest but only succeeded in lodging itself in his thick carapace; almost immediately, a second arrow imbedded itself in his gut, and he collapsed to his knees, clutching the wound and crying out in pain before pitching over on his face.

Ragran's eyes opened wide.

"Go get him!" he roared at Thesilar. "I'll keep them off you!"

The lumbering barbarian hefted himself to his feet and charged at the skeletal archers with an echoing yell, his axe held above his head. On the right, Aestelle, Seeba, and Valletto succeeded in hacking down the small group of zombie spearmen, whilst on the left, five of the undead elves advanced steadily toward Thesilar. Ragran charged straight across the center of the room, another volley of arrows whistling through the air to meet him. One slammed into his leg, another into his shoulder. He kept running. Thesilar quickly slid her bow over her shoulder and sprinted from cover toward where Z'akke lay bleeding on the dusty floor, his hisses and screams of pain audible even over the din of battle.

Thesilar dived down next to him, conscious of the second group of tallspears rushing behind her. She grabbed him under his arms and attempted to drag him back to the barricade but failed to shift his heavy bulk. Nervously eying the advancing zombies behind her, she quickly pulled the arrow out of Z'akke's wound and poured half of a potion over the bloody mess left behind before emptying the rest into the wailing salamander's throat.

The healing magic was instantaneous. His eyes were still pained, but now fear replaced with a furious determination, the salamander mage-priest quickly sat up, retrieved his staff, and chanted a series of hisses and clicks until roaring fire blazed from the wooden pole to incinerate one of the approaching tallspears. Thesilar had barely enough time to drop a second zombie with an arrow to the chest before they were on her. Thesilar and Z'akke drew their swords and charged into the fight.

***

Feeling his draw from the arcane plains running dry – and the characteristic onset of exhaustion with it – Valletto held out his staff and summoned another typhoon of energy, directing the violent wind blast through the ranks of skeletal archers crowding around Ragran. The pulse of energy scattered a trio of the animated elven soldiers back away from Ragran, giving the huge man time to swing his axe and cut down another foe. Bringing up his legion daga sword, Valletto turned his attention back to the more immediate threat of the armored zombies locked in combat with himself, Aestelle, and Seeba. Aestelle snarled as she curved her sword down in a heavy strike against one foe, fluidly following up with a second attack by slamming the cross guard of her weapon into the face of another.

The first zombie, hacked half in twain, staggered back for a moment but then turned to launch itself at Valletto, lashing out with the tip of its long spear. Valletto jumped to one side, batting the attack away but finding himself on the back foot immediately when the zombie swung the deadly pole arm around into another strike. Then Seeba leapt up and knocked the zombie down to the ground, savaging its face viciously until it lay still. Valletto let out a breath of relief.

For the briefest of moments, an image of home flashed into his mind. The terracotta walled house he shared with his wife and children; the similar layout of the surrounding homes, the smell of lavender and olives from the surrounding fields. Every culture had some saying relating to the world being a dangerous place, but the rural outskirts of the City of the Golden Horn were not remotely unsafe. Yet, due to just a handful of ill-thought out, rapidly made decisions, he was now practically buried in the ancient tombs of a powerful evil, possibly to die at the hands of nightmarish creatures from long forgotten graves, left to rot where his wife and children would never know what happened to him and why he left his home so suddenly. The people back home, in their safe houses and secure vocations, could never comprehend the things he was seeing right now, at that very moment. Valletto gritted his teeth. He needed to ensure that these would not be the last things he saw.

Content that Aestelle and Seeba had the last two zombies of this group occupied, he turned back to survey the rest of the battle. Ragran stood his ground valiantly, bleeding from several wounds and trading blows with four of five skeletons that had him surrounded. Z'akke and Thesilar, both wounded, staggered back toward the center of the room as they fought off the attacks of twice their number of elven zombies. Steeling his courage, Valletto let out a cry and charged into the midst of the skeletal archers, striking down at the first as he struggled to barge his way through to Ragran. The skeletal soldier brought up a short, pitted blade to block Valletto's first attack. Anger coursing through his veins, Valletto brought his own sword down again, this time forcefully enough to knock the undead warrior's shorter blade aside. Quickly capitalizing on the opening, Valletto swiped his sword across in a powerful cut and took off the skeleton's head.

His eyes wide in surprise at his own success, Valletto saw another skeleton turn to face him. He risked a quick look over his shoulder and saw Aestelle and Seeba plowing into the side of the group of zombie spearmen attacking Thesilar and Z'akke. Bloodied and exhausted though they all were, yet again they were turning the tide and achieving victory. Valletto allowed himself an exhausted smile as he parried the attack of the skeleton facing him, and countered with a heavy but ineffectual strike of his own. Then the wall at the far end of the room collapsed in its entirety, and a pair of zombie trolls lumbered through the dust to attack.

***

Letting out a grunt, more from the pain of his bleeding wounds rather than any show of aggression, Ragran advanced on the rickety, almost fragile skeleton. He swung his axe around to cleave through the undead soldier's blade and then bite the edge of the weapon deep into the elf's chest. With another snort, Ragran kicked the skeleton off his axe and arced the weapon up, over his head, and then down to split the undead archer's skull in two. That was when the near wall suddenly collapsed spectacularly, flooding the room in plumes of choking dust. Ragran peered through the smoke, coughing and hacking, and saw two tall, bulky silhouettes. Zombie trolls.

"Not again!" Valletto breathed from a few paces behind Ragran.

The muscular barbarian hefted his axe up across his chest.

"We beat their sort before," he grimaced, "and we can do it again."

Simultaneously, a blast of fire pelted into one of the zombified trolls whilst a column of air smashed against the second, inferno and tornado conjured up by Z'akke and Valletto. An arrow punched into the troll held in place by the arcane winds, then a second as Thesilar let fly with her bow. From a few feet away, a staccato explosion resonated around the chamber as Aestelle fired her pistol into the troll set ablaze by Z'akke magic. Yelling aloud, Ragran sprinted at the burning troll with his axe held at the ready. The towering creature paced forward, heedless of the flames eating away at its dead flesh. The colossal creature swiped down at Ragran as he approached with a clenched fist the size of the barbarian's entire torso. Ragran ducked quickly beneath the attack and hacked out with his axe, catching the fist just after it passed him and cleaving off two of the knuckles.

Seeba leapt into the fight with a roar, her claws swiping at the troll's legs as her jaw clenched around one of the monster's kneecaps, which was torn free and spat out after a moment later. Ragran heaved his axe up again but saw a blur out of the corner of his eye just too late as the troll's mangled fist came swiping back toward him. He heard bones break and felt pain shoot up his arm and across his chest as the fist smashed into him, tossing him effortlessly through the air to skid across the stony floor, leaving a smear of blood behind him.

***

Aestelle sprinted across to the blazing troll, wincing as the heat from another blast of fiery magic smashed into the hulking creature's flank. With a rasping, half-choked roar emitted from dry, dead vocal chords, the zombie troll lunged out at her with a deadly fist; Aestelle nimbly leapt over the attack and reached to the small of her back with both hands, grabbing her throwing knives from her belt and flinging them into the side of the creature's head as she jumped past. Landing behind the monstrosity, she reached over her shoulder and unsheathed her greatsword, swinging the blade around into a heavy attack to rip open the zombie troll's back.

Fire, wind, and arrows pelted the troll as Aestelle's blade and Seeba's claws tore at the dead flesh. The creature let out an almost mournful howl and collapsed down to one knee, the flames eating at its dead, blackened skin now dying down to little more than a simmer. Seeba leapt up to wrap her muscular limbs around the troll's neck, knocking it to the ground where the gur panther set about mauling its face and throat. Aestelle dashed over, planted one booted foot on the troll's chest, and drove her sword down into where its heart had once beat. She looked up and saw Z'akke, Thesilar, and Valletto all advancing around the defeated zombie troll. Her eyes widened in alarm. Who was fighting the second troll? She looked across the darkened chamber anxiously.

The second troll stood still, rigid, motionless. A tall, slim figure draped in a black cloak stood before the towering troll, one pale white hand raised up toward the monster's head. The fingers of that deathly pale hand slowly closed. The zombie troll collapsed heavily to the ground and laid perfectly still, any evidence of arcane manipulation and animation now completely gone. The figure turned around. A well-formed, smooth face with eyes of enchanting, dark red regarded her. Aestelle recognized Khirius.

"Vampire!" Thesilar screamed in alarm, notching an arrow to her bow and letting fly.

The arrow slammed straight into Khirius' chest, knocking him to stagger back a pace. With a roar, Z'akke leapt forward with both of his deadly fists blazing with arcane fire. Seeba advanced, eyeing the vampire warily, her teeth bared.

"Wait!" Aestelle shouted. "Stop!"

Khirius pulled the arrow out of his chest and held his hands out to either side passively. Z'akke and Seeba continued to advance, whilst Thesilar took another arrow from her quiver and Valletto drew his sword.

"Wait!" Aestelle repeated forcefully. "He's on our side! Stop, you bloody idiots! Have you not just seen him come to our aid?"

"It's undead, Aestelle!" Z'akke growled. "Snap out of it! Don't look at the thing! It will enchant you!"

"Stop," Ragran coughed, struggling up to one bloodied knee as he held himself weakly in place, holding on to his axe, "I saw that thing help us. Just wait for a moment."

"Wait?!" Valletto exclaimed. "It's a damn aberration! An undead monster! We need to kill it, just like all the rest!"

Aestelle looked around the room slowly. Felled skeletons and zombies littered the tiled floor. Thesilar stared down the arrow on her bow, her gut red with a bloody wound and her eyes drifting in and out of focus. Ragran breathed heavily as he clung to his axe, one arm mangled with a broken bone protruding through torn flesh. Seeba stared intently at the vampire, her beautiful fur matted with blood from her own wounds. Z'akke, his fists still ablaze, eyed the vampire as he limped awkwardly forward. Only Aestelle and Valletto seemed in a good position to continue the fight.

"What do you want, Khirius?" Aestelle called out.

The vampire looked across at her, his expression neutral.

"To end this," he replied evenly, "to help you do what you came here to do."

"Lies!" Valletto snapped. "This thing is one of them! Why are we even entertaining this?"

"Because he dropped one of their trolls by himself," Ragran coughed weakly, struggling to his feet as Thesilar edged over toward her old comrade.

"Theatrics!" Z'akke snarled. "I saw it myself! He stopped that thing from being animated, nothing more! That's easy enough to do when you are the one who animated it in the first place!"

"I didn't animate that troll," Khirius said calmly, "she did. The one not far from here. The one orchestrating all of this. Now listen to me so I can tell you what you are about to face."

"Don't listen to that thing!" Valletto shouted. "Are Z'akke and I the only ones left here with any sanity? It's a vampire! They spout lies to..."

"Young man," Khirius cut off the aeromancer, "I would imagine that I am the first vampire you have ever met. Please save me the lesson in what vampires are and are not, given that your teaching has most likely come from morbid, fanciful stories and plays. You have no idea what I am."

Thesilar lowered her bow. She took a healing potion from her belt – her last – and, still eyeing the vampire, pulled the stopper out and poured it over Ragran's wound.

"You are not the first vampire I have ever met," the elf ranger said, "and I am really rather confident in my knowledge of your sort. Now, say what you came here to say and then we will decide if you are leaving this room on your feet, or in an urn or ashes."

"Thesilar," Z'akke growled, "it's a..."

"Let him speak, Z'akke!" Thesilar urged.

"Why?" the salamander glowered across at the elf. "Why should we? This makes no sense! We are here slaying undead! This thing is undead! What possible reason could it have to want to help us?"

Thesilar looked across at Aestelle and cast her eyes down and back up across the half-Elohi warrior's body.

"Oh, I think I have a fairly good idea what he wants," Thesilar said. "Go on, vampire, tell us what you came here to say."

Khirius walked slowly along the side of the room, his dark eyes occasionally flitting across to eye the poised, bloodied gur panther. Z'akke continued to watch him, his clenched fists still crackling with fire. Aestelle looked at her companions and made a quick assessment as to who was in the worst shape to continue. She checked her belt. Only one healing potion left for herself.   She walked across to where Thesilar crouched by Ragran. The barbarian's arm was healed over from the magic potion, but judging by the discoloration of the skin, even after the magical healing there were still problems. It was clear that whilst the bone was set, it was still brittle and would take time to heal properly. Even with more arcane healing, Ragran would not be lifting an axe with that arm any time soon. Before Thesilar could argue, Aestelle pressed one of her hands against the elf's stomach and let out a pulse of divinity magic to close the wound across the ranger's abdomen. Color immediately returned to Thesilar's face. She nodded in gratitude.

"The main burial chamber is just up there." Khirius pointed to the collapsed wall at the back of the chamber. "Through that wall and then up to the next level. But it is defended."

Aestelle walked over to Z'akke and offered him her last healing potion. The salamander stubbornly shook his head.

"Take it," Aestelle insisted quietly.

Khirius watched Aestelle and Z'akke as the mage-priest took the potion.

"Anything else?" Thesilar smirked warily. "Centuries of knowledge of power crammed into that lithe form, and all you have for us is some simple directions to the next room? Like a deadly house servant?"

Khirius shot a warning glare at the elf ranger.

"This tomb is guarded by an organization called the Coven," the vampire continued. "It is an insidious network of necromancers than originally took root in Basilea but has now spread a little further. You already know that this tomb was built, in secret, centuries ago to house the body of Arteri the Plague. The Coven acquired that information after this tomb was discovered by chance only weeks ago, and they quickly moved in here to claim it."

Aestelle hung her head and let out a long sigh. This was her fault. Or perhaps Orion's. She had wanted to continue to explore the tunnel network when the two of them had stumbled upon it during the summer; Aestelle had been vocal in her desire to see the exploration through to the end whilst it was Orion who had insisted on leaving the tombs to return to their original task. Then again, Aestelle only wanted to see that exploration through because she sensed treasures. There was nothing altruistic in her motivation at the time. She felt her shoulders slump. Truly a fallen hero. But this was her opportunity to rise again. To do the right thing.

"What does your Coven want with the tomb?" Valletto demanded.

"It's not *my* Coven," the vampire replied quickly, "and they want to raise Arteri the Plague, a being of immense power, lieutenant to Mhorgoth himself. To have such a being in a position of leadership would elevate the Coven from a secretive organization skulking in the shadows to a real power in Pannithor. At least, that is what the Coven's leadership believes. For somebody as simple as me, I see a group of fools meddling with a dark power they do not understand and engineering their own destruction. But if Arteri is raised – a lengthy and complicated task to do properly, lest he be restored instead as a simple, mindless zombie – then destruction will not end with the Coven. Thousands will die. Innocent people. That is why I am here to offer my help."

Valletto spat a curse and shook his head.

"A good, noble vampire? There is no such thing!"

"I never claimed to be good," Khirius said, "but this, what you see before you... this was not always me. I did not choose this. I have remained low, hiding away from the world for two hundred years. I have no interest in politics or war. But I have been dragged into this now and forced to make a choice. This is my choice. I am not a good person, but I can at least try to do some good, even trapped in this form."

Valletto swore again. Z'akke growled something in his own tongue which, whilst indecipherable to Aestelle, was clear in its tone – he agreed with Valletto.

"What defends the tomb?" Thesilar asked. "What awaits us?"

Khirius folded his arms, the golden hilt of his sword protruding from within the folds of his dark cloak.

"Arteri's guard," he replied, "his best soldiers. The elite of those who followed him alongside Mhorgoth in life. Much of what you have faced in here has been rather unceremoniously dumped here by the Coven to bolster the defenses, but not all. The Inner Guard were buried with him. As were the skeletal drakons."

"Eg... Dragon?" Z'akke's eyes opened wide in excitement.

"Drakon," Khirius corrected the salamander, "two of them. Tansia was good enough to show them to me not long ago. To remind me of where my loyalties should lie. It did not work."

"Who is Tansia?" Aestelle asked.

"Who cares who Tansia is?" Ragran wheezed, one arm wrapped around his belly. "Did you not hear? Two undead drakons! Aestelle, we have done well with achieving what we have achieved, and I can still stand strong facing some dead guardsmen, no matter how elite they think they are, but drakons? Two?"

Aestelle gritted her teeth and shook her head. No. They had not come so far only to quit now. Of course the mention of drakons left her heart thumping with fear – she would be insane not to feel terror at the thought of facing them – but what use were they to the world as heroes if they abandoned their task at the first mention of something they had not faced before?

"No," Aestelle declared, "we do not stop. We carry on. There could be a row of a dozen drakons up in that tomb. I am not turning back now. We carry on and we finish what we set out to do."

Valletto looked across at Aestelle, the anger twisting his face now replaced with fear. Z'akke nodded slowly.

"Yes," he hissed quietly, "yes. We carry on. There are people who need to be protected from what is in this place. We carry on."

"Right," Valletto agreed, pale-faced, "right. I'm in. We carry on."

Thesilar stood up slowly and folded her arms.

"Who is Tansia?" the elf asked.

Khirius looked down at the ground by his feet briefly. He swallowed slowly, the movements in his face seeming oddly human and natural for a being unanimously associated with dark, unnatural power and evil.

"Lady Tansia is an ancient vampire," he responded. "She is the leader of the Coven's affairs in this corner of Basilea. She is also the one who made me what I am."

The chamber fell silent, save for the low growling of the gur panther, who padded over to stand by Aestelle, her eyes still locked dangerously on Khirius. Thesilar glanced up at Aestelle.

"I told you before we came in that we were underprepared for this," she said, her voice low. "That was before any mention of drakons and ancient vampires."

Aestelle met her gaze and forced a cocky smirk.

"What were you expecting to defend the tomb of Arteri the Plague, Thes? A dozen halfling cooks?"

The elf's stern face slowly broke into a smile and then a laugh.

"Alright, Dee Drinkee Yaydee, alright. We carry on. We all have to die sometime, might as well be for something worthwhile. Except you, old man. I can't carry you any further."

Ragran tilted his head around to face Thesilar, his jaw set in stubborn determination.

"Don't talk nonsense, woman," he grunted.

Thesilar met his glare without flinching.

"Your arm is broken. You cannot hold a weapon, let alone swing one."

The muscular barbarian looked down at his swollen, discolored arm, and then back up at the elf.

"If there is anybody above watching out for us," he grunted, "they saw fit to alter fate for me to have my left arm crippled. But I am right-handed."

Ragran looked over at Valletto.

"Valletto, give me your sword. You are not using it. You have been at the back, using your wizardry. As you should. I need that sword."

"Ragran…" Aestelle began.

"Stay out of this, girl!" the barbarian turned to face her, his eyes narrowed. "You may think you are a veteran at this game, but you are not there yet! I know what I am doing. I was slaying these bastards when you were still mastering your first steps."

Aestelle considered countering, both his ludicrous plan to carry on and his false assertion that there was so much of a difference in their age – it was only a decade, even if her heritage left her looking a little younger than her thirty or so years. Ragran looked back at Valletto. The aeromancer slowly handed across his sword. Aestelle let out a breath and returned her gaze to Khirius.

"And what of you?" she demanded as she made her way over to the first of the felled trolls to recover her throwing knives. "What now?"

The vampire's brow rose slightly.

"I shall come with you, if you will permit me," he answered quietly. "I am no swordsman, fighting never held much of an appeal to me. But I think, given what you are about to face, that I may be of some use."

Aestelle looked around the room at the faces of her comrades; the motley collection of wizards and warriors and their mixed emotions of fear and determination. Nothing more needed to be said. Hefting her blade up to rest over her shoulders, she led the way across the room and up through the broken wall ahead.

Chapter Nineteen

Khirius was the first to enter the main burial chamber. The dim room was much as he left it after Tansia had threatened him with the skeletal drakons; torches blazed along the long walls to either side of him, casting flickering shadows between the alcoves and tall pillars. The gold-trimmed tomb – that small, stone box that had affected the events of so much – waited silently on the raised platform at the far end of the room. Two ranks of five elite elven guards stood rigidly in Khirius' path, their dead, fleshless hands clutching their long, curved shields and deadly glaives. Tansia paced silently across the crumbled tiles near the tomb, her deathly pale, bare feet protruding from beneath her black robes.

Khirius' new companions filed into the room behind him and fanned out to form a fighting line. He pointed to the tall door on the left.

"The drakons are in there," he told the others.

Tansia looked across at the new arrivals and shook her head in disappointment.

"Oh, Khirius," she issued a forlorn smile, "now you think you are a hero. Wicked Ones bless you! I actually do feel a pang of sympathy for you. I feel a little sad that you think you can hope to achieve anything here."

Ragran and Aestelle began to pace forward. Thesilar brought an arrow to her bow and drew back the string.

"We are not here for speeches, Tansia," Khirius said evenly as he drew his sword, "just to end you and destroy that tomb."

Tansia walked down toward the rear rank of skeletal elven guards.

"This empty tomb?" she smiled.

Khirius stopped dead in his tracks.

"She's bluffing," Ragran growled.

"Am I?" the ancient vampire laughed. "Perhaps. Or, considering that you, dim-witted Khirius, have been duped at every turn, perhaps I am now telling you the truth. On the one hand, you may be here to end my reign of terror within the Coven and destroy the tomb. Or on the other? Perhaps this tomb was emptied before you ever even arrived. Perhaps the body of Arteri has already been safely taken away to another location, and I released you because I knew you were stupid enough to bring these mercenaries here to me. These people who are the only viable threat. These people you have delivered right to me. Either way, you shall have to come here to find out."

Khirius' shoulders slumped. He had been tricked, again. Just like when the Brotherhood knight led the attack on his home. Just like when he left his loyal servants unguarded to be brutally murdered. All of it was in accordance with Tansia's plan.

Z'akke was the first to speak.

"Val! Take the left!"

A deafening howl of wind erupted from Khirius' side as a hurricane of magical energy shot from the aeromancer's staff, ripping through one end of the ranks of elven guards and scattering three of them, sending them twirling back through the air. A moment later, Khirius felt his right cheek practically ablaze as fire shot from Z'akke's staff, burning down one of the skeletal guards and setting fire to a second. Ragran, Aestelle, and the gur panther leapt forward to attack. Seeing the gap on the left flank of the guards, Khirius sprinted forward. His dark cloak billowing out as he moved with unnatural speed, he dashed past the opening in the wall of undead soldiers and around to face Tansia, his sword held high. To either side, the tall doors behind the alcoves slid open.

Tansia watched him approach, her red eyes narrowed and her thin, twisted lips smiling. An arrow shot through the line of guards and impacted into Tansia's midriff, forcing her to stagger back and cry out. Khirius seized his opportunity and leapt up into the air, his sword held in both hands above his head. Tansia looked up, held out one scarred hand, and a black beam of magical energy lanced out from her palm and into Khirius' chest, knocking him back as a burning, agonizing force ripped through his body.

***

The simple Basilean daga sword felt too light, almost child-like in Ragran's grasp as he limped forward. His arm ached. His lungs burned. The dark recesses of his mind whispered cruel promises, reminding him of that sense of doom he had before entering the mountain. Telling him that this was the end. But Ragran was a son of the Howling Peaks. A broken body and broken mind meant nothing. He ignored them both and charged down his foes.

Seeba had already plunged headlong into the center of the front rank of elven guards whilst Z'akke continued to blast away at the right side of the glaive-wielding skeletons with magical fire. Ragran and Aestelle met the left-hand side simultaneously, their blades hammering down on the ancient, pitted-bronze shield wall of the once elite, noble elven soldiers. Fighting through the pain, Ragran dragged his wounded left arm up and took a firm hold of the top of the shield of the skeletal elf facing him. With a grunt, he overpowered his animated adversary and pulled the shield to one side before plunging his short, Basilean sword into the undead warrior's chest, twisting it, and then withdrawing the blade. Ragran's foe fell limply at his feet.

To his side, Aestelle let out a cry of pain as a glaive slashed across her thigh. She staggered back, bringing her greatsword up to defend herself from a series of savage, well-drilled attacks from two of the skeletal guards. Ragran booted his closest adversary away and lunged across to the younger warrior's aid, headbutting the first armored guard to the floor with a resounding crack, and hacking down into the side of the second.

Ahead of Ragran, across one of the chamber's long walls, a tall, ornate stone door slid up and open with a rumbling creak. The doorway opened to reveal only blackness, without even a pinpoint of light beyond. With a clatter of bone, a tall figure appeared out of the shadows and took a step forward into the burial chamber. Two long, crooked legs of thick bone paced powerfully out into the open, each taller than Ragran and ending in viciously curved claws. A thick ribcage led up to a stubby neck, atop of which was a long, bony snout lined with teeth the size of daggers, and horns longer than a spear. A pair of slender arms led up to the remains of now skinless wings, whilst a bony tail flickered out from behind the gargantuan, undead best.

Behind the first drakon, a second of near identical proportions clattered out into the burial chamber. Fearing nothing, not even his own doom, Ragran charged at them both. Magical winds blasted into the side of the first skeletal drake, twisting it at the hip and causing the colossal creature to stumble toward the raised platform and the tomb. Ragran hurled himself into the drakon, hacking down with his sword into the creature's knee but succeeding only in chipping away a small sliver of bone. Behind him, Aestelle charged back into the fight against the sturdy, stoic line of elven guards. Thesilar shot an arrow into the side of the first drakon's head, again not even managing to attract the creature's attention, let alone slow it down. Another blast of magical tempest winds from Valletto hammered into the second drake, slowing its advance into the ancient chamber.

Shrugging off the pain and weariness of his wounds, Ragran raised his sword for a second time and brought it down into the drake's knee with all of his strength. The serpentine kneecap dislodged and fell to the ground, and the ancient leg buckled. The drakon towering above him let out a screech, somehow made audible and deafening from the dark magics that animated the creature, and a claw came slashing down to tear at Ragran's back. The force of the blow knocked him to one knee, and before he could respond, a tail swept across and took his feet from beneath him. Ragran stared up at the dark ceiling above, a clawed skeletal foot slamming down atop his chest to pin him in place. His lungs blazing as he struggled and wheezed for air, one arm grabbing uselessly at the claw digging into his pectoral muscles as his other, wounded arm flailed helplessly, Ragran stared up at his doom.

***

Leaning back quickly to avoid a deadly slash from the long blade of a glaive, Z'akke stepped closer to his skeletal assailant once the weapon was clear and swung his sword up into its midriff. Despite the power behind his strike, Z'akke's blade clanged harmlessly against the age-old bronze breastplate, denting the metal but failing to cut through. Wearily, Z'akke brought his sword up again to defend himself as the undead elf guard batted its shield toward him and recovered the glaive to a ready position. Inhaling deeply, desperate to rely on his sword so as not to exhaust himself further still with the continued use of his pyromancy, Z'akke rushed into the undead guard and planted a shoulder against the shield.

Easily overpowering the animated elven corpse, letting out a long growl, Z'akke barged his adversary back against one of the tall, decorative stone pillars with a resounding crunch. Whipping his staff up to deflect another strike from the deadly glaive, Z'akke slammed his sword-arm fist into the elf's face with enough force to knock the lower jawbone clean off. Quickly following up, Z'akke brought his heavy blade down onto the skeleton's exposed neck and severed the head. The body remained upright for a brief moment and then clattered to the ground. Z'akke stepped back and surveyed the scene around him.

Only four of the skeletal guards remained now, locked in a vicious and fast moving melee with Aestelle and Seeba. Near the tomb, the two vampires traded rapid sword strikes and vicious exchanges of dark magic as they attempted to cut each other down. On the other side of the chamber, Valletto quickly cracked open an energy crystal and then desperately sent pulse after pulse of tempestuous winds into one of the drakes, each arcane blast pushing the towering creature back as the aeromancer attempted to hold it at bay, his teeth gritted as sweat poured down his face. Only a few paces away, the second drakon pinned Ragran to the ground in a pool of his own blood beneath a huge, bony claw whilst Thesilar desperately attempted to fight off the undead monstrosity to rescue her old comrade.

Then Z'akke saw the glow. He slowly turned around. The door opposite the huge opening that had admitted the drakes was also open. Z'akke's eyes widened. In an adjoining chamber, clearly visible only a few paces away through that huge doorway, Z'akke saw the largest horde of treasure he had ever encountered. Rows of neatly stacked treasure chests lined a far wall whilst sacks of gold coins lay littered before them. Ancient, bejeweled weapons fit for royalty rested in racks by the chests, and a trio of large, open crates were packed to near overflowing with jewelry and precious stones. His jaw agape, Z'akke's feet monotonously plodded toward the treasure room, numb and oblivious to the fight behind him.

He stared ahead incredulously. This amount of treasure would cover the extortionate quote he had received from the alchemist in Valentica, many times over. After years away from home, years of leaving his young to grow up without their father, years of leaving his clan to suffer their illness with their hopes placed in a handful of mage-priests in foreign lands, Z'akke had succeeded. If the man in Valentica was true to his word, if he truly understood the problem Z'akke had described to him, he would now come back to the Three Kings and all of these problems would be solved. The clan would thrive again. Z'akke could go home to his mate and offspring. The solution stood before him, only yards away.

Z'akke stopped in place. In the space of only two or three seconds, a thousand thoughts raced through his mind. His friends were all locked in a bitter, deadly fight. They were all hurt. Z'akke was hurt, and they had protected him. Healed him. They needed him now. But if he turned away from that treasure room, the door could seal as quickly as it opened. His very best outcome would be if the fight were a success, he would be forced to split that treasure many ways, possibly to the point that he could no longer afford to bring the alchemist to the Three Kings. And then there was the very real possibility that they would lose the fight, given the fearsome opposition they faced.

What use was Z'akke to his clan, and his family, if he was dead? He could easily rush into that treasure room, grab all he could, and then turn to leave. He could still save his clan that way, if he was quick enough to work out what the most valuable treasure was and grab it for himself. But Ragran was in trouble. He was hurt more than any of them and was now fighting for his life. But... Ragran was often mean to him. He bullied him. Ragran was not worth sacrificing the future of his clan over. And Thesilar was there, with him. Yes, Thesilar could save him.

Z'akke's eyes focused on the treasure again. He took another step forward. But his conscience prevented a second step. Failing his friends was his downfall. It had been for some time now. It was persistent. Z'akke faced the opportunity, a unique opportunity, to change who he was and what his priorities were, there and then. To become a better person. And all in the space of those two to three seconds, Z'akke found himself torn between his duty and loyalty.

Z'akke made his decision. Reaching down to his belt, he produced his last energy crystal. A commonplace one, but an augmentation to his powers nonetheless. He crushed the crystal in a tight grasp and felt the temporary surge of magical power course through him. The flow mingled with the fire in his very core. His hands glowed hot as steam wafted up from his snout. He stood taller, stronger, as he tapped into the very essence of his being, the flames within that defined him. Summoning on his mastery of pyromancy, channeling and focusing the fires to his will, Z'akke felt a white hot glow shoot along his arms. He turned to look across the room at the drakes.

Letting out a feral roar, Z'akke sprinted across the chamber. The battle raging between Aestelle, Seeba, and the final elf guards thundered closer with each of his heavy steps. His roar dragged out into a long, deep howl, Z'akke forced the flow of fire through his hand and into his staff. The entire staff burst into white-hot flame as Z'akke approached the fight. Swinging the staff out, he caught the first of the undead elf guards and tore straight through the monstrosity's body, cutting the skeleton and its armor in two. Spurred on into an even faster sprint, Z'akke pelted across the chamber toward the two drakons where he saw the light of life fading from Ragran's eyes.

With a final yell, Z'akke lashed out heavily with his staff and connected with the first drakon's knee, the blazing fury of his attack carving straight through the thick bone. The lower half of the drakon's leg twirled away spectacularly as the entire creature, left without one half of a leg, collapsed down to one side to roll away from Ragran and Thesilar. The undead monster thrashed and twisted on the ground, its limbs a flurry of blurred bone, as the second drakon let out a hoarse roar and stomped over to stand by its crippled mate.

Undeterred, his flaming staff held ready in both hands, Z'akke looked up at the drakon and met its roar with one of his own, head on, as Ragran staggered away from the fight, and Thesilar and Valletto moved up to stand ready at Z'akke's side.

***

Forced back a step with each attack, Khirius brought his blade from side to side as he frantically parried an expert sequence of attacks aimed at every quarter. Her eyes set in determination, her scarred lips twisted in a snarl, Tansia advanced across the tomb's platform. What basic knowledge he had of swordsmanship was now gone; footwork was scattered to the wind and parries centered from the wrist were now replaced in a blind panic with tiring, sweeping movements of the arm as Khirius fought for his very existence.

Dark energy swirled in an expanding sphere around Tansia's guarding hand as Khirius sensed the dull pulse of necromantic energy building from her. With a rage-filled snarl, the older vampire held out a clawed hand, and a beam of purple-black shot out toward Khirius. He deftly leapt aside as the blast of arcane energy smashed into a pillar behind him, scattering chipped stone across the floor of the raised platform. Khirius momentarily considered trying to take advantage of Tansia's lowered blade by lunging in to attack but found his weary body failing to respond. Every inch of his skin ached and burned from Tansia's first attack, and their deadly dance across the tomb platform only highlighted her immensely superior speed and skill with a sword. He was outclassed in every way. He could not defeat her.

Khirius risked a glance toward the door leading to his only potential escape. He saw the barbarian staggering away from the two skeletal drakes, one arm wrapped around his side as he bled profusely. The two mages and the elf tried to do battle against the towering drakons and had succeeded in crippling one of them. Aestelle and the gur panther remained locked in a furious melee with the final few elite guards. There was nobody to help him. Hope seemed to drip from his very pores and drain away from his clouded mind. To rely on complete strangers for help was foolish enough, but for a vampire to look for salvation in Basileans and elves was laughable. There was nobody to cry out for help to. For the first time in two hundred years, Khirius realized that he actually was defeated. This was the end.

Khirius looked back to the horrific, scarred vampire stood before him. He raised his blade again and gritted his teeth. He had never been a fighter and had never considered himself to be brave, but if this was the end, then it was right to at least face it with some dignity. Khirius lunged forward to attack. His first strike lanced forth at Tansia's chest but was batted aside with almost contemptuous ease. He brought his blade back around in a slash toward her head, but this was again parried. Before Khirius could even contemplate a third strike, he felt a sudden flare of pain as Tansia's blade punctured through his gut. He stopped dead in his tracks and looked down at the weapon piercing his body. As he slowly lifted his head, another pulse of dark energy shot out of Tansia's hand and blasted into his body, flinging him backward in a ball of agonizing magical fire.

***

Falling to the ground in an awkward, dusty embrace, Aestelle jabbed her elbow out into the face of the undead elven guard, snapping the animated corpse's head back with a crunch of bone. She reached out for her dropped sword, tantalizingly having fallen only inches away, before her world thudded into a star-filled daze as her assailant smashed a shield into the side of her head. Her vision blurred, Aestelle lashed out with one hand blindly whilst groping for her sword with the other, aware of the shadowy figure looming above her. She heard the familiar, deafening roar of Seeba and made out the fuzzy outline of the huge gur panther as she leapt into the elven guard above her, knocking the skeleton down and savaging it violently.

Staggering up to one knee, Aestelle grabbed her sword and wearily heaved it back up. Her vision cleared just in time for her to see a second undead elven soldier step across and strike with its long glaive, plunging the blade into Seeba's back. The great panther let out an almost human cry, braced up in agony, and then crumpled down motionless to the ground. Despair immediately twisting in her chest like a knife, Aestelle's eyes opened wide and she let out a yell of anguish as the loyal creature who had saved her multiple times lay still in a pool of blood.

Aestelle leapt forward and hacked down with her blade, clanging it against the undead guard's metal shield with a series of savage, heavy blows. Crying out in anger, beating her blade down time and time again, the metal buckled and then the shield fell away. Aestelle kicked the skeleton in the chest with enough force to send it back a pace, arms flung to either side before stepping in and neatly cutting off its head. Seeing the final undead elf staggering back to its feet, she took another pace forward and struck down with a second precise attack, lopping off its skull.

Around her, she saw Thesilar, Z'akke, and Valletto falling back toward the main entrance with arrows, tornado winds, and volcanic fires spewing out at the two undead drakons they faced. Ragran clung to one of the shattered pillars, down on one knee with an arm placed over his bleeding abdomen. Khirius attempted to struggle back up to his feet as the haggard female vampire struck him down with a blaze of obsidian, magical energy. All around her, all seemed hopeless. All seemed lost. Only the door to the exit, mere paces away, looked to be a viable option. Aestelle rushed over to the fallen gur panther and dropped to one knee by the noble creature.

The broken panther wheezed as her chest pathetically rose and fell, blood seeping out from a dozen wounds. The animal's eyes slowly looked up at Aestelle. A curious, sad smile seemed to weakly grow across the creature's face. Pushing through the exhaustion, ignoring the cramp and dizziness from constant use of her divinity powers, Aestelle placed both of her hands down on that final, terrible wound across Seeba's back and fought with all of her focus and discipline to summon the energy for one final, last push of healing magic.

Slowly, pitifully, a blue-white glow emanated from her hands, spreading ever so slightly across the dying panther's body. The glaive wound slowly closed, the ends of the terrible lesion coming together. The dizziness returned, and the glow faded. Dripping with sweat across her entire body, Aestelle fell forward and fought to breath. She looked up at the wound and saw it was half closed, perhaps even enough to stop the poor creature from passing for a few moments longer but little more.

To her left, one of the drakons let out a terrific roar and lashed out with its tail, knocking through the stone of one of the alcoves along the wall as Valletto and Thesilar dived to either side to avoid the blow. The ceiling above collapsed down spectacularly, filling the entire chamber with thick, yellow dust. Her eyes stinging, Aestelle clambered up to her feet and held up her blade. As the dust slowly dispersed, she saw the ancient vampire standing over Khirius' prone form. Only a few feet behind was the stone tomb. It was her only chance.

Her eyes set in grim determination on the vampire, Aestelle sprinted forward across the rubble-strewn floor toward the raised platform ahead. Almost immediately, the scarred vampire turned to regard her and held out a hand, emitting a flash of black lightning. Aestelle dived to one side, rolling behind one of the stone pillars before rapidly hurtling forward again to almost immediately duck beneath a second blast. She reached the vampire and flung herself straight into her first attack, thrusting the tip of her greatsword straight forward toward the undead leader's neck.

With a motion so rapid it appeared as little more than a blur, the vampire jumped back and then stepped in to attack with her own blade. Despite the sheer speed of the vampire's strike, the move was at least predictable, and Aestelle succeeded in parrying the blow and backhanding the vampire across the face, splitting open her mouth. Aestelle stepped in and raised a knee into the shorter woman's gut, striking with enough power to bend the vampire over nearly double and eliciting a cry of pain. Quickly capitalizing on her opportunity, Aestelle brought the pommel of her greatsword smashing down into the vampire's spine with a snap of bone, sending the ancient monster sprawling to the ground where she quickly kicked her harshly in the ribs.

Before she even fully realized that the vampire was recovering, Aestelle found herself forced backward as her undead opponent appeared before her, wide-eyed with bloodied-faced rage as she swept forward with a flurry of sword strikes.

***

Valletto had lost count of how many times he had nervously eyed the doorway leading to the exit. Forced back for step after painful step, his temples throbbing from the exertion of casting spell after spell, their task now seemed completely hopeless as the skeletal drakon advanced on them. Towering up near the ceiling of the chamber, the first drakon's gray-boned visage seemed to almost smile down maliciously at its prey as its tail quivered behind the bulky body. Wind from Valletto's aeromancy only seemed to slow its advance, and Thesilr's arrows and blade were all but useless against such a mighty foe. Only Z'akke's seemingly tireless onslaught of pyromancy seemed to have any effect, just as it had on the crippled second drakon which dragged itself pathetically across the floor in the wake of the first, desperately attempting to rejoin the fight.

"This is useless!" Valletto shouted. "Ragran and Seeba are too badly hurt! We need to leave!"

He looked to his right and saw Thesilar reach up to a near empty quiver, with one final arrow waiting for use. The elf swore in desperation and slung her bow across her back before placing both hands onto the handle of her sword. The elf looked across the chamber to where Ragran continued to groggily stagger along a haphazard pathway, trailing blood.

"Ragran!" she yelled. "We have to go! Get back here!"

"The panther!" Z'akke shouted. "I'll go get her!"

"Leave it!" Thesilar screamed. "It's dead! And we will be soon! We have to go! Aestelle! Get back to us!"

With a shriek, the drakon lunged forward again, catching Z'akke and barging the salamander effortlessly to one side. Its tail whipped out and caught Thesilar, lacerating one of her legs in a shower of blood and forcing a scream of pain from her lips as she crumpled down to the ground. A taloned claw sliced down through the air toward Valletto, but he nimbly ducked beneath it and then jumped back to avoid a second strike. The claw ploughed through another of the chamber's pillars, and with it, another section of roof caved in on the far side of the room where the second door had opened opposite the drakons' lair.

Z'akke, staggering up to his knees from the last attack, looked across at where the ceiling had fallen to block that second doorway, his face falling in despair.

"No," the salamander looked as though he would weep, "no, no, no..."

Thesilar wearily stepped forward to face the drakon yet again, driving her blade up to slice into his ribs with seemingly little effect.

Z'akke continued to stare forlornly at the fallen rocks, somehow now reaching the point of desolation where he seemed to have given up the fight. Dust fell down from cracks in the ceiling above. The entire chamber seemed to tremor. Valletto looked forward and saw Khirius lying motionless on the raised platform as Aestelle and the female vampire traded sword blows. Ragran lay again slumped on one knee, his face deathly pale. Seeba lay motionless where she had fallen. Thesilar, desperately trying to parry blows from the uninjured drakon, quickly looked back at Valletto for the briefest of moments.

"Val!" she shouted. "Go! Get out of here before the ceiling comes down! Go!"

***

Aestelle's sword seemed to jump in her grip, almost wrenched clear of both hands by the sheer force of the vampire's attack. The ancient, crone-like woman flung herself into another series of powerful strikes, both stronger and faster than anything Aestelle could manage herself, but far less skilled. Aestelle ducked, jumped back, and parried every attack coming her way until she saw an opening and, for perhaps the third time in the seemingly endless confrontation, quickly switched the initiative and sliced down with her own blade.

The vampire dropped a shoulder to avoid Aestelle's first blow and then took a second attack cleanly on her own blade. The third strike landed home. Aestelle's blade tore through the vampire's throat, half-severing the deathly pale, scarred neck to the point of revealing the rotten, yellow neck bone beneath. With a gargled screech, the vampire reeled backward, her sword slipping from her open fingers to clatter to the ground. Aestelle brought her blade back around over her shoulder, ready to deliver the killing blow. Before she could swing forward, the vampire was on her again, rushing forward to clamp one ice-cold hand around Aestelle's wrist and the other over her neck.

Unable to move her sword arm against the overpowering strength of the undead monster, Aestelle thought quickly. She grabbed the pistol at her side, cocked the hammer with her thumb, and brought her arm up in an attempt to shove the muzzle against the vampire's chin. Before she brought the pistol up into place, the vampire let go of her throat and grabbed the weapon. Red eyes bored into Aestelle's as the two women struggled for possession of the pistol, hands shaking as the vampire's supernatural strength slowly proved to be superior. Her teeth gritted, her mind determined never to give in, Aestelle could still only watch astounded as her arm was slowly twisted around, the muzzle of her own pistol was pressed against her gut, and the weapon discharged with a violent, resounding eruption.

Chapter Twenty

Aestelle smelled the burnt powder before she felt the pain. The spherical, metal shot plunged through her, causing her to jolt for a moment before her entire body tensed up in silent agony. The smoking pistol and her greatsword fell from her limp fingers. She pressed a shaking hand against the gunshot wound and willed with every iota of her discipline for healing powers to surge forth. Nothing came. Every reserve was spent. She was exhausted, cut open, shot, and now dying. Her mouth falling open, her eyelids heavy, she looked down at the viciously sneering face of her killer.

The pale, wretched vampire smiled up at her in victory. One clawed, cold hand grabbed Aestelle by the hair and yanked her head to one side to expose her neck, whilst the other held a wrist firmly to her side. Her mind still focused, determined, undefeated, Aestelle willed her limbs into resistance, to action, to fight back and win. But somewhere between her resolute, indomitable thoughts and her broken body, the system failed, and her arms refused to obey her commands. She looked up helplessly at the vampire as the hideous creature opened its bloody mouth, sharp canine teeth extending down to position to sink into her throat as the chamber continued to crumble and fall all around them.

Out of nowhere, an arrow whistled through the air to slam directly into the very center of the vampire's chest, stopping her dead in her tracks. A fraction of a moment later, a huge, almost paw-like hand slammed down from the heavens to land on top of the vampire's head. Ragran appeared looming over them both, covered in blood from head to toe, a deep, deafening, and demented howl roaring from his split lips as he stared down at the vampire, wild-eyed. With a hissing snarl, the vampire span to face the baying barbarian. Ragran clamped both of his immense hands on each side of the vampire's head as Aestelle stumbled back away from them, both hands pressed to the gunshot wound in her abdomen. The vampire grabbed Ragran by the wrists and struggled to tear his hands away. Aestelle watched in a blur as all of the supernaturally augmented strength in the world failed to overcome the sheer, brute force of the frenzied northern barbarian.

Still continuing his endless, baying howl, his wide-eyes staring down at the struggling vampire, Ragran dug both of his thumbs into her eyeballs and crushed them into her skull. The blinded vampire shrieked an unholy scream, thrashing wildly in agony as blood flowed down her white cheeks from her empty eye sockets. Relentlessly, Ragran took one of her wrists in his unwounded arm and twisted the limb behind her back until the bone snapped and splintered. He then leant into her, sank his teeth into her half-severed throat, and tore out a chunk of dead flesh before spitting it bloodily to one side.

Aestelle watched in amazement at the ironic spectacle of a mortal man biting out the throat of a vampire until his powerful hands came up, tearing off chunks of flesh from her throat until the neck bone was completely exposed. Howling deeply again, Ragran took a hold of the shrieking vampire's chin with one hand, the neck with the other, and, after several seconds of shaking and struggling, snapped the creature's head clean off her shoulders. The mighty, muscular mountain man held the severed head aloft and yelled a booming, feral roar.

"Ragran..." Aestelle whispered hoarsely, blood trickling from one side of her mouth. "The tomb..."

She looked in desperation over at the stone tomb as the wall behind the raised platform crumbled and fell, the shattered, ancient chamber falling apart all around them with every passing moment. She looked around her and saw Khirius had already come to his senses and fled the chamber, reaching the exit and safety. A few paces behind him, Z'akke stumbled toward the door, weighed down by the bulk of Seeba's motionless body draped across his huge, reptilian shoulders.

His expression still maddened, confused, and erratic, Ragran stumbled drunkenly toward the tomb. He planted one huge, bare shoulder against the lid and pushed with all of his remaining strength. Seeing Valletto reach the safety of the exit shortly after Z'akke, Aestelle recovered her sword and pistol, and limped over to the tomb. She placed one hand weakly on the edge. Pushing for all she was worth, desperate to know the truth, her cracked, bloodied lips recited prayers as she pleaded with the Shining Ones above to grant her the providence she needed to find the body in the tomb, and one final surge of strength to be able to do the right thing and end the unholy creature's wave of terror before it could even begin.

Ragran pushed the lid clear. The stone fell to the floor and cracked in two. Ragran dropped to his knees and pitched forward. Aestelle looked down into the darkness of the tomb. She let out a desperate, agonized cry. The tomb was empty. The body was gone. They were too late. It had all been for nothing.

Then the ceiling caved in.

***

Plumes of dust billowed out of the doorway from the main burial chamber, spewing along the adjoining corridor with enough force to rapidly extinguish every torch along the walls in turn. With the corridor plunged into darkness, Thesilar turned her back on the acrid dust and crouched down to one knee, bending over and covering her head with her arms in an attempt to somehow fend off the clouds and keep them at bay from her airway. One huge, earth-shaking thump sounded from behind her, and the whole mountain seemed to tremor, but smaller rock falls continued afterward like a vicious, thunderous rainstorm. Pain tore through her body from wounds in her legs, stomach, and back. Those awful few seconds of waiting for the rocks collapsing behind her were just enough for her to desperately dwell on the fact that she had seen so few of her companions escape the room. So few of her friends.

The hammering and thumping of falling rocks stopped. Thesilar hacked and coughed as the clouds of dust continued to billow along the darkened corridor, her splutters echoing in the empty darkness. She looked up. To a human, that corridor would be complete and utter inky blackness; to Thesilar, she saw her world dimly and without color, but clearly enough as the dust dispersed. Still coughing, she struggled up to her feet.

She immediately saw a figure in the darkness ahead. That figure stood up and looked around, evidently also well able to see in the dark. The face turned to regard Thesilar; a long, pale face that was blistered and burned hideously along one side, but with eyes that twinkled white in the darkness as they focused on her. It was the vampire, the one they had allied with. Thesilar's hand shot out to retrieve her sword from her side. It was not there. Fear raced through her as she realized her sword was buried behind her under tons of rock, and she was now alone, without her friends.

"Stay away from me!" Thesilar shrieked in terror.

"Wh… who is it?" a groggy but familiar voice murmured from somewhere behind her.

"Val?" Thesilar gasped. "Val! Get over here!"

She turned to look over her shoulder and saw Valletto edging down the corridor, hands tentatively feeling thin air and nothingness ahead as he made his way slowly toward her. Thesilar turned back to look down to the far end of the corridor again. The vampire was gone. She span around in a blind panic, expecting the monstrosity to suddenly be looming over her, but there was no sign of their brief, undead ally. She allowed herself to exhale slowly in relief.

"Thesilar," Valletto called, "are you up there? Did anybody else get out?"

Thesilar heard a chittering, clicking cough from around the first corner of the corridor, closer to the entrance of the burial chamber and the cave in.

"I did… it's… Z'akke… I brought Seeba with me… I…"

A flicker of light erupted from around the corner of the corridor, close to where Thesilar could hear Z'akke's voice. Color dimly re-entered her world, yellows and grays seeping into the rocky walls, ceiling and carved tiles beneath her feet.

"Where's Ragran?" Thesilar called out, stumbling back along the corridor toward the cave in. "He was right behind me... Where's Aestelle?"

"She's not breathing!" Z'akke yelled, his tone panicked. "Help me! She's not breathing!"

Thesilar and Valletto both hurried back toward Z'akke, Valletto faltering as his eyes adjusted to the meager light whilst Thesilar staggered and stumbled due to the pain of her wounds. They rounded the corner, and Thesilar looked down to see Z'akke on both knees, still bleeding from his own wounds, leaning over the motionless form of the bloodied gur panther as a torch blazed in one of his clawed hands. He looked desperately up at his two comrades.

"Help me!" he pleaded. "I can't fix her! Help me!"

Valletto edged forward and gently rested a hand on Z'akke's shoulder. Thesilar stared ahead at the darkened doorway leading to the collapsed room, her eyes narrowed.

"They were right behind me," she whispered.

Thesilar stared anxiously at the doorway, waiting expectantly. The muscles of her gut clenched, and her fingers curled up tightly into the palms of her hands. They were not just her friends. Ragran was like a coarse, oafish brother whilst Aestelle felt like her high-achieving, perfect, but intensely annoying little sister. She loved them both dearly. She let out a long breath. Tears came to her eyes.

There was a sound. Behind her, at the far end of the corridor. Thesilar whipped around to face the direction in which she had last seen the fleeing vampire.

"What?" Valletto asked. "What is it?"

"Something is coming."

Thesilar looked around desperately for a weapon, having lost both her sword and her bow. She drew her hunting knife from her boot and stared into the darkness ahead. Valletto pushed past her and raised his staff.

"Get back, Val," Thesilar urged.

"I'm the only one who isn't hurt!" Valletto hissed. "Stay behind me!"

The noise drew closer. Softly padding footsteps, quick, careful, and deliberate. Barely audible even to elven ears. Then Thesilar heard something behind her. Heavy breathing, labored footsteps, clumsy feet crunching on broken rocks. They were surrounded. Wounded, defeated, mages too exhausted for effective magic and most weapons lost, they were surrounded. Z'akke wearily raised himself back to his feet and readied his staff. Her head turning from side to side to survey both ends of the corridor, Thesilar raised her knife.

Two silhouetted figures staggered out of the collapsed burial chamber, both bent over double and clinging on to each other. One was tall, lithe, and feminine with long hair falling down to one side; the other muscular, powerful and recognizable from the hideous skull pauldron strapped to one shoulder. Ragran and Aestelle stumbled and staggered into the light of Z'akke's torch, both dripping with blood and covered in dust and debris. Aestelle looked up wearily at her comrades for a brief moment, her sword still in one hand, before her eyes closed and she crumpled down to the ground. Ragran remained standing for another few moments, his wounds visibly the worse of the two. He nearly managed a grim smile when his eyes met Thesilar's.

The mighty Ragran swayed on the spot like a young tree in a breeze but then slowly raised one hand. Held up in front of his companions was the grotesque sight of a severed head with empty eye sockets. The bloody pulp's face was twisted into a hideous scowl of complete and utter agony. Thesilar recognized the head as that of the ancient vampire from the burial chamber. Ragran looked across at the salamander mage-priest.

"Z'akke," he whispered hoarsely, dropping the bloody pulp at his feet, "burn it."

With that, the barbarian dropped to his knees and crumpled over on his side.

There was time for neither relief over Ragran and Aestelle's arrival nor concern over their horrific wounds as the soft footsteps from the far end of the corridor grew closer. Thesilar swore out loud and paced down toward the corner in the corridor, her fingers clinging tightly to the handle of her knife. Wordlessly, Z'akke and Valletto followed. The trio rounded the corner. In the colorless dark of the corridor ahead, Thesilar made out four slim figures advancing quietly, bows in their hands and hoods covering their heads. Their movements were slow, deliberate, skilled, but very much the movements of the living. Her heart soared as she recognized them as Sisterhood scouts. Allies. Healers.

"Help!" Thesilar yelled. "We have wounded! Help!"

***

Water dripped slowly from a series of claw-like stalactites extending down from the cave roof, dropping softly into the milky water of the pool below. An occasional, quiet moan echoed gloomily through the cave, all that was left from the rushing night wind outside as it swept across the mountain range. Valletto sat on a broad, broken stalagmite, his chin resting in his hands as he stared ahead into the pool. He had lost track of how many days it had been away from home and in and out of these mountains. And it was all for naught. They had failed. Arteri the Plague was free, at large, waiting for a necromancer with the requisite skill to raise him to an unearthly new existence.

He fished the letter from his wife out of his pocket and read it through again, wincing from the sharp pains across his chest and arms, where light wounds and near misses had scratched a few bloody but superficial wounds. Valletto was the lucky one. Thesilar and Z'akke had both stumbled away with wounds that would take time to heal, but theirs were certainly more severe than those Valletto had suffered. Only time would tell if Ragran, Aestelle, or Seeba would live. Part of Valletto felt a light almost ethereal sense of relief at the thought that his children would continue to grow up with their father, but in direct opposition to this and with equal pull, he felt a cripplingly heavy sense of guilt for merely remaining alive.

Footsteps from the narrow, winding cavern behind him snapped Valletto out of his internal struggles. He looked up and saw Z'akke pace slowly over to him, his scaly belly and one arm wrapped tightly in bandages. The salamander carefully sat down next to Valletto and looked out into the pool below the dripping stalactites.

"Any word from the others?" Valletto asked.

Z'akke shook his head.

"Thesilar is… a little worse than they first thought. They are not letting her walk just yet. I have heard nothing about the others."

Valletto stared ahead. A dozen Sisterhood scouts had swept through the tomb complex to flush out any last traces of undead. If anything still lurked in the maze of tunnels and tombs, it was lying low and silent. For now, the sisters had set up a small field hospital of sorts, a few rows of bedding to look to the wounded whilst the next step in their plans was decided.

"I hope she is alright," Z'akke swallowed.

Valletto looked across at his salamander friend.

"Oh, she will be," he forced a smile. "She got through the Battle of Andro in one piece, and you should have seen the wounds she took there."

The mage-priest glanced back at him, his face a picture of confusion.

"Eh? Oh, I didn't mean Aestelle! I meant Seeba. It's just… we all choose to be here for one reason or another. And sometimes those reasons are good. But Seeba is just an animal. Her choices are made for her, and that isn't fair. She's a living, breathing thing. She doesn't understand what is going on here. She just does as she is told. If anybody deserves to live through this, it is Seeba."

Valletto smile faintly and shrugged. Whilst he saw the salamander's logic, he did not necessarily agree with it. At the risk of sounding incredibly selfish, he thought that if anybody deserved to survive it was him and Z'akke. For their children's sake.

"Aestelle will be fine," Z'akke nodded confidently, "she always is. Very quick healer. It's her heritage, what makes her so special. She'll be fine."

Valletto looked across, now his turn to be confused.

"Her heritage?" he repeated.

"Yes," the salamander nodded, "you know, being half-Elohi. She heals quicker. It's why she..."

Z'akke's eyes slowly widened as his expression dropped to one of guilt and despair. He smacked a clawed hand against his snout.

"You didn't know," he sighed, "I wasn't supposed to tell you that. That's her secret to tell. Please, Valletto, do not tell her you know. She would be so angry! Please do not say anything."

Valletto's gaze scanned across the cave as recent memories, suddenly explained, forced their way to the fore of his mind. Aestelle's uncanny ability to adapt to seemingly everything she tried her hand at, aside from the more obvious and unsubtle beauty she exuded at almost unnatural levels.

"Please don't say anything!" Z'akke repeated.

Valletto smiled across and shook his head.

"Don't worry. I won't say anything. Not a word, I promise."

The salamander's brow slowly settled back as his anxious frown faded away. It was replaced with his more normal, happy-go-lucky smile. Then that too faded away only seconds later.

"You need to go home, Val," the salamander suddenly said.

Valletto looked up.

"Sorry?"

"This... All this running around and taking risks to save the nation. Save the world, I don't know. The world always needs saving, friend Val. The world is always in trouble. You cannot always be the one to save it. You should not be out here. You do not need to be. I... struggle with putting these words together. Not only because this is not my language, but because I do not like telling others what to do. But in my heart, I think you should go home. Back to your family. As soon as you are able to."

Valletto looked down at the letter in his hands. He took in a deep breath.

"I agree," he said after a long pause, "you are right, Z'akke. You are wiser than you give yourself credit for. Yes, I will go, I think. Once I know the others are alright, it is time for me to go home. And this time to stay there. Thank you. You are a good friend."

The salamander's grin grew as his soft, blue eyes sparkled. Again, almost immediately, the smile faded away.

"About that," the mage-priest said. "You are my friend? I can trust you?"

Valletto looked sympathetically across at the heartfelt salamander. Z'akke looked back uneasily. Valletto found himself still surprised that such a hardy and battle-proven creature could still be so needing of friendship, even in those he had known for very little time. Then he remembered just how far from home Z'akke was.

"Of course I am your friend," Valletto replied honestly, "you can rely on me."

"You see," Z'akke continued, "I...well, with our other friends lying gravely injured and the two of us sitting here, not knowing who will live and who will... well, I find myself feeling ever so selfish for bringing this up. But it is how I feel. I should not say it out loud, but it has been so long. Years, in fact. Yes, years of this great weight of responsibility hanging over me. Yet I am not supposed to talk of it. But it feels so selfish, talking of it when the others are so badly hurt."

Valletto watched the salamander awkwardly tie himself in verbal knots as he skirted round and round whatever issue it was that he was trying to vocalize. Valletto suppressed the urge to tell him to get to the point and remained silent.

"When we were in the burial chamber," Z'akke continued, "I saw something. There was an open door. Beyond it, there was a room full of treasure. Piles of the stuff. Enough to solve all of my problems. But when the ceiling came tumbling down, that door was the first thing to go. The others think I am selfish, but the treasure was never for me."

"I've told you this before, Z'akke, but I think anybody who takes a little time to get to know you could deduce that," Valletto said quietly. "And even if the others do lie not far from here, perhaps on death's door, shame on them for thinking so ill of you. Go on, what is it?"

Z'akke looked down at his feet. He took in a deep breath, somehow looking like a nervous child, and then nodded in determination.

"My clan... my high priest, told me not to say anything. It is our clan's great shame. We are dwindling. Dying. Every hatching season, we find more and more eggs are unfertilized. We have no idea why. It has gone on for years now, whatever sickness or disease is tearing through us. If it is not remedied, the Lava Tail Clan will be no more."

Valletto listened intently, his sympathy for his friend's plight growing with each passing moment.

"We were sent out, away from the Three Kings," Z'akke continued, "four of us, from the temple. Our task was to travel to foreign places, to nations of great civilization to find learned men and women who we could bring back to help us. For years, I have tried and failed. I brought a dwarf scholar back once. She knew nothing. Then I found a man in Valentica. A great alchemist. He assured me he could help. But the price, Valletto! The payment he demands! It is unearthly! He knows how desperate I am! He knows how much this means to the clan, that we would give everything to heal this infernal sickness!

"But because he knows we will give everything, he demands everything. I cannot afford the payment. But that room in there! The treasure! That would have paid his cost. At least... I think it would. I... I don't know. It has been so long. I am so tired. I do not even know if the room was real. If I imagined it all. Did you see it, Val? Did you see the treasure?"

A realization took root in Valletto's mind. A seed, an embryo of an idea. His eyes narrowed in concentration. He slowly stood up.

"Did you see it?" Z'akke repeated. "Did I imagine it all?"

Ignoring the query, Valletto ran through a conversation in his head. He quickly explored several different avenues, pathways that could emerge from that seed of an idea. It could work. He felt hope growing within him. He span around to stare down at the salamander.

"Z'akke," he exhaled, trying hard to keep his voice level, not to raise any false hope, "I wish I could help you. I wish to the Ones above that I could solve your problem. But I can't. However, I know a man who can... get things done. You see, Valentica is no seat of academia, not compared to Basilea. If you want wise and learned men and women, you need to be heading to the City of the Golden Horn, not to..."

"I tried!" Z'akke exclaimed hopelessly, "I tried that, and..."

"The man I work for!" Valletto interrupted. "Grand Mage Saffus! Look, if there is anybody in the City of the Golden Horn who can help you, Saffus will know them. Not only that, Z'akke, but Saffus will have influence with them. He is... of a political mind. He has things on people. He is owed favors. I can't promise anything, but I think he could get help for you."

The salamander's eyes lit up as he shot to his feet.

"Really? Are you sure? Val, I have had my hopes raised so many times! Are you sure? I... will he listen to you? Will he help me?"

Valletto took a step back and held out his hands.

"I wish I could promise you something, Z'akke, but I can't. All I can tell you is that I am optimistic. I think it is worth trying. I think this has more chance than some crook in Valentica. And yes, Saffus will listen to me. After the Battle of Andro, when the others were given fame, fortune, and promotions, all I got was a medal. As a legion man, I was told that I only did my job. Saffus resented that. Bitterly. He told me that if ever I needed something, he thought Basilea owed me. I'll call it in, Z'akke. Let's try. Let's try and make this work. Come home with me and we will try."

The burly salamander looked down at the aeromancer, his toothy mouth hung open and his eyes lit up with joy. He rushed forward and wrapped his arms around the human, pulling him into a tight embrace and chittering something in his own language that Valletto could only assume was gratitude as he awkwardly stood still, waiting for the embrace to end.

***

Wiping the sleep out of the corners of her eyes with her thumb and forefinger, Aestelle slowly sat up on her bedroll. After those first few groggy moments of taking in exactly where she was and why, she let out a groan of despair when she realized that she was still inside the tomb complex of Mount Ekansu. She had lost track of how long she lay awake in the dim coolness of the ancient chamber. One of the rooms near to the largest entrance had been utilized as a tiny hospital room for her and Thesilar, where a succession of Sisterhood scouts kept watched and occasionally treated their wounds whilst the others continued to methodically sweep through the sprawling network of chambers and tunnels.

Perhaps an hour, perhaps two, dragged on by as she mentally processed the events of the last day, her actions and her failures. She recalled being overpowered and held still and helpless as the ancient vampire loomed over her, teeth bared. She thought on her wounded friends and what she should have done better to protect them, or be less of a burden in need of protecting herself. She thought long and hard about what to do next and what path lay ahead of her. Then she stopped thinking. Ruminating never did anybody any good. Time to get up and carry on.

Aestelle wearily dragged herself up to her knees on the bedroll. Her sword, pack, and her slashed, bloodied leather clothing waited in a pile at the end of the bedroll. Whilst she lay unconscious from her wounds and after they were treated, one of the sisters had clothed her in a spare set of white leggings and a tunic; clearly intended as an act of kindness and charity, but Aestelle found herself nauseated to be back in the uniform of the organization who dominated so much of her life.

She quickly slid off the leggings and set about tying the tunic tightly around her waist in an attempt to haphazardly convert the drab attire into something more appealing. She hissed in pain as soon as she did so, reminded of the pistol ball that had shot through her gut. Looking down across herself, she saw an assortment of bandaged across an upper arm, opposite shoulder, and one knee. In a sudden panic, she raised her hands to her face and explored her features carefully, but then she let out a relieved sigh when she found no evidence of injury.

"That's your first thought?" a familiar voice said from the bedroll next to her. "'Is my face still perfect?' Not, 'How is Ragran?' or, 'Did we stop the evil from escaping?' or anything a little more altruistic?"

Aestelle glanced across and saw Thesilar looking up from her own bedroll. The small room was dimly lit, most likely in an attempt to allow them to sleep, but even so, she could see similar evidence of wounds across her companion's body.

"I remember that we did not stop the evil," Aestelle swallowed. "Not yet, at least. But it isn't over."

Aestelle crawled across to her pack and retrieved her black, leather belt from her ruined clothing and tied it carefully around her waist before dragging her tall, black boots over her bare legs in an attempt to dilute the Sisterhood aesthetic of her borrowed tunic.

"How is Ragran?" she asked tentatively.

"Well, he isn't dead," the elf ranger said, taking a flask of water from next to her bedroll and drinking from it. "What the long term effects of his injuries will be, I do not think anybody knows."

Aestelle retrieved a small brush from her pack and a salve of polish, and set about cleaning the dried blood off her boots and working the polish into the scuffs and cracks.

"He saved my life," she murmured, "I remember that much. I know I owe him."

"We all saved each other at some point, I think," Thesilar replied, carefully easing out from beneath her blanket and pulling her own boots on over her white Sisterhood leggings, "I think we all remain even."

"And Seeba?" Aestelle asked, again scared of the answer as she feigned mild indifference whilst polishing her boots.

"Recovering."

Aestelle could not hide her relief as she exhaled. Her wounds ached. Her limbs were weary. They had utterly failed in what they had set out to do. But they were all alive, at least. The realization drew a small smile. They had failed for now, but it was not over. Aestelle recovered a small mirror glass from a pouch on her pack and peered into it. She recovered her makeup salves and powders and set to work on restoring the perfection of her face and hair. Thesilar swore.

"Do you ever question your priorities?" the elf demanded with a scowl. "We have just faced death and now all lie here battered and bandaged, and your solution is to check your hair and make-up?"

"Piss off, Thes," Aestelle grumbled without looking up from her mirror, "this is important to me. I often find myself questioning your decisions to go out of your way to say deeply hurtful things to your friends, yet you don't find me criticizing you for it."

"Yes you do! You broke my nose!"

Aestelle looked up.

"And if you put some effort into looking good, I would have had the common courtesy to leave your face alone and break something else instead," she said slowly and admonishingly.

Aestelle looked up in the mirror at the reflection of the jewels and beads woven into her hair. Her eyes came to rest on the solitary blue sapphire, left alone from the others. Her wounded stomach seemed to hurt more.

"Come on," Thesilar said slowly raising herself to her feet, "Z'akke and Valletto have been waiting for you for two days now. Let's go and let them know you are up."

"Two days?" Aestelle exclaimed, looking up in surprise.

"You took a beating, pretty," Thesilar said as she hauled her battered, green tunic on over the top of her borrowed Sisterhood clothing. "Without those sisters and their divinity healing, you'd be dead. As would Ragran. And Seeba."

"They're still all bitches," Aestelle yawned, carefully packing up her make-up pouch, polish, and clothes brushes.

Whatever Thesilar responded with, Aestelle found herself immediately ignoring. Something was suddenly wrong. She found herself stood bolt upright, eyes scanning the corners of the dim room, ears picking through the drips from the ceiling in an attempt to detect anything untoward.

"What is it?" Thesilar whispered.

Aestelle took a tentative pace toward the room's solitary doorway. She sensed eyes on her, something vaguely familiar but far from comfortable. Aestelle pulled her sword scabbard over one shoulder and tightened it to her back, a surge of adrenaline dulling the pain of her wounds to little more than a discomfort.

"There is something here," Aestelle said, her voice hushed, "something dark. This place has not been cleared out, Thes. We are being watched."

Aestelle dropped to one knee and strapped a second belt around her waist, fitting her throwing knives to the small of her back as Thesilar grabbed a hunting knife from the foot of her bed.

"Where are the others?" Aestelle whispered, edging toward the doorway.

"Two corridors down," Thesilar replied, "but... the sisters should be close by."

One hand on her sword handle, Aestelle gently opened the ancient, wooden door. The creak of the rusted hinges seemed like a thunderclap next to the silence of the corridor. Aestelle edged out of the room, Thesilar close behind. She checked to her left and saw nothing. She looked right, and her eyes immediately fell on a slim figure stood in the shadows. She recognized the shadowy form immediately and lowered her hand from her sword.

"You."

Khirius stepped out into the light of the wall-mounted torches. The pale face above the dark cloak was again youthful and smooth, a huge improvement from the burnt, blackened wreck she had last seen when rushing over to fight the ancient vampire who had once made Khirius what he now was.

"I am sorry it took some time to return," the vampire said quietly. "I had to see to my wounds."

"Is that so?" Thesilar replied bitterly. "And tell me, what does a vampire need to recover from grave wounds?"

Khirius folded his arms, his brow lowering.

"I think you already know the answer to that," he said evenly.

Aestelle took a step closer to him.

"Why are you here?" she asked. "Why have you come back?"

The tall vampire's eyes remained locked on hers.

"To see you," he replied simply.

Aestelle turned to lean back against the corridor wall, the sole of one boot placed against the rough stones behind her. In many ways, this was not a new situation. At the age of sixteen or seventeen, she first started to notice the endless male attention she received every time she left the abbey. Four or five years later, free of the shackles of Sisterhood, she was at liberty to act on that attention on a whim and without any consequences save the occasional love-struck, discarded lover who did not have the wisdom to realize Aestelle was not interested in anything long term or meaningful. Regardless, this was not the first time she found herself face to face with an admirer who was utterly lethal and wrong for her in every way.

"Give me a few moments, Thes," Aestelle said, turning to face the elf ranger.

Thesilar's eyes widened.

"Are you mad?" she hissed. "You want to spend time alone with that… thing?!"

"I can look after myself," Aestelle said quietly, nodding to the far end of the corridor and holding up a hand to stop a further wave of protestation from her friend. "Go on."

Aestelle returned her gaze to Khirius, her mind racing through a hundred plans and a thousand different outcomes as Thesilar paced away and the vampire walked over to stand in front of her. He looked down into her eyes.

"I am sorry I did not carry you from the burial chamber when it collapsed," Khirius said. "I did not realize at the time how badly hurt you were."

Aestelle bit back an angry retort. He had seen her shot in the gut, when she stood over his prone, defeated form, defending him with her own blade. He knew. Part of her despised him for that act of cowardice. She remembered the lone sapphire woven into her hair. She felt a wave of warmth as she recalled those days in summer, sword in hand, and back to back with Orion, fighting off waves of Abyssal abominations to save the Hegemony from invasion. She suppressed a fond laugh as she thought on all of the times she chastised him for leaping to her aid, insisting that she could fight her own battles. It would not have done to tell him the truth, to tell him that after fifteen years of bitter, bloody combat, it was nice to be rescued once in a while. It felt good to know the man by your side had your back through thick and thin.

"You are better now?" Khirius glanced down across her.

"Nothing that won't mend," Aestelle shrugged casually, folding her arms.

She watched his gaze, assessing his intentions, thinking through her options and their outcomes. Khirius stepped closer, inside that area that mere friends left between them. Aestelle looked up at him, her silence signaling that she permitted it.

"You will be leaving soon?" the vampire asked.

"It depends on if there is anything to make me stay," Aestelle replied.

Khirius placed one hand on her leg and the other on her hip. Aestelle allowed it. She saw his features darken. This was the moment. The gamble she had predicted in her mind seconds before, where he would lean in to either sink his teeth into her neck or kiss her. It was the latter. Khirius pushed her against the wall and pressed his lips against hers, his hands roaming across her. Aestelle wrapped an arm around his neck and murmured the appropriate sounds of encouragement. She waited, her anxiety building, for that next moment only too familiar to her when a man was so completely and utterly enraptured with her that his senses were clouded and twisted with lust and passion. She sensed that moment.

Aestelle rapidly pulled a throwing knife from the small of her back and rammed it up into Khirius' heart. His eyes shot wide open and he staggered back half a step. Aestelle shoved the heel of one hand into the handle of the knife to force it further in before reaching both hands up to her greatsword and, in one rapid and fluid motion, unsheathing the long blade straight into a downward strike that cleanly decapitated the vampire.

The head rolled away as the body remained upright for a moment longer, staggering back one more step before collapsing down to the ground. Her breathing heavy, wiping the back of one arm against her mouth, Aestelle stared down at the motionless corpse. She muttered a brief prayer for the soul of the man that once was before the monster.

"Thes," she called weakly, one hand clinging to her sword whilst the other ran across her face. "Thes!"

Thesilar appeared at the far end of the corridor. The elf let out a cry and rushed across. She came to a clattering, almost ungainly, halt by Aestelle, her long knife drawn. She looked down at the headless corpse.

"Well," the older woman said calmly.

Moments of uncomfortable, shocked silence passed.

"Well," Thesilar repeated, "that was not the road I was expecting you to take."

"I'm sorry I had to do it," Aestelle whispered, "but I had to do it. You see that? He was a vampire. I could not let him leave. He was not my friend. I had to do it."

Thesilar stepped across to distastefully nudge the severed head further away from the body with one foot.

"You did the right thing, Aestelle," Thesilar said grimly, "no question about it. Don't justify yourself to me, this thing was a killer. A monster. You did the right thing. May this thing's soul burn in the fires of the Abyss."

Aestelle turned away, averting her eyes from the corpse at her feet.

"I think... I think he was once a good man. He did not choose to become this. I struck him down because he was a threat to others. To innocents. But I hope that in doing so, I've given him release. Peace. I hope this curse is over and his spirit can now fly to the Mountain."

The elf swore and shook her head.

"Aestelle, you need to take off that stupid nun tunic because you're starting to talk like one of these overzealous morons. It was a vampire! It had no soul! You killed it, and you saved others from it! Good job! Move on to the next. Stop moping!"

Aestelle swallowed and nodded, returning her sword to its sheath. Weariness returned to her body as the adrenaline washed away, and she planted one hand against the wall next to her to steady herself.

"Go and get Z'akke," Thesilar ordered curtly. "I'll keep an eye on this. But this, all of this... it needs to be burnt. Go and get Z'akke and bring him here."

Aestelle nodded again and walked slowly down the corridor. The old familiarity of taking her orders from Thesilar somehow felt comforting. Being in command was, she now realized, not all it promised to be. At that moment, she was more than happy to take commands and to do what she was told, without the pressure of having to make decisions. Her heart heavy, her fingers pressed against the sapphire woven into her hair, she walked away from the headless corpse behind her.

Chapter Twenty-One

"You're leaving without saying goodbye?"

Aestelle stopped halfway down the smooth, stone steps. A bitter autumnal wind tore through the mountain valley and across the abbey grounds, whistling as it was squeezed between the gaps separating the age-old buildings. The wind tugging at her Sisterhood tunic and loincloth, Aestelle turned to look up the steps, back toward the entrance to the Chapel of the Sacred Devotees. Abbess Decima looked down the steps at Aestelle as the sisters of her order filed out of the chapel behind her in silence.

The memorial service for Sister Superior Joselin and the other sisters who fell in Mount Ekansu had been sobering, sorrowful... all the things it should have been to Aestelle, but it was also closure. She felt some relief in knowing that Joselin's body had been recovered and honored with a tomb in the Chapel of the Sacred Devotees; something the Joselin she knew would have accepted with pride. The chapel – the original building of the entire site – stood at the highest point of the abbey grounds, the hallowed, gray building brought to life only by the exquisite artwork of its somber, stained glass windows. The same building she had knelt next to Joselin in as an adolescent the day they were both confirmed as sisters of the battle line. The same chapel Aestelle had stormed out of in a rage after being absolved following her survival of the Fifth Step.

"Do not look too far into this," Aestelle said curtly, gesturing down at her immaculate Sisterhood uniform. "You said I remained on the Order's books in reserve. Today seemed like a good day to pay my respects to an old comrade by wearing the uniform to her memorial. Tomorrow, I am back in reserve. Gone again, and forgotten."

"Don't be so bloody melodramatic!" the dark-skinned woman scoffed as she walked down the steps to catch up with Aestelle. "You know full well that you are not forgotten here. Those who know you already will never forget you. Those who have never met you have all heard of you and your exploits."

"Yes, well, today is not about me, is it?" Aestelle snapped bitterly as she continued her walk toward the abbey's front gates, where her horse awaited her.

"True," Decima shrugged, "it is just a shame that it took Joselin's death to finally ensure that one day, just one, single day, is in fact not all about you. Come on, Aestelle! That was funny. Even Joselin would have laughed at that. We have paid our respects and we will not forget her. But there is room for some mirth in life."

"Is there?" Aestelle stopped and turned to face the aging sister.

Decima's wrinkled face dropped from a hopeful smile into a despondent, sorrowful frown. At the top of the stairs, the last line of initiates filed neatly out of the chapel and headed silently toward their dormitory.

"What will you do now?" Decima asked.

"Carry on," Aestelle said. "Arteri's body is still out there. I was the one who started all of this. It is my responsibility to finish it."

"Then do it as one of us," Decima said. "You've had ten years away, a decade to do whatever you needed to do. Come back home now. If you want to carry this on, then do it with my help."

Aestelle turned and looked up at the peaks of the mountains above and down to the spire of the abbey. Countless memories ran through her mind. Her shoulders felt unbearably heavy at the thought of returning to the order. She toyed with the idea of some sweeping, heartfelt speech about her liberty and personal choices but decided against it. She shook her head.

"No. I can't come back."

"Can't? Or won't?"

"Won't."

Decima nodded. The wind again whipped up around them, rustling vortices of dry, dead leaves across the smooth stones of the path leading to the main entrance.

"Then head to Tmoskai," Decima said, "that much I know. You see, when you ordered my scouts to cover all the exits to the tomb and kill anyone who came out, I gave them different orders. I gave them orders to let anybody they saw go free."

Aestelle's eyes widened. Her fists clenched. She scowled down at the shorter woman.

"What in the Abyss did you..."

Decima held up a hand.

"Killing them would not have given us the upper hand. I gave orders that anybody who left the tomb was to be followed. We now know of five further sites used by the Coven, and so far, two of those have been infiltrated."

Aestelle's brow unfurrowed. Her fingers unclenched as she took in a breath.

"Very pretty, great with a sword," Decima grinned, slapping Aestelle on the shoulder, "but not much of a thinker. You leave the thinking to me, Senior Sister. Tmoskai. Get yourself north to Tmoskai and wait to hear from me."

***

The torrential rainfall that passed through overnight now gave way to broken, gray morning clouds, allowing pillars of sunshine through to reach down to the wet ground below. Thesilar walked slowly through the streets of Torgias, careful to keep her gait slow but natural so as not to offend the dignity of her lumbering travel companion. Limping forward in an ungainly manner, his progress impeded by both a crutch to support an injured leg and one arm splinted and tied across his chest, Ragran grumbled curses to himself and ignored the stares of townsfolk as he passed them by.

It had been a week now since the failed attack on the tomb at Mount Ekansu, and whilst Thesilar's wounds continued to heal, she still felt pain with every step from a vicious slash across one leg she had received in that final battle. Their packs slung across their back for the long journey, Thesilar and Ragran walked through the north gatehouse – the very gatehouse they had arrived in Torgias from and days later found themselves defending from an undead assault – and out into the muddy road ahead.

"I'm not good at this," Ragran grunted, "farewells, I mean."

"Who is?" Thesilar responded.

"But," Ragran continued, "everybody leaves here with some… story. Something to take home. You all have lives and… meaning. I have no tale to tell, Thes. I have no rich yarn anymore for the bards to sing. I am just… me. A simple man. I just move from place to place. There is nothing more to it than that."

Thesilar looked up at the giant man limping by her side. She remembered when they first crossed paths and the fractures in their relationship that were driven by the crude young barbarian's need for fame, his drive to be bigger and better than the much acclaimed Orlaf. Now a more mature, thoughtful, and altogether more likeable man walked by her side.

"You don't need any more than that," Thesilar said quietly, "you are fine just the way you are."

Several feet up the road, displaced from the mining huts on the right-hand side of the track, their comrades waited.

Valletto sat on the edge of a smooth rock, his horse's reigns in his hands. Z'akke crouched down a few feet away, an inane grin plastered across his face as he tickled the belly of the upturned Seeba, who lay on her back at his feet. Aestelle, returned to her normal salacious appeal in a new set of impractical and revealing leather armor, waited with them with a horse of her own. Thesilar looked down at Z'akke as she approached, marveling at the amenability and compliance of the lethal war cat sprawled out lazily before the salamander.

"Who's a good kitty cat? Who's a good kitty cat?" Z'akke grinned as he continued to ruffle the white fur of the immense gur panther's belly.

Aestelle saw the look on Thesilar's face as she approached.

"Seeba remembers who dragged her from the rock fall, I think," she explained to the elf. "I think Z'akke has a friend for life now."

"You're keeping her?" Thesilar asked.

Aestelle smiled and shook her head.

"I do not own her. She chose to remain in my company. She is not a pet."

Seeba's eyes suddenly opened and fixed on Thesilar and Ragran as they approached. The giant panther rolled over and braced her back, claws extending as she fixed her gaze on Ragran, growling threateningly. Ragran's pained face lit up with a smile. He stared across at Valletto.

"See! You see! Even with an arm and leg hanging off, I'm still the manliest here! Look at that! Look at this hand! I tore the bloody head off a vampire with this hand!"

Ignoring the bravado, Thesilar walked over to Valletto and held out her hand. The aeromancer looked down at it, back up at her, and then tentatively accepted it. She shook the hand warmly and firmly.

"Safe travels, Val. Thank you for all you did here. It is more than you know."

Valletto shook her hand with equal sincerity before stepping across and repeating the gesture with Ragran.

"Thank you both," he said earnestly. "When my children are old enough, one day I will be able to honestly tell them that I once stood shoulder to shoulder with the famed Thesilar and Ragran the Mighty. Thank you both."

A dozen witty retorts that would have destroyed the emotion of that moment shot through Thesilar's mind, but she elected to remain quiet. Valletto moved on to say his farewells to Aestelle as Z'akke walked over to Thesilar and Ragran. He smiled uneasily and offered a clawed hand. Ragran pulled him in for an embrace with a bearlike growl.

"Take care of yourself, Gecko!" the mountain man beamed. "You're a lot tougher than you look! Don't take shit from anybody! You're the toughest newt I know, and don't forget that."

Z'akke grinned happily, grabbing Thesilar and pulling her into the embrace. Wincing, Thesilar obliged with the salamander's wishes until he took a step back.

"I will miss you both," he said simply.

"Which way are you headed?" Thesilar asked.

"The capital," the salamander replied, "to stay with Valletto and his family for a while. I hope then I will be heading home."

"I hope that for you, too," Thesilar said honestly.

She watched as Z'akke tottered over to Aestelle and swept her up in an embrace. The normally stern, egotistical young woman returned the gesture with tears flowing down her cheeks. They exchanged a few quiet words before Z'akke gave Seeba one last, forlorn pet on the chin. Valletto heaved himself up into his saddle, issued a sorrowful wave, and then nudged his horse back toward the gate to head through Torgias and take the road south to the City of the Golden Horn, with Z'akke trudging happily next to him, returning a fond wave to a group of miners' children from the far side of the track as he did so.

Ragran looked down at Aestelle.

"You look after yourself," he said seriously.

Aestelle issued a slight smile.

"Of all the people who owe the most in this group," the blonde woman said, "I feel it is I who am indebted to you. Thank you for keeping an eye out for me. Thank you for looking after me in the mountain."

Ragran let out a low laugh.

"I was just trying to impress you because I still want to nail you," the mountain man beamed through his thick, bushy beard.

Aestelle's laughter joined his. For a second time, Thesilar found herself biting back on an expertly timed pun but decided that it was perhaps too soon to make a joke about the last man wanting to nail Aestelle ending up losing his head over her. Ragran and Aestelle exchanged a brief, backslapping hug before Ragran quickly backed away from the growling gur panther. With Valletto and Z'akke gone and Ragran out of earshot, Thesilar was left alone with Aestelle. She looked up at the younger woman, her protégé, and in her mind, her little sister.

"You know," Thesilar began, "every culture I have wandered through and attempted to understand, without exception, has a phrase or saying about taking certain roads or paths in life."

"Right?" Aestelle answered warily.

Thesilar pointed to the muddy track beneath Aestelle's feet.

"You see," the elf continued, "for most people, it is just a figure of speech. But, right now, for you it is literal. You are standing on the road that will decide your future. North or south. There is the difficult road to happiness, or the easier road. I want you to make the right choice. Because I care."

Aestelle looked to her right, up along the track winding through the muddy hills and toward the frozen, snowcapped mountains leading to northern Basilea.

"I have already told you where I am going," she replied.

"But there is the other road," Thesilar said, "the road south. To the capital, or at least near to it. You could drop all of this and go to catch up with Z'akke and Valletto. Head south. Head to the City of the Golden Horn. Find your paladin. You could go and be happy for the first time in your life."

Aestelle's smile faded. Her beautiful features darkened to something akin to anger and then eased off to anxiety, even fear. She stared to the south. One hand reached up to touch the beads in her hair for a contemplative moment. Then she looked back at Thesilar.

"The easy road is never worth anything at the end," Aestelle shrugged. "I am heading north. I am carrying on this fight. I have a responsibility. I have a task to complete."

"Aestelle, you bloody idiot!" Thesilar snapped. "The road north *is* the easy road! You have already proven countless times that you know how to fight! The question now is whether you have the courage to fix your own life! To swallow your pride and go to tell that man how you feel! That is the hard road worth taking! So you tell me, do you have the guts to do it? Do you have the courage to take that hard road to the south?"

Aestelle again cast a long, forlorn gaze to toward the sunny south of the Hegemony. She stared for some time, her eyes dancing from side to side as if running through a conversation in her head. Finally, she walked forward and wrapped a single arm around Thesilar, pressing her forehead gently against the shorter elf in a brief, tender moment of friendship. She stepped back, all introspection and wistfulness on her face replaced with the more familiar, cocky grin and flashing silver-blue eyes.

"I'm no simpering damsel, Thes," she winked, "I'm a fighter. I'm a Viscountess. I'm a damn hero. A hero on the rise. I'm heading north to cut down an evil bastard."

Thesilar swore and shook her head as Aestelle vaulted nimbly up onto her horse's saddle.

"You haven't learned a damn thing, have you?" Thesilar scowled up at her.

Aestelle flashed a broad grin.

"I never do. Look after that lummox over there. I shall see you around."

Aestelle waved to Ragran, smiled down to Thesilar, and then nudged her horse into a trot along the muddy pathway to the north as she quietly sang to herself, the hulking gur panther padding alongside her. Thesilar watched them go, shaking her head in disappointment.

"What was all that about?" Ragran asked as he limped over.

"Oh, nothing. Just... Aestelle. You see, when I killed the Warlord of Galahir and when you braved the fires of the Abyss itself, we became heroes. We became famous across all of Pannithor. But what we did in the last few days in Mount Ekansu, I think it was every bit as difficult. Harder, even, more dangerous. But the bards will never write tales or songs about it, because we met with no success."

"Alright," Ragran nodded, "I am confused as to where you are going with this."

"My point," Thesilar said, turning away to begin the walk back to the Trade Wind Inn, "is that the five of us have just been through something incredible. A life-changing experience. I, myself, admit to falling off the path a little. To use your northern human vernacular, I'd become something of a dick. But this experience has reminded me about friendship. I am proud to realize that, to realize I am a better person for treating those dear to me with kindness."

Ragran grimaced as he limped along next to her on his coarse, wooden crutch.

"I still do not understand where this is going," he repeated.

Thesilar turned again and pointed at the rider disappearing off to the north.

"We all grow as people!" Thesilar exclaimed irritably. "We all become better! But never her! Never Aestelle! She just carries on being an annoying, arrogant bitch and she always gets away with it! And here we are again, talking about Aestelle! Come on, let's go and get a drink. I'm in no rush, and another week here until you are better placed to travel will do us a world of good."

The two famed adventurers passed back through the gatehouse and into Torgias, their booted feet clipping along the cobblestones of the main street.

"Would you rather talk about somebody else?" Ragran offered.

"Yes."

"How about Guraf?"

"Not Guraf! He really is a dick!"

Ragran boomed out a laugh and wrapped his good arm affectionately around Thesilar's shoulders.

"Come on," he smiled, "let us treat ourselves to a week of ale, good food, and proper sleep. And then to the road again."

Thesilar nodded in agreement.

"Any ideas where to next?" she asked.

"This time of year?" Ragran mused. "Winter is best seen out in the Howling Peaks. Proper mountains, not these little Basilean foothills. A week here, my friend, and then I would consider it an honor to show you the lands of my childhood."

Thesilar's anger dissipated quickly, a smile lighting up her face at the thought as they made their way slowly back to the Trade Wind Inn.

***

Gulls hovered over the fields, their distinctive caws seeming to bring the sounds of the sea, only two miles to the south, with them across the air. Only a few trails of cloud broke up the otherwise clear blue sky above the outskirts of the City of the Golden Horn. In many ways, Valletto was thankful for the positioning of Apagus Hill, the small jutting of agrarian land and neat rows of olive trees that blocked the view to the capital city itself that lay nestled in the lower ground to the east. Even though it blocked the sheer majesty and beauty of the City of the Golden Horn, Apagus Hill did at least give the western out-skirts a sense of tranquil isolation, feeling more like the agrarian lands sprawling out to the north and west rather than the tip of the largest city in all of Pannithor.

The birds chirped merrily from the olive trees to the right of the road and from colorful gardens in the houses to left as Valletto led his horse by the reigns along the familiar route home. Next to him, Z'akke leaned his head back and closed his eyes as he walked with him.

"This is perfect!" the mage-priest hissed. "The sun, the heat… well, it is perhaps a little chilly if I stop to think of the Three Kings. But it is certainly better than the Tarkis Mountains!"

Neighbors in the houses leading along the side of the road cast friendly waves and nods to Valletto as he led his horse along the dusty path. An autumnal morning in the City of the Golden Horn may not have kept pace with the Three Kings for sheer heat, but it was certainly still warm, far warmer than Torgias would ever see even in the height of summer. It was all to do with air pressure, Valletto mused, the falling air to the south and the rising air to the north controlling that vicious flow of cold air rolling down from the snowy, high ground in Tarkis. That scientific understanding of air was what made an aeromancer able to take temporary control of the winds to manipulate them. But, Valletto mused, that probably did not make it interesting enough for him to describe to the more traditionally trained pyromancer who walked along with him. But it was something to think over to avoid the anxiety of facing what lay ahead.

"Just up here," Valletto nodded three houses ahead, "that one is mine."

Valletto's apprehension and discomfort had increased with ev-ery mile traveled south over the last few days, culminating in a near sleepless night only hours before. Now, drained and tired, he dragged his feet wearily along toward his house, resigned to his fate and feeling that it was well and truly deserved. Why had he left? He was lucky to be alive, let alone to be able to walk back to his family with only his wife's temper and his children's disappointment to face.

Z'akke rested a hand on his shoulder.

"Are you alright?" the salamander asked with a sympathetic smile.

Valletto nodded slowly.

"I think so."

"They will be happy to see you, no matter what," Z'akke offered quietly. "We all make honest mistakes. Honest mistakes are easy enough to forgive."

Before Valletto could answer, he heard a scream from ahead. A child's voice, yelling out from the bottom of his lungs.

"Mummy! Mummy!"

Valletto looked up and saw his son, Lyius, sprint through his front garden and barge open the fence, his eyes wide and frantic and his face lit up with a disbelieving smile. The young boy hurtled along the road, his eyes fixed on Valletto. His throat choked, Valletto dropped down to one knee and opened his arms. His son ran straight into him with enough force to knock him back a little, burying his head in his father's chest and wrapping his arms tightly around him. Valletto hugged the boy in and kissed the top of his head, bile rising in his throat from the release of fear and anxiety as he finally held his son.

He remembered standing in the cold night of Torgias town square as he faced down towering, deadly zombie trolls. He remembered the terror of two mountain cave ins and the darkness immediately after them. He recalled facing lines of undead, of trading sword blows with skeletons and zombies, and of staring up at the sheer horror of a skeletal drakon. Throughout all of it, he cursed himself for his stupid decisions, wishing more than anything he could be home in the warm sun and safety of southern Basilea, holding his family close to him.

A shadow fell over him. He looked up and saw his wife, Clera, holding their daughter Jullia. Valletto instantly felt the fear return as he rose to his feet. Clera did not say a word. She rushed across, kissed him, and held him tightly with their daughter between as Lyius hugged his parents' legs.

"Welcome home," his wife whispered.

"I'm sorry," Valletto said, "I won't do that again. I'm so sorry."

Clera stepped back and opened her mouth to speak. She then looked over his shoulder and stopped, her face changing to one of confusion. Valletto turned around to see Z'akke staring happily at the family reunion, dabbing at one teary eye.

"This… erm…" Valletto stammered. "This is Z'akke. He will be staying with us for a while. Just whilst I help him with something. He is a friend. A good friend."

"Hello!" Z'akke bowed his head formally. "My name is Z'akke. I can cook and I am good with children."

Clera looked up at the muscular salamander in confusion. Salamanders were a common enough sight in the capital, and even Valletto's children were accustomed to seeing them, but inviting one to stay in your home was not the norm. The confusion gave way to a warm smile.

"If you are a friend of my husband, you are a friend of the whole family," Clera said. "Let me take your bag. Come on in."

Epilogue

One Month Later

The snow clouds had cleared to the southeast to give an unobstructed view of the half-moon and accompanying stars up above. Her black hood pulled up over her head, Aestelle paced slowly through the snow-covered streets of Tmoskai, her eyes flitting from shadow to shadow as hope faded that she would find her prey. With orders and information irregularly coming to her from the Sisterhood via a series of contacts in the city, Aestelle had found herself somehow playing the part of assassin for the last two weeks, systematically finding and eliminating members of the Coven. With three minor lackeys hunted down and slain so far, she could only guess that Tmoskai had a far greater number of the necromantic bastards infecting its streets than she had initially estimated.

Tonight, perhaps two hours past midnight and with streets empty from the city's curfew, Aestelle had lost her target. A newcomer to the city, a necromancer by the name of Cixus who had managed to shake her off in the maze of back alleys and narrow, winding roads weaving through the old city on the eastern edge of the Mountains of Tarkis. She had found Cixus easily enough; he matched the physical description – tall, well-dressed and with a black beard – and was lodging at the inn named in her instructions. And, like her, creeping around the snow-covered alleyways in the early hours of the morning was no activity for a law-bidding citizen out to do good. But Aestelle was cocky. She was growing careless. She closed with her target too quickly, and once she rounded the next corner, he was gone.

Cursing her own recklessness under her breath, Aestelle spent several minutes checking every alleyway and road for signs of movement, disturbances, and recent footprints in the snow. Despair and anger loomed up inside her. Then she heard a scream. Spinning in place to look toward the yell, she saw a track leading north toward the center of the city. Picking up her pace to a sprint, Aestelle rushed beneath a narrow, rickety bridge and past a brewery, rounding a corner to arrive in a small square.

Lying in the middle of the square was a body. The snow around the motionless figure, illuminated by the streetlamps hanging from the walls of surrounding buildings, was red with blood. Aestelle let out a gasp of sympathy as she recognized the robes of a priest. She rushed across and dropped to one knee next to the man. Pained, gray eyes stared up at the heavens above from an old, wrinkled face bracketed with neat, white hair and a short beard. The handle of a dagger emerged from the man's chest where the blade had been plunged straight into his heart. All of the divinity healing in the world would not save the priest now.

Reciting a brief prayer for the priest's soul, Aestelle looked quickly around her. The priest's footprints were easy enough to make out, as were a larger, heavier set that had come in from the west, seemingly to wait behind a tall barrel outside the brewery before rushing out to stab the ill-fated old man. Those same footprints then disappeared north.

Aestelle heard the crunching of snow to the south. Whipping her head around, she saw a figure haloed in the light of the streetlamps, standing at the edge of the square and staring at her. The figure wore bulky, heavy armor – too good for a mere city guard but still clearly a figure of authority. And Aestelle was crouching over the body of a dead priest, whilst the real killer was escaping to the north with every wasted second.

"Stop there!" the figure commanded; a young woman's voice.

Aestelle leapt to her feet and sprinted north. She heard the armored woman behind her giving chase, but Aestelle knew she was faster. Her feet lightly pacing across the snow as she rapidly followed the recent tracks of her target, she pelted north along the empty road toward the main market square. Up ahead, the killer's tracks merged into a mess of muddied snow where, only an hour or two before, a tavern had clearly kicked out all of its patrons and a muddle of footprints of all sizes dispersed in every direction. Aestelle swore. She looked over her shoulder. The armored woman was still chasing her.

Looking to her left, she saw a wall made up of wooden crates and an alleyway on the far side. There was a flicker of movement at the end of the alleyway, a shadow the size of a man suddenly fading away into the darkness. Aestelle rushed over to the crates, acrobatically vaulting over them to hurtle down the narrow alley toward the shadow. She heard a crash behind her and saw the armored woman smash straight through the wooden crates, still giving chase relentlessly despite her heavy armor. Aestelle picked up her pace and ran to the end of the alleyway.

The path split into three. Aestelle swore again. The narrow alleys and the overhanging roofs above had prevented much snow from falling down to the ground. There was only a light dusting of snow over the cobbles, certainly not enough for significant footprints. There was no time to deduce anything meaningful; Cixus was escaping, and the obstinate woman in the armor was still chasing Aestelle down, clearly believing her to be the priest's murderer. Aestelle picked an alleyway and ran down it.

Her footsteps echoed along the cobblestones, reverberating against the thin walls to either side. She listened out for other footsteps, desperate to find her target, but she heard only her own and the heavy, metallic thunking of her pursuer. The alley met another road, and Aestelle allowed herself a smile as she saw fresh footprints in the snow, the distance between them clearly showing the stride of a man running. But she could still hear her pursuer. Determined to catch up with her mark, Aestelle darted down a side passageway to reach a parallel alley where she hoped to find obstacles that an armored woman could not traverse; walls, empty carts, anything she could clamber over to leave her hunter behind.

Aestelle let out a gasp of frustration as the alley snaked off to the left, away from the main road where she had last followed the snowy footprints. She vaulted over barrels, crates, and low walls, dashing from alley to alley in an attempt to lose her tracker and reinteresect the main road. But she did not know Tmoskai nearly well enough to navigate the back streets at night. The inevitable happened. She turned a corner and found a dead end, the steep wall of a stone warehouse blocking her path. Growling in frustration, Aestelle desperately looked up for something she could climb.

"Turn around and get your hands away from that weapon."

Aestelle stopped. Somehow, with a nearly unnatural display of speed and endurance, the armored woman had kept up with her, through the snow and over the obstacles. Aestelle turned around. The woman, even more dimly lit than before, heaved in exertion beneath her heavy armor. Aestelle pointed a finger at her threateningly.

"Walk away whilst you still can," she hissed, desperate to get past her and resume the hunt before it was all too late.

The woman stepped forward. A beam of moonlight sneaked through a crack in the tall buildings, showing her to be perhaps a few years younger than Aestelle, with a pale face and red hair. A blue surcoat and cloak hung from her ornate armor. Aestelle felt her heart grow heavy. A paladin. Of all the things to encounter in the streets of Tmoskai whilst trying to hunt down and kill a necromancer, she had encountered a paladin. The stoic looking woman pulled a heavy, deadly-looking warhammer from her back and held it across her chest. Her grip on the heavy weapon, the placement of her feet, the calm assurance in her eyes: everything told Aestelle that the paladin was a veteran of warfare.

"Get your hands away from that weapon," she ordered Aestelle a second time.

There was no time for this. Cixus would be gone and his trail lost in seconds. Aestelle had no intention of striking down a paladin, but she did not have time to explain the situation. She needed to fight her way through, just a hit or two. Enough to knock the woman down without really hurting her. It was the quickest option. Aestelle unclipped her cloak and threw it to one side before unsheathing her greatsword and stepping forward into the moonlight. The paladin rushed forward to attack.

Look for more books from Winged Hussar Publishing, LLC – E-books, paperbacks and Limited-Edition hardcovers. The best in history, science fiction and fantasy at:
https://www. wingedhussarpublishing.com
https://www.whpsupplyroom.com
or follow us on Facebook at:
Winged Hussar Publishing LLC
Or on twitter at:
WingHusPubLLC
For information and upcoming publications

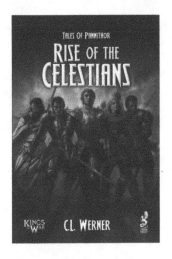

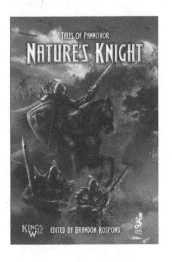

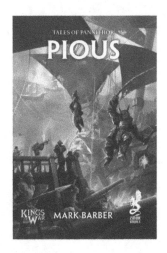